ONLY THE MOON HOWLS

CONNIE SENIOR

Published by Bitingduck Press
ISBN 978-1-938463-49-5
© 2013 Connie Senior
All rights reserved
For information contact
Bitingduck Press, LLC
Montreal • Altadena
notifications@bitingduckpress.com
http://www.bitingduckpress.com
Cover image by Dena Eaton

Iliad quote from from the Penguin publication *THE ILIAD* by Homer, translated by Robert Fagles. © 1990 Robert Fagles.

Publisher's Cataloging-in-Publication
Senior, Constance [1956 -   ]

Only the Moon Howls/by Connie Senior—1st ed.—Altadena, CA: Bitingduck Press, 2013
p. cm.

ISBN 978-1-938463-49-5

[1. Young adult—Fiction 2. Romania—Fiction 3. Vampires—Fiction 4. Werewolves—Fiction] I. Title

LCCN 2012941371

To Moon, with gratitude: this is as much yours as it is mine, and you never gave less than 110% in its making

"There are nights when the wolves are silent and only the moon howls"
~ George Carlin

Prologue

"BRING THE LANTERN OVER here." A ball of light weaves through the darkness of a moonless night, while uncertain steps crunch the gravel path. "Yeah, that's good. Now set it down."

"Jeez, Toby, and you call yourself a wizard," sniggers the boy as he places the lantern in front of a door, barely visible behind the boards nailed across its frame. "Can't even conjure some fire."

"Look, you little twit," Toby retorts. "We're here to break the ward, not waste magic on little conjuring tricks."

Toby grasps a board and takes confident, deep breaths, while the shorter boy fidgets at the outer edges of the circle of light, the gravel whispering under his nervous feet. Restless wind murmurs through the tall pines, whose branches scrape softly against the upper windows and the roof of the dark house. It's been fifty years since anyone lived in the house and the trees have cozied up close to the deserted building.

"Man, these wards are solid," Toby says admiringly.

"Same as before," giggles the other boy. "And you couldn't break them before, either."

"René, you have no faith in me," Toby counters as he walks backward, one step, then two. Without taking his eyes off the door, he adds, "Caleb wouldn't leave that goddamn kindergarten of his to come help us, but he did give me a good idea."

He takes René by the shoulders and maneuvers him until he stands about three feet in front of the door, just outside the left-hand doorframe. Toby takes a similar position on the right.

"This is about it…There, feel it?" Toby hums appreciatively, like a starving man presented with a thick steak. René bounces his head nervously in reply.

"Caleb thinks the ward was set by two wizards, not one, so it will take two of us in just the right places to break it. Okay, move a little to the left. Feel it getting stronger?" Toby is silent for a while, turning his head slightly from side to side. "Feels like Fintonclyde's work, like the wards around the Reserve, but not quite…someone else in there."

"T-T-T-Toby, I don't think I can…" René's teeth chatter.

"Too late to back out, buddy," Toby says. "You were the one begging come back, remember? Well, here we are and even though I know you're a miserable excuse for a wizard, you're going to help me blow this ward."

"Yeah, sure," whispers René.

"Come on." Toby tries to rally his friend. "This is going to be so cool. No one's ever managed to get in, not in fifty years. And it won't be much harder than that ward on the lighthouse. Remember how we broke that? Close your eyes and try to see the lines, punch through them, okay? Ready? One…two…three—"

Boards crack, splinters fly, and the boys stumble backwards, blinded by searing light. A minute, perhaps an hour passes. Toby can't be sure if the light is gone, so scrambled is his vision. He gathers his wits enough to know that he's lying on the ground and, as his vision returns, that he's in front of a ragged hole where the door once blocked entry.

"Shit," he drawls, taking a long time to finish the word, stretching it out to six or seven syllables. "We did it, man!"

He rescues the lantern from under a twisted plank and gets to his feet. "Hey, René, good work." But as he swings the lantern around, he sees he is alone amid the rubble. "René?"

The wind falls silent, but something rustles nearby: a high-pitched squeak in Toby's ear and the rapid beating of wings. Something flies past him, but Toby cannot tell if it went into the house, or exited the house. Then he hears footsteps inside.

"Hey, René?" The silence dampens Toby's confidence. He barrels through the shattered doorway, lantern held high, his panicked scream piercing the waiting darkness. "René! René!"

Book I

A World Apart

1. Trial at Tribulation

WHERE IS HE? WHERE is Toby?"

The old man turned around slowly as the stiff Atlantic wind danced with his long gray beard. A hint of a frown, a brief glimpse of puzzlement, a glimmer of pity in his eyes, then a smile. "Caleb, I didn't expect to see you here." He walked closer, head to one side while inspecting the boy. "You've grown two inches in the last six months, if I'm not mistaken."

"Who cares about my height!" It was controlled anger, not the wind needling through his thin jacket, that caused Caleb O'Connor to shiver. "René is dead and my best friend is accused of—" His tongue tripped, fell, and refused to get up and say the word. "You think I'd stay away?"

"A tragedy," replied Clovis Fintonclyde with a wistful shake of the head. "The Cousineaus are understandably distraught, with all the difficulties they've had. Bit of a panic in the Community, people not knowing if they're going to be murdered in their beds."

"Sophia called me last night, told me about René, and said they'd taken Toby into custody. Where is he, Fintonclyde?"

"Ah, well," said the old man mildly, as if he were still tutoring a much younger Caleb in geography or the care and feeding of dragons. "There will be a trial, of course." He waved a hand toward Tribulation House, the old stone mansion that occupied this tiny island off the Maine coast.

The ancient building on the cliff was officially a museum of local history with such odd hours of operation that tourists never visited. Stone sphinxes flanked the iron gates and looked out across the Atlantic with weather-beaten indifference; a rusty iron fence, leaning hard, tried to shield the building from the spray and surf. Any visitor hardy enough to take a boat out to the remote pile of rocks would find an overgrown brick path and a jaunty yellow sign reading "Closed—We're Sorry We Missed You!"

"Trial?" For the first time, Caleb noticed that the gates leading into the yard of the squat granite building were, for once, open; people had lined up in front of the fence and were shuffling through the gates. He felt as if a large pit had just opened up at his feet. "She didn't mention a trial."

Fintonclyde put a hand on Caleb's shoulder, though it did nothing to quell the shaking. "The outside world doesn't bother with the Community much, as you know, and sometimes, well, it's best if we keep some of our problems to ourselves. There hasn't been a trial since 1942. And that's got folks upset, because we thought we'd executed the lot of them back then and sealed up Lilac House for good. But when Toby broke in, he must have let something out that killed René. Some people are wondering if Toby was in league with… what he found there."

"How can you—" Nearly blinded with rage and confusion, Caleb stumbled, certain he would throw up. "You know Toby. He'll do anything on a dare, the more outrageous the better, but that doesn't mean that he would help a vampire. Because that's what we're talking about here, isn't it? No one will come right out and say it, will they?"

"The Community has to take measures to protect itself," Fintonclyde said. "Surely you can understand?"

"I understand what a kangaroo court is," Caleb snarled. "It sounds as if you and the rest of the Community have already convicted Toby. I want to be in that miserable courtroom. I want to see Toby!"

The old man sighed, the pity briefly returning to his face. "Come along then, but I can't guarantee you anything. It's clear that I can't stop you."

They approached the iron gates. Two silly-looking men in violet chemises demanded rings, staffs, potions or metals—anything they might have on their person that could be used to cast a spell or interfere with the proceedings. Their cheerful dress annoyed Caleb, all the more so when he recalled that within the Community, violet symbolized justice. He feared there was not enough violet in the world for justice to be served that day.

At the head of the queue, a guard looked Caleb up and down, frowning. "Mr. Fintonclyde, sir, you can't bring this…you can't bring him inside," the guard said with casual contempt, as if he expected Fintonclyde to leave Caleb tied to the fence like a well-trained dog.

Caleb almost turned and bolted right then. This was the reason he had left the Community and all of its prejudices six months ago.

"Marcus McNulty, I don't know where you get your quaint notions," Fintonclyde scolded. "This young man has every right to be inside. There is no prohibition of which I'm aware in the Community's laws, and I helped write the 1933 amendments on trial law and the 1947 revision on *habeas corpus.*"

"Beg your pardon, sir," the guard said, ducking his head, "but precautions have to be taken."

"And they will be," replied Fintonclyde. "Now, let me see, I suppose you will want this." He turned out his pockets and handed the guard a collection of metal objects: a brass letter-opener with a dragon's head handle, a set of rusted screwdrivers, and a handful of foreign coins.

The guard visibly cringed to touch Caleb. He ran his hand only over his back pockets, making sure they were empty. Then, with a grunt, he let them pass through the gates.

The crowd pressing to enter the immense weather-scarred doors parted around Caleb and his old teacher, not wanting to get too close. Fintonclyde didn't seem to notice, but Caleb had a feeling that something nasty was going to happen.

Subdued whispers became a roar in the entrance hall of the courthouse, where the high curved ceilings echoed and amplified the sounds of wind, sea, and spectators. The floor was bare stone, the temperature five degrees cooler than comfortable. The somber décor in the flickering candlelight gave the impression of an underground cavern. It scared Caleb nearly to death.

Cedar doors, varnished to a deep violet, led from the entrance hall into the courtrooms. Purple, too, were the robes of the guards flanking the entry to the room. Clusters of showy, bell-shaped flowers—also purple—grew at the courtroom's entrance, out of place with their lush cheeriness. The purple of justice? Caleb sneered silently. Toby Byron would be tried surrounded by purple, with only the judges and the witnesses in attendance.

So that was how they did it, Caleb thought with an odd sense of triumph, giving Fintonclyde a disdainful look.

"Ah, yes," said the old wizard apologetically, seeing that Caleb was eyeing the flowers. "The wolfsbane…It's customary, you know, to keep all Dark influence out of the courts. You'll see they have garlic, as well—"

"I don't care about the *garlic*," Caleb hissed through clenched teeth. He wanted to turn and flee, but the old man held tightly to his arm. "He's my best friend and I'm not even allowed into the courtroom?" As much as he tried to fight it, the stench of the aconite—the queen of poisons—made him back away.

"You can see that it's out of the question for you to be a witness," Fintonclyde said gently, his gaze never wavering. "And I assure you that my testimony and Sophia's will include all of what we know. You certainly don't wish to deny under oath that Toby was capable of breaking the magical wards around the Reserve and, by extension, any ward in these parts?"

"Mistrust" and "Fintonclyde" were two words that Caleb could never have imagined stringing together, even in his mind, so this development devastated him. No one seemed capable of entertaining the slightest doubt that Toby was guilty.

His low-level seethe became a bubbling wrath as he turned his back on Fintonclyde, the noisome flowers, and the courtroom to shove his way out of the cold stone building. His mind raged not only against the old man but also against himself, his naiveté and the irony of his stubborn disbelief in the injustice on display all around him. No matter how many times they had kicked him through the years, he always came running back, wagging his tail like a golden retriever.

A light rain was falling, smelling of moss and ferns, refreshing and pure after the filthy miasma of the Community's "civilization." He knew he had to get off the island before something even more hideous happened. He had been raised as Fintonclyde's ward and read all his books, so knew perfectly well what had happened in 1942 to those accused of being vampires: They had been hanged, staked, disemboweled and their bodies burned, ashes scattered to the wind.

Caleb sprinted across the island and halted at the edge of the water, blinded by rain and tears. He was furious not only at Fintonclyde, but at himself, for running away like a coward while a bunch of crazies put a boy on "trial." He hated himself for not calling the police—and he also hated himself for not having the courage to fight them on their own terms.

The fact was, and he fully admitted it, that he was afraid of the Community. He didn't know what they were capable of. He didn't think his mind was even set up to grasp it. Fintonclyde had managed to teach him a few parlor tricks and ways to get around a dead flashlight battery or a leaky canoe, but they were games for children. Apart from the violence of his monthly transformation, Caleb had a poor grasp of the power that magic could wield, despite all his mentor's efforts to teach him.

The rain had half filled his canoe, which heaved perilously under him when he jumped in. It had been Toby's boat. Toby knew all sorts of ways to make it glide against the current or even skim through the air, but Caleb was restricted to paddling madly, berating the waves with the foulest curses he knew.

He cut around the point well outside of the shore of Tribulation. The tiny hamlet was almost invisible among the pines, a single power line its only obvious connection to the outside world. Electricity had come only the year before, in 1985, and there was still no phone.

Just around the southern point was a different world. When he got to the rocky shoreline of Southwest Harbor, he tried a half-hearted spell to make the canoe jump up onto land, but only succeeded in landing himself in the water. Sputtering, shivering, and swearing, he swam to shore and hauled the boat out by its frayed rope, which he attached to an old post.

The few pedestrians in town threw him hard, cold stares, and he finally realized how distasteful he must look: a weeping teenager, drenched from head to foot.

Caleb briefly held his breath to stop the tears and tore off his soaking coat. Maine had two seasons—winter and the Fourth of July—so he was chilly in his thin jacket, cotton shirt, and jeans, but at least he looked respectable enough to pass among the first wave of hypothermic summer tourists. He smiled at a pretty woman in a sundress and heavy sweater and wondered what secrets she harbored. She had such lovely teeth; had she ever sunk them into steaming human flesh?

As he got into his rusty 1969 Datsun, he pondered his fate. What did it matter whether he killed people every month or was the most reliable, even-tempered SOB around? The results were the same. He was a freak and he would never again have any friends or family of any kind. The title of an old Jack London story flitted through his mind, and he laughed scornfully to himself as he got onto the toll road in Maine. The Call of the Wild—it appealed to his broken heart, but it was absurd. Werewolves were only wolves one, in some rare instances two, nights of the month. They would have no reason to cut themselves off from society and live in the woods.

He headed south, back to the school where he had hoped to find acceptance, or at least anonymity. It was better by far than the Community, but it had not worked out the way he had hoped. He choked with disdain as he thought of his fellow students and all their professors. It wasn't as though he stood out as being particularly weird at MIT—that would be nearly impossible to do. His studies in astronomy offered the perfect excuse for his not working on nights of the full moon. He went his own way and so did all the others. But the banks of the Charles were no place for a werewolf to run free, and even a single night each month spent locked in his apartment took a toll on his health.

The fact was, he hated Boston: the filth, the incessant noise, the cars, the subways, the snobby people. And being so far away had kept him from seeing his friends and realizing just how much they were playing with fire. Now the best friend he'd ever had was going to be put down like a pound puppy. Even worse, his only family was content to sit and watch.

He had wanted to leave that world behind him, and so he had, secretly applying to all the top science schools when he was sixteen. When MIT gave him a scholarship, he'd found an entry to a world where technology replaced magic, and he had desperately hoped it would be a world that he could call his own.

Well, now he would be a better student of sorcery than he ever was of astronomy. He would find a place far from Cambridge where this other world was taken seriously, a world that would teach him the cunning he needed to return to the Community and face Fintonclyde fair and square.

Fintonclyde, the judge, the guards, the spectators—all of them…They would all be sorry for what happened today.

2. Dog Boy

A WET NOSE NUDGED HIS hand. Half-awake, he murmured, "Go away, Toby."

Hearing himself speak Toby's name propelled Caleb into waking, and he found himself staring up into a shaggy face. He had expected to see his best friend, whimpering and panting, down on all fours doing the familiar canine impersonation— "Hey, Dog Boy, time to get up!" Instead, he faced a sheepdog whose brown eyes were partially hidden by long brown and white fur.

The dog licked his face and then sat on its haunches, head cocked quizzically. It was a Toby look: furry, loyal, animal-loving, Toby was ironically (or appropriately) Caleb's first and best human friend. *(What had they done to him?)*

The Charles River was framed in the stone arches of the bridge as a light rain fell, the drops blurring the surface as they landed on the water. A boat approached the bridge's middle arch—a stocky young man with a look of intense concentration rowed a single-person scull. A shaft of morning light punched through the clouds and sparkled on the ripples of the wake spreading out behind the boat.

Caleb's brain streamed an incontinent flood of memories. Seven was too young for a child to leave his parents, even if that was the age at which a werewolf cub's bite became dangerous. Caleb wasn't sure if his family had fully appreciated that, or ever really accepted the diagnosis of the condition that turned their son into a howling, biting monster one night out of the month, and a sniffling, odd-behaving little boy the rest of the time.

He himself, of course, had simply thought he was crazy. When the smelly old man in a pointy hat comes to take you away, even a seven-year-old knows that "residential treatment program" means *loony bin*.

Those first months on Dragonshead Island were so lonely and scary that nothing Fintonclyde did could convince Caleb that the Reserve was a paradise. The old man took him around in his rowboat with no oars and showed him all but the most dangerous corners of his island refuge. To this day, Caleb believed the boat was a trick, with a battery hidden somewhere, but the creatures that Fintonclyde maintained on his island were undeniably magical. An Acadian ghost whose language Caleb never comprehended staffed the lighthouse, and the inlet teemed with tiny, harmless creatures shaped like lions with fins. Billdads, which were like miniature kangaroos with hawk's beaks and webbed feet, fished for them by the shore by slapping the water with their beaver tails.

Inside the log cabin on the island were more books than anyone could read in a lifetime. Caleb owed his academic success not to any formal training, but to nine long winters spent with the history, mathematics, science, and literature found between the damp and salty pages lurking in Fintonclyde's study. Nothing was off-limits or forbidden, and Caleb sensed that even if he were to make inroads into the vast collection, new and exciting tomes would slip in to replace the old ones.

He had no contact with other children for almost five years. Enough people in the Community knew why he was living with Fintonclyde, so the school in Tribulation was out of the question. His wolf-form had more of a social life than his human incarnation, because under the full moon he was able to slip through the wards that kept humans away from the dangerous creatures on the island. He cavorted with manticores and legless, voracious snow wassets that were said to devour any creature hiding in the snow. He played hide and seek with goblins and trolls and talking lobsters the size of ponies. He was less afraid of a griffin than he was of the first boatload of teenagers who came spilling onto the island the July of his twelfth year.

The country's mental health pendulum had swung from helping the mad to punishing the bad, so Fintonclyde's island was no longer a residential treatment program but a "boot camp" designed to scare wayward adolescents straight. They arrived terrified, expecting prison-style discipline, and reacted in a myriad of ways to the wild, unsupervised freedom that Fintonclyde believed was educational.

Caleb had been angry at first when the rowdy throng invaded his privacy. Most of the kids who'd come to the program had been simple hoodlums, but mixed in with the refugees from juvenile detention were kids from the Community, sent to learn some magic from the great Fintonclyde. He could never understand the old man's motivation for taking them in, allowing them to run amok and create messes that Caleb had to clean up.

The few exceptions were as astounding as the rule. By all appearances a good-for-nothing delinquent Mainer, Toby had possessed (still did, for at least a few more hours) a spark of magical genius that made him see that true mischief wasn't spray painting and stealing cars. Magic would let him control the world around him, from atoms to whole islands.

By the time Toby left that September, Caleb had his first friend. And when Toby returned the following year with another brilliant but quirky boy and an intrepid and energetic girl, Caleb's world changed forever. He would have done anything to make himself worthy of the trio: Toby, Sophia, and René. Both of the newcomers were from within the Community, though in very different ways. René Cousineau's parents despaired of his fire-starting and hoped he'd learn enough magic to control it and live an ordinary life. Sophia Daigle, on the other hand, had renowned and powerful wizards in her family who expected her to expand her powers.

Fintonclyde could never understand how much they meant to me, Caleb thought now, gritting his teeth.

He continued to caress the dog as the sounds of traffic on Memorial Drive and of morning joggers on the footpath crept into his consciousness. Soon students would be walking or riding bicycles back and forth across the bridge, hurrying to get to class, and here he sat with his tear-stained face buried in the fur of a stray dog. After his hasty departure from MIT, he'd spent the most of the night walking along the river, up and down each side, crossing and re-crossing whichever bridge happened to be at hand. When he was too tired to walk, he'd sat under this bridge and listened to the water lapping against the bank until he'd fallen asleep. His car waited for him back on campus. He could get in it and drive until he had no money left for gas—anywhere at all—but where and why? Was there any place a werewolf would be welcome? No. Such a place did not exist.

He was free, at least. *(Toby would never be free)*. He would be eighteen in two months and he could find a job, any job.

The wound was too fresh and as much as he tried, Caleb could not stop tears from flowing. Bowing his head, he rubbed his eyes with the heel of his hand. This would do him no good. He'd need to keep his wits about him if he wanted to figure out where to go.

Abruptly, the dog pulled away, gave a short bark, and was gone. Caleb looked up in surprise. Standing before him was a little man in a rumpled overcoat. A pocket protector crammed with colored pens peeked out from his coat and gave the only indication that he might be a professor. Caleb sat up sharply, taking a deep breath to banish the tears that stung his eyes and nose. He eyed the man suspiciously, taking a long moment to recognize him. "Professor Hermann?"

"I had a time finding you, Mr. O'Connor," the man said in a soft voice, his watery blue eyes darting about. "Your car's still parked on campus, so I thought you'd be nearby, but I didn't expect you to be most of the way to Harvard."

"But…how did you…?"

"Shouting that you're a werewolf who's decided to start eating people in the Infinite Corridor," the little man chuckled mildly. "Well, that's going to draw some attention."

Caleb stared at his physics professor in disbelief. Had he really said those things last night?

"Do you mind if I sit? I've been trudging along the river for what seems like hours, though I think, really, it's much less than that."

Professor Hermann didn't wait for a reply but spread his raincoat out on the ground. He taught freshman physics, and Caleb was his best student this term, so he'd been recruited to lead tutoring sessions for the classmates who struggled with the lectures or labs. In spite of this, Caleb had rarely spoken to the professor, who preferred to communicate by leaving cryptic notes for him in the Department Office, always addressed to Mr. O'Connor. The professor looked to be in his seventies, with thinning white hair and a bald spot, now covered by a shapeless brown hat.

"As I was saying, it took a bit of work to find you," Hermann grumped as he balanced a bulging valise on a rock to keep it out of the dirt. Then he sat down, took a deep breath and continued, "Such a promising student."

"Well, make sure the story makes the rounds," Caleb replied dryly. "I'm sure it will be a joke for years."

"Yes, I daresay the students thought it was funny, just blowing off steam during finals. I wouldn't expect them to be knowledgeable in these matters," he explained pointedly.

"And you are?" Caleb's curiosity was piqued, especially since Hermann seemed more curious than horrified.

Hermann laughed faintly, eyes twinkling. "I would like to explain a few things, Mr. O'Connor, if I may?"

3. Holiday in Romania

THREE DAYS UNTIL THE full moon, Caleb was trapped in a rainstorm in the Transylvanian Alps with a crazy old man who probably had never even seen a werewolf.

"Do you need to rest, Professor?" His companion wheezed and struggled inch his way to the plateau where Caleb stood.

"Please, Mr. O'Connor, you should call me Jonathan." Professor Hermann took a couple of ragged breaths, then reached into his coat for the laminated map, which he handed to Caleb.

Drops from his hood trickled onto the two-dimensional mountains as Caleb bent over to read. Landmarks were difficult to see in the dense clouds that hugged the peaks, but he was sure—almost positive—that the road was twisting and turning in a way that mirrored the map.

"We should speak Romanian," the old man added. "We both need the practice."

"Yes…Jonathan." Caleb still couldn't get used to calling his former physics teacher by his first name. He shook water off the map and held it in one hand while he pointed with the other. "We are—" He struggled to switch from English to Romanian. His head buzzed with verb endings and vocabulary. "We are here, I think, because the road turned west—no, sorry, that's not the right word—east just now after going north. We should be less than a kilometer from Stilpescu."

"Very good. I don't know what I should have done without you," Hermann said pleasantly, as if they were on a bird-watching expedition in the Berkshires, instead of slogging along a river of mud in Communist Romania. "Let us press on, then."

Caleb watched the old man stump on ahead of him while he folded the map. Once he had put the map away, he caught up in a few long strides. This wasn't his idea of the walking tour of Europe that Jonathan Hermann had originally suggested. Caleb wondered, as he did with increasing frequency, where the old man was taking them, and to what end.

It was the summer of 1986, and Romania was a closed country in the grip of a dictator. Crossing the border in an official capacity was simply not the way to go about it—whether you were a wizard or a harmless old physics professor. Caleb had followed his mentor over a frontier post in Hungary, at a location that Hermann had termed "unchartable." When Caleb asked whether magic was involved, Professor Hermann simply said that the Communists concealed things better than sorcerers ever could.

There was no magic in their means of transportation. Nothing but their own two feet had carried them from the Hungarian border all the way to the Transylvanian Alps. Spring had not yet melted the snow from the mountain passes, causing the pair to spend extra days in the low-lying town of Rosu, waiting for the roads to clear. Caleb had pressed for details: Why must they visit the mountain village of Stilpescu and the castle on the promontory above? He had been ignored or hushed throughout the journey, even when Hermann ushered him into an old bookshop. As they sat down at a small table, Jonathan told Caleb he was never again to speak English.

Caleb couldn't catch the name of the wizened old proprietor, who handed them a chipped bottle of deep purple glass and made each take a long swig. To chase the bitter taste, the proprietor gave them sweetened black tea. He talked with them for hours, and Caleb was astounded to find Romanian words flooding his mind as he listened. Finally, he and Jonathan began to speak.

"A Polyglot Potion," Professor Hermann explained once he, too, had absorbed enough vocabulary. "It allows you to acquire language the way children do—naturally, free of accent, though of course with practice."

"So you can practice by telling me—" Caleb began, but was waved into silence as the bookseller began again with tales of local history that Hermann seemed to think they needed to know.

Caleb leaned back in resignation and dedicated himself to listening. He had signed up for this adventure, and he had nothing to go back to.

Soon the structure of the grammar began to flow smoothly off his tongue, although the potion frequently made him dizzy and gave him headaches. By the following week, after they left the city and began to scale the mountains, his head was clearer and he felt almost fluent.

It was impossible to escape the chill, even in mid-June. Rain fell straight down, or sideways, or sometimes in several directions at once. No matter how much they swathed themselves in hats, scarves, and raincoats, they found themselves soaked to the skin. The old man did not complain, but with each passing day he had an increasingly more difficult time matching Caleb's pace. Caleb urged him along, anxious to get the professor settled in a safe place before the full moon. The waxing gibbous moon tugged at his insides despite the thick, gray blanket that cloaked the sky.

They both felt immense relief when a bone-jarring gust of wind momentarily pushed aside a fog bank to reveal a collection of houses and the glimpse of a red church roof up ahead.

"We're almost there," Caleb yelled to the lagging professor. He stopped and waited for Hermann to join him, taking his arm and pointing to the vague outlines of buildings. The little man nodded, his eyes—the only part of his face visible within the scarves and hat—tired but alert. They didn't speak again until they found shelter in the village.

The warmth and scents inside the baker's shop almost drove Caleb mad after eight hours in the cold, dank rain. The waitress bustled about, setting their cloaks and scarves to dry near a fire while her husband cut them large slices of steaming brown bread. They sat around a wooden table with mugs of tea, bread, and honey.

"Out in weather like this," the baker was saying. "You speak pretty good, but you're not from these parts, are you?"

They did not try to hide the fact that they were foreigners. Despite their continually improving Romanian, they had the accents of the city, having acquired the language there. The baker seemed to accept them, but he was suspicious of their plan to travel on to the castle.

"I've not seen that old man who lives there," he said, "but he sends his servant down for supplies. If you ask me, it was a bad idea, him coming back to that castle. Better to leave well enough alone."

Caleb looked at him quizzically, but before he could frame a suitable question, the baker's wife chimed in, "The village has enough troubles with werewolves prowling and the things that live in the Petrosna Caves." She shuddered, not wanting to name her fears. "And Castle Arghezi as well, home to…"

"Hush, woman!" her husband said sharply. "No need to bring up the past." He shook his head in trepidation. "These men will see for themselves soon enough." He seemed to consider them insane but harmless. If they wanted to go and get themselves killed, that was their own business. He gave them beds for the night, and shared what he knew about how to find the path to the castle on an old, water-stained map.

Weak sunlight cast feeble shadows in the village square as they set out the next morning. Caleb had held his tongue while they packed and said their goodbyes to the baker and his wife. He didn't say anything as they crossed the little square in the village, the locals silently staring at the crazy foreigners. By the time the village was well behind them, hidden in the misty folds of its alpine valley, the words in Caleb's mouth were a river about to overflow its banks, burst the dam, and drown everything in its path.

"Prof—Jonathan," he said with forced calm, trying to squelch his mounting exasperation and irritation. The rain had ebbed to a light drizzle, and they had stopped to rest by the side of the track. As they shared some of the bread the baker had given to them, Caleb demanded answers. "It's time you told me where we're going. Every time I've asked, you've changed the subject or told me to wait. I'm not taking another step toward that castle until I know what I'm in for."

With just the two of them under the broody sky, Professor Hermann finally allowed himself to speak.

"You might well wonder why I asked you to be my traveling companion this summer," he began.

Caleb chortled at the understatement, but simply nodded his wool-swathed head, afraid that anything he might say would make the old man clam up once more.

"I have observed you," the old man continued, "with the other students and have noted how well you've done in my classes. I observed a few other things as well. How you are invariably absent the day after the full moon, for example, and how you always return with your face and hands covered with scratches."

"I go hiking," Caleb responded in his best tone of scientific scorn.

"Yes, yes," murmured Hermann as if it scarcely mattered. "You in turn may have wondered what I am doing teaching at a place like MIT."

This was a hard question to answer politely. Even as a freshman, Caleb had heard all the stories. "You don't do research," he replied cautiously, "which is a bit odd."

"Yes. The younger faculty consider me quite beneath their notice." Hermann laughed faintly, eyes twinkling. "I earned my position in a less conventional way: I did a favor for the dean, and was rewarded with a permanent lectureship. You wouldn't happen to recall the name of the previous Dean of Science, by chance?"

Caleb was about to reply that he didn't, but the name sprang unbidden to his mind, the way all Romanian proper nouns now did. "Of course, Dean Arghezi—Castle Arghezi? Our old dean is the one who...?" He stopped himself, afraid of being disrespectful.

Every MIT physics student knew the rumors and fanciful tales about Dean Arghezi, and the drama surrounding his last day was no exception. He was mysterious and weird and the students loved him, but the faculty had long balked at his eccentric behavior, and they had finally confronted him about an especially odd demand that they wear silver crucifixes at all times. Right in the middle of the fall term, he had stormed into the University president's office, yelling that he'd had it, he quit. He's rather return to Romania to hunt vampires than spend another moment in that abominable university. Since then, no administrator's portrait was safe from being disfigured with capes, stakes, and fangs.

"But that was a joke, right?" Caleb persisted. "Dr. Arghezi didn't actually move to Romania, did he?"

"Indeed he did," Hermann replied, sounding pleased. "To do precisely as he promised. And now it is time for me to do him another favor."

"The favor you did him involved a vampire?" Caleb had to swallow a snort of derisive laughter.

"Unlike most people," Hermann continued placidly, "you might not be surprised to learn that there are and always have been vampires in academia. It's the late hours and the exposure to an ever-changing stream of the young and naïve that attracts them, I suppose. This particular vampire caused some problems in the upper administration when he began to, er, recruit, if you know what I mean."

"Is that what you wanted me for?" Caleb realized, sarcasm creeping into his voice. "Caleb O'Connor, vampire killer?"

Hermann was unfazed. "Did you know that the blood of a werewolf is toxic to vampires? Drives them mad, in fact."

"I've never even seen—I mean I wouldn't even recognize—" Caleb stopped, aware of the magnitude of the lie he was about to tell. How many hours had he and his friends spent talking about hunting vampires in Maine? It had been a way to occupy rainy afternoons—but except for Toby, none of them had actually done it.

Caleb stalked away from the old man, suddenly unable to look him in the face. The tormenting thoughts returned: If only he'd made Toby see sense, if only he'd been there with him, instead of holed up in his poky basement apartment in Cambridge, doing calculus problems, if only….

Caleb pivoted to face Jonathan Hermann. "Why would I want anything to do with vampires? One of my best friends died, and another took the blame for maybe letting out a vampire. It was never proved, but he was executed by a gang of fake wizards because of it."

"Ah, so that's what happened? Now I understand, I think. Those wizards believed they were protecting their Community." Professor Hermann sighed and stood, gripping his walking stick for balance. "Protecting all of us against an abomination, a soulless evil that fled these very mountains to seek its fortune in the New World."

Caleb shivered, hoping the old man was telling him a tall tale. "And I suppose you hunted down this…thing?"

"Not I," Hermann said mildly. "I heard about the vampire after it had been sealed up—for good, they thought at the time. But I've hunted a few in my younger days."

Caleb couldn't suppress a guffaw. "And that's why MIT hired you to be a monster hunter?"

"Every school should have one." With a wry smile, Hermann reached into his cloak and pulled out a handwritten note. "Read this."

Caleb unfolded the letter, then read quickly as the paper began to dissolve in the rain.

My dearest friend Jonathan,
I write in haste, although I do not wish to neglect inquiring after your health and fortunes. I seek someone to assist me in the dangerous work of keeping the home of my family secure. I believe you know the skills that will be of most use to me. Alas that the best schools in Romania are long closed! If you could perhaps make

discreet inquiries with some of my old colleagues, I would be eternally grateful. I hope that they may know of some suitable candidate. Payment will not be an issue. I hope to receive your reply promptly, as my need is great.

Yours,
Alexandru Arghezi

Caleb thrust the note back at Hermann as though it were a hot poker. "You're not thinking that I could—what do you know about my 'skills'?"

"I have taught many scientists and I have trained many wizards," Hermann replied mildly, allowing the paper to fall apart in his hands and scatter to the wind. "In either case, many of them were more foolish than you appear to be."

4. Interview with a Vampire-Hunter

ASTLE ARGHEZI APPEARED AT first sight to be just another outcropping of the mountains, made of blocks of the same gray stone and draped in wisps of last winter's snowdrifts. Yet as it came into view, there was a regularity, a purposefulness, that marked it as a work of humans. A single tower rose above the two-story wall surrounding the castle, like an arm raised up to puncture the heavens. They could see no more than that until they passed through the massive iron gates.

Before they could call out or ring a bell, a dour man opened the gates for them. Although Professor Hermann called him by name and addressed him in Romanian, Michael said little as he led them across a muddy yard to the main building. The building also had two stories, although the windows of the upper floor were dark. A vaulted roof still flecked with snow, suggested a large hall in the center of the building,

Michael employed a series of gestures incomprehensible to Caleb to open a massive oak door and usher them into a cold stone hall. A few smoky torches lit the way to a broad stone staircase curving up into darkness. Michael took their packs, but advised them tersely to leave their coats on until they reached the Great Hall. They followed him there, accompanied only by the clipped sounds of their boots on the hard stone.

After the dimly lit corridors, the Great Hall was an explosion of color and warmth. Caleb blinked, stopping to let his eyes adjust and to cope with the rush of smells assaulting his half-frozen nose. The hall had a high vaulted ceiling crisscrossed with massive beams, which cast twisted shadows upward. Rugs in maroon and white lay scattered on the stone floor. Tapestries covered the walls with swirls of greens, browns, and reds, giving relief from the endless gray stone. There was little furniture in evidence—an enormous wooden table, half a dozen chairs of different sizes and shapes, a couple of smaller low tables. The decorations were dwarfed by the high ceiling suspended above the uncertain and unquantifiable darkness.

Judging from the odors, this room served as a kitchen for the castle. Caleb's eyes (and nose) were drawn to a huge stone fireplace at the far end of the hall. The tall man standing before it when they entered swiftly turned and strode the length of room, a smile of greeting on his long, angular face. He wore a cloak of deep red that swirled about his heels as he walked.

"Jonathan!" he cried out in English, seizing his friend's hands and then embracing him warmly. "You decided to pay me a visit. Excellent! I apologize for my lack of response to your letters. We have had certain meteorological conditions that impeded all of our usual mechanisms of communication, ordinary and magical alike. But I am pleased that you came. Things will be easier to explain in person. … Oh, Jonathan! It is good to be home. One can't go back entirely… but I had missed this place, and it is my home once again." His English was dramatic but flawless.

Alexandru Arghezi stood a head taller than Caleb, made even taller by his thick black hair, graying at the sides. His face was hard, although it softened when he smiled, as he did now. Dark glittering eyes took in Hermann and his young companion as he helped them off with their coats, hats, and gloves. Michael appeared as if from thin air to help take off their muddy boots, and then disappeared with the whole sodden lot as silently as he'd appeared.

Arghezi fixed his gaze on Caleb, staring at him intently for a moment, which prompted Jonathan to say, "Alec, may I present—" he stopped and began again, this time in Romanian. "This is Caleb O'Connor."

"For thirty years you've been telling me that you would learn my language, Jonathan. I see that it took extreme measures to make that happen." Alexandru laughed and patted his old friend on the shoulder. The smile stayed on his lips as he turned to Caleb and shook his hand, but the dark eyes were calculating and mirthless. "You must be a scholar, if my friend Professor Hermann recommends you."

Caleb stood awkwardly, embarrassed by the description, since he fervently wanted to leave behind scholarship and all it represented. Not wanting to reveal his discomfort, he met the man's probing gaze and answered in Romanian, "School is over for me. I am…looking for another line of work."

Alexandru barked a sharp laugh and dropped Caleb's hand. Clapping both guests on the back, he said, "Come, enjoy the fire. I know you must be chilled."

All three sat at the massive wooden table, bathed in firelight. As Mihail (as he was called in Romanian) served dinner, the two old friends talked of people and events unfamiliar to Caleb. Alexandru explained that Mihail had been a devoted Arghezi servant for decades, and he had even accompanied Alexandru to America to look after him. Now Mihail cooked for him and tended to the sheep, goats, and chickens they kept in the spacious stable all winter long.

Mihail was an excellent cook, and Caleb was ravenous. He wolfed down second and third helpings of mutton stew while the two old men chattered. As he listened to Alexandru's stories, Caleb gazed around the enormous room. The castle was almost four hundred years old, occupied by the Arghezi family for over three hundred of those years. The murky recesses of the rafters reminded Caleb of the great dome at MIT. He wasn't sure why, since the ceiling of the grand entrance to campus was nothing like the vault above him. Perhaps it was the feeling of being dwarfed by the high, curved ceiling that had been built, brick by brick, by the hands of men, and yet was grander and more permanent than the life of any one individual.

During the meal, Professor Hermann grew less animated. The days of trudging in the chill air had caught up with him, and he sneezed and coughed violently while trying to hold up his end of the conversation with his old friend. After dinner, the two travelers sank into high-backed chairs pulled around the fire in a semicircle. The stone mantelpiece loomed in front of them, taller even than Alexandru, who stood next to it as he poured them each a glass of wine.

"The wine cellars here were untouched during my absence." He held the decanter up, and firelight streamed through the blood-red wine. "Although many creatures inhabited the castle, none had the slightest taste for wine. I am quite grateful for that. This 1927 Cockburn would be worth at least five hundred dollars in Boston."

Caleb, who avoided drinking parties and knew nothing of wine, examined the ruby depths of his glass. He couldn't conceive of paying as much money for the contents of a bottle as he had for his car, but he knew that the wine was fragrant and musty at the same time. To his left, Hermann had barely touched his glass; he had fallen asleep in the lumpy leather armchair, the firelight giving his face a fevered look.

"You are—or were—a student in astrophysics, Caleb," Alexandru remarked.

"What?" Caleb had drifted off, entranced by the firelight and unaware of the strength of the wine and the depth of his own exhaustion. "Yes, that's right. Jonathan must have told you," he finished uncertainly.

Alexandru dismissed this with an elegant wave of his hand. "Clovis told me of your plans to go to MIT before I left the States."

"My guardian? You know him?"

How could he have been so naïve as to think that Alexandru wouldn't have known Clovis Fintonclyde? The man had entertained visitors from all over the world when Caleb was a boy: Native American shamans, priestesses of voodoo from the Caribbean, mystics who'd arrive heavily cloaked, speaking languages that Caleb couldn't identify.

"Oh, I know him very well indeed. We have…collaborated…It is astrophysics that protects this castle, you know. The power of Jupiter, Saturn, and the moon combine to create wards against monsters, humans, even animals. The cow barn is constructed entirely from a moonward." Alexandru paused, as if ready to say more, and then shook his head. Instead of continuing, he leaned over and poured more wine into Caleb's glass, then set the decanter down. He took a seat next to the fire in a tall wooden chair with ornately carved back and arms.

"I wonder," Alexandru pondered, "why an adoptee of Fintonclyde's, who I assume has some of the old wizard's talents and inclinations, decides to depart suddenly with no notice to the Community. And now you are here to seek, as you say, another line of work…" In the light of the fire his eyes gleamed as he regarded his guest.

Caleb wondered whether Alexandru had any inkling of what he had brought into the castle that night. The heady wine seemed to have stolen away his normal inhibitions, or perhaps saying it in a foreign language blunted the impact. Either way, he explained, "I wished to leave school, America, everything because Fintonclyde and his cronies blamed my best friend for something he didn't do. I was not even allowed to testify at the trial because I am a werewolf."

Alexandru Arghezi said nothing; only a faint narrowing of his eyes betrayed any emotion in his otherwise unreadable face. From behind Caleb, came a muffled cry and the sound of glass shattering.

Mihail, who had been clearing the table, had dropped a wineglass on the stone floor. In confusion, Caleb turned to see a look of terror and revulsion on the servant's face, a look he knew well and often saw in his troubled dreams.

"That will do, Mihail," Arghezi commanded sharply. With evident concern, he softened his tone and said, "I will clean up the rest. Please take Mr. Hermann to his bed."

The servant approached cautiously, eyeing Caleb as if he might leap up and bite at any moment. Mihail's face was now an emotionless mask, the trepidation pushed beneath the surface like fish under the ice of a winter pond. Keeping as far from Caleb as could, he gently helped Hermann to his feet and supported the stumbling old man out of the hall. Only when the footsteps were completely gone did Alexandru speak again.

"You must forgive Mihail. Werewolves killed both his parents when he was six years old. He has been with our family ever since." His tone was concerned, but otherwise casual, which both surprised and confused Caleb. "Returning here was not pleasant for him."

Caleb realized he was gripping his fragile wineglass tightly, and hastily set it down. He did not know what to say. He felt at once the bitter anger of Mihail's rejection alongside his own memories of being bitten as a small child. The event stood out clearly in his mind, though he had trouble recalling the terror he must have felt.

"Near Amherst, yes?" Alexandru asked thoughtfully, fingertips together at his chin.

Stammering slightly, Caleb told him the name of the little town where he and his parents had lived. "It was over thirteen years ago, when…I was only four. I remember very little."

"Werewolves are not common in New England, not at all. Thirteen years ago…let me think. Ah, Crispin Whitehead, that was the name."

No words could express the confusion Caleb felt at that moment. What was Alexandru saying? He knew the werewolf responsible? Blindly he closed his hand around the glass next to his chair and brought it to his lips, choking on the strong, sweet wine.

"How? You knew—?" he croaked finally.

"We had a federally funded program to track many creatures, including werewolves," came the matter-of-fact reply. "Your government at work, eh? Of course, the general public knew nothing about the program…or the creatures we were tracking. There were never that many on the East Coast, and they tended to be rather territorial. Whitehead was a difficult case. Hmmm.

Emigrated from Britain—kicked out is more like it. He was well spoken, a good chess player, but quite without remorse. He was warned, but…"

"And what happened to him?" asked Caleb timidly, simultaneously fearing and hoping that he already knew the answer. Although the wolf had changed his life so profoundly, he remembered him with something akin to sympathy, somewhere in that corner of his mind where emotions and smells blended. A male, middle-aged… in some ways his father.

Alexandru sighed, releasing his hands in a gesture of futility. "I caught him, caught him in the act. He killed a family of three in the Berkshires. He had been warned, after all."

There was silence, punctuated only by the crackle of the fire. Caleb did not have to ask for further details.

"Clovis Fintonclyde took you in a couple of years later," continued Alexandru. "Quite extraordinary."

"As far as I know, I am the only—the only one of us that he…" Caleb astonished himself by being able to speak at all.

Alexandru rose and paced in front of the fire with his hands clasped behind his back. Caleb had quite given up trying to understand his host. "Not the first that he took in, but certainly the first he attempted to civilize. I was opposed to his little experiment at first, so much so that Clovis and I did not speak for almost ten years. And yet it could prove useful…" He seemed to be speaking to himself more than having a conversation. Abruptly he turned to face Caleb, still clenching his wineglass.

"You are not afraid of other werewolves, I take it?"

"I have never met another one since I was bitten," Caleb confessed, "but I don't suppose I would be afraid."

"And vampires? I doubt you've met any of those," Alexandru stated harshly.

"Some people say that a vampire caused my two best friends' deaths—" Caleb began, but was cut short by a glare from Alexandru telling him to get to the point. "But no. I was not there."

The fire filled in the silence that lengthened between them with a soft hissing. When Caleb did not elaborate, Arghezi raised an elegant eyebrow and continued. "In the West, they talk about vampires and Transylvania and it's a joke. I heard it so often from bureaucrats and even wizards who should know better. But here it is nothing to laugh about. The Undead call to us… and their song is hard to resist." He sank back into his chair and propped his chin on one hand, staring fixedly at Caleb. "Vampires drove my family out of this castle fifty years ago. They occupied it for many years, according to people in the village…no one knows how long. By the time I returned last year, they were gone…they'd been gone for fifteen or twenty years." He did not sound pleased to have missed them, either. "But I will find them."

Caleb began to rouse himself from the torpor of the wine. "Your letter said that you needed help. Is this what you meant, driving vampires from the castle?"

"The castle is quite secure," rumbled Alexandru proudly. "Apart from the planetary wards, traps are set here and there, as well. No—vampires cannot return to this castle, not while I am master of it. But, outside the castle, things are still very bad. For three hundred years, my family has been responsible for keeping this area of the mountains safe. The people in the village below live in fear and that is not right. I have a responsibility to them as well as to myself." He sighed deeply and continued, "But I am not a young man any more, Caleb. I cannot do this alone."

"You would trust a werewolf?" Caleb asked.

"Clovis Fintonclyde trusted you."

Caleb stared down into his wine again, thinking of another question that had nagged him since he had heard it from Hermann "Is it true that vampires don't—that the blood of…of my kind is harmful to them?"

The older wizard laughed sharply. "Yes. Blood from most any mammal sustains vampires. But the blood of a werewolf gives them a kind of dementia, a bit like rabies. They foam at the mouth and are rendered completely insane, sometimes for years. Around here, I expect that vampires have learned to avoid the local werewolf population."

"And if a werewolf is bitten by a vampire?" asked Caleb hesitantly.

Alexandru shrugged. "No vampire will bite you more than once, and it takes three bites before the victim becomes one himself." He grew thoughtful. "I am assuming, of course, that the three-bite rule applies to werewolves. Some say that you become vampires more easily than do ordinary mortals…"

This was finally too much for Caleb, who found that the room began to spin slowly, even though he hadn't moved from his chair. He got to his feet unsteadily, saying, "I'm not sure that I—" He stopped and clutched the chair. Alexandru rose swiftly and took one arm, guiding him out of the hall. Once out of the oppressive heat and flickering firelight, Caleb's head cleared and the chill of the stone passageways refreshed him.

He had no idea where they were going. His host guided him through the drafty entrance hall and into a wide corridor. As they shuffled slowly, Alexandru raised his hand and conjured a bobbing ball of cool yellow flame that floated several feet in front of them. They were surrounded on both sides by ornate frames, each with a little gold plaque glinting on the bottom proclaiming the name of an Arghezi ancestor. As they traversed the long, dark passageway, Caleb noticed that the subjects of the portraits became more modern in appearance and the dates on the plaques more recent. Near the end, his eye caught Alexandru's name along with another: *Alexandru and Mircea Arghezi,* read the gold rectangle. Caleb stopped and looked at the grim and unsmiling younger version of his host next to a younger boy who, even under the layer of grime over the oils, looked beautiful.

Alexandru tugged at Caleb's arm sharply. "Come. You should be in bed."

The final portrait puzzled Caleb the most, but Alexandru hurried him off without giving him a chance to ask questions. The carved gold frame held only charred shreds of canvas, with no hint of what the portrait had once been like. *Ana Maria Arghezi,* read the plaque.

5. Sixes and Sevens

Both Caleb and Professor Hermann caught cold, and spent the next two days by the fireside, wrapped in blankets and drinking a warming potion out of dark blue bottles. The potion steamed and wailed as it descended the throat, bubbling and crying as it ascended into the sinuses to clear them.

As the sun began to go down on their third evening in the castle, Alexandru approached and gestured silently for the young werewolf to follow him. Caleb was already prepared for the night; under the blankets, he wore only a cloak. They went out of the castle, across the courtyard, and out the main gates, facing east where the full moon would soon rise.

Without a word, Alexandru returned to the castle and shut the gates behind him. Caleb removed his cloak and threw it over a nearby boulder, standing naked in the thin, chilly air. As a small child, he sometimes forgot to undress before the full moon arrived, and any clothes he wore during the transformation were torn to pieces. He had learned to carry a cloak, and most of the time the wolf recognized it as something he should pick up and carry with him. Caleb really hoped the wolf remembered tonight, because he had no idea where he'd be when morning came. A large bar of chocolate and an enchanted compass stone were carefully hidden in a pocket, but these seemed pitifully inadequate. *I should have gone to Morocco,* he thought, shivering. *Or maybe California.*

Five minutes later, he had completely forgotten why he didn't like it here. Picking up the cloak, though not sure why he was supposed to, Caleb the wolf stood on the boulder and surveyed his surroundings.

Had he been a real wolf, Caleb would have been a credit to his kind. He was strong and sleek, his gray and brown fur impervious to any weather, a fifteen-mile-per-hour run tiring him no more than a Sunday stroll. His most remarkable characteristic, though, was the same in both his incarnations. The intelligence that made him a studious and thoughtful scholar brought to his canine self a double dose of the mischievous cunning for which the species was famous. Knowing that the castle contained people, he sniffed and pawed at the gates for a way to get in, but quickly abandoned this idea. There was no getting through that gate, but he had all of Romania as his playground.

Picking his way through granite boulders to the highest point of the mountain, the wolf again surveyed the landscape. The valley was obscured by fog, and rain threatened in the form of looming clouds in the west, but the sky was clear over the distant hills in the east. As wolf, Caleb wasn't bothered by the threat of rain. During the frequent storms in Maine, he had spent his full-moon nights scampering around digging holes, chasing whatever creatures he could find, and barking at the only human who dared to share in his monthly exploits.

Caleb didn't remember this explicitly now, nor did he feel the pangs of guilt and remorse that his human self couldn't escape when he remembered Toby. All he knew was that his fondest moments had been spent in the company of a particular scent, which happened to be human. There was no scent of humanity in these hills, and for the moment the werewolf's hunting instinct was quelled by his delight at being swift and free. He stopped at the top of a ridge to point his nose at the sky and gave a loud, chilling howl.

The howl was returned.

Caleb slunk into a crouch, looking quickly around. His vantage point allowed him to see anyone sneaking up on any side, and he waited for one minute, then two. When there was nothing, he gave a series of short, inquiring barks, a "Who's there?" of the canine world.

Similar barks from behind made him leap up and turn around. A furry head had emerged over a pile of rocks, a head much like his own, though no more than half the size. Then a second head, this one more reddish-brown than gray, and the animal slightly smaller still. Then a third, and a fourth.

Wolves. Real ones.

Caleb had never seen a real wolf. The country dogs he'd encountered in rural Maine provided the only practice he'd ever had at canine etiquette. Enough remained in his mind of the human, and of the tame werewolf who'd explored the Maine woods, so that he circled the wolves not only because he was genuinely wary of them but also because he knew that was what was expected. He lowered his head to make himself seem smaller and less threatening, and gave his tail a courteous wave.

They didn't seem frightened. The pack circled closer and closer, until finally they all met in a circle and Caleb bumped noses with the alpha pair: the red female, then the gray male. The two others in the pack appeared to be their young, though not from the same litter. One was full-grown and the other just a pup. They backed off again, then came closer, and then all five squatted back on their haunches and howled together.

When the wolves slipped away through the jumbled boulders, Caleb watched them go with a magical tingling stronger than anything provided by a wailing potion. It was a long moment before he stood up and scampered off over the hills once more.

He chased a rabbit, forded a stream, and encountered a fox. Most of all he ran, over and under rocks, and through the alpine meadows, stopping only for howls of pure happiness. It had been so long since he had run free that dawn was breaking before he realized he should have returned. Howling once more at the setting moon, as if he could stop it in its orbit, the wolf spun around to trace his steps back to the castle and fell on his face.

Five minutes later he was a soaking wet, muddy, thoroughly exhausted and naked human. He'd lost the cloak and wasn't able to feel the pull of the compass stone.

Wrapping his hands around his bare chest against the cold wind, he silently cursed his stupidity, but the night had been so exhilarating that his current misery didn't bother him too much. He'd just have to walk, and he hoped that the paw prints would guide him to his cloak.

"Hey, you!" called a male voice from somewhere nearby.

Caleb flinched. He couldn't imagine a lie that would sound convincing—especially if the voice belonged to a local resident who knew anything about werewolves. Trying desperately to think, he raised his eyes towards the voice and saw a man standing two hundred yards away.

A boy, rather, since he was certainly less than eighteen, maybe by several years. He was dark-haired and pale as a ghost, with the same shadows under his eyes that Caleb knew he had himself.

He was also stark naked.

This neither shocked Caleb nor surprised him too terribly much. Maybe

Romania would be all its reputation had promised.

"Yes, what is it?" he called, hoping his five-hundred-word vocabulary would get him through this. He never should have been running around less than two weeks after coming to this country. He should have had Arghezi lock him in the castle until he knew the language better.

"You're not from around here, are you?"

"No," Caleb called. "I'm staying at the castle."

"What castle?"

"The castle on the mountaintop. Castle Arghezi."

The boy looked wary, then amused, pointing along the trail of paw prints. "That's about ten miles that way," he said.

"Ten miles?" Caleb was dismayed.

"I live just over the hill," said the boy. "If you want to go inside and, you know, get better, you can come with me." He didn't move, waiting for Caleb to respond. It was just like with the wolves last night—these words were a tail wag, inviting Caleb to make the next move.

He didn't have much choice, since his feet were starting to go numb. Could he possibly have anything to fear? The only troubling thing was the boy's terrible thinness—his ribs and collarbones stood out as if they were trying to cut through his milky skin. "Thank you," he said politely and tried to run toward the boy. It was more of a stumble than a run, as the rocks hurt his tender human feet and even when his transformations brought more pleasure than pain, they still took a lot out of him.

"Who's your pack?" asked the boy, when Caleb drew near. Behind him was a trail of his own paw prints, coming from the east and disappearing into the mist. Just on the edge of sight Caleb could make out where several sets of prints had emerged in opposite directions from a large patch of trampled mud—and possibly blood? At least three werewolves, possibly more. He must have passed right by them last night.

"My what?" he wondered, staring at the marks with fascination.

"You really *aren't* from around here," the boy muttered, running his hand through his wet hair. "What are you, German?"

Caleb could see the cottage already, just a few yards ahead, nestled into a cleft cut out of the rocks. It looked warm and cozy, and he wondered if the boy had made it himself. "No, I'm—I'm American," he said in answer to the question.

The boy pushed open the door to the cottage and Caleb entered gratefully.

It wasn't as cozy inside as he'd expected. Downright chilly, actually, and the floor was bare.

"Didn't know they had us in America," said the boy. "Give me a minute, and I'll get a fire going."

"What was that?"

"Fire," the boy repeated. "You know, you burn wood, so that it's warm in here. B-b-but fires don't start themselves." His lips and toes were blue, and he was shivering.

"Oh, excuse me!" Caleb exclaimed. "I guess I thought…I mean, I assumed you were…that you could…I mean, there are magical ways to make a fire in here."

"You're not telling me you can make a fire out of nothing?"

Confused, Caleb went to the stone hearth and did precisely that. He'd been able to call forth Fire for so long, he didn't even remember learning how. He had always thought that werewolves had a spark of magic in them, because of their monthly magical transformations. He might not be skilled at the more impressive magic that Fintonclyde had tried to teach him—and that his best friend had mastered so effortlessly—but he did know how to make a fire.

When the boy saw and felt the flames he drew closer, bringing with him two ancient and moth-eaten woolen blankets from the floor. Wordlessly, he handed one to Caleb and wrapped the other around himself. His eyes were wide with surprise and admiration.

Neither spoke for a long time, concentrating on getting warm. Mastering grammar the morning after a transformation always gave Caleb a headache, and it was especially bad in a foreign language. He stopped shivering and his brain began to thaw. He wondered who this boy was, whether he was alone, and what he meant by a pack.

"Eat anything last night?" the boy asked at last.

"No. You?"

"Couple of rats." He sighed.

With a start, Caleb realized that the boy was thin not because he was ill, but because he was hungry. "What's your name?" he asked, probably just because it was the first Romanian phrase he had learned.

"Grigore," the boy replied, his teeth chattering less.

"Grigore what?"

He looked puzzled, then with a shrug, "Grigore Beta."

This didn't sound like a real name, but Caleb's brain was too hazy to draw any conclusions. "It's nice to meet you, Grigore," he said, offering the boy his hand. "I'm Caleb O'Connor."

The boy stared at his hand for a long time before he shook it. He looked at Caleb as if he'd never quite seen the likes of him before.

"It's a good thing we met," Caleb said with a smile. "I would have been very cold trying to walk ten miles back to the castle without my cloak. Assuming I can find it by using the, uh, compass stone." He was sure he'd got all the case endings and verb conjugations right, and was really quite pleased with himself, but his little speech didn't seem to put Grigore at ease—quite the contrary.

"Ah, fewmets, you dog," he muttered.

Caleb didn't know the word, but the meaning was clear. "What do you mean?"

"A compass stone," muttered Grigore. "You really think you're some kind of wizard, yeah, my tail."

His speech was a bit too slangy for someone with two weeks' worth of Romanian, Polyglot Potion or no. Caleb realized this was the first teenager he'd met. "Oh, I'm sorry, I thought wizards were…trained in Romania, but your wizard school has been closed for many years, so…"

Grigore edged away, his face etched with mistrust, even hatred. "For the love of Selene, you talk like a professor," he snarled. "What's your deal?"

Selene? Caleb wondered. Good Lord, was this some kind of werewolf argot? He didn't know if he was fascinated or horrified. "Well, I was going to be a professor, sort of, I guess," he said modestly, wondering if perhaps Grigore were much younger than he appeared. "I was studying…never mind what, at a school in America, but I left, well…because they hate us." No point mincing words here, he thought.

"You said it," Grigore muttered, moving back to his old spot because he didn't want to be away from the fire, though he still eyed Caleb skeptically. Something seemed to occur to him. "You just get bitten, you dog, or what?"

Suddenly, Caleb felt privileged and spoiled. He thought he'd had it rough within the Community, but he was completely ignorant of how others fared. "No," he answered quietly. "It was when I was four, thirteen years ago."

His companion absorbed this emotionlessly. "You're younger than me, then," was all he said. "I just turned twenty."

Caleb looked in astonishment at this skinny, anemic boy who didn't even need to shave. He must be starving; he must have been starving for years. Did he rely on that single night once a month for most of his food? He stared for a long time, until the boy grew self-conscious and ran his hand through his now-dry hair.

"Um, I'm from Lupeni originally. You know it?" The boy frowned when Caleb didn't answer, as if he couldn't understand how anyone could be ignorant of his hometown. "I was bitten when I was thirteen. The school didn't want me, neither did my parents, so…I'm here. Pack Six, Vlad's our Alpha. That's about all."

This strange talk was making Caleb more depressed than he had ever been. It was hard to imagine enduring all that he had as a teenager—the battle between human and canine urges, the desire to run free mingled with the horror of hurting and killing someone—without the support of his friends, even Fintonclyde. "Do you need anything?" he stammered. "I mean, you saved my life, really. I probably would have frozen to death."

Grigore was trying to be stoic, but there was a gleam in his eyes. "Anything good to eat up there at the castle?"

"Of course there is," Caleb exclaimed. "I can get you some bread…a chicken, maybe." Oh, great, he thought grimly, now I'm going to make all of Pack Six descend on Alexandru.

A thin stream of drool appeared at one corner of Grigore's mouth, which he didn't bother to wipe away.

"Just have to figure out how to get my tail back there," said Caleb, picking up the slang without meaning to.

Grigore grinned. "Can't conjure up a *răsu*, whelp? Thought you were a wizard."

"A what?" Caleb's meager Romanian was taxed beyond its limits. His sluggish mind tried to figure out the word: Breath? No, *wind*. Grigore expected him to call forth Wind? Fintonclyde had taught them all about Elementals, about calling forth Fire, Wind, or Water, about coaxing rocks to split and the earth to open up. Toby loved summoning Wind and gliding like a surfer above the choppy Atlantic waters as he whooped with joy. Caleb watched more than he tried, and when he did try, he often ended up dumped in the water or bounced on the rocks.

"Can't you wizards," a sarcastic smile appeared on Grigore's lips, "just float away home? I'd like to see that." His thin frame shook with laughter.

"Thanks very much for the blanket and…everything," said Caleb. He knew he sounded like a snob at a prep school for the snotty elite, but there was nothing he could do.

"Keep it, you dog." Grigore watched Caleb, unable to take his eyes off him as the American werewolf got to his feet, clutching the ratty blanket. "You know, I can ask Vlad if he'll let you run with us, if you want."

"Yes, sure," Caleb replied earnestly, though the last thing on earth he wanted was to lay eyes on Vlad Alpha. The thought of the luxury he was returning to made him feel guilty. "I should be getting back now…"

Once outside, Caleb contemplated his footprints in the muddy track. Ten miles to the west, in the mountains that were now gleaming in the morning sun, was the partially destroyed castle where he stayed with the old monster-hunter Arghezi. Not what most people would call home, but a lot better than Grigore's bare cottage. He pulled the blanket closer around his shoulders.

Grigore had followed him outside the cottage. "Well, I guess you're one of us and a wizard, too," he said, "but if I hadn't seen you with my own eyes…" He started laughing again.

Caleb opened his mouth to protest that he wasn't much of a wizard, but instead of making a polite and self-deprecating reply, he said something else entirely. The human part of Caleb did not yet have an inkling of what it was to be an Alpha, but the wolf inside him knew that he shouldn't, couldn't, tuck his tail between his legs and limp home in front of a Beta who had the nerve to laugh at him.

"Yeah, that's right, dog," Caleb half-growled. "This is how wizards do it." He raised one hand dramatically—the other was needed to keep his blanket from slipping down in an undignified way—and concentrated on calling forth Wind. Maybe because the bone-tired weariness prevented his addled brain from objecting that he couldn't do it, or maybe because the wolf within him knew that he had to succeed—whatever the reason, everything worked. He realized that summoning Wind didn't require complicated gestures or arcane invocations, just a certain way of sensing and focusing and commanding.

Grigore backed away open-mouthed as a breeze, then a gust, rushed past him and swirled around Caleb. Caleb was equally surprised as the air around him seemed to solidify. Was he really pulling this off or was this a hallucination brought about by hypothermia? He waved to Grigore as he rose up into the air and felt giddy as the ground fell away from him.

"Stay away from the Sevens, dog!" Grigore called after him. "They're bad news!"

Five hundred yards later, Caleb's spell failed and he dropped, tumbling onto the soft grass. He first checked that Grigore was nowhere around, and then he burst into laughter, recalling all of yesterday's animal sounds and smells in peals of pure delight. It had been the most glorious full moon of his life.

In his joy, Caleb never suspected that Castle Arghezi and the wild forest surrounding it would be his home for the next six years.

Book II

A Curious Education

6. The Apprentice

SUMMER CREPT SLOWLY INTO the mountains of Transylvania, particularly to the high, rocky promontory on which the castle perched. Tiny piles of snow still lingered in the nooks of the castle's inner courtyard, which never saw the sun. Only the glass greenhouse held the promise of warmth.

Caleb sat drinking in the June sunlight, its heat collected and magnified by the panes of glass curving overhead to meet the gray stone blocks of the castle wall. Last night had been his first full moon since coming to these mountains, and that meant that he was still weak, not to mention bruised from showing off and from his long walk home. The little greenhouse, which was stuck on the back of the castle next to the library, made a good refuge as the moon began to wane, warming him and revitalizing his weakened body.

The sun was out this afternoon, dancing above the clouds that clung to the lower reaches of the mountains. He sat in a chair—a blanket on his lap, his eyes closed—and smelled the richness of dirt mingled with the scent of daffodils. He had brought a book from the castle library, *Romanian Revenants*, but cared more about the feeling of sun on his skin than about the local Undead.

A door opened with a sharp click, followed by a creaking groan. Caleb opened his eyes enough to see Alexandru step into the greenhouse. The old wizard stood for a moment taking in the smells and humidity, then wound his way through the tables and hanging plants to the corner where Caleb basked.

"How are you feeling, my boy?" he asked. Wood scraped on stone as he drew up a chair and sat down. Alexandru seemed fascinated by the details of Caleb's transformation. After hunting werewolves for so long, his having one as a houseguest was apparently a good opportunity to learn more. (Mihail, on the other hand, had hardly spoken three words to Caleb and avoided him whenever possible).

"The sun feels good," Caleb replied, opening his eyes and smiling at his host. "We never got this much sun on Fintonclyde's little island in Maine."

"Sometimes it is an advantage to be on the top of a mountain, when the clouds go elsewhere. That is why our little greenhouse prospers so." Alexandru waved a hand at the explosion of plants spilling over wooden trays on the tables and hanging down from above. "In only a year, we have brought this back to life, although not like when I was a boy. Then we had old trees and vines hanging down…"

He stopped and shook his head. Remembering was bittersweet to Alexandru; everything associated with his early life at the castle was tinged with both happiness and horror. Caleb had to be content with scraps, snatches of stories from which he tried to understand the puzzle of the Arghezi family and of the castle.

He didn't press Alexandru for more, relieved that the old wizard in turn did not ask Caleb to relive what had happened only a few weeks before on a remote Maine island.

"I see you have begun your reading on our local vampires," he rumbled, gesturing to the book in Caleb's lap. "That is well, for soon we shall give you some practical experience."

Caleb had agreed to accompany Alexandru on a hunt through the local caves. He'd tried to sound casual as he accepted the challenge, as if any American tourist visiting a half-ruined castle in Romania would want to hunt vampires, but the truth was that the memory of his friends' demise haunted him. He blamed the vampires as much as he blamed Fintonclyde.

Alexandru jerked him out of his daydreams with a stern lecture. "In these mountains, vampires are inactive in the winter," he began. "When spring comes, they wake."

"Because they haven't had a…meal all winter?"

"Correct. Vampires do not cease to exist if they cannot get blood. They enter a state of hibernation, sometimes for years, waiting for the opportunity to feed."

How long could a vampire stay dormant? Caleb wondered. It had been more than forty years since that old house in Maine was closed and warded.

"Around here," Alexandru continued, "the vampires begin to stir in May, feeding upon whatever they find—often sheep or shepherds. They are not too choosy when they first wake. If we are lucky, we can catch them before they are fully awake."

"Sheep or shepherds, eh?"

"Vampires have their preferences about blood. In a pinch, any mammal will do, but human blood—with the exception of your own, my dear boy—is preferred. Human blood produces in vampires a state of ecstasy, I suppose one would call it, not attainable any other way, at least so I am told." It occurred to Caleb that Alexandru had personal knowledge about this point, but he seemed reluctant to admit it.

"And so," Alexandru continued, "we shall hunt them. Tell me how we kill them."

"A wooden stake through the heart," began Caleb, feeling a bit like he was back at MIT and cramming for a final exam. The difference was that there would be a field trip associated with this class. "Hawthorn or maple. A single, clean stroke."

"And then?"

"The head must be cut off and the body burned," Caleb recited from some musty book of childhood.

"How long?"

"The stake, you mean?" Caleb asked, feeling fuzzy-headed. He'd never done well in school, either, the day after the full moon. To add to his confusion, Alexandru pulled a wooden stake from his pocket and handed it to Caleb. He ran his finger along the smooth, pale wood from the flat end to the tip. It was about eight inches long and very sharp.

"These are made for me in the States," the old vampire-hunter said casually, "by an Indian shaman in New York. Maple works the best, I have found."

Caleb wondered if Toby had been prepared to meet a vampire on that night. Did he know enough to bring a stake? Of course not. Fintonclyde had never mentioned vampires to them. But had his old teacher ever killed a vampire? The wizard now facing him in the greenhouse had killed at least one.

"How long," Alexandru repeated patiently, "before the body must be burned?"

"Before the next sunset." It was hard not to laugh, to speak with that tone of scorn the skeptics all cultivated. "Otherwise the vampire will…come back to life."

"Excellent," said the old wizard, leaning back in his chair with a pleased expression on his face. "Many have made the mistake of thinking that a simple stake through the heart will suffice—with disastrous consequences."

As Alexandru continued with his questions, assuring himself that the young wizard understood the finer points of vampire lore, Caleb turned the stake over in his hands. Vampires weren't alive anymore. Didn't they deserve to be stopped from draining the living? Wouldn't they welcome death, Nature's final rest for every creature?

Caleb had known since he was very small that other people considered him a monster deserving of death. Not to mention the creatures on Fintonclyde's Reserve, creatures that he grew to consider his friends and family, although to everyone else they were horrors to be (at best) contained, isolated, and gawked at from afar. He knew he couldn't rely on the law to tell him what constituted murder, and pondered obsessively the ethical issues involved with killing anything. In his efforts to construct a consistent philosophy of his own, he usually erred on the side of caution. His human incarnation had never harmed a living creature. He was also quite sure his wolf hadn't eaten anything larger than a mouse, though he often wondered how well his memories of events at the full moon could be trusted.

He dug the sharp point of the stake into his palm. Even if he had killed a person while transformed, even if he were a predator, he was alive, and he killed to feed a mortal body. Vampires were death preying on life, walking corpses, reeking of decay. Life had to be protected, he finally concluded, as he accidentally drew blood from his own hand. It still sounded like a hollow justification—especially knowing that he wished ill on people in the Community—but then, he had yet to encounter the Undead. Without experience it was impossible to say whether he could bear the role of monster killer.

7. The Sleep of the Undead

VAMPIRE HUNTING TURNED OUT to be a cold, uncomfortable, and messy business. Jonathan Hermann declared himself too old and arthritic to hunt again, then without delay returned to the States. At first, Caleb and Alexandru spent days climbing through caves of various shapes and sizes without seeing more than clouds of bats (and a lot of bat droppings). The Romanian didn't seem bothered. In fact, he insisted they bring home several sacks of guano on their first day out, because it made such good fertilizer for the plants in the greenhouse.

Caleb was wedged in a crack between two rough, slimy faces of rock, waiting for the older wizard to catch up with him. This cave, the fourth in as many days, had a narrow and tortuous beginning, although Alexandru assured him that it opened up further on. Caleb's small hand-fire threw a weak, red glow that illuminated the passage only to the next twist.

When he heard Alexandru approach, Caleb continued wriggling through the rocky passage, wondering yet again why he was in Romania, more particularly in a bat-infested cave in Romania. Part of the answer, he knew, had to do with his adventures under the June full moon. Unlike the full moons in Maine, the adventure under the Romanian full moon left him with a keen longing to run wild with others of his kind.

Something more than the wolf's urges kept him here, though. What he had learned from his new teacher was compelling; certainly no school in the world could teach him some of the things he was absorbing. More than that, he began to feel that Alexandru respected him, although the teacher could be harsh when he felt Caleb had made a mistake. That was understandable; mistakes in this desperate land didn't just mean bad marks on an exam, but the difference between life and death.

Caleb felt a sudden surprised vertigo as he stepped into a larger chamber. He stopped and pulsed the hand-fire into the yellow, as a sign to Alexandru that they had reached the cave they sought. He turned slowly and cautiously around, inspecting the rocky roof and walls. The roughly oval chamber measured about twenty feet at its longest. It seemed drier than the passage they had just come through. With a thrill, Caleb saw bits of straw lying on the floor of the chamber. The ubiquitous bats clinging to the ceiling would not bring straw to their lairs, but sometimes vampires did, to make a dry bed for themselves.

When Alexandru emerged from the small opening, Caleb silently gestured to the floor. The pale yellow straw glinted from his magical light. The older wizard nodded curtly, his hungry eyes giving the only indication of excitement. The trail of straw led to one end of the oval, which seemed from a distance to be a dead end. Up close, they saw a jog in the rocky wall, leading to another chamber.

Caleb extinguished his own hand-fire and drew from an inner pocket a lumpy, fist-sized stone. He closed his hand around it as he followed the vampire-hunter around the corner. The little alcove they entered had a thick layer of straw on the floor. Alexandru stepped into the middle of the small space, while his companion hung back near the entrance.

In the light of Alexandru's hand-fire, Caleb saw first folds of cloth and then the pale skin of someone lying on the straw, a boy by his appearance. The young, almost beautiful face moved slightly as the old wizard clenched his hand and caused a brighter light to issue forth. Caleb could have believed that a young shepherd had wandered into this cave for a nap, until the thing opened its eyes.

Dark, empty eyes fixed on them as the creature slowly sat up. Its appearance was nothing like Caleb expected. He had seen ogres, trolls and what he thought was a hydra once, but none of these prepared him for the horror that dwelled in the vampire's black eyes. The eyes lacked any sign of humanity; there was not even a glimmer that would indicate the animal nature that humans shared with monsters. All of a sudden, Caleb felt lost, sucked into the alien vacuum behind those eyes.

"Who disturbs my rest?" asked the vampire softly, as he rose and glared at the grim wizard standing before him. Still Alexandru did not give Caleb the signal, so he watched and waited.

"Many years have passed, Turzii," stated Alexandru flatly. "I thought you were gone."

"And I thought you were dead, Arghezi," came the reply in a cold, hard voice. "You were foolish to come back. She's gone, you know. Fed up with the lot of us."

The old wizard tensed slightly, but his face remained an emotionless mask. "And Cuza?"

The vampire took a step toward Alexandru, who stood his ground. "I haven't seen him in years, but I'll tell him you're looking for him, if I run across him." The creature stepped closer. Alexandru gave a swift glance at Caleb, as the vampire continued, "I know he will want to find you, after what you—"

The vampire launched himself at the old wizard at the same time that Caleb cried, *"Helios!"* and held up the lump of stone in his hand. A blindingly bright light filled the alcove, banishing all shadows and washing color even from the stone walls. The creature had aimed his hands for Alexandru's throat, but at the coming of the light fell to his feet screaming. The sunstone that Caleb held produced a light that, although not sunlight, was sufficiently painful to vampires that it slowed them down. He had not quite believed that this lump of rock, enchanted though it was, could produce such an effect until he saw the writhing form on floor.

Calmly, Alexandru got down on his knees. He knelt on the vampire's chest as if it were a rug, forcing the creature's shoulders to the floor with one hand while extracting a stake from his pocket. As the feeble screams continued, the vampire-hunter plunged the polished wood into the Undead chest so that all but the very end vanished.

The cave grew quiet. Caleb heard only Alexandru's labored breathing and the rustle of bats from the other chamber. Perhaps he would have stood there for a long time, the forgotten sunstone still blazing in his hand, staring at the bloodless face contorted in its final scream. But Alexandru rose abruptly, brushing straw from his clothes, and looked at him.

"So, you see how it is done," he said grimly, while still retaining the air of a professor giving a lecture. He gestured for Caleb to extinguish the sunstone, which he did, plunging them briefly into painful darkness. The silent screams of horror and triumph filled Caleb's brain, and bizarre after-images danced before his aching eyes, monsters more fantastic than any he had ever seen or imagined.

Caleb fell to his knees and curled into a fetal position when he realized who the worst monster was, sitting at his desk with the window open on the first warm night of May, speaking on the phone.

"Hello? Toby?"

"Hey, Dog Boy, what took you so long to answer the phone?"

"I'm studying. I have finals coming up, just after…you know."

"Aw, Dog Boy, you don't need to study–you never did. That's why they let you into that school after all. Anyway, you gotta come up here this weekend. You can't stay down in Cambridge, locked in your apartment."

"But finals start next week—"

"And here's the coolest thing: You gotta come up to help us. 'Cuz we did it, we got in."

"Got in where? Not—"

"Lilac House, yeah, we did it. Well, sort of…"

"Toby, are you crazier than I think you are? Nobody has—does—I mean, it's not—If anyone finds out…"

"You worry too much. We were fine. Okay, René got lost in this tunnel that we found, scared a bunch of bats, and then fainted, but you know what a wuss he is."

"Huh? What—"

"Yeah, well, we got through the wards at the main gate, but we couldn't get into the house. The wards on that house were really solid, you know? But the garage was easy to get into and there were tunnels underneath, one leading to the house and others…well, Sophia figures some of those tunnels go down to the cove where they used to smuggle whisky in from Canada during Prohibition. Cool, huh?"

"Wait a second, Toby. Sophia went with you?"

"She's better than me at undoing wards–not as good as you though, and that's why you have to come up this weekend. She says she won't go back."

"She's smart, Toby, smarter than you sometimes. I wish you'd listen to her."

"But we were really close, and it would be so cool if you could figure out the wards to get into the main house. No one's ever done that."

"You mean no one's ever lived to tell about it. Toby, you can't—"

"Sure I can, Dog Boy, but it'd be easier if you helped me."

"Finals, I've got finals. I'll come up after classes are over–I'll be there all summer, I promise."

"*Right. Yeah. You used to be fun, you know that?*"

"*Toby, I promise I... Toby?*"

Alexandru caught him by the shoulders and shook him. Caleb was momentarily embarrassed, until he realized that the old wizard, too, looked haunted. Caleb resolved to be prepared next time for his personal demons.

They cornered and killed two other vampires that month, before the warm weather made the monsters more elusive. While they did not stop hunting, it became more difficult. Each time, the old wizard questioned their victims about other vampires. Only once did Caleb ask Arghezi once why he wanted to find certain vampires, and Arghezi had turned away in silence. Caleb intuited that it was best not to ask again.

They returned to the castle in silence, and then Caleb was put to work. The rest of the afternoon was dedicated to the study of the rhythms of the celestial bodies that controlled the castle wards. He learned how to read star charts, and where and when to look for planets in the sky, both by season and time of night. Alexandru made him read Greek and Roman myths in Latin and Greek, explaining that the ancient pantheons came closer than anyone else to describing the real magic in the celestial bodies.

After a brief respite when Mihail brought them bread, cheese, and coffee, their real work began. A bright evening star was visible near the thin crescent moon, but Caleb wasn't even sure whether it was Venus or Jupiter. No matter how hard he tried, he couldn't feel anything over the magical surges from the waxing moon. By the time the crescent had set, he was worn out and Alexandru was full of disdain.

"If you need your celestial body to be the size of your head, I'm not sure how much I can teach you," he chided. "Now that that pesky orb is out of our sight, let's try to find Saturn, shall we?"

It was getting late and Caleb was exhausted, but he made an effort. He spent some time prodding around at something that turned out to be Betelgeuse, but finally located the planet climbing in its rising arc. He was sure he felt something there, something feeble that vanished each time a cloud or even a brisk breeze appeared, but something real.

"Yes!" Alexandru cried. "You have it!"

Caleb looked down to see a faint pale blue glow around his fingertips, and then it was all over. He slumped down onto the grass, completely spent, forehead in a cold sweat. "It's nothing at all. You can use this to protect the castle?"

"It took me many years, my boy," Alexandru reminded him. "Many years of patience, study, and practice. We will work on this until Saturn disappears for the season; at least we've made a start."

He didn't sound particularly pleased, but Caleb was beyond caring. It was past midnight, and the smell of chicken garlic soup called from the castle. In a single day he had taken part in his first vampire hunt and been introduced to a type of magic he had no idea existed. The mystery of Alexandru's history with vampires faded to the back of his mind—in time, he told himself. Everything would become clear in time.

8. Fido

FOR A MONTH AFTER they met, Caleb sent food to Grigore from time to time, but he didn't respond to the invitations to meet Pack Six at the next full moon. He spent that night by himself, running through the fields, exploring the mountains, staying far away from the people and villages below. He had yet to meet another of his kind while transformed.

But it was summer, and summer was no time to be alone. Even the wolf pack he'd seen his first night out had a pair of little cubs who'd just emerged from their den. In both of his incarnations, he had sat for hours and watched them playing with their parents.

He couldn't just tell Grigore he wanted to show up. Grigore had to ask Vlad Alpha, who then relayed his response back through the Beta. An Alpha would never deign to speak directly to Caleb. Caleb was amused that the canine alpha behavior was not unlike that he had experienced in the academic bureaucracy.

Grigore arranged for Caleb to meet Pack Six at the cottage half an hour before moonrise, the third since his arrival in Romania. Caleb left the castle a couple of hours before that. His confidence had grown in calling forth Wind, which could carry him swiftly across the high alpine valley to Grigore's cottage, but he still hadn't perfected ending the spell. He decided to walk so that he didn't make a fool of himself by falling on his head in front of a pack of strange werewolves.

Six young people were gathered in Grigore's cottage: five boys and one very skinny girl with hollow eyes. It was instantly obvious which one was Vlad, first because of the way the others surrounded him with an air of protectiveness and respect.

Second, because even in human form he looked like a monster.

When Caleb was a boy, werewolves were never discussed within the Community. But children had a way of figuring out precisely what adults didn't want them to know. For Caleb and his friends, clandestine reading of books on werewolves "borrowed" from Fintonclyde's library was a thrill, though some of what they read made Caleb shiver. The worst might have been the laws that werewolves had to be cremated after death, like vampires, because it was widely believed that they were akin to vampires and could turn into them. Some of the old wives' tales made him furious, especially the idea that a werewolf's bite was dangerous even when he was in human form. But a lot of what they found mostly made them all giggle, especially the parts about the slight physical differences that were supposed to distinguish werewolves from normal people.

But even the most ignorant of lobstermen could not have failed to recognize Vlad Alpha. His hands were large and bony, the nails like claws. His six-foot height and broad shoulders made him less imposing than scarecrow-like. Ungroomed curly hair fell past his brow, and an unkempt beard reached almost to his deep-set eyes. A long, quarter-inch-thick scar ran down the right side of his face, just missing his eye—the souvenir, no doubt, of a dogfight. All of the hair on his face couldn't conceal the contemptuous sneer he had for Caleb.

"Well, Fido," he drawled, "decided to join us?"

"Yes," said Caleb simply, regarding the other with scholarly detachment. Had Vlad been born that way, which was supposed to make it worse? No, he decided after a moment, he's probably just trying to look scary. The thought made him smile—it was what Toby would do.

"The Betas here were telling me you met some full-timers, Fido," Vlad continued.

Caleb wondered what he'd have to do to stop being Fido. "Some who?"

Vlad glanced at Grigore with a look that plainly said, *Where'd you dredge up this moron? "Wolves,* Fido. A mommy, and a daddy, and their cute little puppies." His contempt was accompanied by an evil snarl.

"Oh, yes." Caleb remembered the magical feeling he always got when he saw them. "They're so beautiful, aren't they?"

Vlad flexed his long, clawed fingers. "Not any more." He paused for a terrible leer, showing scraggly teeth. "Now they're a coat worn by a farmer in the village."

"All of them?" Caleb was shocked. He didn't know what to say. "Even the…the babies?" Wonderful, he thought. Cry, why don't you—you'll be Fido forever.

"Don't worry, Fido. Mr. Fatulescu doesn't have long to live." Vlad looked around at the Betas, who all laughed.

"Just about half an hour," Grigore added. "Slightly less."

"We're going to kill him," Caleb guessed.

"Very good, Fido, you learn fast."

This was what he claimed he had come to Romania to do: wreak revenge on humans who killed with impunity. But talking about it like this made it sound more like premeditated murder than instinct or justice. "Do we have to kill—" Caleb began, but stopped at the malevolent leers proclaiming *I knew it* that appeared on the faces of Pack Six. He swallowed and thought fast. "It won't teach him a lesson to kill him. We should bite him and make him one of us."

"Fine sentiments, Fido, worthy of your education," sneered Vlad. "But then what will we eat?"

"He's a farmer, right? Maybe he has chickens."

Vlad extended his arms towards his pack, all of them skeletal and almost translucent with hunger. "You propose to feed Pack Six on chickens?" he asked dangerously.

Caleb took a deep breath and thought of the puppies, unsure of how to answer. The power of the moon caused a tug-of-war inside him between the human and the wolf. One wanted cooperation and the other wanted blood.

Vlad grinned and extended his claws. It was unnecessary for him to demand promises, or to warn, "You do as I say." They all knew that there would be no scheming or conniving once they transformed, and that as long as Caleb didn't openly challenge Vlad's authority, Pack Six could be assured of his loyalty.

Caleb had a hard time believing that the threats to the farmer were anything but talk. It took a lot of discipline and practice for a werewolf to remember any plans he'd made as a person. He doubted that these Romanian werewolves ever found it necessary to exert that kind of self-control.

Or maybe murder came more naturally to them.

A lot of good his Fintonclyde or MIT education had done for him. There was so much he didn't know.

"Come," said Vlad, motioning the others out the door as their bodies simultaneously capitulated to the celestial event.

The members of Pack Six exited the cabin and sought privacy behind bushes and boulders to await their transformation. Caleb did as the others, saying nothing, reflecting to himself that both humans and animals attached great importance to ritual.

As they had retreated simultaneously, so they emerged. The full moon now hung several degrees above the horizon, partially obscured by mist. The wolves mingled for another rite: sniffing, bumping noses, wagging tails to show friendly intent.

Vlad was not the biggest of the pack. Truth be told, he was a rather bedraggled and scrawny animal, with bare patches on his hide. Grigore was actually the tallest, though he too was thin. Caleb's wolf form, nourished by Mihail's mutton stew and coq au vin, outweighed the largest of them by at least twenty pounds.

Size alone, however, wasn't enough to take on the entire pack. In battles of tooth and claw, Caleb was inexperienced and timid. But he had no doubt of the outcome of a battle of wits, and was even now on the alert for signs of gullibility in Vlad.

At the moment, though, he knew that it would be worth his life to approach the Alpha without lowering his head and wagging his tail. Vlad did the same, but as they stood up, neither could resist curling his lip to show the other a fang.

As in his human form, Vlad's teeth were scraggly and broken, the tip of his largest canine fractured to a jagged point.

The wolves took off at last, dashing over the wet leaves, between trees, and up and down hills. They did indeed arrive at a farmhouse, which they approached with a brazenness that surprised Caleb. He followed unquestioningly, though his instincts told him to stay hidden. When Vlad motioned for the two of them to continue on while the others hid, Caleb took the challenge and joined him as they loped up to the dwelling shoulder-to-shoulder. They hadn't discussed whether the farmer might be a wizard, or whether he would take them for ordinary wolves, and at this point Caleb didn't care. He could smell the farmer, stronger and stronger as they went through the wooden door and up the flight of stairs to a small attic outfitted with a straw bed, a chair, and a triangular-shaped window. The man was sitting in the chair, smoking a pipe…and wearing a wolfskin jacket.

With a howl of rage, Caleb leapt at his throat, not caring if the farmer was a wizard and could slay him. He wanted, more than he ever had, to kill.

It was the farmer's own bloodlust that saved him. Having spotted the wolves approaching, he was holding a gun in his lap, and was able to fire enough buckshot at Caleb to throw him backwards.

Ordinary shot, not silver, so he had mistaken them for real wolves. It hurt no more than a softball in the chest would hurt a person, but it still made both werewolves hesitate for a split second—just long enough for the farmer to dive through the window.

Howling and barking, Caleb and Vlad descended the stairs in pursuit. They were somewhat awkward on stairs, though, and the Betas outside had done nothing to stop the farmer, waiting for Vlad's orders. By the time Caleb and Vlad came tearing out of the farmhouse to sniff in the bushes where the farmer had fallen, he had pulled himself out and taken refuge in the grain silo.

Caleb was convinced that, with a minimum of cleverness, they could break their way into the silo. Vlad, however, led them all away, and soon they were tearing across the hills again.

They encountered a small deer, less than a year old, and limping. Vlad and the female wolf brought it down, and they all had something to eat—except Caleb, who sensed that they were all much hungrier than he was. Vlad, too, ate little, perhaps because he wanted to keep his level of bloodlust high.

It wasn't clear if it was Vlad or Caleb who led the pack back to the farmhouse. The Alpha wasn't taking the direct route there, but Caleb's slightest nudges steered him in that direction. This time they approached more furtively from behind the grain silo, which their ears and noses told them was now empty. Peering up, down, and then straight ahead, they saw the farmer lurking in the bushes with his gun.

Something made Caleb hesitate, and Vlad led the attack. Too late, the trained wizard that shared the werewolf's mind realized that the gun appeared to be luminous, as if it carried the magic of the moon that now shone directly overhead.

Silver, the lunar metal. Caleb threw himself at Vlad and tackled him to the ground before he could reach the farmer.

The shot went high, but they heard a squeal from one of the Betas. The slugs had indeed been silver.

Still crushing Vlad to the earth under his 200-pound weight, Caleb watched as the remaining Betas leapt at the farmer before he fired again, and ripped him to shreds.

Vlad struggled, and Caleb stepped off with an embarrassed shake, as if to say *Gee, I must have tripped.* He wasn't sure how the Alpha would interpret the attack. They faced each other for a moment, eyes locked and teeth bared, then turned their attention to their fallen comrade as the Betas devoured the farmer.

Caleb had never even learned the name of the wolf who was shot. He lay very still. Vlad and Caleb nuzzled him, but quickly backed off when they realized the Beta was cold and already beginning to stiffen. Their hackles rising, they licked their lips in a gesture of canine disgust. Caleb had never smelled death before; his curious growl turned into a puppy's whine that lasted until Vlad snapped at the pack. Together they fled, forgetting their dead fellow and the half-eaten farmer as soon as they were free of the scent.

Sated but subdued by their loss, the werewolves returned to Grigore's cottage somewhat before moonset. They occupied themselves with small tasks, grooming and napping, until the sky lightened and they hid themselves away once more.

After the transformation, Caleb was exhausted, but he couldn't bring himself to return to the castle right away. He didn't clearly remember the events of the previous night, but he was uneasy. He knew he had challenged the Alpha, though he wasn't sure to what extent or what it would mean for the future. He also knew that something had happened between the pack and humans, and an odd foreboding told him that he should stay around to see what was going to happen. He had clothes and a vague memory of where the trouble had taken place. The members of Pack Six, equally drained and lazy from their night of gluttony, paid him no heed as he stepped outside to clear his head.

They came just after dawn. Hunters, dozens of them, with everything from clubs and ropes to silver daggers and lit torches. Caleb did what he could without putting himself in danger. Some of the hunters were easy to dispatch magically: a couple of guns exploding in their hands and they were running down the mountain as fast as they could go.

A few of the hunters were also wizards, and they were harder to outwit. The hunt lasted for hours. Caleb's magic did limit the damage: by the end of the day the hunters had killed only one werewolf, along with a teenage boy who was in the wrong place at the wrong time. Tired and confused, Caleb limped back to castle Arghezi as the sun set and the nearly full moon was just beginning to rise.

There had to be a better way to coexist.

Two months later there was no hiding his rebellion. Less than an hour after moonrise, Caleb snarled at Vlad and moved to bite him, fully expecting to be attacked from every direction.

To Caleb's surprise, Grigore was suddenly at his side, as was the young female, Liszka. It was now three to three, and Vlad conceded rather than risk serious injury to himself or to his remaining pack.

Three was a small number, but another pack in the area, Pack Five, was moving to Hungary. Those who didn't want to go divided their loyalties equally between Pack Six and Caleb's group, the new Pack Five. As long as the new pack stayed high in the mountains and avoided the areas south of Grigore's cottage, the Sixes left them alone.

As winter closed in on the mountains, Caleb found himself responsible for five wild, uneducated, starving young werewolves. As much as he hated humans, he knew that his pack would live better lives if they could live in peace with the villagers. He knew there had to be a way, but he had no idea of how to begin.

Lupeni, they called him, after Grigore's hometown, because he was a city dog. The name suited him just fine, and it was better than Fido, after all. As Lupeni, he stood a chance. Caleb O'Connor, ex-MIT student, would never survive in the mountains of Transylvania.

9. ✦ Loyalty

RUMORS OF VAMPIRE-HUNTERS BEGAN to circulate in the village and the surrounding farms. Winter and spring passed with a noticeable drop in attacks by the Undead. However, the reduction in vampires made little difference in the villagers' daily lives. Though they were the scariest creatures of darkness, it was the everyday demons and spirits that demoralized the people of Stilpescu.

A mysterious man appeared now and again to drive the spiridus and balaurs from the rivers and bogs, zmeus from the rocky heights, and şobolans from the cellars. Everyone suspected he was also the vampire-hunter, but they didn't pester him for fear he would vanish as mysteriously as he had come. It had been years since they dared to venture far from their homes; but with the start of a new summer, children again were learning to swim, young men went fishing, and shepherds let their flocks seek out lusher pastures beyond the fences. The braids of garlic tacked to every door grew dry and withered. Howls no longer rented their full-moon nights.

In this interlude of unaccustomed peace, it came as a nasty shock when a pair of werewolves attacked the Muscaturas' boy on his way home from his best friend's house one night.

The boy's father and two local shepherds managed to drive the creatures into an old stable and bar the door before they could kill the child. The weather-beaten wood strained under assault from teeth and claws, but as the sun rose, the howls were replaced by human cries and the assaults on the door grew less effective.

The town gathered to discuss the best way to kill the monsters. Many thought that in human form, a werewolf could be put to death the same way as any other person. Others insisted upon a wooden stake through the heart followed by beheading. Yet others were certain that silver bullets were required, though no one in the crowd was sure where to find any, or whether silver coins melted into projectiles would do the trick.

They were scouring the town for silver and wise old grandparents when the cloaked demon-hunter appeared. Nothing showed of his face but a pair of eyes, which were weary but alert, and he held his hand at the wooden stake in his belt.

"What has happened?" he inquired of Mr. Muscatura in a hoarse voice.

"A—a child," the distraught father replied, unwilling to admit that it was his own son. "Attacked and mauled by werewolves. We've trapped the monsters," he added with some pride, "but no one remembers when we've last had to kill one in this village."

The mysterious man said nothing for a long moment. "Where are they?" he asked finally.

The villagers led him to the stable, where attacks on the door had stopped. Everything was quiet.

Mr. Muscatura cursed expressively, and turned angrily to his son's friends who were gathered at the door. "Has anyone—anything—come out of here?" he bellowed.

They shook their heads, eyes wide with curiosity.

"They're probably asleep," the monster-hunter said in a quiet tone. After staring at the barn door for several moments, he said, "I'll need a length of rope."

"Don't you need silver, a chain or… something like that?" someone called from the crowd.

"That won't be necessary," replied the stranger, without taking his eyes off the door, as if he could see right through it at the beasts trapped inside. The crowd murmured. Could this mysterious monster-hunter be so powerful that he didn't even need silver? What magic did he have at his disposal?

A boy was sent to fetch rope, while the crowd peppered the man with questions about the werewolves. He didn't seem to hear, and he made no answer in any case, resting his head wearily against the door. He roused himself when the panting boy returned, burdened with a thick coil of rope from the blacksmith's. Without a word, the monster-hunter took the rope and slung it over one shoulder.

He motioned for the children to step away. "Stand back," he warned. Then, to the men in the crowd, "Open the door."

The bitten boy's father and the shepherds strode forward, all three removing the bar from the door in a single swift motion. They leapt aside, leaving a clear path between the unknown wizard and the inside of the stable.

The villagers got one good look at the two werewolves inside before the door closed. The barn was quiet for some minutes. Those that pressed their ears to the door heard words, too low to be intelligible, and wondered if the wizard had cast a spell on the Dark creatures inside. When the door finally opened, the stranger emerged, leading two naked and bedraggled young men, practically boys, bound together back-to-back by the very unmagical rope. He jerked the monsters into the bright sunlight, where they blinked sleepily, then his hand moved rapidly through the air, tracing a series of figures in such a way that the air seemed to tingle around him. A wind blew through the crowd suddenly, lifting up the monster-hunter and his prisoners, carrying them away so rapidly that the startled observers had little time to cry out their many questions.

The werewolves gaped in surprise as they found themselves set down in front of Grigore's cottage. The ropes that bound them easily fell away, as they had never been applied tightly. Grins of recognition appeared on their faces as the monster-killer lowered his hood and stared at them for a long moment in silence.

"I missed you last night, Grigore," said Caleb at last. His voice was raspy, and he couldn't suppress a yawn. "I've been looking for you since morning, and it's a miracle I got there in time."

"I can explain, Lupeni Alpha," the younger werewolf began, stammering.

"Please," Caleb winced. "We're friends, Grigore. I think we can dispense with titles."

"Because you don't deserve them." Spiteful as ever despite the close call, Vlad pushed Grigore away and stepped in front of him. They were all so tired from the previous night's full moon that none of their words or actions had the characteristics of a real fight. Their movements were slow, their voices calm, but both Alphas were furious.

Vlad stood not six inches from Caleb, his lips curled into a sneer. "If we don't bite anyone, we disappear, I think you know that. Do you want to see our kind die out?" He didn't utter the worst word one werewolf could use to another—"traitor"—but it was more than implicit in his every drawling remark.

"For every person we bite, villagers come into the mountains and shoot three of us. Is that what you want?"

"It hardly matters if they kill us old dogs." Vlad was not yet twenty-one. "We need pups to keep us going."

This seemed unusually philosophical for Vlad, but he was far from stupid. He had probably been thinking hard about this all winter long—ever since he realized that Pack Five followed the questionable ideal of not biting anyone.

"Attacking small children is a cowardly act, and hardly the way to convince anyone that our kind are anything but monsters," Caleb responded coolly. He glanced at Grigore, who was cowering to one side, letting the leaders of packs Five and Six fight it out.

Vlad threw back his shaggy head, his evil laugh piercing the quiet morning. "But that's just the point," he leered, jabbing a bony finger into Caleb's chest. "We don't have to convince anyone. Once they're one of us, they realize we're superior. Even you are glad you were bitten. Am I right?"

Definitely, Vlad had been thinking. It took a long time for Caleb to formulate a reply. Vlad could be smug because he knew he had the phase of the moon on his side; Caleb's memory was full of yesterday's animal joy, the intense sensations of sound and smell that humans could never know. He had to force himself to remember the lonely nights on the island and the agony of spending full moons in the tiny basement apartment in Cambridge.

"I am glad only when I am free," Caleb managed at last, "and your behavior threatens all of our freedom." Sensing that he'd gained an advantage, he moved quickly. Clever or not, Vlad was not one for subtlety. "If you show your snout in the village at the full moon again, I won't lift a finger—or a paw—to help you. Is that clear?"

Vlad hesitated in turn. Caleb had, after all, just saved his life for the second time.

Suddenly, Grigore slapped them both on the shoulder, smiling uncertainly. "Aw, don't fight, you dogs, OK?"

Caleb took his eyes off of Vlad's infuriating smirk and looked at his packmate. "You're right, little buddy," he said at last, torn between anger at Grigore's betrayal and concern for his well-being.

He realized as an afterthought that he had used the exact words he'd said to René Cousineau when René was forced to play peacemaker between Caleb and Toby on those occasions when tempers—most often Toby's—frayed. Caleb's obstinacy when he was sure he was right coupled with his refusal to lose his cool could drive even best friends into a frenzy.

Vlad shot them both a nasty look and went to get clothes from Grigore's meager collection in the corner of the cottage. He was by tradition unwelcome in Pack Five's territory, but he didn't hesitate to take a bag of food, too. As he departed he snarled at Caleb. "You won't last long," he growled. "Your pack won't survive without biting people."

Caleb watched him go, then looked again at his friend. Grigore should have been with the rest of Pack Five last night, but instead had sneaked into Stilpescu with his old leader. Since their first meeting, Caleb was protective of Grigore, but he knew he could lose control of his pack if he stood silent.

"We made a commitment to each other, Grigore. You've broken that trust. Pack Five agreed we would all fare better if we did not bite people in the village, and now one of my own has violated that pact." Grigore whimpered softly in the corner, too humiliated and frightened to look at Caleb.

Grigore was a lot like René, and Caleb had hope for him. "You don't have to be afraid of Vlad," he told his friend firmly. "He isn't your master. You're a human being, and you can learn to stick up for yourself."

Perhaps Vlad was right, Caleb thought to himself. The Fives were no longer starving. They were robust and healthy and didn't spend their human days stealing the way they used to. Caleb had considered this his greatest accomplishment so far in Transylvania; but was it all for nothing? Did he really want his kind to die out? His spirit was torn with the conflict between gratitude for the comfortable life he had as a human and the hatred for humans that had filled his heart at Toby's trial.

"Get some rest, Grigore," he said wearily. "We're meeting Liszka tomorrow to see about the swamp goblins, right? I'm going back to the castle to rest, too."

The boy nodded, surprised that his Alpha wasn't doing more to punish him for his actions.

Caleb sighed. In many ways, he could rely on Liszka more than on any of the boys. Female werewolves were rare. He didn't know why; maybe it was because little girls were less likely to be running around alone at night, where they could get bitten. Werewolf society didn't have the male and female hierarchies that real wolves did, and the few females had to compete for their place in the male ranks. In some ways this was unfortunate, because Vlad had bullied Liszka horribly. In other ways, though, this unnatural arrangement freed her. She had less instinct to obey the Alpha than the Beta males did, and could readily tell Caleb when he was being stupid. Sometimes he needed that.

She was the most fearful when Caleb tried get the Fives to interact with the villagers, refusing to believe they wouldn't be recognized for what they were and driven out of town, even killed. She would probably never much care for people, but she was the best hunter of minor monsters Caleb had ever seen, and was invaluable in the dirty work of trampling through bogs and creeks to flush out demons. Grigore wasn't bad at that, either, and between them they had managed to earn enough money to feed and clothe themselves through the long winter. Caleb hoped they could get their garden and sheepfold going, too, although the pair of spring lambs he'd gotten from Alexandru had been messily and prematurely devoured at the full moon.

They just needed to learn to use their minds as much as their instincts. Caleb had met people who liked to be bullied before. Some of the inmates at Fintonclyde's "boot camp" had actually been sent there by their parents to toughen them up after one too many beatings in the schoolyard.

Calling on his last reserves, Caleb wearily summoned Wind; but he was not so tired that he missed Grigore's staring at him in disbelief. It was just like Grigore's demeanor when they first met. It did not reassure the troubled pack leader.

10. ❖ Man or Beast?

CALEB RESTED BRIEFLY OUTSIDE the small stable gate to Castle Arghezi. So much summoning on the day after a full moon had exhausted him. He ached, his body crying out for sleep. The luxury of napping in the warmth of the greenhouse or curled up next to the fireplace in his room seemed to be getting rarer as the pack took up more and more of his time.

Life had improved so markedly for all the members of Pack Five in the last nine months. Caleb tried to focus on this as he numbly undid the enchantment on the gate. He made it through at last, resetting the magical ward behind him and dragging himself into the castle through the kitchen doors. Each movement he made, however small, required reserves of energy that he didn't have.

The old kitchens were no longer used, and dust lay thick everywhere on the shelves and tables. A great variety of black pots hung suspended from the ceiling, looking like misshapen beasts imprisoned in some floating dungeon, silently pleading to be released. Paying scant attention, Caleb followed the well worn trail that led out of the kitchen and into the old servants' quarters. This was practically the only living space left in the castle. The upper floor, which had been the family bedrooms when Alexandru was a boy, was uninhabitable. During much of his fifty years' absence, the vampires who had made the castle their own had occupied those rooms. In spite of numerous cleanings, magical and ordinary, they reeked of the Undead. No one ventured up the stairs.

Caleb dragged himself finally into the room where he slept, an unused drawing room off the portrait gallery. Alexandru and Mihail had rooms in the servants' quarters, but Mihail would not tolerate a werewolf sleeping so close. Thus, Caleb had chosen the distant, cavernous drawing room as his lair. At least it had a large fireplace at one end, which provided much-needed warmth, especially on days like this one.

After getting a fire going, Caleb sat on a sofa next to the fireplace, wrapped in a blanket with his legs stretched out before him. He stared into the pulsating flames, his mind too full of the day's events to sleep, even as his body drifted away into some semblance of rest.

Vlad was right: He was a traitor if he didn't want there to be any new werewolves. There was no getting around that. And making new ones meant biting people, biting *children.* Adults didn't usually survive the bite—they died or went mad, unable to incorporate the beast into their already-formed personalities. It was a painful event, one that caused grief to everyone involved…but wasn't every birth process painful?

Not that he knew too much about that. Liszka was the first and only female of his kind he'd ever met, and it was she who told him that they couldn't reproduce in the normal way. The offspring would be born dead, or not at all. It sounded as though she'd had personal experience in the matter, though she provided no details.

Liszka had taught him other, more visceral, lessons. When the moon was full, Liszka and the leader of the Fives coupled joyously as wolves. He knew it, without needing or wanting any explicit memory. She was a gorgeous animal, pure white like a Samoyed. She was a beautiful young woman, too, now that she was well fed: graceful and strong, with glossy hair and shining eyes.

He shut his eyes, forgetting his guilt for a moment in memories of how pleasant it was to be touched, to feel another's warmth, enjoy the smell of her hair, the softness of her face. Before he met Liszka he'd never even kissed a girl, afraid she'd find out his secret and feel as if she'd been tricked into smooching her dog—or even worse, that she'd fear he was contagious. Liszka, too, had been starved for affection, thrown out of her parents' house when she was ten, and they clung to each other in a relationship that was purely physical. It always lost its magic as the moon waned.

She was beautiful and feral and warm, but as a person she was rather dull. She didn't even like to read.

A series of reflections on whether it was possible to teach werewolf gangs to appreciate literature was interrupted by a brief knock and the sound of the wooden door scraping across the stone floor. Caleb didn't turn his head to see who his guest might be, but waited for the visitor to speak. After a minute or two of silence, he sat up wearily, starting slightly as he saw Mihail. The servant ordinarily never spoke to him, and there was a gleam in his eye right now that bothered Caleb.

"Master Arghezi wishes to speak to you," Mihail said coldly, his lips pursed. "He is in his library."

"I am," Caleb could barely speak through his yawn, "very tired, do you suppose it could wait?" He stopped when he saw that this question heightened the servant's smug look. It was obvious that Mihail knew about the events of the previous night. Caleb got slowly to his feet, wondering if Mihail had seen him rescue Vlad and Grigore or if he had just heard the story. Certainly he wouldn't do something so low as to follow him?

Alexandru was sitting comfortably in a chair with a book propped in front of him on the heavy oak library table, reading glasses perched on his nose. "Ah, yes," he murmured as Mihail and Caleb entered, then glanced back to his book. "Mihail, you may go."

The servant did so, with one more malevolent glare at Caleb.

The old wizard did not ask Caleb to sit, leaving him standing near the door, flanked by the enormous dark bookcases that dominated the room. He removed his glasses and tapped them on his book, regarding his guest with curiosity. "I understand that the villagers trapped two of your, er, fellows," he said finally. "And that you took it upon yourself to—"

"To rescue them," Caleb admitted bluntly. Ordinarily, it would have been a tough call as to which of them could cause the other to explode first, but it had just been a full moon. Caleb's emotions were still skewed in the direction of anger and loyalty, and too much complexity was beyond him. Besides, he had spent all morning arguing—and while Vlad the monster got on his nerves, these humans and their smug conviction that it was their prerogative to kill drove him into a blind rage.

"So," Alexandru peered into his book in a pretense of thought, "I can assume that you didn't do with them as the villagers intended?"

"I didn't slay them like vermin, if that's what you mean," Caleb retorted.

"They bit a small boy, nearly killed him." Alexandru was calm as ever, almost dreamy as he looked up and met Caleb's hostile gaze. "They were acting like wild animals, and I have yet to meet a wild animal that can be cured by a strict talking-to."

Caleb was growing angrier and angrier. "Talking is not all I do," he hissed, pacing the space between the bookcases like a caged beast. "Ever since I came to this country I have been trying to help people—yes, people!—who were abandoned by their families and friends to starve. Anyone will act like an animal when he's hungry, and despite the way they are treated, my—my pack are for the most part kind and loyal, much more than I can say for most humans."

Alexandru put down his glasses and raised an eyebrow. "Your pack," he said thoughtfully, as if that explained something. "Pretty ambitious for a city dog like you, isn't it?"

That bit of werewolf slang perturbed Caleb. Alexandru knew more than he cared to tell. "This was the first bite in more than a year," he said coldly, leaning heavily on the massive table that separated the two men, gripping the edge tightly out of both fury and exhaustion.

"Well, then," the anger began to show in Alexandru's voice, "see to it that it is the last."

Caleb bristled, thinking of the hunters who had come pouring into the forest the first time he had run with Pack Six. Had they been trained by Alexandru, supplied by him, even encouraged by him? Why, for instance, had they used silver bullets then, whereas today the villagers seemed unable to come up with any?

Yes, Pack Six had killed a person. But humans wouldn't play the hunting "sport" unless it was skewed one hundred percent in their favor. He sneered at Alexandru the way his wolf-form sneered at Vlad, a gesture common to both dogs and primates. "The last, or what? You'll kill us, is that it?" he snarled. In a flash, he remembered their very first conversation about the New England werewolf whom Alexandru had killed. "Murderer," he said, in a low, venomous tone.

"I have a duty to humans, as do you," Alexandru replied, his voice turning cold. "I warned Fintonclyde that you might run wild one day, and now I see that I was right."

Unable to contain the rage and frustration, which had been seething inside since he first began hunting for Grigore only a few short hours earlier, Caleb blew up. "I want to protect humans! Haven't I tried to keep the pack away from the village?" He pounded on the table with his fists and slammed his forearms onto the unyielding wood so hard that the pain made him dizzy. "I've done all that I can to protect both humans and wolves. What more do you want? If you were so sure I'd run wild, why did you have Professor

Hermann bring me to this godforsaken place?"

Alexandru regarded him with an expression of forced calm, a blankness that Caleb found unreadable and unsettling. He tried to move away from the table, but tired as he was from the day's exertions, he found that his knees would no longer support him. He looked down at his shaking hands and said hoarsely, "Turn me out, then, if that's how you feel. I'll take my chances with my pack."

Caleb felt himself slipping away, his mind and body having gone beyond their limits of endurance. Alexandru must have sensed this, too.

"Go to your room," he said crisply. "I can see that you are in no condition to continue this discussion. We will speak of this matter another time."

Caleb stumbled out of the library and into the Great Hall, conscious of Mihail's eyes on him as the old servant prepared dinner at the hearth. The smells of food cooking attacked him like a horde of rabid dogs, making him realize that it had been a full twenty-four hours since he'd eaten anything. But he needed sleep, needed to be alone.

He dragged himself slowly out into the corridor and down the portrait gallery. He had no memory of how he came finally to his room or to his pile of blankets in front of the fire, but slept a tormented, nightmare-filled sleep for the next twelve hours.

"Where is he? Where is Toby?"

The figure turned around slowly as the stiff wind off the Atlantic lifted his ragged cloak and made it dance. Instead of the familiar face of Clovis Fintonclyde, Caleb was confronted with burning eyes, scabby burned skin, and patchy singed hair framing the face of René Cousineau.

"You're late, Caleb," cackled the specter of his boyhood friend.

"You died," said the dream-Caleb matter-of-factly. "I want to know where Toby is."

René cocked his head over his shoulder at the gray granite building that loomed behind them. "Trial's in there, but it's almost over except for the pyre. It's going to be a nice one." René smacked his cracked and blistered lips, and a rivulet of drool ran down his chin.

Caleb pushed past the laughing René. He began to run along the gravel path, pushing his way into the courtroom. He found himself in front of a wall, transparent in some enchanted way, that let him see into the room where the trial was being held. People thronged him from all sides, making it hard to breathe.

"He's a vampire, my Gran says," said a young woman in a leather miniskirt and electric blue leggings, directly into Caleb's ear. "That's why they're going to execute him."

"No, you've got it all wrong," said a boy next to her. "There haven't been any vampires for fifty years. It was that pyro, Cousineau, that started things, and this guy finished him off."

Scenes from inside the courtroom began to materialize on the enchanted wall. The images were life-size, so it was easy to believe that the participants in the trial could see and hear the crowd of rude observers. Fintonclyde entered and was ushered to his place near the front of the spectators' seats, next to Sophia Daigle.

He almost howled like the beast he was when he saw his friend led into the courtroom.

"Toby, it's me!" Caleb yelled at the image of his brave, heroic Toby, legs shaking and eyes rolling in his head from fear. "I'm here!"

The crowd in the observation gallery fell silent. Toby turned and stared, then slowly pointed his shaking arm in Caleb's direction, his mouth open in a silent scream.

Caleb awoke in a cold sweat, to see Mihail standing in his doorway. The servant was draped head to toe in purple flowers.

"The Master requests your presence at luncheon," he informed Caleb, then backed away and tore off down the hall.

11. Between Two Worlds

BETWEEN SQUABBLING WITH ALEXANDRU, recovering from the transformation, and chores with his pack, it was three days before Caleb managed to get into Stilpescu to check on the boy who had been bitten. All his practice at hunting Dark creatures made it easy to identify the house. He knocked, heard some whispers but no response, and knocked again.

Mr. Muscatura flung the door open, blocking the way. Behind him, his wife put one hand to her chest and the other to her mouth. It was clear that they misunderstood the reason for the monster-hunter's visit.

"Please," Caleb exclaimed, pulling aside his hood. Alexandru insisted upon anonymity, but he doubted that this family would reveal anything. "Don't be frightened. I came to see whether your son has had a healing potion." He didn't even know what the appropriate concoction would be called.

"A cure?" the mother gasped, still with her hand near her heart.

"No, it's not a cure, I'm afraid—but the bite is very painful, and can be dangerous, if it's not treated."

"Why bother?" the father wondered in a low voice, stepping from the doorway and allowing Caleb to enter. "What kind of a life will he have?"

"With some precautions, he will be able to lead a nearly normal life," Caleb lied, the words somehow sounding familiar. "You might not, er, want to tell people, but—"

"We're already planning to leave the village," said Mr. Muscatura. "Too many people know. The brats he played with can't keep a secret."

"Well, if you need me," said Caleb earnestly, "please don't hesitate. There are magical wards one can set up to keep him inside at the full moon, and no one will hear the noise."

Both parents regarded him strangely. After all, he was supposed to be hunting monsters, not giving them advice on escaping detection.

"It might be some time before his bite is dangerous," Caleb added hastily, as if that explained it. "How old is he now?"

"Eight."

"Yes…I can talk to him, tell him what he needs to know to stay safe. It'll be fine." The magnitude of that last lie astounded him. "I'll be back with the potion in a few hours. Don't abandon your son. He needs you now more than ever." Feeling light-headed with the burden of lies and responsibility, he went out the door and ran for the mountains. Without a local expert in dryomancy, these poor people would be entrusting their son's life to someone whose erratic education in America included nothing of the traditional magical remedies practiced in these mountains…and someone whose own parents had given up on him not long after his seventh birthday.

He didn't wish to face Alexandru right now, but fortunately the library was empty. They'd been chilly toward one another since the argument, and it was not the time for squabbles. It was the first time Caleb had taken a close look at the towering book collection, and he wished now he had time to browse. Every book, ancient and modern, on every topic related to Dark Magic seemed to be there, piled two and three deep, floor to ceiling. He was already familiar with the books on vampires and werewolves; none of these featured potions, though. Thinking back to his science labs, he sought out the most battered-looking tomes, the ones with pages out and drips and splotches of questionable substances down their spines.

Healing Herbs was the most stained, but didn't have anything he could use. *101 Common Potions* contained mostly love potions and poisons. Finally, almost by accident, he flipped to a worn and bloodstained page in *Magical Mandrake*. It was a Fang Formula, a treatment for all magical bites, but a note in the margin told him this was the best recipe for the bites of roofdraks, werewolves, and cerberi. Who on Earth had been bitten by a cerberus, he wondered.

Well, now he had the recipe, but wasn't much closer to having the potion. Finding mandrake root would be difficult, unless Mihail had some already dried. He couldn't imagine being able to locate a plant around here, never mind pull it up correctly and dry it—no, he was going to have to ask. Quickly, he scanned the rest of the ingredients: garlic, which they had in abundance; ginger, ginseng, spider silk, nightshade (no wolfsbane, at least)…and a drop of blood from the creature responsible.

The very same creature? Caleb wondered, with a small smile as he imagined going after Vlad with a needle. Reading further, he discovered that any of the same species would do. That made it easy, of course, but he was slightly disappointed at not having an excuse to bleed Vlad. He marked the place in the book with a strip of paper, stepped out of the library, and took a deep breath as he steeled himself for a confrontation with Mihail.

The servant was at the hearth in the Great Hall, standing at a large pot stirred by a three-foot long magical wooden spoon. It smelled of garlic and chicken, and would probably be delicious. Caleb was too nervous to think about food, though. He'd never tried to address Mihail, having previously learned that it was impossible to change those who couldn't forgive him for what he was.

"Er, excuse me," he stammered with his best possible manners.

Mihail looked up and his face froze. They watched each other icily for several seconds.

"I have a potion to brew," Caleb began finally, managing to keep any emotion from his voice, "and there are some ingredients that you might have." He held up the book and opened it to the marked page.

Mihail's face twitched slightly. "Garlic, ginger, ginseng, spider silk, nightshade, mandragora," he recited without emotion.

"Oh, you know it? Good!" Caleb was greatly relieved. "It's not even clear from this recipe whether you drink it or rub it on the… the wound."

"You do not drink nightshade," Mihail informed him in the same flat voice. "It would kill you. You apply the solution to the bite, making sure it penetrates all the way into the flesh. This is for the bite of what sort of creature?"

Caleb hesitated. "It's for the little boy in the village—from three days ago."

"Ah, yes." A malicious smirk appeared for a second on Mihail's lips, then vanished. "One of yours. I'm sure that pleases you."

"It doesn't," said Caleb flatly.

Mihail did not reply, but went out and returned shortly with an armful of vials, bags, and a special coffin-like box from which the dried face of the mandrake peered in an expression of angered surprise. The piece the servant cut from the mandrake root came hurtling at Caleb, who almost didn't catch it in time. Mihail combined the other powders all together into a marble mortar, measuring with an expert eye.

"There are some," he said, turning to face Caleb as he ground the ingredients with a stone pestle, "who may argue that he is better off untreated."

"You mean left to die," Caleb translated. He hated euphemisms.

"His parents will turn him out." He handed the pestle to Caleb, who consulted the book again. The trouble with potions was that you always had to be two or three steps ahead of yourself. "If not now, then when he is large enough to frighten them. That is the silk," he added, "the ginger, and the ginseng. The mandrake root must be boiled for an hour. I trust you can do this."

"Yes," Caleb agreed thoughtfully. "Is it OK if I do it in here? So near the food? I mean, with the nightshade and everything…" The whole business reminded him of organic chemistry, which had earned him the only C of his one year at MIT. He foolishly imagined some kind of magical fume hood designed to trap the noxious fumes.

But Mihail only responded, "Be my guest," and Caleb went to the stone hearth and set a kettle over the fire to start it boiling.

Caleb was surprised and grateful for Mihail's cooperation. Although he kept a wary eye on Caleb, Mihail returned to his cooking. His potion thickened nicely, and the mandrake let out the proper squeals. He needed to concentrate, but he was emboldened by Mihail's kindness. Caleb decided to and try out the lies on Mihail that he had on the boy's parents: that the child could lead a normal life, go to school, be a regular child twenty-eight days out of twenty-nine.

Caleb knew they were falsehoods, and yet he persisted in believing them. Before Toby arrived on the island, had never had a friend, becoming increasingly bitter as he learned how his kind were hated within the Community. As he grew older, he also became increasingly unpredictable and frightening as the monster fought the human for control. Here he was eighteen years old, and he still didn't know who or what he was. How could he pretend that things would be any different for this boy? Perhaps the kindest thing would be to take him from his parents and give him to Liszka to raise.

And yet he believed that things could be different, that this child could learn to master his dark urges before he was old enough to be a real danger. He was confident, yet an involuntary shiver ran through his core; was he simply becoming the next Fintonclyde?

"My mother didn't wish to be treated," Mihail confessed suddenly, as Caleb removed the pot from the flame and waved his wand over it to cool it. "She preferred to die quickly, so that she didn't burden her family."

"I'm sorry," said Caleb sincerely, their eyes fully meeting for the first time since Caleb's arrival at the castle. The servant watched in horror as Caleb pricked his finger with a sharp knife and added a single drop of his own blood to the rapidly congealing formula.

It was almost nightfall before he returned to the village. The castle wards extended nearly all the way down the mountain, which meant he couldn't travel by any means other than walking. He'd covered fifteen miles that day, five of them carrying a large glass vial. Caleb moved deliberately, taking extreme care not to shatter his precious package against the rocks.

He found the mother at home. She ushered him into a room at the back of the cottage where there was a bed of stuffed straw and a reeking oil lamp. Caleb had to get very close to be able to see in the dim light.

Despite his philosophical words, Vlad had not been trying to convert the boy—he had been trying to kill him. An unmistakable mark of his jagged fang ran all the way across his throat, and the wound was red and swollen. The child moaned and burned with fever.

Caleb sat beside the low bed, placing the vial between his knees so he could unscrew the cap. A plume of purple smoke emerged that made him choke. He leaned over the boy, wondering if he were conscious. "This will make you feel better," he promised. "It might hurt for a second, so get ready, OK?"

The boy opened his eyes slightly and gave a low growl. When Caleb went to touch him, he sat up and sank his teeth into his hand.

The mother, watching closely from just behind Caleb, gasped and clutched the wall. Caleb glanced at her, then smiled at the boy. "Biting's rude," he said gently. "Now, growl all you like, but this will help, I promise." Waving away the purple smoke, he splashed most of the vial's contents on the bite.

The red welt caused by Vlad's fang swelled even more, then began to drain a thin black liquid as it shrank back in on itself to leave a scratch no more conspicuous than if it had been from a rosebush.

The boy groaned the whole time, Caleb smoothing the hair off his hot brow and trying in vain to think of something comforting to say. He didn't remember any of this from his own experience, and hoped he'd made the concoction correctly.

After a few minutes the boy breathed more easily, though his forehead was still very hot. Caleb sat at the bedside until the child fell into a deep sleep. As he waited, Mrs. Muscatura came closer, and finally sat on the bed and took her son's hand.

"He hasn't slept well in three days," she said hopefully.

"Yes…" Caleb felt he should apologize. "I haven't, er, ever done this before, so if there are any problems…I'll come back tomorrow, anyway, and see how your boy is doing. What's his name?"

"Bela," said his mother, watching her son sleep.

"Good-bye, Bela," said Caleb. "You'll be OK, you hear?" He handed Mrs. Muscatura the vial. "I don't think you'll need this, but just in case."

She tried to make her son's head comfortable on the pillow. The boy slept on, making Caleb worriedly recalculate how much nightshade he'd added to the pot. He paused once more, and felt Bela's forehead and pulse: cool and normal. It's probably about as exhausting as a transformation, he thought, trying to reassure himself.

Passing by the old stable where Grigore and Vlad had been trapped three days before, he found some kids oohing and aahing over the clawed door. They spied Caleb, greeted him deferentially, and handed him a handful of long, gray hairs. Grigore's. Had Vlad attacked him?

"We thought the fur might have magical powers," they explained.

Caleb took the tuft and stuffed it into his pocket. Around his wrist he wore a cord Liszka had braided from his and her fur that they shed in Grigore's cottage during the spring. It had no magical powers whatsoever, but the white and gray looked pretty together. "You…I…" he stammered. "Can I ask you kids a favor?" he managed finally.

Their eyes grew big and somewhat frightened, as if they expected him to ask for a silver dagger. He put those thoughts to rest quickly. "I want you to make sure the little boy, you know who I mean, is not treated badly. Do you understand?"

They gave nervous giggles. "What if he bites us?" one wondered.

"He can't turn anyone into a werewolf," Caleb responded firmly, "he's too young." He found his confidence again; children always made him nervous. "If you see any trouble, or if anyone plans to do him or his family violence, I want you to let me know immediately. Can you do that?"

They hesitated at first, but Caleb held his ground, hoping that his reputation as a vampire slayer would let him get away with being soft on werewolves. Slowly, one by one, the kids nodded, and Caleb saluted them like a good Young Pioneer before turning once again to the ascent of the long hill up to the castle.

12 ❖ Treachery

MEALS AT CASTLE ARGHEZI were a grim exercise for a while. Alexandru insisted Caleb eat with him, even if they spoke little to each other. However, Mihail had lightened up somewhat, maybe as a result of seeing Caleb's concern over little Bela. Mihail frequently visited Stilpescu, so it seemed likely he knew of the many calls Caleb had made at the Muscatura house to check on the boy's condition. Mihail would at least make eye contact with him while serving food now and did not resist his offers to help clean up.

The old wizard had avoided talking to Caleb since their quarrel in the library the day after the full moon, except to drill him in his lessons and insist that he practice his planetary magic every evening that planets were visible in the sky without moonlight. Tonight the moon was new, and they stood on the grassy outcrop by the castle, looking for Jupiter. It was endless rounds of tedious repetitions of spells, but still Alexandru refused to speak of anything but Kronos and Zeus. Caleb was not entirely sure that he wanted to continue the argument either. He feared there could be no rapprochement between them.

Alexandru even took to departing solo on his forays into vampire country. Caleb could tell where he had been by the dirt and straw on his boots, the bat guano in his hair, and the haunted look that lingered on his face. One evening he returned late, taking his seat at the dinner table just as Mihail had removed Caleb's plate and poured his coffee. Caleb gathered up the book he was reading and his notes and rose to leave, not welcoming another hour of stony silence, but the old wizard gestured so vehemently for him to sit that he did so.

As had become his habit during the previous two weeks, Alexandru said nothing. Caleb ignored him, focusing on his coffee and *Atlas of Magical Wards and Enchantments.* Mihail brought a plate of bread and butter, followed by a steaming bowl of chicken soup. The vampire-hunter took a piece of bread, but seemed to forget what he was doing with the butter knife halfway to its target. His hands sagged, dropping the food onto the table. "A glass of wine," he murmured, turning his head slightly towards the servant. "Or brandy, perhaps…"

Realizing something was wrong, Mihail approached quickly with the drink, unable to hide a look of concern. "What else may I bring you, Master?"

Taking a long sip and steeling his face, Alexandru managed to regain his composure. "Nothing, thank you, Mihail." He waved his devoted servant away.

The quaver in his voice made Caleb look up. Alexandru's face bore a look of horror that reminded him of Toby in that cold, stone courthouse. Their eyes met, and it was a long moment before Alexandru spoke three chilling words.

"*He* has returned," he said.

There was a cry and a shatter of china. Mihail, his face impassive but ghostly white, had dropped a soup bowl.

"Come." Alexandru rose and beckoned Caleb, with a warning glance at the servant. "I think it is time that we put aside our trivial differences."

Advocating the cold-blooded murder of his kind was not exactly what Caleb would call a trivial difference, but his curiosity overcame his anger and he followed the old man into the library. The door magically shut and sealed behind them. Caleb sat in a chair opposite Alexandru and waited, taking in the mud on the other's clothes. Had Alexandru been walking through a rainstorm?

"I do not wish to lose you, Caleb," came the quiet words after some minutes' silence. Caleb looked into Alexandru's face to find a respect he'd never seen before from the old wizard. "I trust you. I have trusted you with my life. If I hadn't, we could not have hunted vampires together." He drew a deep breath. "And now we will be facing our greatest challenge."

Under heavy clouds, a solitary traveler hurried along the dark nighttime road between Orastana and Albimare. The man had a pack slung over one shoulder. Vlad loped easily alongside the road, far enough away that the trees and hedges screened him. Even as a human, he could hunt as silently as a wolf.

And he was hunting tonight. He had watched the man, a farmer, counting the money he had gotten from selling his sheep in Orastana. The man stayed a bit too long in the tavern, so now he was forced to make his way home in the dark, which suited Vlad perfectly.

Vlad did not understand Fido's insane desire to find jobs for the Fives. No one in his right mind would hire a werewolf. The locals knew instinctively what he was; they were always nervous around him, although they didn't understand why. He survived on stealing money or food, whatever he could find. Tonight's quarry seemed to have plenty of money and Vlad aimed to take possession soon.

It began to drizzle as the road wound through the tiny hamlet of Catunescu. Most of the village had been abandoned long ago. A crumbling stone church and a few run-down houses were all that remained. The man ducked into the church as the rain came down harder and a crack of thunder boomed through the hills. Vlad watched him disappear into the dark opening as lightning sizzled and the rain fell in sheets. This was going to be easy.

Crossing the road openly in the driving rain, he stopped at the door to the church. It would be easiest to wait for the man to come out again, Vlad thought, rather than chase him around inside a dark church. A little covered stone porch kept Vlad mostly dry as he scrunched next to the door. As soon as the rain let up, the man would want to get back on the road and then Vlad could jump him as he came out. It seemed like a good, simple plan, the kind that worked best for Vlad.

The rain settled into a steady drizzle, although lightning continued to play across the sky. From inside the church, Vlad heard the faint scuffles of someone walking. The sky went white for a moment from an intense burst of lightning. Vlad expected to hear the boom of thunder, but in the split second before the drumbeat echoed from the sky, another sound caught Vlad's attention. A scream. Faint, but unmistakable, it came from inside the church. The scream was not repeated, but Vlad then heard the heavy thud of something or someone falling to the floor.

Had someone beaten him to the robbery idea? That didn't seem likely. Catunescu had been empty of people since Vlad was a small boy. He didn't expect a thief to spend his nights waiting inside an abandoned church in a town nobody lived in. Perhaps a demon or spirit? Vlad debated with himself for some time, but in the end greed won the argument. He would peek into the church, knowing that his night vision was better than that of any human he might find inside.

Cautiously, he slipped through the partially open door and stood against the wall, surveying the dark interior. Occasional flashes of lightning revealed the church's layout. The windows were up high, meaning that they couldn't easily be used for an exit. In one particularly bright flash, he saw the ruined altar, but there did not seem to be another door at that end of the church.

Good, he thought, only one way out or in. It took a few minutes for him to pick out the figure of a man, lying amidst the jumble of benches in the middle of the floor. He sidled closer, moving away from the door but still hugging the wall. The traveler lay face up, his pack by his side. In another brief flash of light, Vlad noticed that the pack appeared untouched. No one else had tried to rob the fellow, at least. Perhaps the man had tripped over something in the dark…

Greed continued to hold the upper hand in Vlad's mind. He couldn't just leave that pack, now that he was so close.

Dropping into a crouch, he crawled across the dusty floor. Musty odors, dust and ancient incense, mingled with the perfume of rain. Approaching the body, he smelled something else that he couldn't name right away. Tentatively, he touched the body. The traveler's hand felt cold, too cold. Vlad grabbed the pack and was ready to flee when a flash of lightning showed him the man's face. In an instant, he knew that the man was not dead, not yet, and what was worse, he now recognized that mysterious smell.

Vampire.

Of all the stinking piles of dung for him to fall into, this was one of the worst. He had to get out right away.

He stood up and turned toward the door, picking the straightest path through the wooden debris. A faint flutter from above made him hurry all the more, trying not to trip over the benches sticking out at odd angles at his feet. With a tremendous rush of air, something appeared above and behind him. Strong hands gripped his shoulders as he threw himself toward the door. He lunged, but tripped over the leg of a bench, hitting the floor hard while fighting off the fingers that closed around his neck.

The vampire (no question about it now) continued to choke him and he felt himself blacking out. Just try to make a meal out of me, he thought as he passed out.

"Dog." In his haze, Vlad mistook the word as an affectionate greeting from a packmate. "A thief and a dog," the voice continued, bringing Vlad more fully to his senses. He looked up from the floor to see the tall figure of a man, standing over him with a glowing orb in his hand. Vlad had no idea how long he had been unconscious, but he did know that the situation kept getting worse. The vampire must be one of the old ones—not some clueless local who had been bitten and turned into one of the garden-variety Undead, but a wizard. Vlad had never run into one of the old guys before, but he'd heard plenty of tales.

"Cadavru," Vlad spat. "I hope you got a good taste."

Dark, empty eyes regarded him coldly. The face was bony and hard, the skin looking quite rosy for a corpse, but of course the vampire had just eaten. A smile played across the vampire's face, making it seem harder still.

"You think I'll spare your miserable life, dog?" The vampire spoke as if describing a bug about to be squashed.

Vlad sat up, noticing that the vampire held the traveler's pack in one hand. "Just try it, you stinking corpse," he growled.

"I'll admit," drawled the vampire, as he casually strolled toward the door, blocking the only exit, "that killing a dog like you would take some work. But I am feeling quite, shall we say, energetic tonight."

In response Vlad lunged, snarling at the vampire as he tried to pull him down. Pain and bright light shot from the glowing hand, knocking Vlad back to the floor. In the glow of his magical fire, the vampire's face appeared to float above him in the dark, cruel but thoughtful.

"You want whatever's in here, don't you, thief?" He threw the pack at his feet, just out of Vlad's reach. "Hmmmm. I have only recently woken after a rather long sleep. After my meal, I hunger for certain information. Perhaps I would be willing to let you live, if you have something of value to trade."

Vlad glared at him, intrigued, but not willing to give away anything without a better idea of what the vampire wanted.

"What do you call yourself, dog?"

"Vlad," he replied reluctantly as he warily pulled himself to a standing position. He and the vampire were both tall, about the same height, and Vlad felt better being at the same level, although he could not look into those empty eyes for very long. They stood about six feet apart, glaring at one another in the soft light of the orb.

"Well, Vlad, I have not seen too many of my old friends recently," began the vampire. "My old, old friends are neither awake nor asleep. What do you know of this?"

"Vampires have been getting scarcer. People complain more about us, now that they're not getting bitten by you corpses." Vlad sneered, but the vampire was too intrigued by the information to notice the insult. "They say there's a vampire-hunter killing them off."

"Indeed? How long?" The vampire raked Vlad with his dark eyes, impossible to read because they swallowed up rather than reflected light.

"Dunno. Twelve months, maybe thirteen. You know how rumors are."

"And do you know the identity of this hunter or where he lives?"

"No. No one's owned up to it, if that's what you mean. I hear about it mostly around Stilpescu and Orastana."

"Now, that is interesting," mused the vampire, "because I recently discovered that Castle Arghezi is protected by certain magical wards. Who lives there now?"

Vlad knew at least one person who lived there, although he didn't think that Fido was tough enough to kill vampires. Other people lived in the castle, too, but Lupeni never talked about them. Vlad sensed that anything related to the castle could be very valuable.

The leader of the Fives was his own kind, however, and had recently saved his life for the second time. Vlad felt a strange loyalty tugging at him. He never expected to be shielding his rival, but the enmity between vampires and werewolves ran deep. He couldn't sell out a former packmate to a vampire.

"Some wizards live at the castle," he said slowly, "but no one sees them much or knows who they are."

"But you do see them occasionally, don't you?" asked the vampire sharply, perhaps suspecting that he knew more than he was telling.

"Yeah, I guess." Vlad tried to shrug as if it scarcely mattered.

"Perhaps you might learn more? I would reward further information," crooned the vampire softly. "I collect many trinkets which humans, and dogs like you, might consider valuable. If you are willing to tell the truth, that is."

The vampire regarded him coldly, staring with the unnatural stillness that only the Undead could maintain for long. Rain still fell heavily outside, monotonous and hypnotic. Vlad grew afraid that the vampire had seen through him and was starting to think of another way to attack, when the silence was broken by the scrape of canvas on stone. With one elegant boot, the vampire kicked the pack toward Vlad.

"Take your stolen goods, dog," he sneered. "But remember my offer."

Vlad scrambled quickly to grab the pack, hugging it tightly, and edged toward the door as the vampire moved aside slightly to let him pass.

"Suppose I do find out something," he said boldly. "How do I get in touch with you?"

"Others of my kind will know how to find me," the vampire crooned, closing his fist to extinguish the light so that only his silky voice remained floating in the dark. "The Vampire Cuza. That is all you need say."

Book III

I Was a Teenage Werewolf

13. Chasse-galerie

"HEY, DAD, CAN I borrow your canoe to go into the village?"

"I don't know. Are you done with your homework?"

The boy appeared in the doorway of the wooden cottage, looking exasperated, the paddle already in his hand. He was average in height for his twelve and a half years, but quite skinny, and his shoulder-length straight black hair was tied back with a piece of woolly sheepskin. "Yeah, yeah…" he mumbled in response to the question. "I guess I'm done."

"Well, let me see it and you can go." The man the boy called "Dad" sat at a homemade table of raw pine in the center of the cottage's living room. He was not quite old enough for the role, and he looked nothing like his "son." He glanced up from the map and notebook on which he had been taking notes and gestured for the boy to pull up a chair.

"Just a sec…" the boy mumbled, leaning the paddle against the wall and reaching for a sheet of paper tossed haphazardly onto the floor. He unfolded it now gently, and couldn't hide the pride in his face as he gave it to his father. "Most people think the Earth gets in the way of the moon to cause the phases. But see, it's when the Earth is between the sun and the moon that it's full, and when there's nothing in between that it's new."

"Very good. And did you calculate the period using Kepler's law?"

"Twenty-seven point three days," Bela replied proudly.

"OK," replied his parent in the tone of upping the ante. "So why don't we have a full moon every twenty-seven point three days?"

This question puzzled the boy, who sighed heavily. He wanted to be outside in the spring afternoon, not working problems in the cottage—but he didn't want his father to outwit him, either. He reached for the text, which he'd left open on the table, interested in spite of himself. "If I could make sense of these pictures, it would help."

His father frowned. "There should be some 3-D glasses to help you see them," he said thoughtfully. "I hope they haven't been lost." He picked up the book and flipped through the pages, then held it up and shook it.

No glasses, but a small triangle of paper, looking as if it had been torn hastily from another piece, fluttered onto the table between them. A messy scrawl in green ink read, "9 pm SWHarbor, Toby."

The man stared at the note for a moment, then carefully folded it and stuck it into his pocket.

There was a moment's silence, then Bela's curiosity got the better of him. He read English pretty well. "Who's Toby?" he wondered.

"An old friend," said his father quietly, but with a hint of warning that he really didn't want to talk about it.

"Where is he now?"

"He's dead."

Bela nodded wisely. Some of his friends had died, too. He picked up the book again and thumbed through it, as if it would tell him more about the past they couldn't discuss. Coming to a sticker in the front, with a cartoon beaver and a name scribbled in faded ink, he read aloud, "'Caleb J. O'Connor, Physics&Astronomy. What's that all about? Is that you, Dad?"

The man smiled, his eyes far away. "It was, yes."

"What's *IHTFP*?"

"'I Have Truly Found Paradise'—or alternatively, `I Hate This Fucking Place,'" the man chuckled.

The boy snickered at the English and the profanity. "And why does the beaver look like it's, um—?"

The man peeked at the symbol, and smiled. "Throwing up? It's not supposed to. One of my friends hexed it because he was mad that I'd gone off to the city and left him behind."

Bela rolled his eyes. "Mom told me you used to live in the city with humans, but I didn't believe her."

Caleb laughed ruefully. "It's true." He tried not to let the bitterness show in his voice, but he wished Liszka's concept of parental duty didn't begin and end at the full moon. He'd never expected to find himself with a child to raise, but instinct and tradition made the youngest member of Pack Five Caleb's and Liszka's son as much as if they had borne him.

He'd tried, countless times in the twenty-seven months since the boy had joined them, to convince Bela to return to his human parents. They didn't want him, though, and neither did the schools in the villages around Stilpescu. There was still enough magical tradition around that everyone knew what the boy was.

What did one do with a pre-teen werewolf? Caleb had always resented the town of Tribulation for keeping him away, but maybe it had been a good thing. In retrospect his human self had been far too much of a child to deal with the monster's adolescence, and it was no wonder the Muscaturas had treated Bela more like a pet tiger than a son. He was better off here with adoptive parents who understood, who would just send him out in the forest to play if he got a bit growly. Liszka had no trouble controlling him as a wolf, either, even though his head would no longer fit in her mouth. The readiness with which Bela adopted them, calling them Mom and Dad and coming to them with his troubles, made Caleb feel both guilty and oddly gratified. He was pleased he seemed to be able to help Bela, but he felt bad that he had to take him away from his parents to do it, and that he couldn't do more.

At least Bela had constant companionship here at Grigore's cottage, where some member of the Fives was always around, and where they all got together once a month. But the winters were lean and hard, and Caleb had spent many a long snowy night torn with guilt over his cozy fire and home-cooked meals. Mihail's roast beef and venison stuck in his throat as he thought of his foster son out here in a cabin with a half dozen other starving werewolves. He trembled with worry and rage when he heard the werewolf-hunters tramping through the snow on a day after the full moon, and had done a few things to them that Alexandru would doubtless condemn.

But if Alexandru knew, he didn't let on. He had become monomaniacal in his search for the elusive Cuza, demanding that Caleb camp out with him in caves and attics and churchyards for days at a time, casting spells that mostly caught innocent bats. Last time he had cursed a crow out of the sky and, in a fit of paranoia, drove a stake through the poor bird's heart.

As spring slowly crept back to the hills, Caleb's vampire-hunting duties became increasingly demanding. The worst of the cold was past, though, and the Fives were eating reasonably well. Caleb stopped being a den mother and focused mostly on the boy, trying to drop into the cottage often enough to teach Bela a little math, a sprinkling of botany, and hopefully some self-respect.

"You know what, Bela?" he asked gently, somewhat appalled in the back of his mind at how much he sounded like his own parents. "You're really smart, and if you study a little bit, you can be almost anything you want to be."

Bela laughed, his pencil scratching at the paper, a laugh that didn't yet contain a teenager's scorn. "You lived in the *city*," he marveled. "Did you run away into the forest for the full moon?"

"No, I just…just tried to stay indoors."

Bela pondered this, disbelieving. "Indoors? Dunno. I think I'd eat the furniture," he admitted with a smirk.

"Yes, well, I tried."

"Really?" His dad was full of surprises today. "So why did you… I mean… Why would you want to do that?"

It wasn't a bad question. "I suppose there were things I wanted to do, to learn, that made it necessary," Caleb said after a pause. "Humans don't…they don't realize how important our one night is to us, and I didn't know either."

Bela shook his head, his look of mild skepticism becoming replaced with one of total astonishment. "So you pretended you were human just like all the rest of them? And they didn't hear you eating the furniture?"

"They did. They thought it was the neighbors having a party." He winced at the memory of his landlord discovering the holes in the wall. "And whenever I could, I would go back to the forest to be with my friends." He touched the note in his pocket. "They don't all hate us, you know."

"The wizards do," said Bela darkly.

His father's eyebrows knotted. "Maybe you're right. I never told you this, Bela, but I left my country because I lost Toby, my best friend." Seeing the boy watching him with rapt attention, he continued in a mild voice, "We used to do things together at the full moon, things using magic that we weren't supposed to do. We broke through wards and went into the Reserve filled with monsters. There were other wards, too, ones protecting old mansions or parts of the forest. We couldn't figure out their purpose—We broke these just for fun, and Toby continued to do it after I had gone off to the city. One night he got into an old house and let out…something: Everyone said he had let a vampire escape."

Bela nodded his understanding. "You've told me about the vampires in Maine that came over from Europe during the Second World War."

"Some even before that," Caleb corrected. "In fact, from what I've heard, it may have been lucky that the *Titanic* went down, considering what was in steerage. But I don't know if these were the vampires Toby found. They could have been more recent ones." Caleb hesitated, unsure whether to repeat what he'd heard from Jonathan Hermann and the hints that Alexandru occasionally let slip. What did it matter if they were twentieth-century renegade Romanian vampires, as Alexandru had intimated? The end result was the same.

"Did they kill the vampire?" Bela breathed.

Caleb closed his eyes for longer than a blink. "No. The vampire escaped and bit two people and murdered two more. The local wizards blamed Toby for this, and executed him."

Bela slammed shut the astronomy book and gave voice to what Caleb couldn't say. "They blamed Toby because he was your friend," he growled.

Unable to speak, Caleb stared at his own "homework"—a piece of paper where he had been carefully sketching the mountains and their passes into the surrounding towns. He still despaired of making Jupiter do his bidding, but had finally mastered a variety of moonwards of different shapes, sizes, and strengths. These grew weaker and stronger with the phase of the moon, which was exactly what he needed to keep humans and werewolves apart on only that one enchanted night. He had set the wards up on all of the known trails, but the Sixes still occasionally got into the village of Albimare, south of Stilpescu, to bite people. "Were they wrong to do this?" he wondered aloud, not wondering if this was too much moral complexity for a twelve-year-old.

Bela frowned. "If they killed my best friend, I would bite them all."

It was dangerously close to the desire for revenge that had brought him to Romania, and Caleb was not prepared to explore it with his son. He brought the conversation to a halt by telling Bela that he could go into the village but, after a bit of squabbling, convinced the boy not to take the canoe. Making it fly was a very clever Air and Water spell that the Romanian boy had happily adopted from Maine, and Caleb was proud of him, but if any authorities spotted him it would be disastrous.

"Why don't you ride Patches?" he suggested. "Then no one will suspect anything."

Bela smirked sardonically, but went to swap the paddle for a pair of riding boots and bridle. Everyone believed that horses feared werewolves, but Pack Five had found that as long as the animals were kept in the barn at the full moon, they were none the wiser. Soon the boy was galloping down the mountain, and Caleb listened to the retreating hooves for a long moment before returning to his map.

How could the werewolves be getting into Albimare? Descending the treacherous granite cliffs away from the paths was impossible even in wolf form, so they were using a route that he had not yet discovered. He knew they weren't going into the village in human form and waiting for the moon to rise. If they did that where wards were in place, they'd be trapped there until noon the next day. The villagers knew this, and the werewolves knew the villagers knew it. This didn't exactly make Caleb popular among his kind, but there wasn't a pack in the mountains that dared to take on the well-nourished and disciplined Fives.

No, they were entering the town as wolves. But how? Stilpescu appeared safe. No one had been bitten there since Bela. North of Stilpescu, where a gradual earthy trail led to a small farming community, his wards seemed to have held up as well—even the sheep stayed uneaten. There was a complex tangle of trails east of Stilpescu, leading from the Sixes' territory toward human settlements. It was possible his spells had missed a spot, but in order to get to Albimare from there, the wolves would have to make a forty-mile circuit south through the foothills. To the east of Albimare were granite cliffs, which he had not explored further after a nasty fall on his second full moon in Romania.

The long walk south was not out of the question for a wolf pack, but it was far for Caleb right now. He decided to investigate the cliffs first. Maybe they would hold the answer.

14. Moonrise

"LAMIA? YOU OUT THERE?" A firm but worried male voice called into the trees as the sun set over the mountains. Clouds swirled behind the peaks in a fleeting display of neon pinks, oranges, and purples that morphed into the dead grays of late twilight.

Brush crackled as the man pushed aside new spring growth, coming upon a woman standing quite still in a small clearing. Her back was turned toward him and her head was bowed as though she were staring at her feet. Like the man, the woman had black hair. Hers was long and braided in a thick plait that extended down her back.

"We were getting worried about you." He addressed her in English with flat American overtones.

"I wanted to be alone," she replied, also in English, but with a lilting Mediterranean accent. She turned to face him, but her eyes were hidden in the shadows of the coming evening. She stared at him curiously for a moment and then appeared to relax, a smile forming on her lips. "Really, Mike, I can take care of myself. You think a little first-year grad student needs protection?"

He relaxed, too, forgetting whatever had made him apprehensive. "Naw. But this area is riddled with caves, and I—" he stopped as he drew next to her and saw what she had been looking at. "What's that? Some sort of dead animal?"

"A rabbit, I think," she replied cautiously. "Maybe an owl or something got it. I guess you're right, though. We should get back to the camp." She brushed past him, finding a path through the trees. He wanted to say more, but followed her silently instead. They both halted as one howl and then several more echoed faintly from the distance.

"There's what ate that rabbit," he said lightly as they continued to walk. "Dogs or wolves. Hey, maybe a werewolf. Didn't that old guy say something to you about werewolves?"

Lamia stopped abruptly and Mike nearly collided with her. She didn't like the thought of werewolves and wished he hadn't brought it up. He continued to pursue it, though.

"You know, that guy who drove the truck with all our stuff? He was jabbering at you in Romanian for a while. How come you didn't tell anyone you spoke the language?"

"Well, I haven't spoken it in fifteen or twenty years," she answered as she again started up the path. "My grandmother was Romanian and I didn't honestly know if I could still remember much."

"It was pretty handy, your being able to talk to him. I don't think we would have gotten him to give us that extra tank of fuel for the generator otherwise."

"He just wanted more money, that's all," she said dismissively, but he didn't seem willing to let it drop.

"And he warned you about werewolves, right? I could really see that around here. You remember that old story from MIT about the dean who ran off to Romania to hunt monsters?"

She regretted now telling the other students what the old man had said. She thought it would amuse them, a bit of local color, but she didn't want to be reminded of it. Especially now, with the full moon rising in front of them.

Of course, Mike picked up on this next, saying, "Tonight's the night!"

As if on cue, another howl interrupted him. Echoes reverberated for several seconds, telling her that it was close, much closer than before. She stopped again and turned to face him. "Please, Mike, let's talk about something else, okay?"

The howl had gotten his attention. He was willing, more than willing, to change the subject.

She knew he was attracted to her, but she hadn't decided what to do about it yet. It was common knowledge that she was sleeping with Carlo, one of the physics graduate students in their group at the university. But Carlo was back in Bologna writing his thesis. Besides, he was starting to irritate her. He seemed to think that because she went to bed with him he could run the rest of her life, too.

Carlo was on his way out. She'd be stuck with three other students this spring and summer as they set up their high-energy physics experiment in the local caves. There were some possibilities: Mike, who looked Italian but was from New Jersey; Vijay, who was Indian with a degree from Cambridge and a very posh British accent; and the silent Taofang, who hailed from some unpronounceable place in China. Mike thought he was first in line, but she was leaning toward Vijay. He was quieter and seemed less likely to turn into a Carlo.

Lamia sighed inwardly. She was here to start a thesis project on the physics of neutrino oscillations, collecting the nearly massless particles from collider beams in Italy. They were also setting up an apparatus to detect proton decay—though at a predicted rate of one data point per year, it would take at least a century to graduate on this project. The payoff if they saw proton decay was so great that they were all willing to take part in the experiment, though it sparked many jokes about the need for Undead graduate students.

Maybe it would be better to concentrate on her work instead of her sleeping arrangements. She knew it would create all sorts of tension among the group and interfere with the work.

And she loved the work. Until she started studying physics, she never realized the beauty of some of the most difficult of abstract concepts: the dance of subatomic particles existing in their own little realm, pure and not contaminated by the ugliness of the human world. She had had a pretty rough life up until now, which she didn't talk about with the others. Maybe they suspected from all the languages she spoke that she'd bounced around at a few different schools, or maybe they didn't think about it. This project was a chance to get away from her past, she hoped.

"Let's get back," she said with more urgency. They were close to the camp now, passing by the main entrance to the Petrosna Caves in which they had begun setting up their equipment. From the dark cave mouth came scuffling noises and low growls—definitely not made by graduate students, even at their worst. Mike had a flashlight, which he turned on and pointed into the cave.

"Don't—don't do that," Lamia began haltingly.

"Why not? I want to see if the equipment's okay."

Light played over cardboard boxes and hulking shapes covered by tarps just inside the entrance. Lamia gripped his arm hard enough to make him wince. There. Greenish-orange discs flashed back at them. Two—no, four. There was more in the cave than equipment.

The luminous circles vanished, then reappeared suddenly as eyes. At once heads materialized around the eyes, erupting from the darkness like twin rockets on a jet fighter. No dogs, these were wolves, very large ones that were coming at them fast.

Mike threw the flashlight at the attackers, but it bounced ineffectually to the ground, leaving them with nothing but the light of the moon. Lamia could see just fine, and she saw one wolf, the smaller one, leap at Mike, knocking him to the ground.

The wolf was as surprised as Mike by what happened next. Lamia grabbed the snarling beast by its shoulders and pushed it backwards, yelling something in Romanian. She stepped in front of her downed companion and stood glaring at the two animals. They seemed to be reappraising her, sniffing at her while growling softly. After a moment, they backed away, hackles raised, and then abruptly fled back into the caves.

She helped Mike up, staring into the darkness after the departed wolves all the while. Damned wolves, she thought, I shouldn't have come here. I should have known there'd be wolves.

"What happened? What did you do?" Mike stammered semi-coherently, lacking his usual glib physics-student persona.

"I don't know," she replied distractedly, still occupied by her own thoughts. "Scared them away, I guess."

"You sure yelled something that worked. What language were you speaking, anyway?"

"What? Oh, Romanian, I guess." Funny how a language she hadn't spoken for fifteen years still lurked inside, so ready to come out when she least expected it. "I think I said something like 'Go away, stupid dog.' I'm not really sure. We'd better get back to camp and check on the others."

Mike searched for his flashlight in the dark. He was starting to stumble and Lamia swiftly found the flashlight and turned it on.

"You're bleeding," she said with a sharp intake of breath. "It didn't bite you, did it?"

"How did you—" Mike gasped too, as Lamia shone the flashlight on the triple trace of blood running down his left forearm, the track of the wolf's claws. "Jeez. It's quite a scratch," he said bravely as he inspected the wound.

He glanced up to see a frozen mask of what looked like terror on Lamia's face. Her unblinking eyes fixed on his arm and the flashlight nervously danced in her hand. Suddenly, she dropped the light, turned, and ran.

"Just a little blood," he muttered as he picked it up and made his way more slowly back to their camp. "What's wrong, Lamia? Am I going to turn into one now? Transylvania," he muttered. "One day and I'm already a werewolf."

15. Fools Rush In

THE FULL MOON CAME and went, without any rumors of attacks on villagers that Caleb heard about. Then he was dragged into an arduous, three-day vampire hunt with Alexandru that left them both exhausted and edgy. The old wizard refused to say precisely who Cuza was, or why he was hunting him so assiduously, and the old church in Catunescu where they'd holed up for twenty-four silent and tense hours yielded no further clues.

The moon was in its second quarter before Caleb got around to visiting the cliffs above Albimare. A rainstorm had erased any possible trails or paw prints, and he didn't know where to begin looking. Tired, hungry, and frustrated, he wandered past the cliffs and took a circuitous route into the village via one of the paths that he'd warded some time ago. Maybe he could put magical shields over the individual streets, if need be, but he'd never tried that. The smaller the area, the easier it was to build a ward. What he really hoped to find was one single, narrow access point into the village that could be taken care of with a three-foot-wide barrier.

From a small café on the edge of town he could see the stone cliffs, every bit as sheer as he suspected. He knew the werewolves weren't using magic to descend them—they hardly knew any in human form. Munching on a chunk of black bread softened by a rather thin and greasy red-pepper soup, he continued to gaze out the window, hoping to find a clue in the jagged rocks with their clouds of oddly flitting birds.

But no, he realized suddenly, they weren't birds at all. They were bats, and they were coming and going somewhere in a clump of aspens just by the base of the mountain. Leaving the waitress an extra-large tip because she looked hungry, Caleb left the café and made his way quickly to the stand of trees.

He had to get down on his belly and crawl through the dense grass and wildflowers to find where the bats were coming from. Sure enough, it was the mouth of a cave, about half the height of a man: or exactly the height of a wolf. Sticking his head into the darkness, he sniffed—then, feeling stupid, conjured a small flame. A nose would be much more useful than eyes here, but even this inferior sense told him everything he needed to know.

Just inside the mouth of the cave was a nearly skeletonized body, and beside it, a gnawed leather satchel. The largest bones had been fractured and the marrow sucked out, and the imprints of the teeth on the bag were too large for any ordinary wolf. In addition, the bag had been systematically ripped apart with obvious cunning. Only a few of the contents remained, some dried fragments of herbs…vervain and moonwort, two magical species that had to be harvested at the full moon.

If he'd had the wolf's 100,000 odor receptors he would've been able to say just which member or members of Pack Six had been here. With less than a tenth that, all he knew was that the cave stank of bats, decay, and wolf pee. Did the tunnel continue upward and emerge somewhere above the cliffs? He increased the light from the flame, but that helped little in the velvety darkness. The path did continue on, but it stayed narrow, and he found himself crawling more than once. This wasn't the ideal form for worming his way through low-ceilinged passages.

The occasional bat skimmed past him, startled by the light and movement. Bats didn't bother him, after years of prowling the local caves with Arghezi. Even as a kid, he was more fascinated than frightened by the bats encountered in the old houses on the Maine coast. René had been scared of bats, Caleb remembered, with a sudden vivid image of his friend's scarred, lopsided face and that silly amulet he always wore.

A voice from the darkness completed his thought. "Hola, Dog Boy. The gang's all here."

Caleb sat back on his heels, astounded, not caring that he scraped his head along the roof of the cave. He had heard that voice in his dreams so many times that he was almost unsurprised, as if the five years since his best friend's death had shrunk to an instant. "Toby?" he whispered, feeling too foolish to say it aloud.

"The very same," the voice replied. A face, still as young and insouciant as ever, appeared grinning in front of Caleb.

His instincts told Caleb to watch out, that something was wrong, but irrational hope won out. "You're here? You...escaped? Or are you here, exactly?" Was Toby powerful enough to escape the Community? If he was that powerful, there was no telling what he could do.

The boy showed his teeth and laughed easily. "You might say we all escaped." He smiled. "Look behind you. Know who that was?"

Caleb remembered the body at the entrance. "No, of course not."

"No, of course not," Toby mocked, cackling. "Great gods, are you stupid. Would a little flesh and blood help?"

The skeleton sat up, and pieces of sinew and skin seemed to appear patchily over its bare bones, leaving a face cratered with scars. Caleb recoiled in disgust as he recognized this decaying version of his old friend René.

"B-b-but that can't be," Caleb stuttered, brain working furiously as he looked for some contradiction to which he could cling, like a drowning man reaching for a life preserver just beyond his fingertips. "René was burned to ashes in the fire."

"You don't believe that, do you?" Toby cackled. "René was smarter than any of us thought. I tried to tell you, you moron, but you were too busy playing at being a good little MIT student. Pitiful, really."

Caleb's hope crumbled, and he realized in a flash that this wasn't Toby. He didn't know what it was or what it wanted, but he knew he had to get out of the cave and fast. He felt lost and disoriented, unable to remember where he had come in. He thought he had turned to run, but somehow he found himself crawling towards the specter, over and over again. It taunted him and mocked him, but if it wanted to kill him it didn't seem to quite know how.

It was the skeleton, resting at peace once again, that finally saved him. He knew its feet pointed towards the entrance and, gripping onto its shoes to keep from losing his sense of direction again, he heaved himself out of the cave mouth to lie panting in the aspens. Night had fallen. His head hurt abominably and his stomach churned so that he felt as though he'd never eat again.

He didn't know how long he lay there, but the waxing moon was halfway to setting by the time he was finally able to get to his feet. He vomited twice on the way home, arriving at the castle at the end of his strength. Alexandru was just taking a nightcap; he made Caleb sit down at the table and had Mihail bring him a bowl of soup.

Caleb's stomach revolted at the sight and his head spun. After an embarrassing dash for the bathroom, he returned apologizing and tried to tell the old wizard about what had happened.

He'd expected the story to sound weak, but instead he saw Alexandru's face grow pale. Mihail whisked away the soup and brought over a tightly capped blue bottle. "Drink this," Alexandru told him.

Caleb removed the stopper and sniffed. "Who? What—?"

"Do as I say," Alexandru commanded in a voice edged with panic.

The potion tasted of old tea and grass, not at all unpleasant, and Caleb swilled it willingly. He didn't feel any different afterwards, but saw the others relax visibly as he drained the bottle.

"That was not your friend you found in the caves," Alexandru told him at last, gesturing to Mihail for a cup of herbal tea. "It was perhaps the Darkest creature that these mountains hide, and I hope that it will not have lasting effects on you." His panic subsiding, he became scholarly again, stirring two creams and one sugar lump into the thick black brew. "Quite odd indeed that a leptothrix should take the form of your old friend. They are usually local around here—victims of one of the many massacres to plague this region."

"A leptothrix?" Caleb wondered. He smacked his lips; the potion had a funny after-taste, like tuna fish. "Is that some kind of ghost?"

Alexandru shook his head in disbelief. "My boy, I think the only reason you escaped is that you didn't know what you were up against. Some kind of ghost, yes."

"But he—it knew things about me, about Toby and René and Lilac House."

"A leptothrix is the ghost of someone strong and talented who has died unfairly with ambitions unfulfilled. He then feeds off these traits in others. It usually takes no more than an hour before they have taken everything from a man—his memories, his strength, his hopes and dreams—twisting everything he loves into something he hates." Alexandru paused and frowned at Caleb. "Lilac House? What did your friend have to do with that cursed place?"

"You know it?" Caleb stared open-mouthed as memories erupted from the dark corners where they'd been chained since the day of the trial.

"Know it?" Alexandru snorted. "I was the one who created the wards fifty years ago after the local wizards botched things. I had only recently come to America, and Fintonclyde had the sense to ask me to help him. I don't think he could have defeated that nest of vampires on his own." Alexandru's dark eyes drilled into Caleb. "What do you know of this place? You've never mentioned it before."

"I've been trying to forget it for the last five years." Caleb sighed and told Alexandru the parts of the story he knew, or thought he knew. He realized as he spoke that he had stayed in Romania to keep these memories at bay, and that they still hurt as acutely now as they had when he was a naïve seventeen-year-old.

Alexandru rose from the table and paced while Caleb talked. Mihail hovered in the background and regarded his master as if he were about to explode.

"The whole house burned to the ground, you say. Are you certain?"

"Nothing was left standing, or so I heard. No one should have been able to get out alive. And yet, the next day, a couple of people were attacked in Southwest Harbor. No one would say it out loud, but they thought it was a vampire."

"Perhaps local gossip was wrong, my boy," Alexandru finished grimly, "because if not…let's just say that you were lucky to leave Maine when you did. Those are no ordinary vampires. All of the wizards in the area could not succeed in doing more than containing them behind walls—walls that we hoped would last many lifetimes."

Alexandru sat down and signaled Mihail for more hot water. "The more immediate problem is the leptothrixes. Those caves are probably crawling with them, and you should consider yourself lucky to be alive and sane after your encounter."

"How did I get away?" Caleb felt another wrench of nausea as he recalled the false Toby's cruel taunts and how they had deadened his senses. "Do you suppose my, er, my kind are more resistant?"

"Who knows, who knows." Alexandru put down his teacup. "They're too dangerous to do research on—and few would acknowledge that your kind have the positive traits on which they thrive."

Caleb drew a sharp breath of indignation, then thought of someone else, someone even he had perhaps misjudged. "The—er, my, um,… oh, dammit, the *werewolves* have been sneaking through the caves into Albimare. Do you think the leptothrixes affect them even in wolf form? Maybe that's why their leader is the way he is—heartless and evil."

Both Mihail and Alexandru gazed at him with heavy irony, but at least in Alexandru's case he recovered himself quickly and gave a reasonable response. "A leptothrix does not necessarily make one evil," he corrected. "It leaves one empty. I imagine that evil quickly arrives to fill the void, however. Victims are said to be unconscious of what they have lost, but to grow angry and resentful, much like the spirits who were forced to leave this world too soon."

"I imagine that a wolf would be somewhat resistant, at least—" Caleb began.

"Only a fool would go near those caves," Alexandru interrupted in a low tone. "Consider yourself lucky you were able to get home at all. We still don't know if this will take a toll on your powers or your wits. Risk them at your peril, because I will not endanger my own powers to save you."

16. The Calm Before the Storm

THE DAY BEFORE THE full moon, Caleb went to work on a special project. After dinner at Grigore's cottage, he hauled out a large canvas-wrapped parcel that he'd been keeping at the castle. The smell wouldn't bother a human, but to a werewolf's more sensitive nose, it smelled of death and danger. He sat in the doorway to unwrap it, but still the odor made both Liszka and Bela pinch their noses. They were the only ones in the cottage that evening, enjoying a cozy meal with the door open to let in the fragrant breeze that signaled the start of the alpine summer.

"Daughter of Hyperion, is that what I think it is? Don't you dare bring that into the cottage!" Liszka exclaimed, pushing away her unfinished dessert.

It smelled vile to Caleb, too, but he had considered all his other options, and this was the best of a short list of improbable and impractical ideas for solving the mystery of the Petrosna caves.

"Liszka, I'm…er…trying a bit of an experiment, so maybe if you could lead the Fives this month…?"

"Experiment? Is it dangerous?"

He had to remind himself that she wasn't saying this because she wanted to stop him, but because she was ready to offer to fight. "No, no," he assured hastily. "Not in the slightest. Bela, do you remember some of the old stories about werewolves, about other ways of transforming?"

The boy had appropriated his mother's discarded apple cake and was jamming it into his mouth. "Uh, sure," he said between chews. "How to be a wolf in five easy lessons, right? Like drinking a potion or putting on a magic belt."

"Old wives' tales," Liszka snorted. She left the table and walked to the doorway, looking over Caleb's shoulder as he pulled back the canvas to reveal a dusty gray pelt. The whites of her eyes showed as she growled, "Where did you get that?"

Caleb didn't reply, figuring Liszka could infer all she needed to know. They had both been there last fall when the farmer's widow had called the band of monster-hunters to figure out the noises in the barn. Pushing aside harnesses and empty grain sacks hanging on a wall, the werewolves had seen the coat that had caused the farmer's death.

Caleb had coughed, then made a lame remark about dust and moved away quickly before the more hot-headed of his team said something unfortunate. They did a cursory job on their task and left, most of them swearing never to return unless it was to kill and eat the widow, too.

But Caleb later remembered the wolfskin as he pored over dusty old books in Brasov. A wolf belt could allow a man to change into a wolf at will, but accounts differed as to how one actually went about making a wolf belt. Some books insisted that a pact with the Devil was required, while others said that the belt must be made of a hairy hide, but did that mean a wolf's hide or a werewolf's hide? In either case, Caleb felt repulsed. He might have told Vlad once or twice that he deserved to be skinned, but he didn't mean it literally.

One book, a French translation of an Arabic translation of the original Greek, prescribed a ritual for creating a wolf belt that involved the skin of a true wolf. A person who donned the belt could transform into a wolf at will. Unlike the true werewolf, who became a beast under the full moon, the transformee would retain some capacity for rational thought. This method of transformation was not without its dangers, as stories were rife concerning those unfortunates who had gone mad or got stuck. Caleb didn't think he'd have any trouble coping with the smells and sights of being a wolf, but he did worry about changing back. Was it merely a matter of taking off the belt without opposable thumbs, or was there something more subtle and sinister going on?

At least he had the ingredients without having to resort to any more violence. Having killed once over this particular coat, he felt as if it belonged to him.

"If the wolf belt works as advertised," Caleb remarked as he forced himself to touch the pelt, spreading it flat on the ground, "I'll able to get into the cave, past the leptothrix. Even though it will be a full moon, I'll keep my human mind, which means I can see if there are werewolves using the caves to get down to Albimare."

"A human's mind in a wolf's body?" Liszka challenged. "What kind of sheeprot is that?"

Bela looked at his mother with sympathy. "Why have paws and teeth if you don't know how to use them?" They both rolled their eyes in agreement that Lupeni Alpha had crossed the line from eccentric to barking mad.

"Well, Bela, it's all in the name of science."

Caleb's remark elicited guffaws from the boy, who had heard that line all too often from his father. Caleb didn't respond. Instead he took out the notes he'd written during his research on how to make a wolf belt, determined to pull an all-nighter if necessary.

He didn't go to Grigore's cottage the following night, since he worried that Liszka would try to follow him in case he got into trouble. She never quite trusted his skills as a wolf. Alexandru let him out the gates as on his very first full moon at the castle, but this time the air was warm and he enjoyed sitting naked in the grass watching the sunset.

"Here we go," he said out loud to the rocks and the grasses as he looped the belt across his chest like a sash and fastened it. "It's all in the name of science."

The pain of transforming was something they were all used to. It even helped to unite them, to get them ready for a night of hunting, like a tribe's warrior initiation rite. Caleb was somehow disappointed, then, when he felt nothing but a vague stretching sensation and raised his hand to his face only to discover that it was a paw.

No, it wasn't right at all. Walking on all fours felt funny because he was thinking about every move. He wanted to grab things with his fingers, forgetting that his teeth were better for the purpose, and his mind was cluttered with a stream of interfering thoughts—What was that noise? What was that smell? What should he do next?—precious moments wasted as he pondered rather than acted.

He set out at a lope through the woods to the caves. Before going to Brasov he'd found the upper entrance, high in the hills where he would never have thought to set a ward. All he had to do was go in, find a narrow passage with enough available rocks, and cause a cave-in so that the Sixes couldn't pass through. The thought of the leptothrix didn't even occur to him, which almost certainly meant that he was immune.

Reaching the entrance to the cave, he sniffed once and plunged through the underbrush. There had been humans here very recently, and he hesitated, waiting for a twinge from the overwhelming killer instinct that had been part of him for eighteen years.

He didn't so much as growl.

Not even when he broke through into the cave's main chamber and found a complex array of scientific apparatus that all smelled human. Some of it hung from the ceiling, some was scattered on the floor. Huge blocks of metal (iron; it had the tang of blood) stood stacked along one wall. Green video screens blipped and bleeped in patterns of smooth or square waves.

There was no one here now, though, and he stepped nimbly through the main cave and into the narrower passage that led down, presumably into the village of Albimare. Leptothrixes swirled around him, but they didn't seem to notice him, and he felt no emotions whatsoever. He could sense them only as a swirly, smoky presence, like the remnants of a bad campfire. It was so dark that even the wolf couldn't see, but his fur and whiskers sensed the size of the passages and where the stone gave way to soft earth.

Some distance from the village, he began to dig at the roof of the cave. It was hard work, and he was there for many hours, but he grew neither tired nor bored. At last, the faintest hint of a breeze alerted him to a breach in the tunnel's structure, and he began to back away.

The cave-in was larger than he intended, stretching ten or twenty feet, and he found himself pelted by clots of earth and falling rocks.

As the cave fell around him, he scrambled up the narrow passageways, bursting into the large chamber full of equipment. The wolf was suddenly face to face with a very surprised young man. Giving off a burst of fear-smell, the man turned and ran. The wolf sniffed the equipment briefly, confirming what he suspected on his first visit to the chamber.

He followed the scent of the human and soon stood at a large entrance to the caves. There was shouting in the distance; presumably the man was alerting others. Caleb slunk through the trees, keeping himself well hidden, until he saw a camp composed of a large pavilion and several small tents with a Jeep parked nearby. The shouting man was rousing others from the tents. Three others emerged, two men and a woman.

The man yelled, in English, that he had seen another wolf. That made it seem likely that the Sixes *had* been using the caves to get to Albimare. Well, Caleb was fairly certain that the way would be barred from now on. As the four campers hiked along the path to look for the elusive wolf, Caleb thought he'd better be going.

He had a lot to think about as he limped back to the castle. Dawn had broken, the moon had set, and his body was confused and sore. It didn't expect to be a wolf after moonset, giving him strange tugs and twinges in his face, paws, and spine.

Not just wolves occupied his mind, however. He wondered about the people he'd seen: they'd spoken English and had a cave full of electronics. Spies? A CIA plot in the mountains of Transylvania? More worrisome, however, was the faint but unmistakable trace of vampire that he'd detected in the main cave.

Leptothrixes and vampires together in the same cave? He wasn't sure they could co-exist. Perhaps that was why no one had made a thorough investigation of the Petrosna caves before. The grim task seemed to be called for now, although he wasn't sure how to carry it out.

17 ✦ A Tangled Web We Weave

IN THE THIRD QUARTER Caleb finally felt up for the journey south to investigate the caves in a normal human way. In Rosu he learned that the four people at the camp were students from a university in Italy. He was astounded—the political situation in Romania must have undergone a complete upheaval in the five years that he had been living in the castle. He had heard nothing of this, had no idea, and only knew that more hunters had been spotted in the forest within the past year. He hoped that wasn't a harbinger of things to come.

Maybe he was getting anxious over nothing. After all, Hermann had slipped into Romania during the Communist repression. Perhaps the "physics grad student" thing was a cover story for the CIA, and they had come here to see the vampires and werewolves that had so interested Dean Arghezi back in the States.

Of course, they might see a lot more vampires and werewolves than they bargained for.

Grim thoughts occupied his mind as he made his way along the dirt track leading to the camp. An argument was taking place as he came in sight of it, conducted in bad Italian. That is, two very angry people, neither of whom spoke Italian well, were yelling at each other.

One of the combatants was the man that Caleb's wolf had startled in the cave. He was a stocky man in his early twenties; he looked Italian, but he had an American accent and a vocabulary he'd probably picked up in his grandmother's kitchen. The other man appeared to be a local who had driven to the camp in a battered black car. The only other vehicle in the camp was the Jeep.

From comments that the Romanian made when he lapsed back into his native tongue, Caleb concluded that the man was trying to shake down the students for money with a story about needing a license. Smiling to himself, he moved behind the black car and surreptitiously waved his hand.

"Excuse me," he said in Romanian, as he stepped around the front of the car and into the fray. "Is that your car? I think it's on fire."

Furious words ceased as both men turned to look first at Caleb and then at the car. White smoke with a hint of green (he was proud of that little touch) came pouring out of the back seat. With a startled cry, the car's owner yanked open the door and began throwing dirt onto the "fire."

The smoke quickly vanished, leaving the man surprised and angry. Before he could resume the argument, Caleb said to him quietly but forcefully, "I think that you should leave these people alone, otherwise something else might happen to your car." He wasn't really very good at human threats, but this sort of thing had always worked for Toby, he remembered.

"You going to curse my car or something?" accused the man. Even non-wizards understood about hexes and curses in the mountains of Transylvania.

"Something like that," replied Caleb mildly.

The man glared back, but got into the car without saying another word. With a great shudder and a cloud of blue smoke, which came from underneath the car this time, the sedan lurched out of camp and down the track.

The student turned to stare at Caleb, not saying anything at first. Incredibly, Caleb noticed that another student, an Asian, had been sitting in the large pavilion the entire time. His attention seemed to be glued to a computer of some sort, but he would occasionally move his hands furiously. Otherwise, he paid no attention to anything else.

"Jeez, first a sleazeball and now a damned hippie," muttered the Italian-looking man in English.

Do I look like a hippie? Caleb mused to himself. He remembered seeing clusters of them in Harvard Square when he was a student, with their long hair and frayed blue jeans. He never dreamed that he'd be adopting their dress one day. But his life hadn't turned out as expected in most other ways, either.

"I am, er, a botanist, actually," Caleb said in English, feeling the words emerge slowly, like bears waking from hibernation.

"Oh, you speak English." The other man looked startled and perhaps slightly embarrassed. "Hey, thanks for chasing that guy away. I couldn't figure out what he wanted and Italian was the only language we had in common…

Oh, hey, my name's Mike Ferraro." He stuck out his hand brusquely in a way that would have proclaimed that he was an American, even without the distinctive accent.

"Lupeni," Caleb replied, shaking Mike's hand. "That fellow wanted you to give him money, although I don't think he had any good reason for it."

"Too bad Lamia wasn't around," Mike said brightly. "She's Italian, the only Italian in the bunch, but she speaks Romanian and about ten other languages. She would have chased him away." He stopped and looked over Caleb's shoulder. "There she is…Hey, Lamia! We've got company!"

Mike waved, and Caleb turned to see a woman walking unhurriedly toward them. She was thin with long, dark hair pulled back behind her head. In spite of the overcast morning, she wore a large floppy straw hat and dark sunglasses, looking as if she had just stepped from some Mediterranean beach rather than out of an alpine forest in Transylvania. Only her clothes proclaimed her to be a student: the ubiquitous blue jeans and shapeless black T-shirt.

"I speak nine languages, actually, and my hearing is very good," she said as she approached the two. Her full mouth curved into a mischievous smile. She spoke English with a lyrical accent that was as beautiful as Mike's was flat and uninteresting. "I understand we have a hippie visiting us, or perhaps a botanist?"

"This is Lubin—I didn't quite catch your name," Mike blustered with the proud air of someone who can't be bothered with such trivial details.

"Lupeni," finished Caleb and extended his hand to the woman.

"Lamia Borgheza," she replied, taking his hand. Hers was cold, but she smiled up at him warmly. He found it impossible to guess what she might be thinking behind those dark glasses, but was intrigued. The handshake took long enough for Mike to start making small coughing noises. Caleb dropped her hand, amused, and wondered about the relationship between the two.

"So, what brings you to our little side of the mountain?" Mike inquired roughly, trying to win back center stage. "You collecting plants? You said you were a botanist, right?" He clearly did not believe Caleb, who silently agreed that his cover story was a bit farfetched.

"I'm collecting some rare specimens of *Dianthus callizonus* that grow close to cave entrances." Caleb wasn't quite sure that it grew anywhere near caves, but it was the best he could do. It was one of the ingredients in the fever-banishing potion he fed to his packmates when they had colds or the flu.

"Ah," Lamia said in round, knowledgeable tones, "perhaps you mean

Dianthus spiculifolius? Callizonus, with the beautiful pink flowers, only grows in Piatra Craiului, but I have seen a few *spiculifolius* growing around here."

"Yes, of course," Caleb replied quickly. It would be just his luck that these students would turn out to be botanists. He wondered how he was going to turn the conversation around to wolves. Why hadn't he said he was a zoologist?

But Mike, eager to claim the conversation back, did it for him. "Aw, Lamia, you're not an expert on flowers, too? You're going to make Mr. Lubenny think we're here to study nature or something. We're just humble physicists, y'know." Mike eyed his fellow student slyly and addressed Caleb. "You don't know anything about wolves, do you? We seem to have lots of those."

Lamia shuddered slightly and Caleb guessed that this was the desired effect of Mike's question. "You have seen wolves?" he inquired levelly. "There aren't too many left up here, from what people tell me. There are quite a few dogs, though."

"Seen 'em!" Mike snorted. "I was attacked by them, right Lamia? And they weren't dogs!"

An attack would almost certainly mean a werewolf. This month or last month? He didn't see any of the Sixes last week when he visited the cave, but he had spent much of the night inside.

"How long ago?"

"End of last month, right after we got here. I went chasing after Miss Nature here, and as we were coming through the woods back to camp, two of them jumped out of the cave at me." Lamia seemed calm during this recital, but Caleb would have liked to have seen her eyes. Her body seemed to grow more tense and more still with each syllable of Mike's story, even though her face was impassive. "Lamia scared them off, yelled something in Romanian. Not before one of them scratched me, though."

"Oh?" Caleb asked cautiously. The timing was about right for the full moon before the most recent one. "Just a scratch? No bite?" Lamia looked up at him with a sudden, startled motion and then turned away quickly. "Sometimes those scratches can turn nasty. I have…had them myself. Did it heal?"

"Stupid thing keeps hurting," Mike said as he shoved up the sleeve of his shirt to reveal three long scratches on his forearm. The traces were black, an unnatural shade of black, with red puckering around the edges. Werewolf scratches were not deadly, but they could fester if left untreated. Caleb put out his hand, wondering if this was Vlad's work, causing Mike to wince even before contact with the scab.

"I know of an herbal remedy that will help that heal," Caleb promised. "Something I've picked up since I've been here. If you like, I could make some and bring it back for you."

The wound should heal with a simple Canine Poultice Potion, provided a bit of wolfsbane was mixed in. Perhaps he could get Mihail to help out. That would give him an excuse to come back and learn more about the wolves and the caves.

"Well," drawled Mike, "I don't know. It'll probably heal on its own."

Surprisingly, Lamia spoke up, saying, "Go on, Mike. I'm sure our botanist can mix the right things together. He probably won't make it any worse than it already is."

"Oh, what the hell," Mike grinned with a nod.

Relieved, Caleb sprinted back to the castle and prodded Mihail out of his afternoon nap to help with yet another potion. It must have been Caleb's imagination that the old servant had grown used to him over the years, because his immediate response upon being asked for wolfsbane was, "So, cleaning up after your friends again?"

Not only that, but he went into his bedroom to collect the plant. He probably draped the stuff around himself as he slept.

Caleb tried to be brave as Mihail returned with a flowery sprig, but it went beyond ordinary disgust: the plant just made him back off. It was all he could do not to flee from the room.

Mihail watched with malicious delight as he completed the poultice. "Works well, doesn't it?" he wondered rhetorically. "Like vampires and garlic."

"Something like that," Caleb said with forced cheerfulness, thinking he should be grateful that these tricks really worked. Garlic had saved him and Alexandru more than once, for it held Romanian vampires at bay indefinitely. It was better than sunlight, which only made them feeble and to which some of the old-timers seemed entirely resistant. Alexandru had explained that these rules were not universal, though. As close by as Slovenia, vampires only came out at night. In Russia, allegedly, they emerged at noon. "And luckily, wolfsbane isn't a critical ingredient in the local cuisine," he added.

Mihail turned his liquid dark eyes on Caleb, his face full of fear and rage. "Do you think the castle grounds were planted with garlic to season legs of lamb?" he inquired with sarcasm born of helpless terror.

Caleb shivered as he realized Mihail's hostility was not directed at him personally, but that he was just as afraid of whatever Alexandru sought as the old wizard himself...if not more afraid. The days of uncertainty, of Alexandru's fraying temper and occasionally irrational demands, had taken their toll.

"No, I supposed it was to keep the vampires from moving into the castle again," he began, thinking.

He was cut off by Mihail's harsh cackle. "Ah, no, they did not move *in* to the castle before, Mr. O'Connor," laughed the old man. "Rotten from within, it was."

Caleb thought of the missing portraits in the gallery, and he began to understand. "So then..."

But Mihail was returning to his duty, and the potion reminded him to be wary of his partner in this conversation. He wasn't quite ready to discuss his fear of one Dark creature with another.

"Here you go," he said, his expression closing as he handed Caleb a stoppered flask. "Why you need it for a mere *scratch*, I do not know, but..." He leered. Clearly he thought Caleb was lying about a bite.

"It was a student, with a group from a university," Caleb explained. "They're doing some kind of experiment in the Petrosna caves."

Mihail snatched the flask with an intake of breath, then reconsidered and handed it back. "Adults don't survive werewolf bites, you know," he said darkly.

"Yes, I know."

"I thought you would," muttered the old man, watching Caleb stroll insouciantly from the room with the flask tucked into his pocket.

18. Calypso's Cave

WHEN CALEB RETURNED TO the Petrosna caves the next day, he found yet another student in the pavilion. The area consisted of a large tent with its sides rolled up and mesh netting hanging all around; the interior contained several tables with computers and piles of books and papers. The student, an Indian by his looks, stared fixedly at a computer screen watching bright squiggly lines dance.

"Er, excuse me," Caleb began as he stood nearby, just outside the netting.

"What is it?" the other began in a crisp British accent, without taking his eyes from the squiggles. When he finally looked up, he seemed startled to see a stranger.

"Oh. Sorry," he said, still lost in whatever he had been working on. "You're that fellow Mike told us about, eh?"

"Yes. I'm looking for Mike, in fact. I brought something for him. Is he here?"

"He's on shift," replied the student, as if that explained everything. Responding to Caleb's puzzled expression, he jumped off his stool and pushed aside the mesh curtain. "Sorry. He's up at the caves taking data. I'm Vijay."

Vijay offered his hand and Caleb shook it, musing that he had gotten out of practice shaking hands. Sniffing noses was more his style, but he didn't think these students would understand or appreciate that greeting.

"I'll just go and get him, shall I?" Without waiting for a reply, the student disappeared up the path, leaving Caleb to stare at the computer screen. He wondered if the wiggles were tracking particle decays, with some vague memory of why this should be done in a cave. Protection from solar neutrinos, maybe? He stepped into the pavilion and surveyed some of the piles lying about, thinking that he could at least understand books.

That was wrong, of course, since most of the books turned out to have incomprehensible titles filled with words that Caleb didn't even know existed. Particle physics had not been a particular interest of his, and the time he'd spent as a science student seemed as if it had happened to someone else decades ago.

One corner of the tent was piled with books of another sort, books about history and literature in a surprising number of languages. Most he didn't know, but Greek and Latin he had studied with Fintonclyde, simply because he'd had a voracious desire to learn anything he could find.

He picked up a copy of *The Iliad*, turning to the beginning to see how well he could do with the Greek. Words and phrases leapt out at him as he stumbled out loud through the opening lines:

> *"Rage—Goddess, sing the rage of Peleus' son Achilles,*
> *murderous, doomed, that cost the Acheans countless losses,*
> *hurtling down to the House of Death so many sturdy souls…"*

He broke off, thinking sharply of Toby, not wanting to hear more about the doom of one of the greatest of tragic heroes.

"Well, the hippie knows Homer," said a dry voice from behind him. He turned to find Lamia, her face shaded by the enormous hat, but without her dark glasses today. A pair of intense violet eyes bored into him as if he were an odd specimen in a zoo. There was something about her eyes, something at once familiar and alien.

"It's been a long time," he said, hastily putting the book down. "I wasn't sure if I could still…"

"I don't care for *The Iliad*, myself," she said slyly, as she entered the pavilion and appraised Caleb carefully. "Not enough interesting female characters. Pleading Thetis and dreary, tortured Helen are about it."

"Ah," he smiled at her, "perhaps you prefer *The Odyssey* and the clever wife, Penelope?"

She shook her head, but smiled back at him.

"Circe, enchantress of men, then," he said, feeling oddly buoyant as his brain worked in ways long forgotten. "Or the nymph Calypso, who wants to make Odysseus immortal so he will stay with her forever?"

She approached and he smelled her perfume, musky, sweet and unsettling, and as familiar as her eyes in some odd way. "Calypso, I fancy," she said softly, perching on a stool and looking up at him with a newfound interest. "She lives on a lovely island far out to sea."

"Isolation is what you crave?" Caleb asked, surprised at himself for wanting to continue the conversation. She laughed in response with a trace of bitterness.

"I'm here, aren't I? But I suppose that you must like isolation as well." She didn't give him time to reply, but stood abruptly, saying, "Mike and Vijay have gotten into an argument—they usually do. I'll take you up to the caves."

He followed her along a path that wound through the trees for about five hundred yards. A wall of granite loomed suddenly, proclaiming their arrival at the flank of the mountain. Caleb could see thick black cables on the ground, snaking into the entrance to the cave. An unnatural glow issued from the dark opening, indicating that this wasn't the lair of a dragon or a chimera or any other creature in Caleb's experience.

An argument was indeed in progress; he'd heard similar ones in the halls of MIT. The cosmic irony of finding himself once again among physics students was almost too much. For a brief moment he considered that they all might be leptothrixes playing an elaborate trick on him—then he decided they were all too dorky to be soul-sucking Dark creatures.

"The whole idea of proton decay is based on the simplest possible Unified Field Theory, SU(3) cross SU(3) cross U(1). There's no reason nature has to make everything the simplest way." That was Mike, playing the devil's advocate in what sounded like his usual manner.

"But would it be any surprise that the vector boson mediating baryon number non-conservation would have finite mass?" Vijay replied in a tone of calm reason. "We have already seen the unification of the electrical and weak forces. Why not the strong force?"

Hundreds of steel boxes, three feet across and taller than a tall man, were stacked two-deep throughout the cave. Metal tubes of every description were scattered around the stack in chaotic disarray. Someone had made a half-hearted attempt to pile them up, and there were two people right now engaged in layering them around the stack. Other metal boxes were arranged so that the conical holes in their centers faced the ceiling. Bits and pieces of hardware dangled from every surface, most of it wrapped in tape and plastic so that Caleb could not even begin to guess what it might be. Dozens of computer screens scrolled constant streams of numbers, and occasionally the streams would stop, causing Mike or Vijay to hammer at the keyboards and curse.

"Hey, you two," Lamia said with practiced tones, "you're not going to construct a Grand Unified Theory just yet." Both men stopped reluctantly.

Mike noticed Caleb and broke into a broad grin. "Hey, I didn't think you'd be back," he said, the argument having been forgotten. "Did you really bring some Transylvanian potion?"

Caleb smiled. That was exactly what he had brought, although a few years previous he would have been as scientifically skeptical of it as they were. He flashed back to his drive to Boston the day of Toby's trial, and the "magical courtroom" that had had no magical ways of finding the truth. Had any of that actually happened?

"Let's see your arm," he said, stepping toward Mike and shaking his head to banish the memories. Treating wounds was something he had grown familiar with. The Fives got themselves into plenty of scrapes, both in human and in wolf form, although Caleb wasn't as certain about the healing powers of humans.

Mike rolled up his sleeve to reveal the scratched landscape on his arm. Caleb got the flask from the canvas bag on his shoulder along with some bandages.

"Can you, er, give me a hand?" he asked, turning to Lamia. He realized all of a sudden that the Poultice Potion, containing wolfsbane as it did, was not something he cared to touch. He handed her the flask as he took Mike's outstretched arm. "Unstopper it, and pour a bit on," he directed her.

The potion smoked slightly as the flask was opened, and even more as Lamia dribbled it along the scars on Mike's arm. He winced, clearly trying to be brave, saying, "Whoa. What is this stuff?"

"Mmmm. Herbs mostly," Caleb replied as he inspected the wound. The redness was starting to decrease. Mihail had never failed him on a potion, perhaps making it worth the cold stares and harsh words he usually encountered from the Romanian servant.

"Apply it twice a day for five days," he said brusquely as he wrapped a bandage around the wounded arm. "I'll come back and check on it next week. It should be healed by then."

"Think I'll have a scar?" Mike grinned at him. "Souvenir of Transylvania? Hey, at least I didn't turn into a werewolf."

Both Lamia and Caleb shuddered at his words. Caleb wondered once again at her seeming familiarity with the subject. He put the remainder of the bandages back in his bag and wished to be gone from the cave. He detected no vampires today, although his human senses were far inferior to those of the wolf. Perhaps it was the lurking presence of leptothrixes somewhere in the labyrinth of caves that made him uncomfortable.

"We should let Mike get back to work," Lamia said suddenly. "I'll walk you back to the camp. I'm not due on shift until after dark."

As they left the caves, Mike and Vijay resumed their argument. This was as much a part of being a physicist as all the dancing squiggles. Caleb was quite sure he preferred the werewolves.

As if reading his mind, Lamia said, "The argumentation gets wearisome, but physics is beautiful, really. The problems are so hard—a lifetime could be spent just in preparing to understand—and your mind has to stretch, to reach out to grasp them…" She broke off, embarrassed, and looked at her feet once again. "I'm sorry. I don't expect I can explain what it's like for me."

Caleb remembered what had originally drawn him to science, and realized there were some things he hadn't left behind. When he learned a complicated enchantment like the moonwards, he had to seek out just the right balance in his mind and in the external world, and it all had to come together as a conceptual whole.

"Your mind creates something from nothing," he mused as he walked. "No, that's not right. You take from the chaos around you and build something that didn't exist before. It *is* beautiful."

She stopped walking and Caleb, lost in thought, didn't notice for a moment. He turned back to see her staring at him with an expression rendered unreadable by the dark glasses.

"Yes," she said softly, "perhaps you do understand."

Lamia walked quickly up the path, eager to be gone from the lights and the noise of the camp. Not that it was all that noisy tonight, especially with Mike up in the caves. He could carry on enough conversation for all four of them if need be.

She held a flashlight in one hand, although she didn't need it. She was perfectly familiar with the path now, even in the dark of early evening. As she walked, she thought about Lupeni, the alleged botanist. He was no more a botanist than she, probably less of one since she had almost taken a degree in botany at one point. She had her suspicions about what he really was, leading her to wonder once again about the wisdom of coming here.

Why had she come? Working for Professor Gamberi at the University of Bologna was definitely an opportunity she could not pass up. All she had to do was to collect enough data this summer and she could spend the next five years analyzing it back at the university; that would be enough to earn her a degree. Four months in Transylvania wouldn't be so bad, or so she thought initially.

But the wolves. She had forgotten about the wolves. And there were other things, too.

"Mike?" she called as she entered the cave, bathed in the green light of the oscilloscopes. He wasn't hunched over the console as usual. Maybe he was further back tending to a piece of equipment.

Lamia wove her way through the tall racks of instruments, skillfully stepping over cables. He wasn't behind any of the racks either. It wasn't like him to leave an experiment in progress. She turned on the flashlight as she emerged back into the center of the chamber, playing the light into the darker corners.

There. On the cave floor behind a packing crate, the light picked up something white. Lamia switched off the light and moved cautiously to investigate. As she came near, she saw the body of a man stretched out, the head and shoulders bathed in darkness. Those were Mike's shoes. She knelt down, shaking him roughly.

"Mike? Are you all right?" But, of course, Mike wasn't going to answer any time soon. That much was obvious from the first touch. More than that, she knew what had happened, something that frightened her even more than werewolves. She stood, conscious that someone or something had come up behind her.

Why did I come back?

Taking a deep breath, she turned, coming face to face with a pale man whose dark eyes leered at her hungrily. Recognition flooded his face, mirroring her own.

"Emil," she said crisply to the vampire, not pleased at all to see him. "It has been a long, long time."

19. The Sheep Look Up

CALEB AND GRIGORE HERDED a ewe and her two lambs up the narrow mountain track. The sheep bleated as they were forced to thread the narrow rocky clefts, and the men worked hard to keep the sheep from tumbling off the rocky ledges. A thick fog wrapped itself around the top of the mountain, cutting off the warm midsummer sun of the pass.

"Grigore!" exclaimed Caleb. "Watch that ewe! She's too close to the edge."

The ewe stumbled and disappeared, her angry bleats echoing through the mist, calling out to the remaining animals. Both men moved cautiously toward the cries, but halted when it became obvious that the ewe had slipped off the edge of the track and tumbled down to a nearby ledge. In spite of their mother's insistent calls, the remaining sheep—all this spring's lambs—huddled behind the men.

"I am sorry, Lupeni Alpha," Grigore replied timidly.

"She's not very smart and this mist is getting thick," Caleb reassured Grigore, clapping him lightly on the shoulder. He alwayss winced when Grigore addressed him as Alpha; he had hoped that oldest friend in the mountains could dispense with it when they traveled without the pack.

"Grigore," he said after a thoughtful pause, "this might be a good time for you to try to summon Wind."

"Oh, no," replied the other nervously, "I've only practiced on small things and—"

"Nonsense. What good is it learning spells if you don't practice them?"

The lost ewe continued her loud cries as they talked, and the lambs nudged the two wizards nervously. In ten months of practice Grigore had learned a few simple spells. With the exception of the boy, Bela, none of the other Fives was remotely interested in learning magic—but Caleb was pleased with even that much progress. Unlike Fintonclyde, Caleb was not driven to teach all of the packmates under his care.

"Close your eyes and focus, just as we practiced," Caleb prompted gently.

The wizard-in-training nodded, raised his arms and muttered the words of the spell under his breath, his eyes closed tightly in concentration. The bleats of the lost ewe grew closer and Caleb could just make out her fuzzy head appearing out of the mist. Grigore opened his eyes and gasped, startled that he had actually done it. Unfortunately, this revelation broke his concentration and the sheep disappeared from sight, baaing bitterly. They could hear her hooves scrambling over the stones below.

"Son of a rabid dog," cursed Grigore, stamping his feet. Caleb ignored him while he called to the ewe. She soon reappeared, frantically struggling but otherwise unharmed, and tumbled to the ground at their feet. She would have gone off the edge again if Caleb had not grabbed her, kneeling and throwing his arms around the large woolly neck.

"That was very good, Grigore," he said as calmly as he could over the ewe's bleats. He tried to sound encouraging, despite the mouthful of wool and sharp kicks from the sheep's hooves.

"Stupid sheep," muttered Grigore. "We were better off stealing them."

"You cannot mean that," Caleb said sharply, rising to meet the younger wizard's eyes.

"No, Lupeni Alpha." he murmured, ducking his head to avoid the other's glaring disappointment. "But…" Grigore spoke haltingly, but with an edge of determination in his voice. "Wolves aren't—aren't sheepdogs. In the old days, we—"

"Stole sheep and bit people and were continually hunted down and murdered. Do you want to go back to that way?" Caleb sighed and shooed the sheep together. The lambs nuzzled the ewe, happy to be reunited.

"Too many humans, that's the problem," spat Grigore. "We should just go somewhere else."

It was an old argument. Some of the werewolf packs had, in fact, left the mountains, but leaving would not make the problem go away. Caleb had been fighting this particular battle since he had challenged Vlad Alpha and created his own pack. Grigore had been one of the first to take Caleb's side; hearing Vlad-like sentiments from Grigore's lips was an unsettling surprise, especially now, when it was becoming increasingly clear that the dictatorship was releasing its grip on the Romanian cities. Soon there would be ordinary people coming to play and work in these hills, and if they couldn't coexist, it was the werewolves who would lose. There was no place left to hide.

As they coaxed the sheep back up the trail—not unlike persuading water to flow uphill—Caleb tried again with Grigore. "I'm not cut out for herding sheep myself, but raising a few sheep gives us freedom, you know that." Grigore walked beside him with eyes downcast and said nothing. Caleb continued, "We'll trade the lambs for some chickens at the castle and then perhaps even have some eggs to sell in the village. More freedom."

"Yeah, I guess," he mumbled, "freedom is good. But what good is it if—" Grigore halted and the sheep jostled around him, unhappy that something blocked their path.

"Yes, what is it, Grigore?" Caleb asked with patient curiosity.

"Well, um, we might have our freedom here, but for how long? All the packs get smaller every year. Bela's the last one to join the Fives and that was…thirty months ago, at least." Grigore began haltingly without meeting Caleb's eyes, but talked faster as he went along, as if each word fueled the next. "Twelve months ago, we lost Andre. If we stay here, how long until we are—until we disappear?"

Grigore managed in the end to raise his face and confront his pack leader with a mixture of fear and resolve in his eyes. Too shocked to answer, Caleb turned away and wrangled the wandering sheep. He felt angry, betrayed in a way, by words that he would only expect to hear from Vlad.

"We'll always take in new members," he replied with a calm he didn't feel, "but we have to find some kind of balance here. We can't attack humans and provoke them to kill us."

He paused, struggling to find the words to convince Grigore. At that moment, however, the great standing stone marking the end of the trail loomed out of the mist. They had their hands full keeping the sheep away from the sheer cliff at the east side of the castle so that they could be herded around the west wall toward the stable gate. By the time they all arrived at the rear of the castle, Caleb thought it best to leave the argument for another day. Instead, he would try teaching Grigore a bit more magic.

"The castle is protected by a lot of elaborate enchantments," Caleb said as they collected the sheep around them, "but the locking spell on this gate is not much more complicated than the one I showed you. The main gate of the castle has a more intricate ward on it. Even I don't know how to release or set that one properly."

The small wooden gate stood before them. Three times the width of a man and twice as tall, it was only small by comparison to the main gate. The gate was flanked by the smooth gray stones of the castle wall that curved over the top in a graceful arch. Caleb raised his arm and gestured for Grigore to do the same.

"Remember the locking spell on your cottage?" Grigore nodded uncertainly and Caleb continued, "The enchantment on the gate is much the same, but there are six serae magi to activate instead of three. First, find the points. Go on."

Grigore raised his arm, looked at Caleb doubtfully, and then turned toward the gate. With his fingers extended, he gestured around the perimeter of the gate. First one spot and then others began to glow with a faint blue light. He gained confidence with each glimmer.

"Good," Caleb praised. "Now once you can hold all the serae of the enchantment in your mind, the words to release the spell are portales minor."

Taking a deep breath, Grigore closed his eyes, waved his hand once more, and said, "Portales minor."

The entire gate flared briefly with the same blue light. The apprentice wizard opened his eyes and grinned as Caleb patted him on the back. After swinging the gate open using a large iron ring, they both began to push the sheep through the portal. When the last lamb had passed into the castle, Grigore made to follow, but something sent him reeling backward onto the ground.

"I forgot to mention," Caleb said, suppressing a laugh as his companion picked himself up, "that there's more than one enchantment on this gate."

"But how did the sheep get through?"

"Wizards and other magical creatures are barred by another spell that does not affect animals. It is based upon the planet Jupiter, and extends all around the castle so that you could not, for example, climb over the wall."

"What about wolves?" puzzled Grigore. "I mean our kind."

"Good question," he responded. "Werewolves are magical creatures and would not be able to get in. The spell is far too complex to be broken simply, but a skilled wizard can make an opening in it for a short time. I don't expect you to be able to do this. It takes considerable practice to master. If you do it wrong, you can get stuck in the field of the enchantment—which isn't pleasant, I can tell you."

Grigore watched raptly as Caleb moved his hands through the air in a complicated figure. A glow, the same blue of the locking spell, filled the open space of the gate. Caleb gestured for Grigore to enter and then followed rapidly as the luminous blue field faded. He closed the gate behind them and reset the locking spell. Both men turned their attention to the scattered sheep, bleating and clattering over the stones of the castle yard.

As they worked at getting the sheep settled in the stable, Mihail appeared, standing in the doorway with his arms folded in contempt and disapproval. After a few minutes of the servant's silent vigil, Caleb figured that he had something he wanted to say—probably not within earshot of Grigore, who Mihail would guess was another werewolf.

"Good morning," Caleb said pleasantly as he approached the stony-faced Romanian.

"The master went out early this morning and has not returned," declared Mihail, "and I have just come back from the village."

"Oh?" Caleb queried.

"You have not heard, then," replied Mihail smugly, as he always did when he had the upper hand.

Caleb shook his head and waited, realizing that the man had more than the usual gossip to relate.

"One of your students at the Petrosna caves was bitten by a vampire."

20 ❖ Vampire-Hunter!

"HEY, LOOK AT THIS." Mike sat up on his cot in the students' pavilion outside the Petrosna caves. He was still weak, unable to get out of bed, and trying to banish the chill in his bones under the late afternoon sun. There wasn't much more he could do; he certainly wasn't going to risk having a blood transfusion in Romania. In these last days of Communism's ascendancy, anyone close enough to the big cities was beginning to hear about dictator Ceaușescu's forced fertility program, the orphanages filled with children who had never left their cots, AIDS. The horror in the doctors' faces as they examined Mike's neck wound had, he thought, much more to do with unconscious knowledge of the suppressed epidemic than with ancient mythology.

He propped himself on his elbow, pasty white fingers gripping a yellowed volume. It belonged to Lamia, one of her few zoology books in English, *Arachnids of the Carpații Meridionali.* It looked to be about a hundred years old, but the local bugs probably hadn't changed much. "There's a Romanian indigenous cave spider that evolved underground, cut off from sunlight for over five million years, with nothing to eat but other creatures. It has no eyes and is a pure carnivore."

Vijay chuckled low in his throat. He was sitting on the ground, a multimeter propped between his feet as he prodded a complicated circuit board placed on a sheet of Mylar. "Oh, indeed, Mike. And I suppose it's a meter high and can drink two pints of blood in a sitting." He switched his probes, muttered something about capacitance, and reached for a soldering iron lying nearby.

"Well, a bat, then." Mike unconsciously fingered the bandage on his neck. "They did give me a rabies shot, right? I bet they were thinking bats."

Taofang was immobile at his computer but for his fingers, seemingly a ventriloquist as he spoke in staccato, scarcely grammatical sentences. "No vampire bats outside Latin America. Charles Darwin first European see one."

"Well, so what do you guys think?" Mike's voice had a note of forced calm. Too bad Lamia wasn't here to set them straight, he thought. She knew more biology than the rest of them put together, and had a Romanian grandmother besides. But she was asleep in her tent, exhausted after a long night with the Cerenkov detectors. They could only get good data with them a few nights a month, when there was no moon. "What is the scientific origin of Romanian vampire myths?"

It was too good to pass up. Even Taofang turned his head, memories of all Mike's verbal zings stretching his face into a leer. "Vampires," he and Vijay said together.

"All monster myths have some basis in fact," Mike declared. "Werewolves, of course, are an archetype for man the hunter. We have always been ambivalent about being killers. And vampires…"

There was a crunching in the leaves. Mike whirled, still jumpy, and saw that hippie botanist, his hand clutching something hidden in a sack. He had a friend with him, too, who looked Romanian and who was also lugging a bag.

"Oh, it's you," Mike said coolly, but his usual bravado wilted like a day-old salad, and he seemed almost glad to see the mysterious maker of potions. "Got any bottles of smoking magic juice in there?"

Caleb winced when Mike's arrow hit a little too close to the target. Without much encouragement, Mike launched into his story at length, while Caleb fretted about the sun rapidly approaching the horizon.

"You haven't been to the cave yet?" Caleb demanded when the story finally wound down.

"Just getting my strength back and then I'll go up there. Lots of work to do," Mike replied thinly, his courage gone past wilting into an advanced state of decomposition.

There was a rude laugh over by the computer. "Sure, Mike, and you bit by spider," Taofang chortled.

"There's a scientific explanation!"

"Maybe, but you still idiot."

"The road to hell is paved with not understanding your instruments," Mike insisted.

"Says you." Taofang was laughing at what was apparently an ancient joke. "And two weeks ago wolf reset amplifier gain? Saved whole night data."

"Really?" Caleb wondered. His memories of the night spent wearing the wolf belt were much clearer than usual, but he certainly didn't remember pawing at the amplifier gain. "Well, Mike, I'm sure the wolf recognized you were an idiot," he said truthfully, causing gales of mirth from the other two.

Mike chortled good-naturedly, but his eyes widened as the "botanist" reached into his bag and came up with an eight-inch, polished, gleaming wooden stake.

"Come along, Mike," said Caleb. "Shall we do an experiment?"

There were several reasons for Caleb's impatience. The first was that there was less than a half-hour until sunset. The second, and perhaps the most serious, was that he wasn't even sure that sunset would be critical. Unless they had been powerful wizards in life, vampires who had been Undead for less than fifty years had to return to their coffins at night. But the older ones could sleep anywhere, or even walk about in the daytime. If he had a choice, the vampire would probably not return to the cave where he had already been seen. So if he didn't find a vampire in the cave, Caleb would have to go hunting around, which was not an attractive prospect at night with the moon the slimmest crescent that would set with the sun.

The fact that any reasonably strong werewolf could gut a vampire the way a cat does a mouse was plenty of incentive for most vampires to sleep through nights of the full moon. The dislike of the Undead for moonlight went deeper than that, however. While many animals could see well in dim light, they were blind in total darkness. Vampires were not. On the darkest nights, under a new moon or a densely overcast sky, vampires could hunt without risk of being seen by their prey.

Additionally, lurking in the back of Caleb's mind were the leptothrixes. The area of the cave where Mike was leading him was nowhere near the path he had blocked two weeks ago, but he was still worried about being driven away from his target by the malevolent simulacrum of his long-dead best friend.

"Here," said Caleb. "Wear this." He handed Mike a thick braid of healthy, pungent garlic.

"You're kidding."

"Quite the contrary, there's a scientific explanation." He had to remind himself not to get too sarcastic, but those last two words seemed to work like…well, like magic.

Mike was quiet for a moment, leading Caleb through the cave by the light of the non-magical flashlight. "Yeah," he said at last, though in a hushed voice. "People thought to be vampires were actually suffering from a disease called porphyria, which leads to defective hemoglobin production. They were anemic unless they drank blood, and garlic made it worse. Here!" he cried, his raucous tone returning. "This is where I got bitten."

Caleb gestured for Mike to stay behind and disappeared into the passage with the stake, the flashlight, and his Romanian companion.

"…By the spider," Mike continued, talking to himself. "Garlic made porphyria worse because…because…gee, I forget, some enzyme defect. It was common in Eastern European royal families hundreds of years ago, because they married their cousins and things…Nowadays porphyria can be treated with blood transfusions. Almost anything can be treated…" He touched his neck nervously. "Except rabies, but there's a vaccine. That's the origin of werewolves, I suppose…real wolves are shy of people and don't bite…"

Immersed in such thoughts, Mike jumped as Caleb's feet poked out, and he came out of the passage backwards. He was dragging something, something that almost got stuck in the narrow tunnel.

It was a body, the body of quite a large man, with a stake driven through the heart.

"Rabies!" cried Mike.

Now that he was free of the tunnel, Caleb picked up the body and carried it back through the cave's main gallery. "Excuse me?" he wondered courteously, as Mike came panting after.

"Did he die of rabies? How long has he been dead? Why did you put that stick—?"

"Somewhere between one and fifty years, I would think." Caleb thought fast. He had told many lies in his lifetime, and many of them he had enjoyed. People would provide their own details to believe what they wanted.

"Oooh…" Mike breathed. "Because he was mummified in the cave, right? There's not enough humidity for him to decompose, and very few bacteria. There are so many caves around here—that's why the vampire myth—" Mike chuckled knowingly, and reached out a finger to prod the waxy corpse. "It's OK, the doctor in the village gave me a shot. It's probably bad for the cave to have him in there. Good thing you found him."

"Yes," Caleb agreed thoughtfully. "We'll have to burn the body, because of the possibility of rabies, you know."

"I can help," Mike volunteered. "I've been vaccinated."

It wasn't quite dark outside, though the sun had set. There were no clouds, and some pink rays still reflected off the granite peaks and forests of quaking aspen. The student pavilion, where everyone seemed to have remained during the adventure, was also lit by a kerosene lantern.

Caleb deposited the body just outside the tent and was thinking of something to say when Mike started bellowing and thrashing his arms.

"Rabies!" he screamed. "Someone in the cave had rabies! Fifty years ago! He's dried out like a mummy!"

"IT ISN'T RABIES," Caleb shouted. "There is always a slight risk of it because of the…er…caves, and the bats, but the chances that he actually had rabies are very slim." He sneaked a peek out of the tent to make sure the vampire remained safely staked.

That wasn't much fun for Mike. "Yeah, you're a botanist, what do you know?" He suddenly thought of something. "And the wolves, what about the wolves? Wandering around in here, touching the apparatus…"

Oh no, Caleb thought, swamped with guilt at having drawn attention to his persecuted cousins. "Wolves in Romania do not have rabies," he declared, having no idea if that was true. "Sometimes they behave oddly when they have…eaten poisonous plants. In addition, they are an endangered species, so you are not allowed to kill them."

"Who said anything about killing?" Mike wondered.

"Hmph," Caleb grumbled suspiciously. "For the last time, this man did not have rabies…but we should burn his body anyway. Do you have a source of fire?"

Mike thought for a second, then a broad grin stretched over his face. "I've got an acetylene torch!" he bragged.

Caleb really didn't care about the source, as long as the vampire was disposed of. It had indeed been a relatively new vampire, unable to leave its resting-place before sundown, and the whole affair would have been perfectly straightforward if not for Mike's flights of fancy.

It was an odd parade of humans and werewolves that wound its way out of camp to an isolated spot to dispose of the vampire—or desiccated victim of a cave spider, depending on the point of view. Caleb volunteered to carry the body. Grigore silently accompanied him, seeming bewildered as much by the odd behavior of everyone at the camp as by his inability to understand the language. Finally, Mike and Vijay tagged along, toting lanterns and working through the details of the explanation for it all.

When the corpse was alight, Caleb took the stake and placed it into Grigore's hand. "Thanks for helping out, Grigore," he said to his friend. "Nice job." The young Romanian grinned proudly.

Back at the camp, listening to Mike fill his friends in on the details of the hunt, Caleb decided his work there was done. Between practical jokes, mummification, and rabies, the situation was explained sufficiently to satisfy Mike. He was already arguing with Vijay about how to determine the age of a desiccated corpse, and Taofang was offering to make an animal hologram.

There was one more person to consider, however, someone who might not accept the stories of rabies and mummies so readily. He approached the Chinese graduate student at his computer, waiting for a lull in the conversation.

"It's not a German Shepherd," he couldn't stop himself from inserting when he saw the hologram.

Taofang looked up. "Sorry?"

"Never mind. Where is Lamia?"

"She in her tent," he replied casually, directing his attention back to his computer screen. "But she came out. Just went into trees, near caves."

The final twilight of the afternoon was fading as Caleb started up the path to the caves. He expected to find her inside; instead, he just made her out in the darkness, sitting on a rocky ledge about twenty feet from the main entrance. Her knees were drawn up to her chest and her long, loose hair spilled over them like a dark river.

She could have been a statue adorning some secluded mountain garden, sitting so still that she gave no notice of his approach.

"Er, excuse me," Caleb began, uncertain of how much to reveal, "there was quite a bit of excitement at the camp this afternoon. I don't know if you heard…"

"My hearing is excellent," she murmured, her face buried in her knees and shielded by her hair.

"I want to explain what happened," Caleb said, taking a seat on the rough granite ledge. She dropped her arms stiffly and moved away slightly, turning to stare at him with those odd violet eyes, which hid rather than revealed her feelings.

"I would be very interested to hear what you have to say," she replied coolly, a hint of challenge in her voice.

"I think you know more than the others."

"You're not a botanist. Is that what you mean?" Lamia snapped. "You are an American wizard."

Caleb picked up a handful of small pebbles and rattled them in one hand, letting them dribble slowly to the ground. For a time the clinking of the rocks was the only sound. "You were on to me from the first, weren't you?" He smiled at her. "I take it that your Romanian grandmother was acquainted with magic?"

She did not return his smile, but replied through tight lips, "Yes. She told me many stories of things that live in these mountains." She shook her head suddenly and looked away, concluding in a hoarse whisper, "I should not have come."

Caleb was about to ask another question when she turned to him, her face now darkened by shadow and more unreadable than usual.

"You killed him, didn't you?" she accused roughly, her voiced tinged with horror and perhaps even a little relief.

"The vampire? Yes," he responded simply, curious to hear more about what she knew.

But she did not volunteer anything further. "Poor Mike," Lamia sighed, rising abruptly and dusting bits of gravel from the back of her pants. "I should go see how he's feeling."

With that, she strode past Caleb toward the camp, the conversation clearly at an end. He had many questions, but suspected that getting the answers would be as easy as pulling teeth from a dragon.

21. Down the Rabbit Hole

"How's Mike?" Vijay looked up from the console, his face splashed with green and blue light from the oscilloscopes and computer displays, the only lights in the cave.

"He's sleeping. His color looks a bit better," Lamia shrugged. "You should get some sleep, too."

"Sure," he yawned in response. "What a day, eh? You missed most of the excitement." His dark eyes sparkled with the memory. "I can't believe you slept through the whole thing. That botanist pulled a guy out of the caves, bitten by the same, er, spider that bit Mike."

Lamia wondered whether Lupeni had put a spell on Vijay's mind or whether he actually believed the fantastic story of the cave spider. The American wizard thought she needed protection. He was wrong.

Pushing those thoughts aside, she approached the other student to check on the current state of the experiment. She stopped short a couple of feet away.

"Vijay, you've got garlic in your pocket."

"Yeah," he grinned, "I forgot you don't like the stuff. I was humoring that Lupeni chap. Just forgot to take it out of my pocket. A bit absurd, isn't it?"

"Well," she said lightly, "if vampires really existed, I suppose it might be useful. Show me what we got from the Cerenkov detectors last night."

He happily recounted the events of his shift, including an anomalously high background of neutrino events that he thought might tell them about a supernova. The data from the events could also be used to look for neutrino oscillations, something he had always been interested in but couldn't get their advisor to care about. Vijay certainly didn't want to be a graduate student for 10^{33} years, waiting for protons to decay.

After hearing all this, Lamia shooed him back to the camp, relieved to be alone with numbers and abstract concepts once again.

She hummed softly to herself as she created a graph of energy distributions in three dimensions, looking like a fairy castle as it rotated slowly on the computer screen before her. Once, a long time ago, she wanted to live in a real castle. Now she longed to lose herself in the realm of subatomic particles. The real castle hadn't worked out very well.

So intent was she on the unseen world of baryons and leptons that at first she did not notice the presence of another in the cave, did not see any movement reflected in her computer display. A faint rustle, not of bat wings but of fabric, informed her that she was no longer alone. She turned to face two dark orbs, the eyes of someone standing right behind her. With an unsettling jolt, all thoughts of physics fled from her mind as she recognized the jutting nose and angled cheekbones of one whom she hoped never to see again.

"Cuza," she said coldly in Romanian. "I thought you might show up."

"Emil told me he had seen you, but I scarcely believed him," said the vampire with an air of conquest, now that he was sure of her identity.

He looked exactly the same as the last time she had seen him, twenty years ago. The Undead did not age, need not reflect the passage of time at all. *But I am not the same,* she thought, desperate to force away the memories that his haughty face called forth.

"You have changed," he marveled, as if reading her mind. "Your eyes. Something is wrong."

She laughed harshly, hopping off the stool and moving away from him. "A human thing called—" She stopped, realizing she didn't know the Romanian word for contact lenses. The language she knew was from another time, another world. Why bother explaining it to a vampire, though?

"What do you want from me?" she asked, eyeing him warily. "I told Emil that I wanted nothing to do with the whole lot of you."

"Of course, my dear," he replied smoothly, the old steeliness creeping in underneath. "That is what you said when you left. But, you have come back to us, have you not?"

"No," she growled, turning away from him and staring intently at a different monitor, this one for controlling the argon that filled the metal boxes of the detectors. She typed furiously for a minute, as if she could make the vampire vanish the same way she controlled the gas.

"Then why have you come?" he inquired, still sure he knew the answer. "Emil told me some story about these humans, but I did not believe it."

"I hear you left the castle," she said, pointedly ignoring his question. Focusing on the argon pressure became increasingly difficult as Cuza drifted toward her, hovering at her back.

"Things became difficult in the mountains," he mused. "The living became scarcer and more cautious. We scattered to find better hunting."

She laughed, in spite of the loathing she felt for the vampire who had once been her lover and much more besides. She had always been the one to keep the peace among the group at the castle, interceding in their pointless arguments over events that had happened decades earlier. Their long days of boredom were filled with endless rehashing of the past. The next meal was about as far into the future as they thought. She had finally grown so disgusted that she left, hoping to find something better elsewhere. She had drifted to Bucharest, Athens, London, New York. The vampires she met in those cities were more cultured, had more to talk about, but also remained focused on the past. She wanted to learn new things—obviously an alien concept for the Undead—and so embarked on a career of sorts, skipping from one university to another. Incredibly, the voyage had returned her to the mountains she had fled, and now to the presence of Cuza.

"And you live among these humans now, and they think you are one of them," he spoke the words hungrily.

She moved away from him again, and toward the towers of metal boxes stacked to the ceiling. She felt the rough surface of the metal and tried to put her mind inside the boxes with the argon atoms, waiting patiently for the next neutrino to come whizzing by. But the call of the past was too strong.

"I don't feed on them, if that's what you mean," she responded harshly, turning to face him with her back against the tower of detectors. She stroked the metal with her hand, as if the lifeless metal could overpower the lifeless vampire before her.

"No?" he inquired with much curiosity, drawing closer. "How could you resist so much, so close?"

"I have not had—it has been five years since I—" she faltered.

"No human blood at all? You deprive yourself so, my dear." His surprise turned to a seductive whisper. "Have you forgotten what it is like?"

How could she explain? She had not forgotten, in the same way that a heroin addict never forgets that roaring thunder of sensation that sweeps away the mind and the self, leaving only raw pleasure so intense that it would hurt, if feeling pain were possible. But the ecstasy of human blood left the brain fuzzy and confused, filled only with the lust for more.

She had come to appreciate the pleasure of a fine, sharp mind, the joy of being able to shape complicated concepts the way a sculptor works in clay. She was willing to give up human blood for that joy, but Cuza would never comprehend that, and she told him so.

"You cannot possibly understand what I have become," she said coldly, wishing he would leave her to the peaceful solitude of the oscilloscopes and displays.

"I know what you are," he crooned, drawing near enough to brush her cheek gently with his hand. She froze, momentarily hypnotized by his empty eyes and soft whispering. Languidly, he drew his hand down, the fingers curving possessively around her neck with the gentleness that she remembered. The gentleness that stood in stark contrast to his cruelty.

"You may become a human on the outside, but you will always be one of us," he whispered, brushing his lips softly on her hair, on her cheek, on her neck.

"You're wrong," she cried, pushing him away with both hands. "I have changed and I want nothing more to do with you."

After he had gone, she sat for a long time bathed in the green and blue lights of the familiar instruments, heedless of the pulsating blips and flowing numbers. She knew he would be back.

22 ❖ Dogfight

As June became July in the mountains above Stilpescu, the profusion of pinks, whites, reds, and yellows gave way to rich summer green. Stands of birch and beech formed canopies with their deep green leaves and bundles of catkins. In the meadows between trees, tall tufted grasses extended awns to tempt the birds and bees. The flowers that remained were of a large and hardy sort: daisies and black-eyed Susans with broad, flat leaves, clover, and dandelion, some beginning to fluff with seed.

The lush and peaceful scenery soothed Caleb's irritability as he walked in the grasses, between a row of aspens and a forest of evergreens, on his way to Grigore's cottage. It was less than half an hour till moonrise, but he didn't hurry. It wasn't just the imminent full moon that was making him snappish; he didn't want to run into Liszka while they could still talk, and risk a replay of the arguments they'd been having ever since he blocked the cave to Albimare.

There was a reason he hadn't encountered Vlad's pack at the caves last month. Liszka knew he planned to pass through the Sixes territory, and she suspected that if Vlad caught Caleb there, alone, he would kill him. So she had directed the Fives to loiter around their mutual border, provoking minor skirmishes throughout the night that distracted Pack Six from Caleb's work.

When Vlad found out a week later what had happened to the cave, he was furious. Liszka now insisted that the Fives had to attack, to drive the Sixes out of the strip of mountains between the castle and the Petrosna caves. The others were leaning towards agreeing with her. The fact that she was a female complicated matters: She didn't have to challenge Caleb directly in order to become leader. Either member of the alpha pair could make decisions, and the final authority would rest with whomever the group considered the better leader.

Caleb would readily admit that he didn't fit that description. He carried too much of the human into his plans, feeling almost apologetic for pulling rank and wanting to settle their differences without a fight if at all possible. The Fives territory was already twice the size of the Sixes, and contained the fertile, rabbity meadows that made navigating the mountains easier. It would be painful and pointless to go on the offensive…and if they did fight, he didn't want Bela involved.

Liszka had regarded him with scornful astonishment at that last sentiment. Bela in wolf-form was as big as some of them now, and had proved himself on the night Caleb was absent, although Caleb had refused to hear any details. She went so far as to suggest that the wolf belt was still affecting his mind, and had no qualms about telling him that it was the mother who made the final decision when it came to the pups.

"He's just a kid," Caleb had objected.

Liszka tossed up her hands in disbelief. "A kid is a goat, Lupeni," she said.

So he wasn't particularly looking forward to the night ahead. First he'd have to see if the pack was still obeying him, or if Liszka was going to lead them all off on a hunt for Vlad.

She is wrong, he thought, wincing at the thought of their bitter arguments. He wasn't ashamed of what he was—no more than she was, at any rate. She just had different ways of showing it. It wasn't something he expected Grigore to understand, but Liszka was intelligent enough to know that making peace with the villagers was their only real hope.

He didn't want his kind to die out. They didn't have to bite to reproduce: while the young of two werewolves would not survive, the offspring of a werewolf and a human was a healthy young werewolf. Few of either kind knew this. Caleb had recently met the first child of such a union that he could find. Contrary to all legends, the girl was good-looking and healthy, more well-adjusted than he had been at that age. Such a simple fact, and yet he himself hadn't known it until now.

Intermarriage would help both kinds—dispel fear, increase diversity, and improve the werewolf gender ratio. But it would be impossible as long as each group was convinced the other was out to kill.

He arrived just as the first sliver of the moon emerged above the horizon. The Fives were coming out of the cottage, taking their places in the grasses and trees. Caleb chose a secluded spot in a clump of birch, relieved at not having to speak, his head starting to hurt. Hopefully last month's experiment with the wolf belt wouldn't carry over into tonight.

The six members of Pack Five gathered around Lupeni as he emerged from his hiding place, nuzzling him and pushing their noses into his muzzle. It would've looked threatening to an observer, all those teeth so near his lips and throat, but the ritual comforted him. It meant they accepted him as their leader and were waiting to follow orders. With a glance at Liszka to assure himself of her cooperation, Caleb took off across the fields at a run, tail held high.

They spent the evening at the northern limits of their territory, as far from the Sixes as possible. There was a creek there, running low in the summer drought, and they did some fishing. Bela had never tried this before, and the first time he scooped a paw into the water and came up with a fish, he was so surprised he dropped it with a startled bark.

The first hint that something was wrong was a scent of blood.

Detecting it simultaneously, the Fives all raised their noses, sniffing. Not wolf blood, or human blood…it smelled of prey, rabbits perhaps, or squirrels. Turning to look in the direction of the odor, they saw a pack of wolves standing nearly motionless on the riverbank.

It was Pack Six. Not only Pack Six—there were more of them than usual, coming up the bank one by one. The Fives were outnumbered two-to-one; and Vlad, clever schemer that he was, had made sure they had eaten their fill before seeking out the enemy. There was now less chance that they would tire of the fight and give up to search for food. Blood and fragments of small animals still clung to their lips as they regarded the Fives with hostile snarls and growls.

In the split second that Caleb hesitated to think, there was a flash of white. Liszka dashed up the riverbank and threw herself on Vlad, knocking him backwards, her teeth in the loose skin just below his throat.

Caleb sprang to her defense, but he was less experienced at fighting and didn't anticipate the Sixes attacking from behind. As he tried to get a grip on Vlad, he felt a sharp pain as fangs bit into his Achilles tendon. He whirled around, snapping.

Grigore and Bela came next. Grigore helped Caleb drive back the Sixes—and the Fours, who'd joined up with the Sixes—while Bela tackled Vlad from behind. The surprise attack knocked Vlad to the ground, where Liszka was able to undo her hold and get a better one higher up, right over the arteries of his neck. She gave a low growl, one that called Caleb away from his tangle with two scrawny Fours and over to her side.

She repeated the sound, this time with a note of interrogation: she was asking whether she should give the shake of her powerful neck that would kill Vlad. Looking around at his enemy's gashed and whimpering minions, cowering back at the fall of their leader, Caleb called her off.

They flanked Vlad then, growling low in their throats, letting him know that next time he wouldn't get off that easily. The scraggly black wolf shook himself, rounded up his followers, and fled.

The Fives sat down to lick each other's wounds and finish eating their fish. But they'd scarcely settled in when their rivals were back, sneaking up through a grove of aspen.

The fight went on till dawn. Vlad had noticed Lupeni's inexperience with rear attacks, but Lupeni caught on quickly and managed to give Vlad a nasty chomp in the hamstring. They may have been outnumbered, but the Fives were strong and healthy, and only single-minded determination made Vlad drive his exhausted allies into the fray time and time again.

As the sky began to lighten, Caleb led his pack back towards Grigore's cottage. He didn't want them to be stranded and hurt when they transformed back—but Vlad was relentless. The Sixes continued to attack all the way, nipping at their heels, lunging for their shoulders.

Dawn came at last. The Fives had prevailed, and Caleb watched the Sixes trudge away through the trees, limping and miserable. He quickly turned his attention to his own pack, glad that he'd spent the week stocking up on healing herbs and potions.

"Is everybody OK?" he asked, before even taking stock of his own injuries.

There was a chorus of "yes"es; the Fives seemed almost proud of their wounds, their fight, their victory. Caleb went to the shelf for potions, thinking how lucky he was to have werewolves for patients. No matter how terrible they looked now, he knew from experience that they'd be up running around by the next day.

"Who needs a poultice?" he asked, carrying the flask of potion over to the hearth where Liszka had started a blazing fire. "Come on, don't be shy."

Grigore held out his arm. "Here, I got bitten."

"Me too," Liszka admitted, pulling the blanket she was wrapped in off her shoulder.

Caleb cast a look over at Bela. He was nodding off to sleep in front of the fire, seemingly unhurt. Maybe Liszka was right; for an animal, he was almost fully grown. She was right an awful lot. "Do you think we'll see them again?" he asked, applying the potion to the teeth marks over her shoulder blade and neck.

"No," she declared firmly, "they're no match for us."

She gasped slightly as the poultice entered her wound, then interrupted Caleb's sigh of relief with a scowl. "But don't think you've seen the last of Vlad. I've known him since I was ten years old, and all that time I've been waiting for the chance to kill him."

There was no anger in her voice, for she had asked Caleb's opinion and followed it willingly. She just sounded slightly wistful, and he had to ask himself yet again whether he had done the right thing.

Book IV

When the War Came

23. Interview with a Vampire

THE DAY HAD BEEN hot, unusually hot for July in the mountains, but after sunset, the air turned cool. Vlad enjoyed the breeze, which made the leaves of the tall aspen around him whisper softly. That was about the only thing he enjoyed as he limped down the dusty road to Catunescu in the darkness of the new moon.

Vampires like the new moon; werewolves do not.

Vlad was going to meet a vampire and was feeling none too pleased.

After the rout of his pack by the Fives two weeks earlier, Vlad had become increasingly desperate to rid the local mountains of Lupeni. None of the members of his own pack understood. They had taken to avoiding the subject when they met him. In fact, he suspected that the other Sixes had been avoiding him altogether since the full moon, but he didn't care.

As the moon waned, he searched the mountains for a vampire, any vampire. The vampire he finally found, sleeping in the loft of an abandoned barn, had been quite surprised that a werewolf would seek him. The surprise turned to shock, however, when the vampire heard Vlad's request to set up a meeting with the most powerful vampire in the region.

The meeting had been arranged, relayed through the vampire-intermediary, for the spot where Vlad had first met Cuza. At the new moon. Vlad had no say in time or place, and was forced to make a twenty-mile journey on foot on his least favorite day of the month.

Still favoring one leg because of a bite that was slow to heal, Vlad came in sight of the little church in the deserted village of Catunescu. The building loomed suddenly, a luminous white monolith like the face of a corpse. Its tall roof towered above the decrepit houses of the village, although the cross that once adorned the very top had fallen off. More of the building had crumbled since Vlad had last come this way, he noticed as he approached the large wooden door. Ever since his chance meeting with the vampire fifty months before, he had avoided the ruined church. Now desperation drove him here.

Vlad grimaced to recall that he had barely survived his first meeting with Cuza, but he knew tonight that he had information that the old vampire wanted—enough for a trade, he hoped. He carried a wooden stake in his pocket just in case he needed it, because he intended to survive this meeting, too.

The door itself was shattered, hanging open. Vlad pushed the remnants aside and stepped into the dark interior. The cloudless night gave only star-light for illumination, so he paused just inside the door to light a small torch of wood and pitch. The yellow, smoky flame provided a small circle of light, showing the jumble of broken benches near the door and the deep shadows of the ruined altar at the far end. He stayed close to the door, not willing to venture further inside.

Overpowered by a sudden gust of air, his torch went out and the church filled with a gravid darkness. He swore loudly and threw the useless torch down, just as he heard crisp footfalls approach. A looming figure materialized before his face, the features dark and unrecognizable, the very negation of light. But Vlad recognized the voice; a lifetime would not be enough to forget that steely drawl.

"Well, the dog has returned," said the voice of the vampire. Vlad could picture the sneering face, but could not see anything except the outline of a head at about his own height.

"You will excuse my preference for darkness," Cuza said, drawing to within several feet of the werewolf. "I would not like to call too much attention to this meeting. Certain individuals seem bent on finding me, and I have no desire to be found."

As Vlad's eyes adjusted, he could make out the pale, angular face and the dark sockets that held terrible, empty eyes. He felt grateful that he did not look upon the eyes of the vampire directly. Somehow this enabled Vlad to retain his courage, enough to say, "Yeah, maybe they'll catch you one of these days, you rotting corpse."

"Mmmm. I see that your manners have not improved since our last meeting," said Cuza in a soft, nearly pleasant tone as he circled around the werewolf. "But you are hunted yourself, are you not? I saw you limp as you came in. A dogfight, perhaps?"

Vlad said nothing, holding his temper, remembering why he had come.

"You came because you need my help," Cuza whispered harshly at Vlad's back, "but I do not wish to involve myself in wolf business. Do you have something of interest to me?"

"Yeah," Vlad replied stiffly. "You said you wanted to know who lives in the castle. Well, I can help you on that score."

"Indeed?" laughed the vampire, continuing his circuit and returning to face Vlad. "You knew something even four years ago, didn't you? Now it is worth your while to tell me. Why is that?"

"*He* lives in the castle," Vlad began. "A werewolf, I mean."

"Make yourself clear, dog," snapped Cuza. "You ask me to believe that a werewolf lives in Castle Arghezi?"

"He's not like the rest of us," countered Vlad. "He's foreign, from America. He's been at the castle for, um, sixty-one months."

"Does this mysterious American werewolf have a name?"

"Lupeni. That's what we call him," Vlad said weakly, then continued, "I don't know what his real name is."

"A rival of yours, this Lupeni?" asked the vampire curiously.

"Bastard," spat Vlad. Cuza chuckled softly and came closer, within a foot of the werewolf, who stiffened but held his ground.

"I see how it is," mused the vampire. "Now, what else can you tell me about the castle? Others live there, yes?"

"Yeah. Two other wizards, I think. One goes down to Stilpescu sometimes. I've never seen the other one."

"Foreign wizards, like this Lupeni?"

"I don't think so." Vlad shook his head stiffly. "The guy who comes down to the village, he talks like he's from around here."

"But you have never been to the castle, have you?" Cuza asked shortly. "Your information is of little use to me, dog. I already know that there are several wizards living at the castle. Why should I care that one of them is a dog like you?"

The vampire bared its teeth at him. Even in the dim starlight trickling through the door, Vlad could see the expression of disgust on the waxy,

Undead face. Vlad licked his lips nervously, fingering the stake in his pocket.

"He's a vampire-killer," he blurted out. "Maybe they all are. Grigore's seen him kill a vampire."

"Ah. This begins to interest me. Who is this Grigore of whom you speak?"

"A werewolf," continued the nervous Vlad, "in Lupeni's pack, but I talk to him sometimes. He tells me things because he's not very happy. With Lupeni, I mean. He's been inside the castle and last month he was with him when he killed a vampire at the Petrosna caves. Grigore watched the body being burned."

"Emil! I—" Cuza broke off angrily and took several sharp steps, pacing behind Vlad who turned to stare at the vampire, satisfied that his information had unsettled him and seemed especially valuable.

"At the Petrosna caves, you say?" muttered the vampire. He vampire returned to face the werewolf, an undercurrent of anger now present in every word.

"Can you get into the castle?" he snapped.

"N-n-no," faltered Vlad. "Grigore told me there's more than one enchantment to get through. He learned how to do a gate spell, but there were other spells, some of which even Lupeni doesn't know." Vlad halted and screwed up his courage in the face of the grinning vampire. "Look, wouldn't it be a start just to get rid of Lupeni? I mean, he's hunting your kind and all."

"A start, you say," replied Cuza thoughtfully. He was silent for a long while. Vlad tried to suppress his nervousness, fondling the stake and calculating the number of steps to the door.

"You will need my help to kill this Lupeni," the vampire said at last. "I can see that you have tried and failed, you miserable dog. But I will help you and we will not fail. That will be a good start, indeed."

24 ❖ Siren Song

ALEXANDRU, IT IS GOOD to see you," beamed the old man as the two wizards approached him. He sat on the low wooden fence marking the boundary to a small farm.

"You look well, Lucian," returned Alexandru. "Hard to believe that it has been nearly sixty years."

Lucian was near in age to Alexandru, and his hair and long beard were shot with white. He jumped off the fence spryly to embrace his old friend. Caleb hung back, taking in the small farm still visible in the lingering light of the clear summer evening.

Tonight they were hunting a vampire who chose the new moon to prey on the living.

"I am so glad that you came," said Lucian, stepping back and taking in his old friend. Dropping his voice, he continued, "Mihail said that you could help us with our problem."

"Please, tell me what is troubling you," Alexandru urged. He gestured toward Caleb. "You may speak freely in front of this man. He assists me in these matters."

The old farmer sighed, relieved to unburden himself. Clasping both hands together, he began, "My grandson Stefan has been troubled by fever this summer, it seems. Twice after the new moon he has been sick for a day or two, weak and unable to rise. He feels fine after a few days, but we notice he has bites, some on his neck. We question him, but he knows nothing, says he gets bitten by a lot of things."

"Have you or anyone else noticed anything on these nights?" Alexandru asked thoughtfully.

"It is summer," shrugged Lucian in reply. "Stefan sleeps in the hay barn."

"I would like to see your grandson and examine these bites," Alexandru said promptly, although it was clear to Caleb that he had made up his mind about their origin. Lucian led them down a dirt track toward a one-room farmhouse where he lived with his son, daughter-in-law, and their four children. With so many in the house, it didn't seem strange that Stefan might choose to sleep in the hay barn.

"A relatively new vampire," murmured Alexandru to Caleb as they walked, "who hunts primarily on the new moon, I should think."

"And you believe the vampire will attack the boy tonight?"

"The pattern seems clear," he responded. "I do not believe you have been in this situation. I must warn you that when he attacks, it can be... difficult to separate the vampire from his victim."

"Oh?" Caleb was intrigued. His previous hunts with Alexandru had been confined to rousting sleeping vampires. It was unusual to have the chance to catch a vampire in the act.

"As this is the third attack," Alexandru said slowly, as if lost in a dream or perhaps an old memory, "the victim, this boy Stefan, will resist us. He may try to help the vampire, in fact." He pitched his voice even lower, making it difficult for Caleb to make out his words. "Contrary to what you may think, it is not painful to be bitten by a vampire. I am told that it—that there is a certain pleasure..."

Once again, Caleb wondered where Alexandru had come by this information. There was a melancholy to Alexandru's demeanor when he spoke of such things, as though he had learned them first hand. How could that be? Caleb debated whether he should press for answers—but they reached the door of the house and there was no time for questions.

The tiny kitchen was full of the family finishing their supper. Both men were introduced as old friends of Lucian's, nothing more. Stefan, a robust boy of sixteen or seventeen, cheerfully shook their hands. As Caleb made small talk with the boy, Alexandru watched him closely, inspecting his neck, no doubt. Once they had been introduced all around, the family went back to clearing dishes. Stefan excused himself to finish a few chores and get ready for bed.

The two vampire-hunters went outside with Lucian and sat on rough wooden benches at the rear of the farmhouse, in sight of the hay barn.

"Well?" asked the old farmer nervously.

"You were right to call on me," Alexandru replied. "I believe that your grandson has been bitten by a vampire, one that we have missed somehow. We will station ourselves in the hay barn tonight. I would ask you and your family to stay away, no matter what you might hear."

Lucian nodded solemnly. Caleb's mind drifted to his long-ago home in Maine and how much his life had changed; he could not imagine an American farmer, no matter how isolated, inviting wizards into his barn to catch a vampire.

The two wizards silently entered the barn before the boy finished his chores in the house. After inspecting the ground floor and loft, they hid among the bales of hay near the nest of blankets that served Stefan as a bed. They heard him climb up the wooden ladder to the loft and settle himself in with much creaking of the boards, his breath revealing that he had fallen rapidly into a deep sleep. Caleb wondered how long they would have to wait and fingered some of the items in the bag he carried: stakes, sunstone, a long rope of braided garlic.

The wait was not long. Soon after the boy fell asleep, the soft whisper of bat wings fluttered in the rafters. Alexandru tensed, gripping Caleb's arm. Both got out their stakes, but as usual Caleb waited for a cue from the older wizard. Alexandru took the garlic braid in one hand, but otherwise remained still, listening carefully.

Soon after the beat of wings died away, they heard another whispering sound from above, a voice chanting or singing softly. The loft creaked, although they could not see anything from their spot directly below. Someone moved above them, the singer of the song. The boy moaned in response, turning heavily above them. Fear? Pleasure? Caleb was not sure, particularly after what Alexandru had told him earlier.

Caleb could distinguish no words in the song, yet, he understood it, or thought he did. A welcome release. An opening into another place—dark, secret, and mysterious. The promise of—

His hand closed around the sunstone, gripping it tightly as if to push away the wordless, tuneless song. *Poor boy,* he thought, *he's not much older than Bela.* Of course, Bela would never be bitten by a vampire, which made Caleb feel even more for Stefan.

A nudge from Alexandru's elbow brought his mind back to the barn. They exchanged glances and emerged from behind the piles of straw.

Who was more shocked, the vampire or the vampire-hunters? The boy, lying down and only semi-conscious, was perhaps the only one not surprised by the sudden appearance of two men kneeling next to him. Caleb took his feet and Alexandru the head.

A woman crouched over the boy, head bent low. Caleb should not have been startled to find out that the vampire was female—they had killed several in the last five years—and yet the figure of a strange woman preying on the boy shocked him nonetheless.

She froze, her long brown hair brushing the boy's bare chest like an icy waterfall, and her face twisted into a grimace of fear and hatred. A dark void filled with loathing, her soulless eyes regarded the two strangers. Then she moved, raking her hands down the boy's body and raising her arms, and Caleb realized just in time that she meant to turn into a bat and escape.

"Helios," he cried hastily, and thrust the sunstone toward her. With a cry of agony, she collapsed in the bright light onto the boy's prone body. Alexandru threw the garlic braid around her neck, dragging her toward him so that she was pinned against him, facing Caleb and the boy. She choked and struggled as if the garlic burned. Was it like a silver cord to a werewolf? Caleb wondered.

Her hands reached out for Stefan, calling his name over and over in a strangled voice. The boy's eyes opened, with the wild, disoriented look of a sleeper. He sat up clumsily, seeing only the vampire, and lunged, arms outstretched toward her, shouting incoherently. Caleb threw down his stake and grabbed Stefan with one arm thrown awkwardly around the boy's chest. Stefan's hands plowed furrows in the hay on the loft floor as Caleb dragged him back, away from the vampire he yearned to reach. In spite of Caleb's greater strength, the boy fought him hard. Caleb was forced to toss the sunstone onto the floorboards and grasp Stefan's arms with both hands, pinning them behind his back.

"Neva, Neva, Neva," the boy sobbed. He stopped fighting his captor, but continued to quake, his chest heaving with enormous, ragged breaths.

"Sleep, boy," intoned Alexandru coldly as he pointed his hand at Stefan. Caleb felt Stefan slump in his grip and laid him gently on the hay that lined the loft. He picked up the sunstone once again, winded and shaken by the sudden assault.

The vampire struggled weakly, the combination of the garlic braid around her neck and the sunstone proving too much—indications that she was a young vampire.

"Neva. That is your name?" questioned Alexandru harshly, angrier than Caleb had ever seen him on a vampire hunt. He had always been cold and dispassionate, even at the mention of Cuza, his maniacal obsession. Was there something about this particular vampire? Did he know her? But she did not seem to know him as she answered weakly.

"Yes. What is it that you—?" She faltered. Perhaps she was a bit slow to realize that the two men meant to bring her a final death.

"You!" she cried with more animation, her dark eyes drilling into Caleb. "You killed Emil! And the others."

"Who is Emil?" Alexandru asked curtly.

"He is—was my…I met him three years ago, while I was still—"

Human. Living. She could not say the words, but it was clear that she was a young vampire and Emil was responsible. She looked frightened, and that, too, betrayed her short time as one of the Undead.

"At the Petrosna Caves, you killed him," she finished weakly.

Alexandru gave Caleb a furious look; clearly, he was still angry that Caleb had killed Emil without him, depriving Alexandru the chance to interrogate the vampire about Cuza.

"Do you know other vampires?" queried Alexandru. "Have you met Cuza?"

"Yes. Once," she shivered. "Emil knew him. He's an old, old vampire. Emil was…scared of him. They talked about the killings." She struggled weakly, realizing anew that those same vampire killers held her prisoner. Surely she suspected what her fate would be.

"Do you know where to find Cuza?" The old vampire-hunter's words were clipped, but still angry.

"I don't," she began, licking her lips and giving Caleb a pleading look. "But I could find him for you, if you want. If you let me go."

Alexandru allowed himself a sharp laugh, although his face was set in a grimace. Caleb noticed that he had released the garlic from his free hand and replaced it with a stake from his pocket.

"You pollute the living," Alexandru intoned, his fury transformed into icy resolve as he raised the stake above his head in a gesture unseen by the vampire. "You deserve no more than this."

She had no time to reply, or even cry out, as he plunged the stake into her heart.

When Alexandru released the vampire into a crumpled heap between them, Caleb saw that the old man was shaking, obsessively fingering the garlic braid. It was all Caleb could do not to ask Alexandru why this vampire affected him so strongly.

Caleb extinguished the sunstone, blinking in the afterglow for a few moments before helping Alexandru move Stefan back into bed. The boy slept an untroubled, charmed sleep.

Neva rested, too, in the final sleep that vampires defied. Even at the new moon, when the wolf in him was at an ebb, Caleb felt the song of Nature. It told of the coupling between birth and death, of how Life rose and fell like a wave in an endless sea. Life was so precious to Caleb; he knew he would never understand the vampire's hunger to step outside these bounds, to feed on the living without being part of the fabric Life.

"Shall we finish?" he asked, hesitant to break into Alexandru's reverie.

Wordlessly, the old vampire-hunter nodded. Caleb picked up the lifeless body and the wizards left the barn in search of a secluded place in which to burn the corpse.

Few words were exchanged as they completed their work. When it was done, Alexandru turned to his companion, looking exhausted and many years older.

"I must speak with Lucian and the boy's parents," he said hoarsely. "Wake the boy and bring him into the house. He should not sleep alone."

Back in the loft, Caleb conjured a ball of light and found Stefan lying on the straw, still sleeping peacefully. The boy had a future now, one that involved growing up, growing old, perhaps having children and watching them grow. He could not help but think of Bela again, wishing those things for him, the only child he might ever have.

Pushing those thoughts aside, he worked a spell to undo the sleep that Alexandru had imposed on the boy. Stefan opened his eyes suddenly, staring at the wizard with scant recognition.

"How do you feel?" Caleb asked quietly.

"Where is she?" cried the boy, as he cast about the loft and realized they were alone. He sat up quickly, searching frantically, and then grabbed Caleb's tunic, shaking him as if to extract the lost vampire.

"How much do you remember, Stefan?" Caleb gripped the boy's wrists gently, but firmly. The boy still had the look of incoherent dreams about his eyes. He yielded to Caleb's grip, lost in a waking dream.

"She was so beautiful," the boy murmured, "and she came…it was a secret. Don't tell, she said, and I'll take you away to where it's always…Neva, her name…so beautiful." Caleb could almost hear echoes of the song of the vampire in his words.

"Neva was a vampire," he said to the boy, sounding more harsh and cruel than he had intended. The boy shook his head and became more agitated. "She came back for the *third* time tonight. Do you know what that means?" Caleb took Stefan by the shoulders as the boy squirmed, rolling his head from side to side as if to deny everything but his memories.

"Do you know what that means?" Caleb repeated, staring intently at the boy's face, forcing him to meet his eyes.

"I would have been—" Stefan broke off, cradling his head in his hands after Caleb released him from his grip. When he looked up after a moment, his eyes seemed fully conscious, the dreams replaced by horror at knowing what might have been.

Caleb could not get another word out of him, but managed to persuade him to walk on his own and climb out of the loft. Back in the farmhouse, the entire family was awake and waiting. They surrounded the boy loudly and tearfully, not noticing in the least when the vampire-hunters slipped out for a silent journey back to the castle.

"Brandy," called Alexandru wearily as they came inside the entrance hall, shedding their cloaks and bags. Mihail was awake to greet them; Caleb again wondered if he had some magical way of anticipating his master's every need.

A fire still burned in the hearth of the Great Hall as they sat at the table. Uncharacteristically, Caleb welcomed the strong drink. The common human vices didn't appeal much to werewolves; the harsh flavors of alcohol and tobacco hurt their heightened senses. This was fortunate, he supposed, as the Fives were difficult enough to discipline without their being a bunch of drunks. But on the new moon, after a vampire hunt, he didn't refuse the deceptively smooth brandy Mihail poured for them.

"The boy will be all right, then?" Caleb ventured.

"With time he will recover," sighed Alexandru, swirling amber liquid shot with firelight in his glass. "With each bite, the victim becomes more…vulnerable, more susceptible to the vampire's song. But, yes, he will recover."

"He wanted her so terribly much," mused Caleb. "I would not have believed that the victim could desire so completely to—"

"The victim always does," growled Alexandru, setting his half-drunk brandy down violently and rising. "Resistance becomes impossible, until there is nothing left but death."

With that, he strode from the room, leaving Caleb confused at his parting words. Mihail glowered at the younger wizard as he removed the glass from the table.

"You should not upset the master by bringing up things long forgotten," he said through thin, tight lips.

"What do you mean?" Caleb asked, but as he spoke, the answer became clear. "There was another boy, like the one tonight, wasn't there?"

Mihail froze with the crystal glass gripped tightly in mid-air.

The fearful truth swept over Caleb in a crushing wave. "Mircea Arghezi was a vampire? Alexandru's brother?"

"We fought," replied the servant, turning away abruptly. "But he was stronger than all of us that night."

25. The Feminine Mystique

THREE DAYS BEFORE THE August full moon, Caleb sat with Liszka in the cattails by the creek, watching the sun go down. They were barefoot, basking in the sun; Liszka had a line with a worm on it but wasn't actually bothering to fish. Weary of their arguments, which were always the same, Caleb made his decision.

"Would you like to lead the pack?" he asked quietly. "I know you'd be a great leader."

"If you hadn't offered, I would've fought you," Liszka said bluntly, leaning back to catch the last warm rays from the western hills.

"There's no need for that." Caleb tried to smile. "Let's do this amicably, shall we?"

Liszka looked surprised. "We could be amicable and still fight."

That was why she would make a great leader. As their predatory instincts waxed along with the moon, she began to make plans—ones that would be difficult to carry out in any detail once they were transformed, but which at least would provide some structure for how the group would spend the night. She didn't waste her energy snapping and quarreling the way the others did, or in suppressing her urges, like Caleb. It seemed so silly and futile now, the way he had prided himself in controlling his behavior so that Toby could not tell what phase it was until the very moment Caleb slipped into the Reserve to transform.

He didn't want to fight Liszka. He thought of her with her teeth in Vlad's throat, and of the nightmare that made her awaken clawing and growling—a saber-toothed cat straight from the Ice Age, a fear not learned from her own experiences but imprinted somewhere in the collective pre-history of canine kind. "No, that's all right, I'd just as soon skip that part. Take care of Bela, please, and I…I'll try to make sure Vlad leaves you alone."

"What?" She threw down her fishing rod. "Vlad? Let that mangy cur come near me, and I'll kill him."

No, he didn't want to fight Liszka. "He disturbs me," he said carefully. "I worry that he might…might try something worse than attacking Pack Five."

"What can he do, the toothless old mutt? I can take care of myself, Lupeni." Her eyes blazed with anger and pride. "Don't think you're leaving to protect me." She suddenly had an idea that made her scowl. "Or that you can hunt him down yourself. Vlad is mine to kill."

He felt the wolf in him growl competitively, but squelched it. "OK, OK, I'm sorry. I just don't want you to have to answer for mistakes I've made."

"Not everything you've done has been a mistake," Liszka told him honestly. "We have food, and money, and we're organized."

He grimaced, not entirely sure that organized werewolves were exactly what the world needed.

"But you went too far," she persisted. "It's unnatural. Raising sheep is unnatural, but that's OK, it helps us. Not biting people…" She shook her head in disgust. "Are you still going to keep those cursed wards up?"

"Of course." He interrupted before she could get too angry again. "They work both ways. We can't get into the villages at the full moon, but the humans can't get into the forest. They have their territory, we have ours. It's fair."

"They're the enemy," she raged, digging a clump of mud from the ground and heaving it into the river. "Never mind `fair'!"

"Now you sound like one of them." Had he really said that? Did he really hate humans? If so, why did he feel the imperative to protect them?

"So? If they do it, so can we."

"But then they call us monsters."

"Who *cares* what they *think?*" She stood up, brushing grass and flowers from her front. "You think too much, that's your problem." She hunted among the reeds for her shoes.

Caleb stayed seated, watching a fish jumping in the water. "We should think. We aren't animals," he said.

Her look of utter bafflement at that statement confirmed that he would never succeed as a pack leader. "Oh, never mind," he muttered, and stood up too. "We're still friends, aren't we? You'll come to me if you need anything, if you have any problems?"

"Of course." She pushed her hair out of her face, streaks of red shimmering in the sun. She'd just had her twenty-first birthday, which a couple generations earlier was old for a Romanian werewolf. It wasn't so old anymore, especially for the Fives. There was no reason to go back to starving and being shot. Surely she could preserve what he'd accomplished without distorting her goals with utopian dreaming, as he had done?

"Promise," said Caleb.

She looked confused again. Wolves didn't need to promise, because they didn't lie. Or so said tradition. "Promise," she said, humoring him.

It was the friendliest conversation they'd had in many months. "Good-bye, Liszka," he said, and squeezed her hand. He reached to the sky to summon Wind for the trip to the castle, not wanting to return to the cottage one last time. It wasn't that he wouldn't be accepted, or even that he would never run with them again, but Liszka's cockiness only served to increase his concerns about Vlad. He intended to make his departure as abrupt and obvious as possible so that the leader of the Sixes would think that Liszka had taken over by force, that she hated Caleb. Maybe then she would be safe for a while.

Deep down, where he was ashamed to admit it to himself, Caleb knew that his motivations were not entirely about providing Bela with a conflict-free puppyhood, or even about protecting the pack from humans and other werewolves. A small but significant part of his reason for leaving was that this was the only way to break up with Liszka…and he was beginning to suspect that there were other women in the world, ones who might even deign to speak to him.

Was it anything to feel guilty about? Their relationship had lasted four years, and they had parted friends. She didn't need him trying to turn her into someone like himself, confused and conflicted.

A thought entered his head, like a small trickle of water snaking across a leaky dam. He saw again the odd, violet eyes of the mysterious Lamia. WHY? burst through his consciousness suddenly, almost making him shout out loud as he flew. Now that he allowed himself to think of her, even vaguely, the contradictions and mysteries came flooding into his head as if the dam had burst.

Why was Lamia a physics graduate student? She clearly was as magical as Caleb, perhaps even as Alexandru. She had known for certain that Emil was a vampire, and she had driven away Vlad on a night of the full moon. What would make her spend so many years in academia? In several disparate fields of study, too, judging by her books. It was odd, too, that she scarcely looked twenty—though perhaps he had grown used to werewolves who lived hard and died young.

"I should not have come"… those were her words. Why?

Of course, he had tried a similar life himself, but that only made the whole thing more fascinating. He couldn't help wondering if she felt as miserable and out of place in the caves as he had been in Cambridge, doing homework problems and taking the subway and constantly yearning for something else. He wanted to think that Lamia, too, had a secret, that she might be the one person he'd ever met who could truly understand.

With this sentiment he touched down a quarter mile from the castle, and started up the stone path. His lighthearted step was short-lived. In only a few feet, he found himself face to face with Vlad.

Caleb took the offensive, knowing that worked best. "What are you sniffing around here for?" he inquired coolly. "No bones today." He'd never quite forgotten that "Fido" business.

"I wouldn't hold my tail so high if I were you, Lupeni," Vlad snarled. "I have ways to break into this pile of rubble that you could never guess."

Much too arrogant to keep a secret, Caleb decided in a flash. "Oh, yes?" His voice purred with an exaggerated calm. Sometimes being able to keep his cool near the full moon could pay off. "You and the Fleabite Army of 1602?"

It didn't look as though Vlad had anything with him—camera, bag, anything that Caleb should inspect or confiscate. The sarcasm infuriated Vlad, and he stood blocking the trail as if Caleb were the trespasser, twisting his hairy face into the intimidating scowl that had helped him stay leader for so long.

"One skilled wizard could get through that dog door," Vlad growled, waving his arms as if ready to hit Caleb.

"Which is one more than you have on your side," Caleb retorted, stepping aside as Vlad lunged and watching calmly as he nearly toppled down the rocky trail.

Stumbling, Vlad regained his footing and stalked away. He pretended to mutter to himself, but obviously he intended for Caleb to catch every word. "I have friends," he growled. "Ones you wouldn't dare approach. You kill them because you're scared of their power…and they've only just started feasting on those humans you try to protect."

So he's been speaking to a vampire, Caleb thought, trying to stay cool although his skin prickled at the thought of the hunt ten days ago. Surely it was an empty boast that Vlad had incited Emil to bite Mike…

"Those students are gonna be dead meat on the full moon!" Vlad turned and shouted as his parting shot.

Vlad teaming up with vampires to eat the students? It sounded like another ill-conceived threat from the dim but vicious leader of the Sixes. But still, he should check on all of them, probably keep them out of the caves three nights from now.

He started up the trail, smiling at the thought of the explanation Mike would conjure to explain this.

But Lamia would understand.

20. Amateur Naturalist

Just what we needed!" Mike's voice boomed before Caleb could even enter the compound. "A botanist!"

Caleb sighed as he pushed through the grasses and made his way to the grad students' pavilion, watching Mike dig through his bag. He was impatient. It was two days until the full moon, and he didn't want Vlad—or worse, Vlad and his vampire crony—preying on unsuspecting physicists when he'd be worse than useless himself.

"Look at this!" Mike ran forwards, bearing in one hand one of Lamia's botany books, and in the other a grapefruit-sized fungus. It was green on the top, with a ring around the stem like a fairy-sized miniskirt and a bulbous golfball base.

Magical flora, Caleb could do. "*Amanita phalloides,*" he said simply. "One bite is certain death."

Mike dropped the book and the mushroom on the ground, holding his hands away from his body as if the toxin could leap onto him from his tainted fingers.

"It has certain uses," Caleb continued, bending to retrieve the dropped items. The mushroom was fresh and would come in handy. "Repelling flies and mosquitoes. Identifying silver objects, which the fungus will tarnish."

"Really?" Mike looked skeptical, eyeing the poisonous growth with distaste. "I'll stick with DEET. And there are other ways to recognize silver."

"Indeed," Caleb agreed. He placed the book into the large wicker basket he carried, then carefully laid the mushroom on top, shielding it with some wax paper. "Which reminds me…I came to warn you all to stay away from here at the full moon."

As he'd hoped, Lamia, sitting several yards away, heard these words and approached with curiosity.

"What?" Mike exclaimed. "What are you talking about?"

"Haven't you ever heard silver called the lunar metal?" Caleb wondered with partially feigned surprise. "Anyway, the purpose of my visit was to tell you about an exceptionally strong tide that is occurring this month. It will lead to enormous swarms of root moths, which bats will feed upon before they seek caves in which to hibernate." He took a deep breath. Some of this was based on slightly modified facts from the newspapers, but most of it was just made up. "It is important not to disturb the bats in August, because they need to eat as well as find a roosting place."

Holding his toxic hands out like a sleepwalker, Mike still had to be difficult. "So we stay out of the caves at the full moon, the bats eat and sleep, and everyone's happy?"

"Er… yes," said Caleb, knowing it was stupid and glancing towards Lamia for help.

"How do you know it's exactly at the astronomical full moon?" Mike demanded. "The moon can be 97 to 99 percent illuminated for several days."

"I know," Caleb interrupted with some impatience, hardly needing to be lectured about his most and least favorite celestial body. "But—"

"—The tide doesn't hit its maximum until the astronomical full moon," Lamia continued, betraying nothing. "It's at the very peak that the insects swarm. I know about this. We'll have to protect the equipment."

"Yes," Caleb agreed. "You can cover everything to protect it from dead moths and bat guano…apart from that—"

"—I want to make sure it's safe from any wild animals that might be roaming around," she interjected meaningfully.

"Dunno." Mike was a tough customer. "We're nowhere near the ocean, so where are these bugs coming from? Lakes and rivers don't have lunar tides."

"The Black Sea," Caleb and Lamia said at once.

"Really? We're near the Black Sea and you didn't tell me?" Mike would've given Lamia a playful nudge except that he was afraid to touch anything. "Let's go to the beach one of these days, give Gamberi the slip…you probably look great in a bikini with that diet you've been on."

Caleb scowled to himself. Lamia seemed ready to go along with his plan, which he had expected, since she knew what roamed the mountains at the full moon. Mike was a harder sell and the other two students, trance-like in front of their computers, hadn't even looked up.

"You'll have to protect the equipment and, well, it's probably a good idea to spend the night in Rosu because, er…the bats are noisy all night," Caleb said haltingly. "I've checked and there's room at the inn there."

"Aw," Mike said dismissively, wiping his hands on his shirt and then thinking better of it, "a little noise never bothers me. I was an undergrad at Columbia. Talk about noise all night, try living in Harlem."

Very little of what Mike said was relevant, but Caleb continued anyway, "And there's a big festival in Rosu, the annual Garlic Festival." Mike nudged Lamia in the ribs and she looked mildly irritated. "They're showing some American films, too." Caleb was getting desperate now, thinking back to a poster he saw on the wall when he stopped by the inn to check on a room. "Eastwood something or other."

"Dirty Harry!" came a garbled shout from Taofang who looked up from his work excitedly. "Fistful of Dollars! Good, Bad, Ugly!"

The Chinese student's babble was incomprehensible to Caleb, but Mike got excited, saying, "Go ahead, make my day!" which provoked idiotic laughter from Taofang. Vijay looked as confused as Caleb at this exchange, while Lamia maintained an impassive scowl on her face.

"What is it that you two are talking about?" Vijay asked after some of the laughter had died down.

"Man, oh, man," Mike sighed contentedly. "Clint Eastwood…you're gonna love this, buddy."

Caleb met Lamia's eye just long enough to be satisfied that he had made his point, then spun around and left through the underbrush. Mike's silly fungus had reminded him that he was late stocking up on herbs for the Fives, and brewing remedies for the aftermath of the inevitable battles.

He came upon a patch of feverfew, pulling out a few large clumps with their miniature daisy-like flowers. Werewolves didn't get colds often, but their bites festered, and a tea made of the leaves and flowers would soothe their fevers. St. John's Wort would make them all less snappish, and white valerian helped them sleep.

He came upon a patch of sumac, but wasn't sure if it was the poisonous variety, and didn't want to be tormented with itching until the full moon renewed his skin. Remembering the book in his basket, he extracted it gently from under the poisonous mushroom.

The little field guide was yellowed, the binding cracked. In the upper left corner of the inside cover, in a delicate, almost feminine hand, was written *Arghezi.*

Odd, Caleb thought. How did Mike get this? The writing was not Alexandru's.

But the book told him not to touch the sumac, so he quickly forgot the mystery and pressed on through the woods, reveling in the warmth of the summer afternoon and its profusion of botanical colors. He filled his basket with lavender, rosehips, and fruit, humming as he nibbled wild strawberries along the path for home.

27 ✧ Go Ahead, Make My Day

"C'MON, LAMIA, THE PARADE'S started!"

Mike dragged her through the crowded main square of Rosu as if she were a rag doll. Of course there would be a parade. Festivals always included parades, and the Rosu Garlic Festival was no exception.

People milled around dressed in mixtures of "city" clothes and "mountain" clothes. The former were drab and cheap-looking, while the latter dazzled with their intricate colorful embroidery. The bright clothing reminded her of a childhood in Tîrgovişte, which she hadn't thought about in a long, long time. Amazingly, the costumes of the mountain folk hadn't changed much in seventy years.

But the crowds. Too many people in a small space made her anxious, ready to pounce. Mike did not believe her protests that she wanted to spend the afternoon reading in their room at the inn. If she humored him and watched the parade, perhaps she could slip back to the room later.

"Hey, guys," Mike bellowed as they caught sight of their fellow students, "look who was trying to study. Jeez!"

Vijay and Taofang grinned at her. Even the normally dour Chinese student seemed relaxed today, no doubt looking forward to the festival's evening cowboy movies. They were all standing on the sidewalk in front of the town hall, a drab concrete building made festive for the day by a colorful banner proclaiming the health of Communism as well as the festival. The town was similarly a mixture of old and new: The old white-washed church in the square was flanked by centuries-old, graceful stone buildings, stoically co-existing with new concrete monstrosities that sprouted like weeds.

Mike eagerly explained about parades from his childhood in the Italian neighborhood in New York City where his grandparents lived. Lamia was thinking of similar parades she endured when she was a girl. She would be dressed in a starched white dress with ribbons in her hair, not the T-shirt and jeans she sported today. Better not think about that, she scolded herself. The contrast was too great and, after all, she wasn't even human any more.

Instead, she concentrated on the people marching in the street in front of them, just coming into sight. The mayor was there, and a little old priest from the church, dozens of school children, a brass band and dancers in colorful costumes. The men wore brilliant white trousers overhung with dark tunics, and the women had swirling skirts held up with lavishly embroidered belts. All sported braids of garlic around their necks, which bounced cheerily as they marched arm-in-arm.

"So, what did the guy at the hotel tell you about this thing?" Mike shouted as the band passed directly in front of them.

Lamia smiled tightly, a grimace really, and said, "The festival has crafts, food, contests. The food will be full of garlic, which I'm sure will please all of you." The others laughed, knowing her dislike for garlic. "You can probably get your fortune told. There will be dancing." She gestured at the flushed faces of the young men and women marching before them. "Young men tradition-ally pick their wives by how well they dance. Quite simple, no?"

"Yeah," piped up Mike brightly, "and since the girls are all wearing garlic necklaces, a guy can make sure he's not marrying a vampire, right?"

Everyone but Lamia laughed heartily. But Mike was so engrossed in his own tales, he did not see that Lamia was not amused; nor did he see her slip quietly into the throng.

Lamia shut the heavy wooden door of their room at the inn and stood leaning against it, relieved to be out of the crowds. The room had a turn-of-the-century feel to it, reminding her of her grandmother's room at her parents' home in Tîrgovişte. It was such a distant memory; after so many decades, it was hard for her to even believe that she did, indeed, have a Romanian grand-mother. Lace curtains covered the windows, flanked by heavy embroidered drapes. Large, dark furniture filled the room—a tall dresser and an even taller wardrobe, a small writing table, a nightstand with a ceramic pitcher and basin. The large bed was a four-poster with a gauzy white canopy floating above. There was a sofa, too, where she had insisted on sleeping.

Only one room had been available at the inn, the fanciest one, which locals probably couldn't afford. The cost was a pittance for her group, since Western graduate students were rich in comparison to Romanians. The owner of the inn had been particularly happy to receive hard currency, lira from the students' lab in Italy.

She closed the windows and drew the heavy drapes shut, but could not block the cacophony of music and crowd noise. Of course, the ubiquitous smell of garlic could not be avoided, either, with all the garlic necklaces and special dishes.

Garlic was one of the few things her companions could agree on, since they rarely agreed on physics or anything else. In spite of coming from completely different cultures, Mike, Vijay, and Taofang all loved to cook with garlic. At the camp, she usually spent mealtimes in her tent. She didn't need to eat, and the smell of whatever they cooked up made her weak and irritable—exactly how she felt now as she paced the room. She tried reading first a textbook, then a magazine. From the wall, dictator Ceaucescu smiled at her grimly in a badly done portrait.

Coincidentally, he grimaced at her from the pages of her magazine, *The Economist*. She had once thought about getting a degree in economics, but the magazine subscription was all that remained of that enterprise. It hadn't worked out, probably because she cut so many classes at the London School of Economics. How could she attend class when she spent her nights roaming the streets of the city, drinking blood? That was before she realized that she would have to give up human blood if she wanted to study any subject seriously.

According to her magazine and the portrait on the wall, Communism still held the country in its tight fist, and it seemed certain to continue into the next century. All that meant little to her. She had never been affected by Romanian politics. The castle, where she lived for thirty years, had been too isolated. After leaving it for good, she tried to forget her native country, quickly discovering that the West held nearly infinite possibilities for a vampire who wanted to better herself.

All she wanted now was to get a degree and a research position. Switzerland or California would suit her. She could remove herself entirely from the larger world of politics, as well as from the realm of wizards and vampires, in favor of the captivating world of particle physics.

It was particle physics, not politics or garlic, that now caused her to pace restlessly around the room. She needed an uninterrupted summer to make those measurements in the caves. Professor Gamberi, her research director at the university, was suspicious of her, and made it clear that she'd have to go to greater lengths to prove herself than would the others. Maybe he didn't trust women, and held the traditional view that women had no legitimate role in physics. Or maybe he was skeptical of that overly glowing recommendation from Professor Mannheim at Stuttgart. Perhaps its enthusiasm did lack credibility. She knew it wasn't sincere; Mannheim had promised her a good letter if she left quickly, and no one would mention the technician with holes in his neck who had to take medical leave for "pernicious anemia."

The work had to go on this summer, and if some of the students on the project were injured or if some of the equipment in the caves was damaged, it might bring a halt to the project.

The American wizard, Lupeni, knew something was going to happen in the caves tonight, and it had nothing to do with moths or bats. He clearly knew what had attacked Mike in May, so it was likely that he now knew werewolves would be running loose at the camp. She had always feared those monstrous dogs, after thirty years at the castle listening to their senseless howls during the full moon. She was astonished that she had been able to fend off the two wolves attacking Mike; but having done so, she was now confident she could do it again, as long as there weren't too many of them. She shivered as she remembered that werewolves usually ran in packs in these mountains.

An idea occurred to her. There were spells for repelling werewolves, and she knew where a patch of aconite grew. She had come across it recently while exploring the camp. If she picked the flowers and draped them around…

What on Earth was she thinking? Did she actually mean to go back to the camp?

It seemed the only way to protect the equipment. The idea of a pack of werewolves bumping around the cave upset her terribly. Why would Lupeni think they would do that? They were mindless, vicious animals, after all.

She rummaged through the others' bags, looking without success for the keys to the Jeep. Mike must have them, protecting his proclaimed right as an American to do all the driving. The journey from Rosu back to the camp wouldn't take very long for a bat, although it would be tiring because the sun was up. Even though she hadn't used any other spells in years, she routinely practiced flying as a bat. It was simply too handy to give up.

Would she meet Lupeni if she went back? She pondered that as she searched for paper and pen to write a note. He remained a mystery: not a hippie, not a botanist, more than a foreign wizard on holiday. Why was he here? Why was he killing vampires? Certainly his coolness at disposing of Emil meant that he had killed others.

A heroic American crusader bent on making a reputation as a vampire killer? No. Lupeni was too educated, too intelligent and well-spoken to be here simply to make a name for himself.

An exile? A criminal? Not quite, but there was something about him that suggested those possibilities. She detected a fragility in him; under the steely calmness, he kept a dark secret at bay.

Well, she had a rather large dark secret herself.

She perched on the edge of the bed with pen and paper, but couldn't focus on the simple note she needed to write. Instead she thought: *He kills vampires and if he finds out what you are, you'll be next.*

Funny, she didn't mind if Lupeni rid the mountains of other vampires, like Cuza. She shivered at the thought of their last meeting. She wanted nothing to do with any of them. Would Lupeni understand that? she wondered. Would he believe that a vampire could go against her nature so completely? No. Of course not. Sometimes, even she did not believe it.

She swore at herself. Writing this note was taking far too long, and one of the others might come back to check on her soon. Maybe she shouldn't bother with the note…No, if they found her missing without explanation, they would search for her, and she did not want anyone else at the camp that night.

She applied herself and finished, explaining that she had left one of her lab notebooks back at camp and found someone who was going in that direction to give her a ride.

She was pretty sure she could get back to the inn by morning. Perhaps if she could remember a few simple protection charms, she could get back sooner—maybe even before her companions discovered she was gone. The food and movies would keep them occupied until well after midnight.

If she met Lupeni at the camp, she'd deal with him. He was a wizard, after all—he should understand that she could and would protect herself from werewolves.

When was the last time she even spoke with a wizard, a living one? Fifty years? After she left the mountains twenty years ago, she avoided anyone from that world, for fear her secret would be obvious.

And now she was speaking to a wizard who killed vampires.

She tried not to think about that, instead remembering when Lupeni came to fix Mike's arm, and that startling conversation about Greek poetry. Did he really fancy himself to be a modern Odysseus? He was an odd one, but he had none of the ruthless deviousness of the man from Ithaca.

But perhaps Lupeni had not been far off the mark to connect her with Calypso, the nymph who held Odysseus prisoner for love. She would have made him immortal so that he could stay with her forever if Athena had not intervened. Homer might have been describing a vampire. But vampires never love anything except their next victim.

Lamia stood, flinging the note on the bed, and tried to focus on the task at hand. The instruments at the cave needed guarding and that's where she was going.

"You're really missing some awesome stuff," Mike boomed as he flung open the door. He stumbled over one of the bags in the dim interior of the room, but kept talking as he found his own bag and began pawing through the contents.

"This old lady told our fortunes and I think Vijay's gonna get a Nobel Prize or something. Get this: A tall, dark stranger will make trouble for me. Can you believe it? They always tell you that sort of stuff. Probably Professor Luca trying to fail me out of quantum field theory."

Mike pulled off an extremely mud-stained shirt and struggled to get into a clean one, chattering non-stop.

"And they had this contest for catching sheep. I only entered 'cause Taofang said I couldn't do it. Looked easy—they were in a little pen—but, oh, man! Maybe I had too much of the local beer. I dunno, but those suckers can run pretty fast. I'd make a lousy shepherd. Really took a dive into the mud getting that stupid—"

He was speaking to an empty room and finally woke up to that fact.

"Lamia? You in here?" Mike cast around the dimly lit room, as if she were hiding behind the furniture or the thick curtains blocking the windows. Noticing that the bathroom door was closed, Mike pounded on it, shouting, "Hey, you OK?"

His yelling and hammering brought no response. He rattled the doorknob and barged in when he found it unlocked.

"What the hell...where are you—?" Mike stopped short. There was no place to hide in the small, empty bathroom. Festival sounds drifted through the tiny open window over the old fashioned claw-footed tub.

Well, she didn't just fly out the window, he thought with a scowl, then stomped back into the room and roughly flung open the curtains. He didn't understand what was going on and that always made him angry.

Finding Lamia's note did nothing to calm him down.

"She's nuts," he muttered to himself as he crumpled the note and sent the wad whizzing across the room. "Wolves, spiders, bats. What a crazy country." He jingled the keys to the Jeep in his pocket.

"Seems like I'm gonna have to protect her..."

28. With Friends Like These

ITH ONE GLANCE TO the east and one to the west, Caleb figured he had just under twenty minutes left in human form—just enough time to double check that the students had stayed away from their camp.

He was so sure he'd find no one that he didn't see her until she moved. Coming to a screeching halt on a breath of wind isn't possible, so he swooped around and dropped from the air in a sudden motion that would have impressed even Toby.

"Lamia!" he cried, running up to her at one of the computers in the pavilion. The others were still covered with plastic, but this one was completely unwrapped and she was settled in with a big notebook and a variety of pens and pencils, clearly intending to stay the night.

"Lupeni," she responded calmly, not looking up.

"But you shouldn't—it's not safe!"

"It's werewolves, isn't it?" She looked pleased as he flinched, and showed him the pile of purple flowers among her writing implements. "I grew up in these hills. I scarcely need an American wizard to tell me about those monsters."

"But—" He didn't have time for subtlety. "There's a werewolf I've been hunting," he explained in a rushed breath. "He knows I'm after him and threatened to eat the graduate students at the caves. He is not a wizard, when human, but when he's a wolf—"

"Perhaps you are concerning yourself overmuch with our monsters," Lamia replied coldly. "Romania has had vampires and werewolves for thousands of years, and you, a foreigner, take it upon yourself to eliminate them?"

"No, no, it's not that at all," Caleb exclaimed. He wanted to explain, but complex Romanian sentences were beyond him so close to his transformation. "Really, be careful! I have to go now," he added, turning and running for the underbrush as he felt the ache in his bones that signaled the change.

Caleb did not hear the rustling in the leaves or the quiet murmur of a hushed voice. Cuza slapped his hand over Vlad's mouth as he saw Lamia raise her head to listen, and reached into his pocket for a dagger that he pressed into the werewolf's hand.

Vlad looked puzzled, but quickly caught on as Cuza gestured towards the seated graduate student. With a swift pounce, Vlad planted himself behind her and held the blade to her throat.

Lamia screamed.

Caleb, no more than ten yards away, plunged pelican-like to the ground, catching his foot on a tree branch and falling on his face. Did he dare go back? It couldn't possibly be a werewolf attacking her, since he was still human himself. Maybe a vampire.

That possibility convinced him. She'd promised she knew how to drive off werewolves, but if it was a vampire, the Wolf could help.

Caleb was caught by the moonrise before he even had a chance to take off his clothes. Five large bounds took the gray wolf back into the camp.

Caleb hid behind a clump of tall grass, watching his enemy. His fur bristled to see Vlad circling Lamia and growling, not attacking her, though she wasn't holding the wolfsbane. His snaps were half-hearted, his tongue lapping occasionally with disgust and even fear. What powerful magic could make Vlad so uncertain?

Caleb never got an answer to his question. As he hid in the undergrowth, growling softly, he was distracted by a roar of tires and a screech of brakes as a Jeep tore into the campsite. The man who jumped out looked plenty tasty, and Caleb and Vlad paused only briefly to snarl at each other before they flung themselves at him.

"Help!" thundered Mike, pushing himself against the car's grille as Vlad swiped him with a huge paw. "Lamia! Why did you come back here?" he cried reproachfully, barely dodging a clash of jaws.

Lamia grabbed the aconite and held it out in front of her, thinking fast. While werewolves could and did gut vampires, the Undead were not their favorite prey, and they would back off quickly when injured or frightened. It was much harder to make them surrender a chance to bite or devour a person.

Finally she gave up on flowers and started hurling balls of green fire. The first caught the black one in the rump, and he sat back and rolled in the grass, howling.

The gray one was smarter. She could see the calculating intelligence in his eyes as he anticipated each fireball and deftly sidestepped it, getting his body behind Mike's and pinning the American to the ground.

Fortunately, the other wolf helped her out. After easing the sting of the fire with his tongue, the black one leapt for the gray one, fangs planted firmly in his neck. In this position Lamia was able to send a ball of flames at both, burning the black one's nose and setting fire to the gray one's whiskers.

They yelped, pawing at their faces and dragging their snouts along the ground. She was about to turn away and check on Mike when the wolves, half-blinded by fire and seeking cool and shade, chased each other into the cave.

The apparatus! This was precisely why she'd come back here tonight. Forgetting her fellow student, bleeding and perhaps bitten in the dirt, she tore towards the cave after the animals.

Only moments had passed, but the werewolves were nowhere to be seen. Still, they couldn't have caused more damage if that had been their intent— and perhaps it was. She didn't know what the creatures thought about, and she was still struck by the cleverness of the huge gray and brown animal, who had dodged her fireballs as if they were playing tag.

She quickly set about surveying the apparatus. Most critically, sharp teeth had chewed the rubber lines running from the argon tanks, releasing gas into the air. Low-oxygen sensors sounded alarms throughout the cave, their high-pitched wail likely to have been responsible for driving the wolves away.

Argon is a harmless, inert gas, except when it begins to replace oxygen in an enclosed space. Humans and animals can't sense the absence of oxygen, only the presence of carbon dioxide, and so will breathe pure argon without any feelings of breathlessness or pain until they fall unconscious and die. The students had all been carefully trained to run from the cave if the sensors sounded, and not to return until they stopped beeping.

Fortunately, Lamia wasn't alive. The shrill cries of the alarms bothered her intensely, but she couldn't shut them off; if she did, she would have no way of knowing when it would be safe for breathing creatures to enter the cave again.

She tore strips from her T-shirt and stuffed them into her ears. It only dulled the sound, but she had to get to work—shutting off gas tanks, looking for the lines that had been chewed and digging around for replacements in cardboard boxes. Surely low oxygen would kill a werewolf? she wondered idly, as muffled howls filtered through the cotton. It was hard to tell how far away they were with her ears plugged. The animals could have been deep in the unmapped recesses of the caves, trapped and suffocating. Or perhaps the argon wouldn't travel that far into the minor passageways? This was a purely intellectual exercise to someone who hadn't needed oxygen for fifty years.

Lupeni will be proud of me if the wolves die, she thought suddenly, but quickly got back to business. Replacing the gas lines wasn't hard, but then she had to check the argon pressure in all of the metal boxes. She wasn't sure if any had lost gas, and she had to make sure that there were no other leaks. To do this she had to unwrap and boot up all of the computers that had been carefully shut down before the trip to the village.

If the others came back from the garlic fest and found her in here with the alarms going…Well, almost better to be revealed as a vampire than to be expelled from graduate school again.

This was her fourth try at a PhD, and she'd gone all the way back to the first year of university to provide herself with a respectable physics background before applying to this program. The undergraduates in physics had accepted her, at least, which was certainly more than she could say about her fellow students when she first went to college as a psychology major.

"Accepted" was too strong of a word, of course. The physics undergraduates had silently tolerated her presence in study sessions in which no one spoke in anything but equations, there was rarely any food, and the greatest possible accomplishment was to call your colleagues morons.

The perfect field of study for a vampire.

But that was why she had avoided "hard" science for so long: It would prove to her that she had lost every human quality. After rejecting the cold, merciless, gossipy Undead society, she had hoped to find, somewhere in herself, something that could connect with people and recapture some emotion, some warmth. She didn't find it in psychology, where her fellow students speculated endlessly about her—Anorexia? Depression? Dissociative Personality Disorder? Sociology and economics were even worse. She'd despaired at her lack of inspiration and lapsed once more into drinking human blood. By way of scandal or simply boredom, she had always left, off to another school where she could use only her most recent credentials to hide a history that went back many decades.

Mike, Vijay, and Taofang didn't ask why she never ate. They were impressed by her lack of emotion (even when she had papers rejected!) and too intimidated by her command of nine languages to press for details on how she had acquired them. If she could manipulate Maxwell's equations and solder a busted circuit board, she was one of them.

So she was determined to prove herself now. The argon wells were soon sealed and filled once more, their pressures equalized, and neutrino capture events registering dutifully. The data were noisy, though. Had the wolves torn at the shielding as well?

She pulled aside the remains of the plastic installed to protect against bat guano and checked the metal rods that encircled the containers of gas. Sure enough, several had been knocked free, and she struggled to replace them. Eight feet long and unwieldy, they were a job for two or three people, and it was a couple of hours before she completed the task.

Once more she went over the gas lines, electronics cables, everything that snaked across the floor for an animal to trip over or gnaw. The cables to one of the oscilloscopes had been dislodged, but that was an easy fix. As she fired up the equipment around it to make sure everything worked, the oxygen sensors abruptly stopped their piercing wail.

With a sigh of relief, Lamia removed the cotton from her ears. She no longer had to worry about anyone coming in, and everything she knew how to test was operating perfectly.

A far-off howl and the scrabble of paws on rocky soil told Lamia that the werewolves were still alive, one of them at least—and a look outside the cave showed the full moon edging close to the horizon.

It was the black one who emerged from one of the narrow corridors of the cave, his rear still charred from the fire and his muzzle and paws dripping blood. She threw wolfsbane at him and blocked his exit before he could get near any of the equipment again, and she wasn't going to let him run. Controlling him with the wolfsbane and her sheer will, she led the humiliated wolf slowly over the wires and out the main entrance like a good puppy.

She breathed a huge sigh of relief as the gas continued to flow and the oscilloscopes flickered, her mind hardly registering the eerie sound of the werewolf's triumphant howl, followed by the sounds of footsteps in the leaves. Human footsteps, so the wolf must have transformed.

Human footsteps! She had forgotten all about Mike! Had her fellow student spent all night outside the caves? If the werewolves had bitten him, it didn't matter—he would die. Still, she couldn't just leave him there. Cautiously, she crept from the cave and saw in the light of the setting moon Mike's body, lying pale and still near the Jeep. A cold ground mist crept through the camp, extending ghostly tendrils toward the lifeless form.

Several things were wrong. The moon was still above the horizon, so the wolf could not have regained his human form. She had distinctly heard human steps in the leaves; how could a person have come so close to a werewolf without being attacked? And why would the animal ignore a perfectly edible human, even a dead one?

Mike was not dead, she found as she approached him and lifted his cold, bloodstained arm. He had been bitten by a vampire. Again.

29. Lunacy

DEEP DOWN IN THE Petrosna caves, three feet into the collapsed area, Caleb growled with rage as Vlad's triumphant cry claimed the territory. They had chased and fought each other all night. Caleb had been in the cave only once—and then only into one of the passageways, and under the influence of the wolf belt—and he had come out by far the worst. He was lost in the twists and turns of the cave, with no idea how to get out except by digging through the cave-in he'd caused two months before. His bruised and bitten muscles rebelled at the slightest movement, sending constant jolts of pain that obscured the ones that signaled the dawn.

After he transformed, Caleb lay a long time without moving. Not having claws made it harder to dig, and he was bigger and stronger as a wolf than as a person. Worse, his human self felt panic and apprehension that an animal could not. How long could he live, lost in a cave without water? Did he even know which way was up?

He also remembered what he had found last time he was here: a skeleton, a human skeleton. He'd accidentally crawled over it in the dark, feeling its rounded rib cage, its jutting jaws, the last scraps of its decaying meat.

Death always made Caleb think about Toby, who was never far from his mind in any event. Was there even that much left of Toby, after five years? Had his bones been consigned to the waves off the Atlantic coast...or did the executioners burn the body like that of a plague-riddled vermin? Caleb felt cold, much too cold to move, his fingers turning to ice. The tears welling in his eyes froze his lashes like pellets of sleet. He wondered if there would be something familiar and recognizable about the skeleton of a best friend, or if it would be just another pile of bones.

As if in answer to his thoughts, a face emerged from the darkness, leering into his own. Just enough flesh remained on it for it to be called alive, but every bone and sinew stood out in horrifying relief, the specter all the more hideous for its resemblance to the laughing boy that had been Toby Byron. "I almost got them both," it hissed in a low voice. The eyes were sunken and depthless, like a vampire's. "René—always following us around—I could see he would be dangerous in the future. And Sophia…" The face twisted into a rictus of hatred. "She sat with the old man at my trial. I've had my revenge since then, though."

The specter gestured off into the distance, as if towards a movie screen. Blood chilling with horror, Caleb saw his remaining childhood friend torn to pieces in the all-too-human jaws of Monster René. The shambling hulk's charred skin flapped in blackened strips and its face was cratered with scars in the place of ears and nose.

Up in the caves, Mike slept peacefully at Lamia's feet as she recorded and analyzed data. She didn't dare take her eyes off him again, because a vampire Mike was not a pleasant thought. At least it looked as if the werewolves hadn't bitten him, though they'd certainly scratched him up pretty thoroughly. It was probably the smell of fresh blood that had attracted the vampire, who might have started licking from the wounds before making his own puncture opposite that of the first vampire to feed on this unfortunate American physicist.

Unless, she thought grimly, the vampire had been here the whole night, watching or waiting for something else, Mike's wounds just a lucky midnight snack. The footsteps she heard just before moonset must have belonged to this vampire, which explained why he wasn't attacked by the werewolf…and there was only one vampire she knew who dared to hunt at the full moon. The same vampire who had already been here once, who wouldn't give up easily on his craving to win her back. Who might even sink so low as to consort with a dog, if it suited his purpose.

Cuza.

Her thoughts were interrupted by faint howls and moans from the cave that suddenly turned into clear English syllables. She thought at first it was

Vijay—just what she needed, two bitten colleagues in one night!—but the accent wasn't quite right, and after a few sentences she knew.

"No!" the voice cried, with anguish that was unfathomable to one who had felt little emotion for fifty years. "She didn't want them to kill you. It wasn't her fault!"

Lamia's face hardened. So Lupeni had gotten lost in the caves, no doubt going after that werewolf he was hunting. He must have been successful, and that was why only one had come out. She hated and feared Cuza, and despised werewolves, but somehow neither was as bad as the thought of a half-mad American lying in wait like some kind of wizard Captain Ahab. Was he trying to escape his own darkness by killing all monsters? Such a philosophy could easily make a person go too far.

She had a good mind to let him die there, but the cries grew more piteous, and grated on her nerves even if they didn't tug at her heart. If all of the equipment was OK, and Mike looked stable, she might just poke around in the passageway and find out what was going on.

"Dog Boy, old pal." The words were Toby's, but the hard, evil tone was not—and the hand he extended to grip Caleb's shoulder was a bony claw.

Caleb was too numb with cold to feel it, nor could he feel the icy tears running down his face, except when they stung the burns left by Lamia's ball of fire.

"Even if you won't join me, there's no escaping what you are," the de-mon-Toby continued, its horrible arm elongating like rubber as Caleb pulled away from it. "You're evil, old buddy, and you wanted to turn René into a monster even more than I did." Here it stopped to throw back its head and laugh, showing yellow teeth.

Caleb pressed his hands over his eyes, but that didn't block the vision, and his cry of "No!" came out just a whimper.

When he suddenly felt a touch on his face, it seemed as soft and warm as a kitten's paw.

"This place is full of leptothrixes, Lupeni," Lamia said matter-of-factly. "I can't drive them off, but I can drag you out of here."

The words meant little to him, but he didn't protest as she took his wrists and started pulling him after her up the narrow passageway. In his demented state he wasn't sure if she was a continuation of the vision or a real person, or even if he was truly being moved or if he was still huddled in the cave waiting to die.

When they were in the main cave, Lamia let go of him and he collapsed in a heap. She glanced around, seeing no one but the unconscious Mike. He would be out for days this time.

Did Lupeni spend the night in the caves? Did the werewolves attack him? What an idiot, she murmured as she grabbed him under the arms, forcing him to stand. "You can't sit here like this, everybody's going to come back soon." She snaked her arm around his waist, guiding him through the racks of equipment and toward the mouth of the cave. "This way—and don't trip on the cables. It took me all night to fix them, after those wolves got through tearing around. I should have let you finish them off—"

She stopped in mid-sentence. She saw his burned face, burns caused by her fireball—and blood from deep puncture wounds smeared her shirt. It was his blood, and it was not entirely human.

30. The Eye of the Storm

REALIZATION LURCHED INTO HER head as they stumbled out into a heavy fog, creeping in with the dawn as often happened on the mountainside. Lupeni hadn't been attacked by werewolves. He *was* a werewolf, the gray one, the one with the spark of cunning in its yellow eyes.

He knew a lot about werewolves because he was one. Knowing this caused more confusion in her mind, not less, and she was struck with a crazy impulse to laugh. Werewolves were the lowest class of Dark creature: mortal, uneducated, unpredictable and vicious, with an animal shyness of humans except on the one night per month they tore them apart. She couldn't reconcile her few encounters with "dogs" with this confident, articulate American wizard.

He had been bitten on a hunt, she guessed, and somehow had been powerful enough to survive. Perhaps he even continued to kill other werewolves the way he did vampires. Certainly he did not consort with them, since he had come to warn the students, a clear betrayal of his kind. This would explain, too, why he could not return to his home country, a single night of carelessness forcing him into perpetual exile.

He moaned incoherently, something about a stakes and burning, and struggled as if fighting off an imaginary enemy. She forced them both down the path and into the fog.

"Come on," she urged, baffled why she was rescuing someone who should be her enemy. Overhead, sunlight danced through scattered clouds, the last pink of dawn just fading. Around them, however, a thick mist swirled through the trees, obscuring all but the closest parts of the path.

Lamia was rough with Caleb, forcing him to keep moving, although he seemed too weak and insensate to go on. In spite of the frosty cold of his skin, he felt alive beneath her fingers, like any other human. But werewolf blood flowed in his veins. Did it matter? She had sworn off human blood, after all.

A battle raged inside Lamia. The old fear of werewolves, the ever-present lust for blood, and the desire to be free from her past all clashed mercilessly. She felt as confused and muddled as if she had been feeding from humans. She needed to get him cleaned up, dressed, and on his way before things got even more complicated.

Once in the camp, she pulled him toward a wooden tank next to a coiled green rubber hose. She turned the spigot up full blast and sprayed him with cold water, removing blood and dirt and making the long gash on his chest start bleeding again. He stood without making a sound. She was gentler when she got to his face, turning down the water pressure and brushing off the smear of mud and tears with a light touch.

"Where are your clothes?" she asked, turning the hose on top of his head to rinse his hair.

He shook his head to indicate he couldn't remember, not even able to make sense of the words.

Lamia sighed, looking at him with exasperation. A naked, bleeding guy should have been a vampire's fondest wish, but his blood was about as appealing as a can of dog food.

"Come on," she said roughly. "You can stay in my tent until you make sense. I don't want to have to explain this to the others."

She got him in motion again, leaving him at the entrance to her tent where he swayed unsteadily and shivered. After laying a plastic tarp across the tent floor so he wouldn't bleed on everything, she shooed him inside and promised to borrow some clothes from Vijay.

Caleb's teeth were chattering, and it was an immense effort to speak. "Potion…in my pocket," he managed. "The leptothrixes…have to drink…"

"Oh, is that your problem?" she exclaimed in surprise, going out past the camp to rummage in a trampled bush that looked exactly like where a wolf would hide. Sure enough, she found a pair of shredded jeans and a ripped oversized linen shirt with several small bottles still tucked into its pockets.

Some minutes later she crawled into the tent, pushing the bundles in ahead of her. "Here," she said curtly, handing him the bottles.

He closed his eyes and drank from more than one of them, shuddering from more than the cold. When he opened his eyes again, she saw the human intelligence had returned, yet underneath his clear-eyed stare lurked the irrational beast.

"Why?" he asked through chattering teeth.

"Why am I here?" she said casually as she laid out squares of gauze and noisily ripped pieces of white tape into precise lengths. "To protect valuable equipment from rampaging werewolves, of course."

"No," Caleb shook his head from side to side, and couldn't control the shaking that started from his shoulders and moved downward. "Why did you save me?"

"Why did you lie to me?" she hissed at him through clenched teeth. "You're a werewolf! You didn't want to protect any of us. You just wanted to run loose in the caves with your disgusting pack of wild dogs!"

"Vlad is not…one of mine," he said firmly, struggling with himself for calm. "Yes, I was hunting him. He attacked my pack last month, and even his own has deserted him."

"Your pack?" she spat at him.

"The strongest and best organized in the mountains," he replied calmly. "You have been less than truthful yourself, Lamia," he added, a hint of something—anger or betrayal or surprise—creeping into his tone. "You're a vampire."

"And you're a vampire killer, aren't you?" she said in response, drawing away from him quickly. "Emil wasn't your first victim. What makes you do it? Just your filthy instinct, wanting to roll in something dead?"

"You could have left me to die in the caves," he observed in a detached manner that brought the wild dog to heel. "You could have killed me easily any time since then. But you didn't. Why, Lamia?"

She didn't answer. Instead she turned her attention to the array of gauze and tape she'd laid out on the tarp in front of him.

"Here," she announced, holding a bandage in one hand as she roughly pulled his arms down to expose his chest. "I'm going to put a bandage on this wound. It's the worst one." She smoothed the gauze and applied some tape to hold it in place.

"What are you?" he breathed into the absolute stillness of the tent.

She stood suddenly and moved behind him, unwilling or unable to confront the question in his eyes.

"I don't know any more," she replied slowly and cautiously after a long pause in which the sound of his breathing alone filled the space between them.

Lamia groped for a blanket, unable to take her eyes from the filigree of scratches etched across Lupeni's back. She draped the blanket around his shoulders, but still she didn't speak. What was she? Why had she come back? An hour ago, even ten minutes ago, she might have known the answer to those questions.

What was he? She thought she knew who he was, too, but that kept changing. If he had a pack, it meant he kept company with other werewolves, and had probably been one for longer than she suspected. The realization hit her suddenly, painfully, that if she could only figure out who he was, she might know herself again.

But that was crazy.

She pulled off the bloodstained shirt she wore and put on a clean one, wrestling to free her hair where the shirt tangled on her hair clip, a heavy gold piece she had gotten from an old gypsy in Bucharest years ago.

"I was, am, a vampire, it's true," she said harshly as she stood and returned to face Lupeni. He huddled beneath the blanket, regarding her with that same cunning she had seen in the eyes of the gray wolf last night. "But I don't want—I didn't come back for that. I want something different for myself."

She broke off, still unable to meet his eyes, and knelt to collect the scraps of tape and paper wrappings. Then she picked up his clothes and shoved them toward him roughly. They were in shreds, but he could make do.

"You'd better go," she said, desperately trying to add some note of finality to her voice. She was afraid now, afraid of what might happen if he stayed.

"Yeah," he mumbled and tried to stand. His head brushed the roof of the tent as he swayed unsteadily, holding onto the clothes as if they could support him. He almost toppled over but she stood quickly, grabbing his arms and pulling him down again. He didn't resist, but continued to stare at her, his tangled and matted hair falling all around his face.

He looked like a wild animal all of a sudden, and she needed him to look human. Gently she pushed the mess away from his face and gathered all the snarled strands together, letting them rest over one of his shoulders while she undid the clip from her own ponytail. Her hands glided over his neck as she fastened the gold piece in his hair. Those eyes of his were fixed on her own. Beyond the gray vortex, he waited.

Caleb raised a tentative hand and stroked her cheek. It felt smooth and cool. Was it what he expected? Surprisingly, her lips were warm when he kissed her a moment later. Perhaps they shared all the warmth they had between them as they clung together.

He wanted to surrender to her, but struggled against a craving to bite her. His werewolf wanted to sink his teeth playfully the way he did with Liszka, the only other female he'd ever known in this way. He was mad with a desire to nourish Lamia with all his warmth, until he would be left a cold and lifeless husk.

He felt his wolf growl gently as he kissed her, and then almost succeeded in banishing the beast as she pulled back slightly from the kiss. She kissed him gently along the line of his jaw, under his ear, and down his neck. He plunged his fingers into her hair, which was redolent with her perfume. The long, dark strands slipped through his fingers like fine sand at the beach.

They clung to each other, oblivious to the darkness and confusion churning outside. For an instant, the clouds ripped apart to let loose a shaft of sunlight—a gift from the gods—to light up their lonely struggle. For an instant, their darkness was banished and they could both remember what it meant to believe in beautiful dreams.

31. Who's Got Your Back?

HE'D NEVER SEEN HER at the castle before, but even from far off she was unmistakable, with her windswept red-brown hair and her short summer dress of undyed wool. She ran straight and fast, disappearing from view as she approached the high outer wall.

Caleb turned back to his gardening, knowing she had a quarter mile up the rocky trail before she reached the castle. This early autumn afternoon had brought the first peepings of the bernacae, and he was in the greenhouse seeing if they were ready to hatch. The green, leafy pods, held to the trunk by their beaks, would die if they hit dry ground. If they fell into water, they split down the center and small birds with black webbed feet emerged. The bernacae acted as messengers between the worlds of land, air, and water, able to speak to fish, birds, and people. In his irreverent inner mind, Caleb called them "vegetable ducks."

The pods seemed in no imminent danger of bursting, but to be safe he dipped a pail of water from the running spring along the greenhouse wall and placed it under the tree. Then he left the castle by the stable gate to greet the leader of the Fives.

The tanned young woman came sprinting up the path, bare feet impervious to the gravel.

"Hi, Liszka," he said politely. "It's been a while. It's good to see you."

She rolled her eyes in disgust at his dry pleasantries, and kissed him on the nose as if they were still mates. He had forgotten how nice she smelled.

"I'm not here to chat, Lupeni," she said, her voice tense. "There is something I need to tell you. The Sixes have deposed Vlad."

"Well, that's good, isn't it?" he asked in mild surprise.

"Deposed, not killed," she clarified, beginning to sound angry. "He came back to his territory at the new moon covered with wounds and crying for his parents. Something destroyed his mind."

"All right," said Caleb calmly. "Why don't you come in and have some tea and tell me what you know." He knew that she'd be hungry after running here, and having something to eat might make her a bit less temperamental.

Liszka scrunched up her face in annoyance that he didn't seem to be taking this seriously, but she stood patiently as he undid the wards and let them through the old kitchens and into the Great Hall.

Mihail gave Caleb the glare he reserved for werewolves in the castle, but he courteously served them tea and meat pies in front of the fireplace. He seemed somewhat daunted by Liszka and she, in turn, was taken aback by him, fighting laughter when he said, "Will that be all, Mr. O'Connor?"

After bringing their food he departed stiffly to his room, where he could sulk among the garlic and wolfsbane.

As Caleb had expected, she was hungry, eating with gusto as she told a wild tale about Vlad plotting with powerful, ancient vampires. They were all supposed to converge on the castle at the next full moon to kill Caleb and the other wizards.

"Who told you this?" he asked, trying to cover his skepticism.

"Sasha Alpha, the Sixes' new leader. He didn't even have to fight Vlad to take over. Vlad lay on the ground for three days, crying. I think the vampires tortured him."

"He got too close to a leptothrix, most likely," said Caleb, wondering what illusion would so torment Vlad. He had certainly shown up at the caves last month, battling Caleb in the only way he knew. And there had been a vampire there who had drained Mike for the second time, but it was hard to imagine the events were related.

Liszka growled, pouring her teacup full of milk and drinking it straight. The Fives didn't have any cows and she clearly enjoyed the treat. "You don't believe me," she accused. "I wouldn't come out here for idle gossip."

"Yes, well," Caleb smiled, "our kind do tend to be hyperexcitable, don't we?"

"Hyperexcitable," she snarled without irony. "Would you rather believe a vampire?"

As he was quite incapable of answering that question, Liszka growled again and said, "You are one sick puppy, Lupeni."

"It isn't that I don't believe you," he assured her as calmly as he could. Her challenge unsettled him; she obviously knew all about his friendship with a vampire. "But what powerful wizard vampire would run around at full moon with a werewolf in tow?"

She had no answer to that, but she and Sasha did know that Vlad possessed more information about the castle than he could probably learn on his own or by spying on the Fives' conversations. He knew that it was difficult for vampires to get in, had even said something about "wards" and "Jupiter."

"The vampire may know some way to get a werewolf into the castle, even if he can't get himself in," she suggested hesitantly, looking around the room as if the magical wards would be visible. Apart from the ubiquitous hanging braids of garlic, and a few strategically placed mirrors that might have served in happier times for dancing couples to improve their steps, there was nothing that suggested the castle presented any barriers to the Undead.

Caleb was finally beginning to share Liszka's concern, but only a little. Werewolves were magical creatures like wizards, and wouldn't be able to get past the wards. Even if they did get in, there wasn't any way as far as Caleb knew for them to open the gates to vampires. Of course, his knowledge of the Jupiter wards remained weak. He had given up on planetary magic, and Alexandru had despaired as well, the whole idea a sore spot between them.

Even assuming the wards weren't threatened, there was a puzzle here, and the pieces didn't fit together: Mike's encounter with a "spider," twice; Lamia; "powerful vampires," plural. Although Lamia had never hinted that she knew of the castle—and he couldn't imagine that she did—her powers would make her attractive to other vampires, possibly even the dreaded Cuza.

He had to ask Lamia, although he knew that this was just an excuse to see her again. Even sitting here with the beautiful Liszka he could only think of the other—cool and sinuous as opposed to hot and muscular, intellectual as opposed to cunning, mindful rather than precipitous.

He had to stop the reverie before it led down wholly inappropriate paths. "I won't be too useful against wizards once the full moon rises," Caleb admitted, "but I suppose I could stand outside the castle at sunset."

"We'll come too," Liszka declared.

It was said unsentimentally, but it was the highest compliment she could have paid him. Perhaps she just wanted to get her paws on Vlad, but Caleb was touched nonetheless. A cruel former Alpha would be shunned or killed, like Vlad. One who had been respected would be tolerated on occasion, like a crotchety old grandparent who still deserves a Sunday afternoon visit. But for the pack to come to the defense of an ex-leader meant that they considered him both exceptionally kind and wise.

"If Vlad were to get into the castle, Al-…the other wizards would kill him," he began, then stopped as a terrible idea hit him.

They both frowned, thinking the same thing: if Vlad got in, so might they. Alexandru might not even recognize Caleb, never mind believe that he was there to defend the castle. And, of course, Caleb would bite Alexandru, given the opportunity.

"Do they have any weapons that could hurt us?" Liszka asked, shrinking in apprehension from this cozy room that was suddenly a hunter's lair.

No wizard's curse could kill a werewolf in wolf form, but Caleb was certain Alexandru had a supply of silver bullets somewhere. He wondered about the ethics of finding them and disposing of them before the full moon, but that really wasn't a discussion he cared to have with Liszka, whose attitudes he knew full well. "It'll be OK," he reassured. "I'll take care of it."

After she left, it only took him a few minutes to make the decision. Liszka was willing to risk her life to help him—and to risk Bela's life, too. Caleb couldn't stop thinking of the boy, who he still thought was too young to take part in the pack's more dangerous escapades. Alexandru had killed werewolves before, and from everything he'd said on the subject, the old wizard was none too contrite. Caleb had no right to expose the Fives to that.

Mihail was still locked in his room, where he would probably remain for several hours. Alexandru was out, in the village, maybe, or off on one of his solo hunts for Cuza. Apart from the servant's bedroom, then, Caleb had the run of the castle, and he made haste to search it before the old wizard appeared.

It was difficult for him to move silver magically, but not to find it. When he concentrated, stepping slowly about a room with eyes half-closed and senses extended, the lunar metal raised the hair on the back of his neck. As he crept closer, it began to burn his hand. He was sweating as he approached Alexandru's massive oak desk in the library.

There was a single box of silver bullets in the topmost drawer and it was half empty. Gripped with a sudden rage, Caleb made a thorough investigation of every room in the castle, including the upstairs where the stench of vampire still lingered. He tiptoed on the crumbling stairs, hoping Mihail wouldn't hear his footsteps—and hoping, too, that the servant didn't possess a cache of weapons along with his pots of aconite.

Except for Mihail's room, Caleb had been exhaustive in his search; still, he had a nagging sense that he was forgetting something. He reexamined the silver he had found. Apart from a few spoons, a goblet, and some jewelry, the single box of bullets was the only silver he found that could hurt anyone. After a moment's hesitation, he decided the other objects were harmless.

He took the half-empty box and pitched it down the mountainside.

32 ❖ Addicted to Blood

THE WAXING MOON SHONE weakly through the trees, lurking there and waiting until the sun went down to rule the night. Lamia watched the American vampire-hunter go, rising on his gust of Wind and briefly cutting across the moon, off to wherever it was that he lived.

After only three weeks, she knew Lupeni better than she had any lover in the last fifty years, except perhaps one. But there were many things they still kept from one another. She avoided saying where exactly she was from and did not mention her thirty years' stay at the castle. And he did not tell her where he lived or why he had come to this country.

Did it matter? Perhaps all that mattered was to touch him and to feel his touch.

Lamia ambled through the trees back towards the camp, her thoughts still on Lupeni. His fingers were rough, although so very gentle when they caressed her. But his hands had killed her kind on more than one occasion, and could kill her just as easily. When he touched her, she felt pleasure, raw and powerful, and the distant echo of something else, a sweet and tantalizing nothingness. He could give her either.

What did she want?

As the sun set, bats began pouring out of the caves, squeaking eagerly in anticipation of the evening's hunt. She looked up through the leafy canopy and saw them darkening the deep blue sky. Not since she was a little girl had she been frightened by bats. Lately, though, the sight of them only served to remind her of Cuza. She had not talked to him in over a month, but she was sure that he was the bat she saw nearly every afternoon, spying on her.

Odd that he had stayed hidden for so long. That didn't seem like him.

She could deal with Cuza, she felt sure. But Lupeni...The desire she felt for him reverberated inside her, ever present, never entirely silent. The ageless song of hunger and fulfillment. The song of the vampire.

Possess the one you love forever, that was what drove vampires to bite once, twice, then three times. She thought of former lovers: Ioncu, Stephen, Christoph. She had made them hers forever, or so she thought. But it never seemed to work out somehow. She grew bored with them, and they with her. In the case of poor Christoph, becoming a vampire drove him insane. Perhaps it was better that she couldn't possess Lupeni in that way.

"Lamia? Did you hear what I just said?" An irritated voice jolted her out of her reverie. She hadn't even noticed that she had wandered back into the camp. Now a peeved Vijay stood before her, trying to get her attention.

"What?" she mumbled. "Did you say something?"

"Remind me never to fall in love," he snorted derisively, then seemed to recall his purpose in life, saying, "You said you would help me set up tonight's experiment, remember?"

"Yes. I don't want you up in the caves by yourself," she replied with slightly more composure.

"I am willing to humor you," he frowned, clearly not believing as Mike did that danger abounded in the mountains. "But let's get started on some reasonable time scale. Minutes, not centuries."

"Of course," she said more crisply. "I'll just get my things." Happily, Vijay headed back to the pavilion as she called, "But wait for me before you go up there!"

First, though, she should check on Mike, make sure that he was in his tent with plenty of garlic. The thought of the American physics student as a vampire made her shudder. He would become even more irritating, she was sure, and his jokes wouldn't improve either.

"Mike? Are you in there?" She called from outside his tent. The stench of garlic was strong and kept her from going in.

"Yes, Mother," came Mike's grinning reply as he stuck his head out through the tent flap. "Come to tuck me in? Kiss me goodnight?"

She had to laugh in spite of herself. Mike had not lost his sense of humor after all that had befallen him. She admired him for that.

"Hey, I borrowed a couple of books from your tent, a little bedtime reading since you won't let me out at night."

"More botany books?" she said, slightly angry that Mike had been searching her tent. "I didn't think I had any more on that subject."

"Astronomy," Mike corrected. "Guess what's coming up next week?"

"The Harvest Moon?"

"Better than that. Jupiter is going to be occulted by the moon not long after sunset! A complete occultation in northeastern Europe. We're lucky to be in the country to see it. You can bet I won't be in my tent wrapped in garlic that night!"

Lamia bid him good night with a chuckle and headed for her own tent. She wanted to get her pot of wolfsbane—she had taken to carrying it whenever she went to the caves. Inside, books were scattered everywhere, evidence of Mike's borrowing expedition. She found the flowers and stacked the books so that she wouldn't trip over them later. *The Donbury Uprising and the Wizard's Covenant of 1578* was lying on top of one pile. She wondered if Mike had skimmed this tome.

Decades ago, when she was newly a vampire, she remembered sharing books like this with the one or two others at the castle. At the time she felt more connected to Romanian society, and eager to learn all she could. Where were they now, the Undead whom Cuza had gathered around him? Emil was dead, she knew. What about the others?

She shivered suddenly to remember Slaba, a young vampire who had made the mistake of biting a werewolf. His screams had rocked the castle for weeks. Finally the others locked him in the tower, but there was no place to escape the sound of his madness. He had not survived long, though, because he was too insane to eat and would not take any rest. In the end, there was no pity from any of the other vampires, just relief to be free of the din.

But Slaba was a very young and weak vampire. Would an older vampire survive biting a werewolf? She had no direct evidence, because none of the older vampires made such foolish mistakes. And she should not either.

Lamia stood quickly and left the tent, trying to shake the memories as well. She soon discovered that Vijay was not at the pavilion. Only Taofang sat amidst the chains of garlic, like a bunting at a festival.

"Where's Vijay?" she inquired sharply.

"He not wait. Go to cave," came the staccato reply. Taofang did not bother to look up from his computer screen.

Wishing she had someone to swear at, Lamia left the camp briskly. She navigated expertly through the dark woods now, familiar with the path after three months on the mountain. As she entered the cave, she caught sight of Vijay at the main computer console and felt relief. Her complacency was short-lived, though. When she drew nearer, she saw that he was slumped over, arms and head resting slackly on the keyboard of the computer terminal.

Hesitantly, she approached and inspected his neck, finding no puncture wounds. He seemed to be sleeping deeply. Was he merely tired or had she interrupted someone?

"Show yourself," she demanded, turning and gazing impatiently about the cave.

"Ah, you've come," said a silky voice as Cuza emerged from behind one of the black metal towers of neutrino detectors. "I've been waiting for you. Now we can begin."

"What have you done to him? I warned you to leave them alone!"

"Done to him?" replied Cuza, gliding across the cave and facing her across the limp body of the student. "I merely sent him to sleep. I wanted to share him with you…as we did in the old days. That's why I waited."

A smile twitched at the corners of his mouth, his pointed canines winking at her in the odd light of the instruments. A long time ago they had shared sometimes, leering at one another over the body of their victim. She especially remembered Mircea—such a beautiful young boy.

"I told you," she spat forcefully, "I will not. I'm not going to do that anymore."

"So you say," he purred, but his voice became harsher. "But it is not natural. No, it is insane. And now you take as your lover that abomination, that killer!"

Lamia had seldom seen Cuza this angry, and never with that edge of fear in his voice.

"I know what I'm doing," she said slowly and evenly. "I do not need you to protect me."

"Oh, but you do," replied the other vampire, his voice regaining its usual control. "You do not belong with these students or with that monstrous dog, but with your own kind. We shall take back the castle, hmmm? It will be just you and me this time, no others."

"The castle?" She nearly choked on the word. "It can fall into ruins for all I care! I never want to see it again."

She found that she was gripping the edge of the computer table, causing it to rattle slightly. Cuza stared at her unhurriedly, as if weighing his next words with great care.

"Arghezi lives at the castle once more," he hissed. "Aren't you curious to see him again?"

"Alexandru? At the castle?"

"Oh, you did not know," crooned Cuza, softening his tone. "Well, I only found out recently myself. He lived in the States for many, many years, but returned to hunt us, looking for you, no doubt."

"He's welcome to the castle," Lamia said decidedly. "You and he can fight over it, if you want it so badly. Now get out of here!"

"You are making a mistake, my dear," came the patient reply, "if you think that you can leave all this behind." Cuza stroked the neck of the sleeping student, who shuddered slightly in response. "This is what you are. You cannot escape. Why should you deny what you are? Come, drink with me."

Fascinated, almost against her will she watched his long, white fingers caress Vijay's smooth skin. She fought back memories of so many other victims, trying to forget the slow and sensuous dance that led to—

"GET OUT!" she shrieked at him, unable to flee herself. He continued his hypnotic stroking and stared at her with the intensity that only a vampire or a bird of prey can muster.

"Do you think perhaps that the American werewolf will save you?" sneered Cuza. "He will be the death of you, my dear."

"He hunts vampires. I know that," she glared at him. "And I hope he kills you!"

"Ah, but do you know where he lives? Do you know whom he serves?"

The question startled her. Of course she didn't know where he lived. Why did it matter? She was confused, slow to respond, so he continued, "He lives at the castle. Arghezi brought him over from America, to be his hunting dog…"

"No. You are mistaken," she said quickly, fleeing in confusion not to the entrance of the cave, but to one of the dull metal towers. She backed up against it and stared at him, horrified by the implications of what he'd just said.

"You're lying," she growled in a low tone. Even as she spoke, she knew Cuza was right. Where else could Lupeni have gotten all of his science books, if not from the castle? Yet he had failed to recognize her own collection—or kept his discovery to himself.

Cuza saw realization blossom on her face and smiled at her invitingly. Neither vampire moved for several long minutes, then he leaned over Vijay's limp body and slowly made contact.

She knew what it would be like, knew how he would savor it like a slow kiss, first tasting the skin and then sinking, sinking into the flesh while the blood began to flow...

Watching was agony, so she turned away and rested her forehead against the cool and lifeless metal. He could have Vijay. She wanted no part in it.

But Lupeni: What was he? Monster? Changeling? Could he be as cold and cruel as the Alexandru that she remembered, the one who raged at them and vowed to exterminate them all? She thought he loved her, she sensed it in the way he touched her and looked at her on those endless afternoons spent in her tent. And what had she felt? Hunger, desire, perhaps something more.

All of that lay in ruins now, a crumpled heap of experience that no longer made any sense. She was certain now that Lupeni knew who she was—had perhaps come from the New World to hunt the beings that had been her companions decades ago. She ought to go, leave the cave before Cuza finished feeding on the grad student. Shaking all over, she forced herself to move, turning away from the wall of metal.

But Cuza stood there, not six inches from her, blocking her way. He smiled sensuously and she saw the blood glistening on his teeth. The smell overpowered her. She wanted to run but was paralyzed. She could only watch with frightening anticipation as he raised his hand, blood on his fingertips—*no, no, please, not that*—and lightly touched her lips.

Like a jolt of electricity on a living body, the blood sent her rigid with spasm. In an instant it was no longer merely a taste or a smell, but a force that roused every cell in her body to cry out. He kissed her and she tasted more, which only increased the frenzy. Why had she stopped? Why had she cut herself off from this—

Words failed her entirely as he pulled away from her, still smiling, and gently guided her across the cave.

"I meant to share with you, my dear," he whispered, urging her toward the body. She could have found it in the dark, the lust was upon her so strongly now.

Lamia's entire world contracted, focused on the warm body before her. She drank eagerly and stopped feeling or tasting or smelling or hearing. She had no senses, no mind to process information. White-hot pleasure ripped through every cell, exploding the body, disconnecting the brain. Time stopped. Reaching for the fulfillment only found in oblivion, she was…

…jerked back. He held her and spoke to her, but she couldn't comprehend. Why did she stop? She needed more. Why couldn't she have more? Words began to make sense, and she moaned as he talked.

"You have returned to me," he crooned, caressing her face, kissing her gently. "You are still hungry, hmmm? Come with me, my dear."

33. Along Came a Spider

ALL OF A SUDDEN, they claim never to have heard of him," Alexandru brooded, regarding his lamb stew with a dark stare that threatened imminent eruption.

"Hmmm?" Caleb asked insouciantly, eating with appetite as he paged through *Troglodyte Today*. "When all the vampires know Cuza, it's good, but when they deny it, it's bad?"

"This is how he works," Alexandru replied, so sternly that Caleb put down his journal. "He terrorizes the weak, forming a circle of servants whom he swears to secrecy." His tone remained steely, but a shudder passed through him that the servant didn't fail to notice. "Thank you, Mihail," Alexandru murmured, as his wineglass was refilled. He drained half of it in a gulp, and added in a strained voice, "My brother…and my wife…She may still be running free somewhere, and I never give up the search."

"Ana Maria was—?" Caleb widened his eyes in surprise, ignoring Mihail's vigorous head-shakes behind Alexandru's back. He had long since stopped noticing the carved gold frame in the portrait gallery near his room, which held only charred shreds of canvas. Neither Mihail nor Alexandru ever spoke of Ana Maria Arghezi, Alexandru's bride of sixty years ago. Caleb wondered suddenly what she had looked like. "And you could…could kill her?" burst from him unexpectedly.

"She died the moment she was bitten for the third time," the old wizard declared, draining the rest of his glass and handing it to the servant for yet another refill.

Alexandru had lost interest in the food, so Caleb appropriated the loaf of bread and spread it with fresh sweet butter before dipping it into the thick stew. He could never understand people who stopped eating because they were upset. "But don't you think…" he began, "that it's possible for a vampire to—to change his nature? To give up human blood?"

Mihail emitted what sounded like a scream, and Alexandru choked on a mirthless laugh. "They cannot give up blood the way we might pipe-smoking or spirits," he said, in a tone that was unmistakably scolding. "A vampire is passionate, not in any human way…and what he loves, he must possess. Do not think, my young friend, that because you are immune to their bites, you are also immune to their call."

The old wizard rose from his chair with effort, assisted by Mihail. The servant darted furious looks at Caleb as he helped his master to bed.

Caleb didn't notice the glares; before Alexandru could finish his warning, Caleb had returned to reading about bat transfigurations by non-vampire wizards and finishing his dinner. He wasn't particularly worried. Surely Lamia wasn't going to risk "rabies" by biting him? Except for their lovemaking, she was passionless and unemotional, and she'd said herself that she wanted Cuza dead.

He looked up only as wood scraped against stone, and found himself facing Mihail's liquid black eyes. The servant waited a minute, maybe two, frowning at Caleb's failure to display respect for Alexandru's pain.

"Those were the *Mistress's* words," the bitter old man said at last. "She believed that a vampire, that a monster, could change…that he only desired to be with her, rather than to devour her as you do a boiled potato!"

The last words were delivered in a staccato bark, and Caleb, surprised, spat out the potato he was chewing.

"It happens from within," Mihail pondered, his distant eyes no longer seeking Caleb's attention. "All the wards in wizardry will not protect from that. Mistress Arghezi was one of the most powerful magicians in the country…I fear that for the master as well, it is too late. And for you, I have little doubt."

He had finally succeeded in making Caleb lose his appetite, though the young American wizard registered no emotion. When the servant departed with a tray bearing brandy and a hot-water bottle for Alexandru, Caleb slipped out the stable gate and took off in the direction of the Petrosna caves. It wouldn't hurt to check.

The moon would be full in two days, and a silvery light illuminated the forest. Before meeting Lamia, Caleb had rarely gone out at night in human form, and was always surprised by how dark and quiet the mountains seemed. Only with effort did he see a number of nocturnal hunters as he flew by. He spied the telltale tufted ears and bobbed tail of a lynx; the orange-green flash that could only be the eyes of a wolf; and a large, stealthy owl, its gaze on the prey the cat had chosen as its own. Was Lamia out tonight, too, hunting rabbits?

The panicked voice, speaking English, was shockingly loud after the hush of the forest. It wasn't a voice that Caleb recognized. A Romanian accent, he thought at first, and then realized it wasn't. Italian, that was it.

He sprinted up the pathway to find the camp in chaos. Enormous boxes were everywhere, metal rods and containers and equipment tossed haphazardly into them. Caleb only recognized Taofang, the Chinese student. The other three there were strangers, and all four were shouting.

"Forty gigabytes of data, wasted!" roared the Italian—a scruffy, bearded middle-aged man in baggy shorts and a T-shirt that read "Physicists do it with Models." This must be the research director from the university that Lamia had talked about, Caleb guessed. Physics professors looked the same everywhere. "If you stay for two more weeks, you might get enough for a paper. The neutrino events are almost convincing."

Even Taofang, usually ensconced so firmly at his workstation, would not be budged. "Not me. I leave before full moon."

The Italian and his two younger companions threw up their hands in disgust. One said something in Italian that neither Caleb nor, apparently, Taofang understood.

"That's right," corrected the older man, switching from good-natured outrage to dangerous fury. "If you abandon this experiment, you will never get a PhD. Not from my lab. And there are precious few others who would hire you, after this! In fact, I'll see that you never get into another school, anywhere on this planet! And you quit because why—you believe in *vampires?*"

"Mike bit," Taofang said. "Vijay bit."

At that, Caleb pushed his way through the boxes and the shouting and stood in front of Taofang. "What's going on here?" he demanded. "Who's been bitten by what?"

But the graduate student kept his eyes on his boss, clearly someone with nearly life and death power in the world of science, and ignored Caleb utterly.

"A spider," spat the Italian professor in disgust. "You are running around like little babies because of a spider bite."

"Is not spider." Taofang shook his head. "Mike very sick, three days, like rabies."

Caleb felt his stomach jolt. Surely Mike hadn't been bitten for a third time? Giving up on this unrelenting conversation, he started exploring the rest of the camp. The tents had been taken down, and the pavilion was nearly dismantled too, though a lantern shone on an otherwise bare folding table.

"Lamia!" Caleb called, knowing if she was anywhere nearby, she could hear him. "LAMIA!" he tried again, slightly louder.

But it was Mike who came out of the cave to greet him. "Aha," he chuckled, "it's the vampire botanist."

"Werewolf," Caleb corrected impatiently. "Where's Lamia? Did you get bitten again?" As Mike approached, Caleb could see that he was draped head to toe in garlic.

"Not me." He seemed inordinately amused, perhaps at no longer being the only victim. "I was sleeping innocently in my tent, draped in garlic like your girlfriend told me to do."

Caleb let out a long sigh of relief. "Vijay, then? What bit him?" he demanded, praying for wildlife.

"Same thing that bit me, man. Passed out in the cave, just like I was. Last time I was out for three days. Three days! Even when I rolled my motorcycle going ninety I wasn't out for that long. And you can't get a blood transfusion in this third-world hellhole."

"Does Vijay have garlic with him now?" Caleb persisted before Mike's outburst turned into an irrelevant rant against the Communists.

Mike laughed scornfully, even though he had enough on himself to repel all the vampires of Transylvania. "More than me," he admitted. "I piled it all over him. Want to see?"

"Yes, that's a good idea," Caleb agreed, relieved that while Mike may sneer, he was at least prepared to take advice—and he had finally figured out Caleb was no botanist. "And Lamia?" he asked, as they picked their way through the boxes.

It was too late to get more information. Mike had been intercepted by the angry Italian, who by now had reduced Taofang nearly to tears.

"Tell him is not spider!" Taofang pleaded. "Tell him is dangerous…"

"Duuude." Mike turned and faced their advisor, but even he lost much of his scornful tone as he addressed the irate physicist. Mike pulled down the neck of his T-shirt to show off his twin vampire bites. "Not a spider," he said, firmly.

The two cronies pointed at the garlic bulbs in Mike's pocket, and the ring of them around his forehead, and started laughing.

"Ridiculous!" fumed the boss. "Superstition! You come to Transylvania, and your heads are full of Hollywood! You jeopardize your careers over fairy tales!"

"Better than jeopardizing my life," Mike replied boldly.

The younger visitors spoke in English for the first time. "Not sure of that," said one, laughing bitterly.

"You're dead to physics, Mike," said the other.

They were both thin and terribly pale, with circles under their eyes. They could be mistaken for vampires, Caleb thought. Maybe Lamia wasn't the only one back at that university.

Mike glared at each of them in turn. "Fine," he said at last. "You take the data."

"That's your job," said the first. "We're postdocs. We analyze."

"You get your degree, you can be like us," added the second.

Mike looked at them one more time, then tore the braid of garlic off his head and threw it at them. "Hell, no," he said. "I'm going to become a botanist."

Stomping away to dramatic effect, he almost ran into Caleb, who was trying not to laugh at Mike's declaration.

"Show me Vijay, please," Caleb said quietly. "I'd like to be sure."

"Yeah," Mike agreed. "I thought Lamia would've told you."

Caleb slowed his pace without noticing, an ominous worry building in his core. "I haven't seen Lamia for several days," he admitted. "Did she say she was going to find me?"

"Nah." Mike shrugged. "She disappeared the night Vijay got bitten. We thought she was going to go get some herbs from you, but she never came back."

34. Short Leash

THE TOWER LOOMED ABOVE the rock formations, a sullen beacon against the late afternoon sky, reaching up to pull down the heavens. Was it calling her home or warning her away?

Lamia could not see the rest of the castle from her position behind a low rock ridge, but her memory filled in the hidden parts: the high wall of dark granite clinging to the steep cliff like hardy gray lichen; the inner courtyard paved with close-fitting stones; the great vaulted roof; the high narrow windows lining the library and Great Hall. She saw it all as if she were flying, for that was how she had arrived at the castle many, many times. Soon, Cuza promised, she would fly there again.

Her hand traced the whorls of lichen on the rock beside her: tough, gray life imitating cold, gray stone. Pale white fingers caressed the rough surface—soothing, lulling, controlling—in the same way they might stroke the neck of a victim, undead flesh imitating life.

The large wooden gate menaces her, looming like an enormous brown bear ready to devour her. As it swings open to reveal an inner courtyard and castle of dark granite, she does not feel comforted. A man takes her arm, guiding her through the gate, whispering with pride, "This is your home now."

Lamia froze. Memory, human memory, seized her brain and forced her to relive what she thought had died. She could not consciously call forth many memories from that time before she joined the Undead, but when her brain was addled as it was now, the recollections often came to her unbidden.

She was no longer human and felt it keenly as she once more hunted with Cuza. Each night they had found a new victim, until she had reached that delicious state of unknowing, of uncaring. For days now—How long? A week, since the moon would be full tonight—she had feasted on humans, gorged on the one thing she'd denied herself for five years.

Why had she stopped? She could not recall. How could she give up that utterly numbing pleasure, when every cell in her body thrilled to the taste-touch-smell of human blood? Sex was nothing by comparison, a feeble reflection of a blinding white light in a scratched and dusty mirror.

Why had she stopped? All those years, she tried to forget what it was like and had succeeded in blunting the memory, her mind telling her body lies. Mind had nothing to do with it, though. Now her arms, legs, fingers, toes tingled with each movement, no matter how minute.

Vampires, although capable of some emotions, lose the subtlety of human feelings and are like creatures who look at a rainbow and see only red-orange-yellow-green-blue-violet—not the thousands of subtle shades in between. Human blood, hot and indescribably tangy, restored some of those emotional hues as it delivered its load of ecstasy. Her body still sang with the feelings of her recent victims: worry from an old woman, twin surges of fear and lust from a girl, anger and desire from a young man. All the lovely and terrifying emotions collided, and she felt almost alive again.

But today it had faded, this explosion of emotional color. Today her mind was beginning to reassert itself because Cuza had insisted that they not feed last night, saying that there was much to be done on the full moon. She resented that, but he promised her more after they had taken the castle.

Cuza. Scheming and ambitious as ever, that one was. But after all these years apart, he still desired her, which was oddly comforting somehow. She felt safe when he caressed her and spoke soft words, remembering dimly the girl who had fallen under his spell over half a century ago.

She plays chess in the library with the darkly handsome visitor. He listens to her raptly, resting his smooth pointed chin on his hands. She tells him of her secret hopes and he drinks them all in with his fathomless black eyes. The servant glowers at her as he brings them tea, but she pretends not to notice, enchanted by the attention paid her.

Cuza, of course, still considered her to be his possession, gloating each time he touched her, his eyes devouring her with every look. And the cruelty she remembered had not diminished either. He could just as easily taunt her as kiss her, occasionally raging at her for abandoning her kind and for taking up with the American werewolf.

Lupeni. She didn't know his real name or why he lied to her or how he fooled her. She tried very, very hard not to think of him at all, hoping the tide of blood would drown those feelings, would build a wall between her and the enigma of the wolf who loved her. That was a lie, too, probably.

Lamia thought about the tower again, so she wouldn't have to think about her brief doomed affair. The sun sagged toward the horizon, flitting in and out of clouds. Now and again, the side of the tower would be bathed in its waning light, yellow for now, but surely the sun's last rays would turn it a bloody red.

In her lap she held the small glass vial that Cuza had enchanted so that it was bigger inside than out. He obviously had something large he wished to put in it, although he hadn't told her yet what it might be. The vial hung on a thick gold chain; he gave no explanation for this either. Cuza hadn't changed in his obsessive desire for control and secrecy. He had a plan for entering the castle, that much was certain, and he would tell her when the time was right. Until then, she tried to sink back into the memory of bliss that still echoed within her body and forget about those who lived within the castle walls.

A faint sound, the sudden rush of air: In an instant, Cuza and another man stood before her. The vampire held the human stranger by the scruff of the neck with one hand, and with the other grasped a large wrought-iron cage. An evil-looking black raven peered up at her from between the bars.

The stranger was as tall and as gaunt as the vampire, but there the resemblance ended. His dark, greasy hair and scruffy beard hung about his face, making him look like a wild animal. And he acted the part, whimpering as Cuza dragged him by the collar of his ragged shirt and threw him roughly to the ground.

Lamia roused from her hazy thoughts to stare at the man glowering up at Cuza, hatred and fear at war on his face. This pitiful creature obviously had something to do with getting into the castle, although she couldn't understand what. Then she recognized him and saw the joke.

"A werewolf?" She couldn't contain herself any longer and started laughing hysterically. How dare he lecture her about associating with werewolves? "You're consorting with a werewolf, you bloodless bastard!"

"Keep your voice down," hissed the vampire with a cold glare. "This one is merely a tool and not a pet." He obviously failed to see the humor in all this.

"He was the one at the caves," she said as she hopped off her stone perch and walked around the heap of a werewolf. "He tried to kill me last month, and at your orders, I take it."

"Not kill you, no," Cuza retorted. "His job was killing the other. You were merely the bait, my dear. But he wasn't very good at that little job. I have a simpler one for him tonight, however, one which I am certain he can carry out."

"What—?" the werewolf started to ask, but Cuza kicked him sharply in the knees, causing him to cry out in pain.

"You will speak only if I require it," he said contemptuously, directing another kick at the huddled man on the ground. "We have only a few minutes before moonrise. Take off your clothes."

After the werewolf had complied, Cuza reached down and pulled the man up by his hair, forcing him to stand, naked and cowering before them.

"Have you prepared the vial?" Cuza asked her. In response she gave him the innocent-looking little flask, its delicate glass stopper attached to a thick gold chain. He held up the chain, swinging the vial gently, almost hypnotically.

"When the time is right, our little wolf will carry this into the castle for us." He gave the werewolf a shove to indicate that he should start down the path that terminated in the stable gate. "There will be a few surprises inside that should shake things up a bit. And then we shall fly into the castle as I promised."

35. Harvest Moon

THE PREVIOUS MONTH HAD turned the hills above Stilpescu from deep summer green to an autumn patchwork of scarlet, orange, and gold. In the red rays of the disappearing sun, these colors and the lengthening shadows that devoured them seemed not beautiful but ominous, as if fingers of blood were leaking between the alpine peaks and spreading through the forests and meadows.

Whether this was an animal thought or one of an increasingly worried human, Caleb wasn't sure, but he decided on the latter after a look towards the opposite horizon still showed no sign of the Harvest Moon.

He sighed and sat down on a rock, pulling his cloak around him to dispel the autumn chill. The equinox had passed, and for the next six months his nights as a wolf would be longer than his days as a human. Alexandru had let him out of the castle early tonight, perhaps because they were both nervous: The old wizard wanted to make sure the wards were secure before any werewolves appeared. Uncharacteristically, Caleb looked forward to meeting Vlad as a wolf. Talking would be useless, he was now convinced, and he did not have any weapons to protect himself if Vlad should show up early and challenge him in human form.

Caleb had told the old wizard nearly everything, recounting Liszka's warnings and the events at the caves last month. Neither took Vlad's boasts seriously, but Alexandru was certain that only one vampire would hunt at the full moon accompanied by a werewolf: Cuza.

It was already early afternoon when Caleb began his story. Alexandru had been out late the previous night and had taken his breakfast in bed. There remained only a few hours to strengthen the defenses on the castle. First they went over all of the outer wards again, Alexandru lecturing with resignation about the pull of Jupiter that Caleb had never been able to master.

Then they moved inside, and Caleb saw for the first time how every room had been designed to bar vampires, even should they manage to breach the gates.

An *Allios* spell stopped only the Undead from passing through the doors and windows. It was a pity that this complex and difficult spell couldn't be performed on the entire castle. The spring in the greenhouse ran all around the perimeter of the castle to stop vampires, who couldn't cross running water. The mirrors in the Great Hall could be lowered to cover all four walls, so that a creature with no reflection trapped between any pair of them would see into infinity and be killed. They hung garlic from every corner and promontory, and scattered mustard seeds around on the floor.

"It is a myth that vampires don't like mustard," Alexandru explained distractedly, falling into the role of teacher despite the situation. "But the seeds will stop them for some time, as they cannot pass them without stopping to count each one. They count quickly, however," he added bitterly, and after that would say no more.

When these preparations were complete, Alexandru went into the silent stone room at the base of the tower and pulled a series of iron levers that creaked in rusty protest. Caleb considered the room a "prison" because of its heavy door and grilled windows.

Then Alexandru took hold of a three-foot handle, tugging futilely for a few minutes before he enlisted the other's help. Together they managed to turn it in a full circle, and Caleb could see metal cables disappearing through the walls.

"The Undead can be cut, crushed, and mangled as much as you or I," Alexandru explained unnecessarily, as though Caleb hadn't fought and killed his share of vampires by now. "It doesn't kill them, of course, but it stops them in their tracks, and sometimes the simplest methods are the most effective. I developed these traps while hunting werebears, and I got the idea from a hunter who killed bears of the more ordinary variety."

The man is a common murderer, Caleb thought, amazed at his own fury at this monster-hunter who did not draw the line at victims who were outside life. Caleb was very glad he had disposed of the silver bullets. He didn't trust Alexandru to spare the lives of any werewolves who might enter the castle, and even less to be able to recognize them individually, despite detailed descriptions. Liszka was easy, as she was pure white with blue eyes, but Bela looked a good deal like Vlad—not surprisingly, as it was Vlad who had bitten him. Caleb would never forgive Alexandru if he killed his foster son.

It was several minutes before he could contain his anger enough to ask what the handle did, or where these traps were located.

Alexandru smiled grimly. "They are everywhere. Outside the greenhouse, in the floors of the Great Hall, one in the entrance hall. I would advise you to tread lightly, though the stones under which the traps lie will give off a faint violet glow. Vampires are creatures of the night, you know," he added with some pride, "and so they cannot perceive blue or violet."

This interested Caleb, though he wondered how a wolf would see it. As light, certainly, which should be enough of a warning—perhaps even as bluish light. Over the years, he had learned a lot about his half-remembered perceptions of how the wolf saw motion and color and detail. Wolves could see color, but mostly washed-out versions of blue and yellow. He would check the traps, marking them with something they could see if he didn't think the violet light was enough.

He was worrying for nothing, he scolded himself. No werewolves were going to get into the castle. The planetary wards would operate as they always had. Although the primary ward was weakest at the full moon, because it was intended for vampires, its residual strength along with the Jupiter ward would be more than enough to keep out any wizard.

There was still something that nagged at his mind, though. Perhaps Lamia, for he had told his mentor none of that story.

Guilt preyed on him now, as he sat outside waiting for the moon to rise and nibbled half-heartedly on a bar of chocolate. It tasted vile, either because of his nerves or because—as Toby used to say when he raided Caleb's bedside table—chocolate wasn't good for dogs. He folded it up again and stuck it back into his pocket, taking out a small autumn apple. It also tasted mealy and unpleasant, but he finished it anyway.

Certainly it wasn't a fatal mistake to neglect telling Alexandru about the vampire graduate student? A Romanian woman from an unknown century, Undead for an indeterminate number of years, she would have no reason to be interested in the castle. Unless there was a vast vampire society of which he knew nothing, all working in concert. From what she'd told him of flighty, gossipy bloodsuckers, this seemed unlikely.

He turned towards the eastern sky, waiting patiently for that eternal celestial event that seemed delayed tonight, as though Selene's chariot had broken a spoke. The sky was darkening, and a very bright star was visible in the southeast, slightly yellow as it rose above the horizon. No, not a star, he realized, this was Jupiter—which he'd given up on, its magic unreachable to him. The planet called forth memories of the graduate students, though he wasn't sure why.

Why had Lamia disappeared without telling Caleb, or her fellow students, or her employer?

Would he ever know? he wondered, still looking at the bright planet but unaware that a special astronomical event was due that night. Even in its path across the sky, Caleb had never seen the full moon as a sentient creature, and so as its reddish crest appeared it didn't occur to him that its orbit would carry its upper edge across Jupiter in the southeast. The occultation was in his notes, he had even been the one to point it out to Alexandru, but all the idea gave him now was a lingering sense of doubt.

His thoughts were cut short by moonrise. As the transformation began, he was sure that he heard screams not far away.

As always when there were humans to be smelled, the wolf pawed at the gates of the castle, trying to find some purchase for tooth or paw. At the sound of a lupine cry, he dropped back on all fours and turned. He heard it again, a growl from beyond the jumbled rocks surrounding the castle walls. He trotted cautiously up the path leading away from the castle. By the smell, Vlad was nearby. Something slammed into him with a growl as he rounded a large pile of rocks, knocking him to the ground.

No longer able to wonder if an orchestrated plot was at work, all he could do was fight. He twisted his flank out of the black wolf's jaws and backed away, snarling. There was no time to pounce before he found a shining cord draped around his neck.

The cord was silver, and Caleb howled in pain and rage. Since his first few transformations in his parents' home he had not been confined, and he had never been forced to walk on a leash like a domesticated cur. Even through the thick ruff of fur on his neck, the metal burned and he backed around in circles in a vain attempt to escape it.

His howls grew as the end of the cord flew into the hand of a corpse, which jerked him roughly towards itself. The stench of decay filled his nostrils, nauseating him, his instincts screaming to plant his rear feet in the abomination's stomach and scatter its dead guts.

Another set of footsteps came up the stone path. Caleb had to rely on his hearing since his nose was so contaminated by the smell of vampire. The wolf heard a human voice, a female voice, but was confused as his overloaded senses told him she, too, was dead. He laid his ears back, whining with frustration. She seemed not to fear him, and as she grew closer he sniffed again to confirm his first impression.

Whimpering like a puppy, he scarcely noticed he was tethered to Vlad, or where the vampires were dragging them.

"You're not going to—?" wondered the now-worried female voice. Then another voice, a male voice. One so full of the uniquely human enjoyment of cruelty that the fur on Caleb's back stood up as though he had been a scared beagle, rather than a two-hundred pound werewolf who spent most of his days as a fully qualified wizard.

"Kill them?" Cuza laughed. "Certainly not. They will come in useful, just not yet." As he spoke these words, the vampire looked up towards the bright planet that meant nothing to the wolf, and at the sphere of the moon inching in its direction. "And we don't wish the old fool at the castle to hear our little pets playing, do we?"

With a snap of his fingers the vampire created a pit in the rocky soil, into which he hurled the wolves with a jerk of the silver cord. The leash then undid itself from their necks and coiled around the neck of the pit, forming a low fence that threw the animals back as they attempted to leap it.

Trapped, with nothing to do but fight, fight is what the two wolves did. They knew each other so well by now that they did little damage, each coming in for a quick snap of jaws before he was forced to back off again, as choreographed as a boxing match.

Lamia backed away from the snarling pair in revulsion, while Cuza lingered to watch, his satisfaction a dark inversion of her disgust. She, who had not felt cold for fifty years, shivered and wrapped her arms around her thin chest. Wolves howling around the castle had unnerved her then and did so now. Why had she come back?

"The lunar ward is weakest when the moon is full," Cuza was explaining, having tired of the dogfight. "The Jupiter ward will fail for one hour tonight, as the moon covers the planet in a spectacular occultation that I'm sure your physicist friends will enjoy. With those wards out of the way, living magical creatures will be able to get in. That's why we need Rover and Speckles here." He indicated the snarling and bleeding wolves with cold amusement. "But this isn't why I brought you tonight.

"With the aid of a raven and the appearance of Saturn, a wizard can disable the Jupiter ward with a Kronos curse. A wizard more powerful than myself, unfortunately. The two of us together should be able overcome the ward. And that, my drunken darling, is why I need you with all your wits about you. Just one night, and then you can feast as you have never feasted, forever. I promise you," he paused as Lamia quivered in anticipation, "I promise you the blood of Alexandru Arghezi himself!"

Firelight dances before her eyes, bathing them all in yellow and orange hues. Her husband tells a joke, laughing, and she must laugh, too. The boy smiles; he is so beautiful, his delicate features unlike the hard angular ones of his older brother. The boy—he is my brother now, she corrects herself—looks at her with dark, uncertain eyes.

Lamia's mind was just clear enough that she wondered if she were thinking straight. Coming down off her blood high, what she wanted most was more blood to help her forget the pain, and she had wasted most of the evening pleading with Cuza to let her go hunting. She looked between her two lovers: the ancient one, with his threats and promises, and the new one, reduced to savagery in a bloody pit.

"What do you think of your American wizard now?" sneered Cuza as if reading her mind.

Was it only her fantasy that had imagined intelligence on the face of the gray wolf last month? Face crusted with blood and foam and slobber, he was nothing more than a beast. How could he do this to her?

"Your dogs won't be much use to you soon," she said with a laugh as cruel as Cuza's—or perhaps more so, as it was calculated. The wolves were tiring. Their tongues hung out and their tails drooped.

"They will revive when they get the scent of human blood." Cuza smiled. "They prefer human blood, as we do."

Lamia looked up hopefully, thinking there might be the chance to get some—just a little—somewhere, to ease the longing, the emptiness.

But he shook his head. "Tomorrow, tomorrow," he repeated "...and tomorrow, creeps in this petty pace from day to day, to the last syllable of recorded time."

"A tale told by an idiot, full of sound and fury, signifying nothing," Lamia snapped. Cuza had never been intelligent or educated: just smooth and full of pithy quotes. Unlike Lupeni—but no.

The veiled insult only served to make Cuza smile. "Of course, the Kronos curse will not suffice to get us safely into the castle," the vampire continued, with another look towards the rising moon. "Arghezi has put an Allios Spell on the gates, which I have detected from outside the castle, and will certainly have done the same on all the doors and windows. You should remember that spell will not allow us to pass. Thus, even after the major wards surrounding the castle are breached, these dogs will be able to enter, but we will not."

"Arghezi will doubtless have minor traps inside as well that we will want to disarm," he continued as he pulled objects from his pockets and arranged them on the ground in front of them, lit by the full moon as if it were day. "A simple Desiccation Demon will take care of the running water nicely." The creature was encased in a small glass box, kicking and punching the walls in a frenzy. "The garlic will provide nesting material." Here he produced an egg, the shell off-white and papery like the root vegetable itself. He then indicated the gold chain around her neck, where she held the vial of dark blue glass, and gestured for her to remove the stopper.

The spell he had performed would allow all these things and more to be stored inside the vial, but if the glass broke or the stopper came off, all would be released. She held out the container and he transferred the struggling demon into its new prison, then tapped each of the objects on the ground, causing them to rise up and float inside.

"But, even if all these things work," she said slowly, her mind still not functioning properly, "we will not be able to pass through any door or window in the castle, right?"

A secretive smile formed on his lips as he produced a leather bag from the folds of his robe. He pointed his finger at the bag and opened it deftly with one hand. A swarm of small brown insect-like creatures flew out, hundreds of them, each no bigger than a thumbnail and flying so fast that she could barely make them out. A green haze emanating from Cuza's fingertip enveloped the cloud and he coaxed the large glowing haze into the vial. Lamia quickly stoppered it.

"What are those and how do they help us get into the castle?" she puzzled.

"Those are cedar beetles, somewhat magically enhanced so that they should be capable of eating through a good sized tree in about eight hours."

"But we're not anywhere near—" She stopped herself, remembering suddenly that the huge beams forming the roof of the library and Great Hall were made of long, straight trunks of cedar. She smiled, appreciating anew his obsessive deviousness.

Catching her smile, he replied with obvious pleasure, "This delicate piece of glass will not last long around the neck of a wild animal, especially in the thick of a fight. Breaking it will release enough to wreak havoc with Arghezi's protections against our kind. And any other traps or snares I hope will be disarmed by our lupine friends."

"Lupeni is—is going to die?" Lamia quavered, her emotions see-sawing between malicious glee and weepy despair. She needed human blood or she needed two weeks of physics and rabbits.

"Not before he kills Arghezi, I hope," smiled the ancient vampire. "There is a reason I chose these brutes to deliver our gifts to the castle, rather than tie them around the neck of a sheep or a frog. Add that to the fortunate coincidence of the occultation on the night of the full moon. They will kill your old husband, your first lover, Ana Maria." He spoke the name with sarcasm, but it was the name itself that made her wince.

"But...but..." She was unable to find a protest that didn't invoke sentimental feelings for either Alexandru or Lupeni, feelings she herself was trying to fight.

"Come," said Cuza, pocketing the vial and looking up at the slow but steady progress of the moon toward its meeting with Jupiter, "let us collect our hunting dogs. The fun is about to begin."

30. Night of the Werewolves

ALEXANDRU ARGHEZI SPENT THIS night much as any other, taking his supper in the Great Hall and retiring afterwards to his ornate wooden chair in front of the fireplace. Instead of his customary glass of red wine, however, he had a pot of strong black tea, and his eyes kept straying from the ancient and battered *Atlas of Magical Wards and Enchantments* to the viewhole he had conjured in the castle wall. Traveling through the stone walls of the kitchen and the stable gate, it shaped the granite into a transparent lens that magnified images from several yards around the rear castle entrance. It was not a trivial spell to keep going, and he could feel the drain on his energy as the night progressed. Around his throat he wore a braid of garlic, for vampires preferred the neck, while in his lower pockets he held springs of wolfsbane that would meet werewolves at nose level.

For the first time he watched all of the details of Caleb's transformation, observing how the werewolf carefully folded his clothes and placed them on a rock before changing, and even noticing that he kept his eyes on the eastern sky. Some sort of reverence to the moon goddess, he wondered, or something else?

Caleb was easily the largest werewolf the monster-hunter had ever seen. He eats well here, Alexandru mused, unafraid as the enormous animal placed his paw right over the transparent spot. The wolf seemed to be well acquainted with the principles of fences, gates, and doorknobs, as well—and perhaps also with magical wards. The beast figured out quickly that he wouldn't get into the castle, and turned around to trot off down the stone path to the east, away from Stilpescu.

It had been several years since anyone in the village had been bitten. The moonwards worked well, and Alexandru had trusted Caleb to maintain and reset them as necessary. Caleb performed this task ably and willingly, even managing to ward areas that no local wizard would dare approach, such as the caves above Albimare. Five years ago Alexandru would not have believed that such a creature—such a person—as that could exist, but now he trusted Caleb more than any other. Yesterday's rather vague warnings would come to naught, the old wizard was sure, but he meant to show that he was always alert and that he took no hint of Cuza lightly.

He shut his eyes, dozed a little, the strain of maintaining the spell for the viewhole becoming too great. When he had first sworn to kill Cuza, he had been a young man, proud, energetic, and rash. Now he was old and tired, though perhaps wiser. Of course these concerns would mean nothing to a vampire. When and if they met, would they recognize each other? Did vampires understand aging, and would Alexandru's human mind comprehend a face that hadn't changed in half a century?

He wasn't sure what awakened him from his reverie. Not a noise, certainly, as the viewhole transmitted only images. The magical lens was beginning to darken and blur, so he tapped it once more and inched his chair closer, eyes riveted on the stone path and the stable gate.

"Some more tea, please, Mihail," he said in a tense voice without turning his head.

The servant rose behind him with a clank and lumbered off to the hearth. Alexandru had tried to convince him that he would be better off able to move freely, but Mihail had insisted upon ringing his wrists, ankles, and neck with every item of silver jewelry he could borrow for the night. Rosaries and watches and engagement rings and necklaces, anklets for dancing girls and a brooch from the last century covered him head to toe. Combined with a showy waterfall of purple flowers spilling from his pockets and twined in his hair, he looked like an ancient and bearded bridesmaid.

He brought the tea, clanking all the while, and Alexandru began to relax until, all of a sudden, movement caught his eye. Someone—something was coming up the path.

It was a white wolf, shining bright in the moonlight. A female, he saw, and not a large one. Then were two others, though she was clearly their leader. Caleb had mentioned them, Alexandru recalled vaguely. It didn't occur to him to try to remember their names, but it comforted him that so far, nothing truly out of the ordinary had happened. The second wolf had ungainly limbs and a fluffy neck ruff that testified to his youth. The third was an ordinary gray, like Caleb but without the brown markings on his face.

The white wolf led her followers to a rocky outcropping where they sat with their noses high, listening, watching, and sniffing. Unlike domestic dogs, they were stealthy and alert, their body language muted. They didn't bark or wag their tails or hang out their tongues, and when all three tensed simultaneously with the slightest baring of teeth, Alexandru grew nervous too and followed their line of sight.

This time the gray wolf that appeared was Caleb, but almost unrecognizable as the proud, strong animal he had been scant hours before. Scratched, covered with blood, cowering, he was being driven up the path by—

There was no longer any question of recognizing that face. Unchanged it was, with cruelty and evil that were as eternal as the Dark Magic that animated the Undead features.

Alexandru rose from his chair, placing his teacup carefully on the hearth. "Mihail," he said tensely, "O'Connor's warnings were correct. He is here."

The servant's cry was muffled by the jewelry and flowers, and Alexandru had to force him to approach the viewhole so that he might believe.

Mihail took a brief look, then sprang back with a scream. "He has—he has—"

"Werewolves, yes. They are not his willing companions, you see the silver chains around their necks. What he wants with them, I cannot say."

Mihail fingered all of his own silver, almost incoherent in his terror. "But I… but no—But one of them is—"

"One of them is O'Connor, yes. If he gets in, though that shan't happen, we will spare his life. The others we can kill."

This was clearly not the point Mihail was trying to make. "Not the wolves," he stammered, gesturing and pointing at the lens like a foreigner trying to order pastry in a bakery.

Alexandru approached and regarded the scene once more, then shut his eyes for more than a blink. When he spoke, his voice carried anger and resignation but little surprise. "Ana Maria," he said. He smiled wryly as his former bride blew apart the stable gate with a well-aimed spell. It would take more than that to allow her into her old home.

"Ana Maria—and, and him!" babbled the servant, clanking. "That means—it means—"

"That they are hunting together once more," said Alexandru coldly. "That she is still bound to him by what she called love, over fifty years ago."

"Not him—*him!*" Mihail looked just about ready to faint or throw up, whichever came first. "O'Connor!" he cried, the strain of too many names that could not be pronounced finally getting the better of him.

"O'Connor? But he is their prisoner."

"He said vampires could change, could stop drinking—Those were…they were the Mistress's words."

"Mihail!" Alexandru snapped, drawing close to the servant as if about to slap him. "O'Connor is my trusted companion, and I forbid you to accuse him of consorting with Ana Maria. If it were not for his warnings, we would not be so prepared tonight, and we will both be grateful for his help come morning." His face grew hard. "Right now it is up to you and me to keep our heads. In the library, in the uppermost drawer on the left-hand side, are a gun and a supply of silver bullets. You may fetch them, but as I have told you, we will spare O'Connor."

Having a task seemed to allow Mihail to get hold of himself. He turned clumsily, about to shuffle into the library, when their ears rang with a re-sounding crack. A golden thunderbolt shot from a clear starry sky to strike the ground immediately in front of the stable gate.

The viewhole dimmed just as they caught a glimpse of a large black bird fluttering through the ruined gate, and Mihail's screams were inaudible over the squeals and wails that began to emanate from the stone walls.

All color drained from Alexandru's face. "The ward has been breached," he whispered, but to himself, the magical alarm bells making conversation impossible. "The Jupiter ward." He waved his hand, quieting the alarms to a less painful level, though the walls continued to complain as though they were tender. "I see now why they needed the wolves. We are safe from vampires for the time being, but there is nothing to keep living magical creatures out of the castle."

As if on cue, a concert of howls arose from just outside the walls, within the castle courtyard.

Alexandru listened carefully. "We'll have a spot of bother if all five get in," he said, a false lightness replacing the ice in his tone. "Get those bullets, Mihail…but we spare O'Connor."

"He brought them here!" the servant cried, perhaps unheard, and he turned and forced his reluctant bangled feet across the stone floor into the library.

The gun was in fact where it was supposed to be, and Mihail clutched it to his chest, nearly weeping. But the bullets, where were they? Shouldn't they be with the gun? Panicked, he turned out drawers and kicked the desk, scattering purple flowers all the while.

Suddenly there was a crash and splintering of glass, and the heavy door leading to the greenhouse flew open with the weight of a two-hundred-pound animal. The old servant found himself, for the first time since his early childhood, face-to-face with a werewolf. He didn't know whether it was O'Connor, nor did he care. It was a monster, covered with blood, oblivious to the shards of glass in its fur and paws and leering at the human in the way a famine victim stares at a bowl of porridge. As it howled, Mihail turned to run, tripped on an anklet, and fell flat on his face.

The werewolf approached, then took a whiff of the aconite and retreated back into the greenhouse. It was Caleb, in fact, and he knew the castle—well enough to know that the greenhouse was the easiest way in from the courtyard, and well enough to find the library from there. He wasn't about to try to cross all that wolfsbane, though, and he went back to find Liszka chasing Vlad past an angry Venus Mantrap. Bela was paddling around in the spring, trying to find his way out past meowing pussy willows and a couple of bernacae.

There was a snap and a yelp, and Caleb approached the noise carefully, a wary eye on the Mantrap. But it was one of the hunter's traps that had caught hold of Vlad's hind leg at the thigh, digging its rusty jaws deep into his flesh. The stone under him still glowed blue, and a whisper from his human incarnation stirred in Caleb's memory.

Liszka growled in his ear and he backed off. She was the leader now, and the helpless Vlad was hers to kill. Not staying to witness the spectacle, Caleb helped Bela from the spring and headed through another door into the old kitchens. His ears pressed flat as death cries issued from the greenhouse.

Frightened Grigore joined them, and it was three werewolves who opened the latched door from the greenhouse and wandered into the last room before the Great Hall. They could smell Alexandru now—tainted only slightly with wolfsbane—and they didn't linger. The door out of the kitchens was locked, but Caleb hadn't forgotten all the tricks of his Maine days. He stood on his hind feet, inserted a claw, and listened for the tumblers in the lock to fall.

They were in the Great Hall. Mihail had vanished, trembling and incoherent in his room, leaving Alexandru alone to face three werewolves.

The old wizard summoned his strongest curse and hurled it at Grigore, who stumbled and fell like a tranquilized bear. The spell gave Caleb and Bela enough time to attack, and Alexandru barely had the chance to levitate himself to avoid their snaps. He took off through the castle at a stone-hopping run, changing direction over and over the way rabbits do, leading the wolves towards the stones that gave off a bluish light.

The combination of his vague human memories and Alexandru's stone-hopping dance was enough to tell Caleb to avoid the blue ones. This slowed him down. He began to feel his exhaustion from the ordeal earlier in the evening, and it was difficult to change direction quickly with his large body and long legs. Alexandru was getting away, but somehow the wolf no longer cared, slowing his pace and allowing Bela to pass.

Back in the greenhouse, Vlad was dead. Liszka had been furious to find his throat protected by thick gold chain. She tore at the soft metal and flung it aside, finally getting her target free as her enemy gave up the fight, paralyzed with the pain in his leg. Once accomplished, the act disgusted her and she fled from the sight of the dead body, following the scent of her pack through the open doors to the kitchens and Great Hall. The small sounds of breaking glass had not registered with her, nor did she take note of the noises she left behind: faint buzzing, a gurgle and hiss of water turning to steam, and then a crackle of dry leaves and the topple of a tree.

Grigore was just awakening on the floor inside the Great Hall. Liszka helped him up with nudges from her bloody snout, and she sat back to utter a triumphant howl that would tell her pack they had won.

Her howl was cut short by a cry of pain. Even a werewolf is grieved when her child is hurt, and the suffering voice was Bela's. Liszka went tearing over the stones, Grigore trailing groggily, sniffing Bela's trail until she found him in the entrance hall.

Bela had, like Vlad, been caught in a trap, and Alexandru was advancing on him. Liszka and Grigore sprang at the wizard, not to eat him but to protect their cub, heedless of danger to themselves.

Caleb had other ideas. Those blue stones meant something to him. He sniffed his way into the prison room where he had been earlier that day, smelling his own human scent and knowing somehow that it was friendly, trying to remember what it was he had to do.

There were dozens of levers and pulleys in the room, but only a few that smelled of recent touch. Caleb leaned his paws against them, one at a time, puzzled at their mechanism. Turning wheels and pulling handles were not natural motions to him, and he pushed and gnawed futilely for a while before a lever began to move and loud creaks came from all over the castle.

He had sprung the traps. Exiting the prison to see what the noise had meant, he found Bela unconscious, cursed by Alexandru as he stood in the trap. The wizard was just managing to hold Liszka and Grigore at bay, and as Caleb approached, began levitating the body of the young wolf to hold their attention.

All three watched in horror as Alexandru lifted the apparently lifeless wolf, the youngest of the Fives, the only cub to join their ranks in years. His body fell with a thud inside the prison room, and as his parents ran to his aid, the door was slammed and barred behind them.

Showing no more emotion than if he'd put the cat out for the night, Alexandru secured the steel bar (what he would have given at that moment for a silver one) and went to find Mihail in his bedroom. The servant was sitting bolt upright in bed, clinging to his garlic and purple flowers and moving his lips in supplication to some unknown force. Any sounds he may have made were covered by the ever-present whimper of the damaged wards, but at least the wolves were silent now, walled within the thick stone.

"A—a—are you h-h-hurt, Master Arghezi?" Mihail stammered, faithfully sticking to his duty till the last.

"For now, I am unharmed," Alexandru replied grimly. "But we must both rest while we can. We haven't seen the last of the vampires."

He didn't show it, but he was exhausted. Once in his bedroom he fell immediately into a dreamless sleep, lulled by the moaning walls. The crackling of the desiccated greenhouse and the steady crunching of thousands of cedar beetles went unnoticed as midnight turned to twilight, and twilight to dawn.

37 ✦ Day of the Vampires

WELL BEFORE DAWN LIFE stirred on that cold, gray promontory in the Carpathians, home to Castle Arghezi. Soft moanings issued from the walls inside, remnants of the alarms that told of the breach of the Jupiter wards.

One human was awake, while another slept. Four werewolves were semi-conscious, all wounded to some degree. The fifth werewolf was neither awake nor asleep. His lifeless body lay among shards of glass and the ruins of a once-thriving greenhouse. The floor was covered by toppled trees wreathed in brown leaves, gnarled bare vines, and piles of yellow-brown leaves drifting as if winter had already come.

Humans and near-humans were not the only living creatures in the castle. A few birds flitted about the high-ceilings of the Great Hall and library. Small and cream-colored, they darted silently and swiftly, seeking something over the doors and windows. Occasionally a bird found its mark and then flew through the library, carrying a cream-colored burden in its claws. It escaped into the chilly pre-dawn air through the large, jagged hole in the glass wall of the greenhouse adjacent to the library.

More life, hard to see or to hear, gnawed and chewed with ferocious hunger high above the shelves and books of the library. Thousands of nondescript brown beetles happily munched on the thick beams of cedar supporting the roof. They had been feasting most of the night and had not run out of their favorite food as dawn approached.

Outside the castle, sheep huddled in the stable in the shadow of the outer wall, together with an irritated cow who expected to be milked before too long. Faint rustlings came from the sheep and occasionally soft lowing could be heard from the cow. There were no living creatures on the other side of the wall, yet two figures robed in black stood before the thick stone wall ringing the castle. Before them yawned an arched opening, the broken and twisted remains of a wooden gate lying on either side of the portal.

The two might have been statues carved from a fine, luminous marble. A tall, thin man with a sharp face, dark hair and eyes blacker than pitch stood next to a gaunt and graceful woman, shorter than the man with long dark hair flowing unbound down her back. Neither moved as color seeped from the eastern sky, fading as if the plug had been pulled on a sink full of water of the deepest blue. Neither moved as pale birds bearing bulbs of garlic soared silently over their heads. Neither moved as the round swollen moon flirted with the mountains on the western horizon.

A movement from inside the castle, not a bird but a human in the greenhouse, roused the man to speak.

"He lives," hissed the man to his companion, "and the time has not come to enter the castle. Let us move before we are seen."

The woman allowed herself to be guided away from the archway, giving no indication that she had heard or understood what he said. She stumbled and the man took her in his arms to keep her from falling, circling her waist securely with one hand while languidly stroking her cheek with the other.

"Soon," he whispered as he stared into the inky blackness of her eyes. "Soon we will feast on him, and on any others remaining in the castle."

She trembled, shivering like someone who had spent too long in icy waters, although she could not feel the cold.

"And the others?" she stammered through chattering teeth. "If any of the others are alive…"

"We kill them first, of course," he replied smoothly, tightening his grip on her waist. "The werewolves have served their purpose. They are of no use any more."

She nodded slowly, not meeting his eyes. The taste of human blood, the smell of human blood menaced her by its absence, hurt her because she wanted it so badly and was denied. Soon I will stop thinking about anything, she thought. Soon I will be released from this need.

He let her go, a wickedly pleasant smile on his thin, bloodless lips. In an instant, the two figures vanished and two black bats fluttered above the castle walls, heading in the direction of the four-story tower on the east side of the castle. The side of the tower facing the dawn was now brilliantly lit with the first harsh yellow rays of sun, which the bats avoided. They settled on a window ledge on the shadowed western side, the perch giving them an excellent view of the vaulted wooden roof of the castle.

Alexandru Arghezi stepped over the large pieces of glass as best he could, although his feet crunched harshly on the small shards he could not avoid. His pre-dawn survey of the castle had revealed surprisingly little damage, considering that last night a pack of werewolves had free reign inside for a brief time. Furniture had been knocked over in the Great Hall and library, but the wolves had not had time to destroy much else before he had confined them to the tower room.

Except the greenhouse. How could wolves, even werewolves, wreak such havoc? A rough circle of about six feet in diameter punctured the outer glass wall. Some jagged glass pieces remained, hanging precariously as if about to plummet to the ground. Tendrils of lead, which had supported the panes, curled at the edges of the rent, looking like the blackened fingers of roasted corpses. Elsewhere inside, tables had been toppled and the pots that had rested on them lay scattered and broken randomly on the stone floor. The body of a black werewolf, an average-sized male and one of the ones that Cuza had held prisoner, lay sprawled on the floor. The dried and crusted blood adorning the large wound on the beast's neck told the tale of its death.

They would just as soon kill each other as eat humans, Alexandru thought angrily as he levitated the creature up and out through the wolf-sized hole in the glass. He caused the body to fall with a heavy thud to the ground outside, not wishing to see the sickening transformation that would come soon, turning the dead wolf back into some semblance of human form. The foolish idealist O'Connor talked about them as if they had some kind of animal nobility, but Alexandru had trouble believing it, especially after last night.

With the beast out of his sight, Alexandru saw that the damage to the greenhouse was too extensive and too unusual to have been caused by werewolves alone. Every single plant was dead, and there had been hundreds of them. The pots resting on tables or the floor, the hanging baskets held from great iron hooks on the stone wall, all were filled with shriveled death. The enormous Venus Mantrap lay on its side, no less of a corpse in some ways than the werewolf, its large leaves blackened and curling at the edges. Withered leaves in shades of brown, yellow, and dull green mingled with shards of glass on the floor, or clung to skeletal remains of plants he could no longer recognize. The spring had dried up completely; only the dead bodies of a few fish and bernacae marked where it had been.

More than werewolves, his old foe Cuza was responsible for this destruction. A Desiccation Demon had obviously been at work in the greenhouse, and Alexandru did not doubt that any other water in the rest of the castle would also have vanished. Searching the detritus on the floor, he came across a pale white eggshell, almost a complete half and larger than both of his hands together. Allium birds, he remembered, made their nests from the papery skins of garlic. Release enough of them from a magical egg and they would take all the garlic they could find, flying off to nest.

With a mixture of disgust and appreciation for the horrible cleverness of his enemy, Alexandru threw down the shell, smashing it on the hard stones. The white fragments mingled with glass and dead leaves in a mosaic of ruin. The two werewolves captured by Cuza must have brought these things into the castle by some means that Alexandru had yet to determine. Was this all they had brought? A more thorough search of the castle was called for.

First, however, Alexandru assured himself that the Allios Spell on the greenhouse windows still held. This powerful enchantment, which repelled the Undead, required the heart of a dead vampire to protect an object like a door or window. Alexandru had collected plenty of these in his hunts, but had none on hand currently. He was relieved that the greenhouse was still protected, as were all the other exterior doors and windows.

A vampire couldn't walk through any door in the castle; a bat couldn't fly through any window. Yet Cuza had carefully prepared the way, as if he had some means of gaining entry. This thought made the old wizard slightly nervous, though he would not admit that to himself. He suddenly felt too exposed in the greenhouse and made his way slowly back into the library.

He stood briefly in that room, taking in the high shelves that reached up to the dark roof beams. Books crowded almost to the ceiling, for wizards never worried about needing ladders to reach the highest volumes. He wondered if he should take the time to look up other magical means that Cuza might use to get into the castle. As he righted a couple of fallen chairs, he found a handful of dead beetles on the floor. They were small and unremarkable. Probably they had been swept in from the greenhouse by the invading werewolves, he thought. He threw them down and left the library. Perhaps there would be time later for research. For now, he could not imagine how Cuza hoped to gain entry except by force.

Dawn was breaking. He could see it on the tips of the mountains visible to the north of the castle. Mihail must be roused, and the werewolves as well. When the vampires attacked, he would need all the allies he could get.

Crossing the Great Hall, he caught sight of himself between two large mirrors, and was reassured that not all of the defenses against the Undead had been toppled. The bulbs and braids of garlic that had graced the walls last night, however, had been stripped to the last clove. The image of Cuza came into his mind: tall, arrogant, and looking just as Alexandru remembered him from their last meeting. Last night the hated vampire had stood confidently outside the castle, holding two werewolves on leashes like tame dogs. This had not seemed surprising to the old wizard, since he knew well from experience how werewolves could be subdued with the appropriate silver objects.

Seeing Ana Maria had not surprised him either. Although six years of hunting vampires in the mountains had turned up no mention of his former bride, he always knew she would return—and that she would return with Cuza.

Regret was not something that often troubled Alexandru, but he keenly regretted ever admitting the smoothly mannered stranger who arrived at the castle over five decades ago. An old friend of his father's—that was how Cuza had represented himself, and they had all believed him at the time. For who would suspect a vampire, one of those creatures of Darkness that crept about in the night, of showing up at the door and inviting himself in?

He had been foolish not to read the signs. The smiling stranger's stay lengthened, and Alexandru had been pleased that his lonely wife and shy brother had someone else for company. He was young then, only a few years out of school, concerned with building up the library and with scholarly research. He had not encountered a vampire except in textbooks or in tales from his long-dead father. He did not see the cancer spreading throughout the castle until it was too late—too late for Mircea and for Ana Maria.

How she had railed at him in the end, telling him coldly of her devotion to the stranger who he now knew to be one of the Undead. *He loves me and needs me,* she had declared, *which is more than you ever did.* The words meant nothing to him, for by then he was numb from wave upon wave of betrayal and death. Her dark empty eyes (why hadn't he realized how she had changed?) told him everything he needed to know. His wife was dead, replaced by a cruelly accurate copy, a simulation of life, an abomination.

In the end he had left the castle. He'd known that he was no match against her and Cuza together, and there had been Mircea to deal with. Now it seemed very likely that he would get the opportunity to meet the two of them again, but this time he was not alone. With these thoughts, he hurried to wake the others and begin the preparations.

"Mihail," he intoned from the door of the servant's bedroom, "it is dawn."

The old man was asleep sitting up, one hand clutching a sprig of wolfs-bane, extending it towards an invisible phantom. He'd slept in all of his silver jewelry, all except the brooch, which had apparently been too uncomfortable and lay in a crumpled heap by the bed. His eyes sprung open at his master's call.

"You have nothing more to fear from werewolves," Alexandru informed him somewhat tauntingly. "In fact, they will be able to help us against a worse threat."

At that thought, Mihail's hand went to his neck to feel for his braid of garlic. It was gone.

"Allium birds," his master informed him darkly. "There is no garlic left in the castle, nor water. There is no time to waste. I need you to prepare a potion."

38. Hopeful Monsters

DAWN OFTEN CAUGHT THE werewolves by surprise. When the sun went down on the night of the full moon, they imagined they had always been wolves and always would be, living their twelve hours as if they were a lifetime. Locked in the prison room of Castle Arghezi, behind the high wall that screened the eastern sky, Caleb, Liszka, Bela, and Grigore anticipated no end to their eternal night.

None had slept, occupied with their own wounds and those of their packmates. Grigore was the only one uninjured, and he dutifully licked the punctures on Liszka's neck and shoulders from her battle with Vlad. She was impatient, though, shaking him off to attend to Bela with a concern that was fully maternal.

The young wolf had been unconscious when he was dropped to the stone floor of the prison room. Unable to anticipate his fall, he'd landed at an odd angle that had wrenched one shoulder and broken several ribs. At least his neck and back were unhurt, as Liszka discovered when she nuzzled him all over, instinct telling her the difference between sleep and paralysis.

Worse than the fall, Alexandru's trap, intended for werebears the size of African lions, had severed Bela's right rear paw at the ankle. His entire leg was covered with blood and, unhindered by human disgust or pity, Liszka had spent the night cleaning him up and stopping the bleeding. The magic that let werewolves take lead bullets and killing curses made their wounds heal quickly, but they were still mortal. They could suffocate, break bones, or bleed to death. Any injury unhealed at dawn would become that much more painful, as a werewolf in human form healed only slightly more rapidly than an ordinary wizard.

When Liszka tired, Caleb would step in to help. But most of the time he spent pacing, pawing at the handles and gear levers as if they would tell him what to do. For the first time ever, his wolf incarnation felt guilty. Liszka had led Pack Five to his defense, and her cub had been injured by humans. In a head-lowered, tail-between-his-legs kind of way that admitted of no excuses or apologies, the big gray wolf knew that it was all his fault.

As dawn broke he nuzzled the exhausted Liszka, somewhat surprised that she accepted him without anger, laying her bloody white face over his shoulder in a gesture of weariness and friendship. They stretched out on their sides to transform, quietly enduring one more pain among many.

The stings of his dozens of werewolf bites, and the burns around his neck from the silver cord, were nothing to the human Caleb compared to the pain of responsibility and guilt. "I'm sorry," was the first thing he managed to say, grateful for the darkness that concealed the others' wounds.

Liszka said nothing, taking Bela's head gently in her arms, afraid now to look at the mangled leg she'd spent all night licking. The boy was barely conscious, which was perhaps a good thing.

Half by instinct and half by intellect, Caleb knew that Bela had lost a lot of blood and would need to drink. Casually, for it was a very easy spell, he summoned Water from the greenhouse spring, cupping his hands in anticipation.

He frowned as no water appeared and tried again, forcing his foggy mind to concentrate. He was in worse shape than he thought if even this spell was beyond him. Standing with effort, he went to the unyielding stone door and tried again.

Still he was unable to call or sense water. It was as if none remained in the castle. Had Alexandru strengthened the defenses? It seemed unlikely, and he had no trouble summoning clothes and blankets from his bedroom. Cautiously, afraid to stir up either of their emotions, Caleb approached Liszka and gave her a pillow and blanket for Bela and a set of clothes for her. Grigore hung in the background, miserable and cold, and took a bathrobe with a silent gesture of thanks.

Liszka slipped an old MIT sweatshirt over her head, shivering in the chilly darkness, then pulled on the matching pants. She helped her son into a more comfortable position than the sphinx-like crouch he'd retained as he transformed, covering him with a blanket. Bela's face was chilly and dry, and he needed fluids. But try as he might, Caleb couldn't summon any water.

He could have opened the door with a simple spell, but he doubted that he'd find water more easily by running around the castle, especially as weak and ill as he was. Finally the idea occurred to him to give up on the running spring and feel for fluids in the kitchen. A bottle of wine came first, which was not the thing for an injured, dehydrated werewolf, but on the second try he obtained two liters of fresh apple cider.

Drinking was nearly a miracle for Bela. He still moaned quietly in pain, but his eyes grew clear and he was able to speak a few words. As he dropped into a peaceful sleep, Caleb and the other members of Pack Five finished the juice and lay down to rest. They were all asleep as the first rays of the sun peeked over the castle wall and through the tiny barred window of the prison.

Caleb wasn't sure at first what awakened him. Filtered sunlight dotted the stone floor, illuminating the three werewolves who had given him their unquestioning loyalty for fifty-eight months. And now, when he was no longer their leader, they had come unbidden to his defense. Grigore slept soundly over to one side, his skinny body wrapped in cloaks and blankets against the chill. Liszka and Bela were both sitting up, the mother murmuring words of comfort into her son's ear. Bela looked tired but no longer in agony, the pain replaced by dull dread as he wondered if he was crippled for life.

Despite his guilt, Caleb was proud of Bela, who healed so quickly and was so brave. He'd seen the boy show up abandoned in the forest when he was nine years old, because that was just what the local villagers did when their children were bitten by werewolves. Smart, strong, uncomplaining, Bela had rapidly become a full member of the pack as well as a skilled wizard-in-training.

Caleb hadn't given up his role as Bela's father when he resigned as Alpha, which gave him both gratification and worry. His days were too chaotic for him to always be there, with his second life as a vampire-hunter at the castle, and he suspected he was too irresponsible and conflicted to be able to offer anyone else parental advice. He could give Bela books and grade his homework, sometimes even pat him on the head, but he never really knew the boy. He didn't even know how much his personality traits, both positive and negative, came from the bite he'd received from Vlad.

Was it right to be proud of him for being brave, or was that to be expected of their kind? Certainly Caleb had never considered himself particularly courageous, especially not now, as he called himself a coward and a traitor. The Sixes called him "mad dog" but Vlad's mocking "Fido" was more apt, his dealings with humans putting his own pack at risk. This was part of the reason he had resigned as their leader.

Liszka and Bela had not defended him only to have him abandon them. He would see to it that they had futures, both of them, and Grigore, too— but just what futures, he couldn't imagine. Even now, after all these years, he didn't know if his kind belonged in the city, or even whether they were human. Which was more of a lie, his time at the university, or his greater number of years as Lupeni Alpha of the Transylvanian Alps?

He sat up on his blanket and moved closer to Liszka, who had probably kicked him in her sleep. He wondered if all couples had this bed-hog problem. "Are you all right?" he asked Bela gently, hating himself for the trite phrase, always somehow embarrassed when people were injured or ill.

The boy growled noncommittally and finally turned his red and feverish face to Caleb, showing the only emotion he was really good at. "Kill him," he snarled.

Caleb was startled, but realized when Liszka growled approvingly that it had been her idea.

"You warned him," she said angrily, though with no surprise. "You told him who we were, and described us, and he tried to kill us."

She hadn't been there to hear the description, and the fact that she trusted him so implicitly made Caleb feel even worse. It was true that he had tried to make Alexandru understand how much the white wolf and her young black companion meant to him. He was horribly dismayed that the old wizard hadn't been able to subdue them without hurting them, but he was sure Alexandru would apologize and make amends. Something must have happened by accident, something he had missed or forgotten. Most likely he had mistaken Bela for Vlad.

Caleb was formulating a reply for the glowering Liszka when there was a loud metallic scrape at the door of their prison, and the sound of muttered spells. Liszka pulled both Bela and Caleb closer to her. Grigore awoke and came to huddle on Caleb's other side, blinking with sleepy fear.

Alexandru strode into the room, neatly sidestepping the pool of Bela's blood. "Ah, I see all but one of you survived," he said cheerily. "Good. I'm having Mihail brew some Poultice Potion now, so you'll be useful when the vampires arrive."

In a split second, all of his excuses for this human fell to pieces in Caleb's brain. Alexandru could see the blood, he could see that Bela could barely sit up and that all of them were dazed with grief and pain—and "useful"? "All but one," as if Vlad were the equivalent of one of Caleb's pack?

Caleb was furious. The fact that he had no words to express his bonds to Liszka and Bela made it all the worse. If he derided Alexandru for injuring his wife and son, it would make no sense to the old wizard, for by human laws they were not. His mate and pup? Even worse, when what angered him was being treated like an animal.

Then Alexandru walked calmly over to the levers and moved to reset the traps.

There was only one thing Caleb could say, and that was a low, angry growl that would have made any listener wonder whether he had transformed back.

His growl was not alone. It was almost inaudible, in fact, over those of the other Fives. Beside him, Liszka tensed as if preparing to spring.

"Don't touch that." Caleb knew where his loyalties would lie if Alexandru attacked Liszka. "Don't you dare."

The old wizard turned, and regarded the wolf pack with a stony face that betrayed nothing. But he took his hand off the lever and backed out of the room, magically locking the door behind him.

"You see?" Liszka demanded. "Kill him."

Caleb stood up to follow Alexandru, but nearly fell over from stabbing pains from ankles to neck, souvenirs of a nasty tangle with Vlad and the vampires, of which he now remembered little.

Had it been Cuza last night? He couldn't begin to guess, and efforts to recall only drove the memories still deeper. Walking stiffly out of the room, trying not to move any joints or muscles more than necessary, he wondered if he could get past his differences with Alexandru enough to ask.

He knew the old wizard well, and could forgive much if he had finally been confronted with his arch-nemesis. Like Caleb, Alexandru often reacted to panic by becoming excessively cool and collected, and all Caleb expected of him now was an apology to Liszka and Bela, an acknowledgment that they were brave and hurt but that he was asking humbly for their help.

It's simply a matter of respect, he told himself. If there was one thing he couldn't endure, it was someone who treated others as inferiors when they were in no position to fight back.

He found Alexandru in the Great Hall, standing watch over Mihail as the latter added sprigs of flowering dogwood to the Poultice Potion—that instead of wolfsbane, since the werewolves didn't want or need an antidote to their own magic. Dogwood would heal the bites and scratches as well as cure fever. As usual, the Romanian servant was as canny a potion-brewer as any MIT chemist.

Just watching it bubble made Caleb feel better, even as he battled exhaustion, pain, and anger. He hadn't seen Mihail's fancy-dress of last night, or at least didn't remember it, and now was somewhat startled to notice that the servant wore a mirrored ball gown.

This was not the time to worry about transvestite tendencies. "I believe you owe Liszka and Bela an apology," he said coldly, wondering which of them would lose his self-control first on this grim autumn morning.

The brief puzzled look on Alexandru's face—clearly he had forgotten their names—enraged Caleb so much he almost didn't hear the words. "I only did what was necessary," the old man said. "It's too bad, but when your kind pose a threat—"

"We were a threat to no one," Caleb hissed. "You could have worn wolfsbane and retired to your room until dawn, rather than play games with your own life and the lives of my family."

He could only guess what Alexandru had done, but his guess was good enough, as it made the monster-hunter flinch. "I am not one to hide in my room," he responded, self-control weakening. "I shan't do so today, when Cuza returns—and neither shall you."

He's giving me orders, Caleb thought in surprise. It was almost funny. "I will do what I can for my loved ones, but don't be so sure that I will risk my life for a murderer."

39. The Gang's All Here

CALEB'S CRUEL WORDS FINALLY melted Alexandru's cool. "I hired you to hunt monsters, not to consort with them," he bellowed, his yell causing Mihail to startle and drop his pestle into the potion.

The werewolf stayed calm. It was always easier when he felt he was winning. "Someday you might ask yourself just who is the monster," he rejoined casually.

Alexandru's response was to look Caleb insolently up and down, his eyes lingering on the clots of blood and matted hair on his clothes, the face shadowed from a night of sleeplessness and the strain of the Dark magic that powered the transformation.

"Perhaps it's you," the old wizard inquired pointedly, "who has been killing hunters who come into the mountains?"

"Killing, no." Caleb smiled. "Scaring, yes. It's too bad, but I only did what was necessary," he echoed. Caleb was no longer a teenager—he was twenty-two—and he would not let the old wizard patronize or intimidate him, nor would he apologize for what he was. "Perhaps you should consider not only the opinions of your own kind, but try to see yourself as others do," he declared. "But I don't suppose that will happen until the day you die."

"Which will very likely be this morning," said the old wizard in a quiet voice. When this silenced Caleb, he told matter-of-factly of the Allium birds, the desiccated greenhouse, that he had seen Cuza just outside the stable gate. The Jupiter ward could not be reset until after nightfall, when the planet reappeared, and even then Alexandru wasn't sure he could overcome the Kronos curse. "There is no good in a vampire," he said, regaining his cool, professorial tone. "He is coming to kill me, and you too, I expect, and I do not know how many allies he has gathered around him."

Caleb remained unconvinced. "Cuza may be evil," he agreed, "but what if I told you of a vampire who has lived as a human for more than a decade? Abstaining from human blood and living only a—a life of the mind?"

"I would tell you it cannot last," Alexandru replied.

"And that's where you're wrong," Caleb retorted, now angry in his turn. "And a bigot."

Alexandru didn't get a chance to respond, as there was a sound of footsteps and dragging fabric behind them. The old MIT sweatpants were much too big on Liszka, who'd tried unsuccessfully to roll them up around her ankles. She glared at Caleb, who after six years as her mate and co-Alpha knew that look. *Kill the human, Fido.*

Alexandru, of course, didn't know Liszka. "You don't think I'm a bigot, and a monster, do you, young lady?" he wondered, his condescension making Caleb want to tear his eyes out.

Liszka wasn't much for verbal duels. "A monster? No—you're a human," she said somewhat timidly, not knowing that to Alexandru that was a compliment.

"Which means you behave more viciously and ignobly than any monster," Caleb translated.

Liszka growled in agreement, and it wasn't clear how Alexandru was going to respond. The Fives' leader glared at him, circling nearer, suspicious that he had magic that, this morning, could kill her. She was not without magic of her own—Caleb had seen her defeat magical creatures twice her size—but she wouldn't last long against a powerful wizard, if it came to that.

Her appraisal of the wizard was interrupted by a sudden, splintering crash from the library.

Groaning and creaking noises from the library preceded the final collapse of the roof. The thick cedar beams holding up the roof had been flexing for some time, growing progressively thinner as the relentlessly hungry beetles ate through them—but the sounds had gone unheeded as tempers flared.

At some point, one beam became so weak that it bent instead of flexing. The sharp crack could be heard throughout the castle, waking Bela and frightening Grigore in the tower room, and silencing the murderous argument in the Great Hall. The loud report was followed by an avalanche of sounds, as the shelves tumbled down like a house of cards under the weight of the wooden roof and books flowed along in a chaotic jumble. A few books spilled out of the library and into the Great Hall, skidding across the floor to meet Alexandru, who had forgotten the werewolves and run to the open door.

Several centuries of dust billowed into the Great Hall, temporarily obscuring the old wizard from view. The others heard him coughing and momentarily saw him again, peering into the destruction now visible in the former library. Caleb hurried to his side, hearing the roof of the Great Hall creak ominously as he ran, and wondering if they would all suffer the same fate as the books soon.

"There," muttered Alexandru, looking up through the large hole which now graced the roof above the library. "Two of them, as I guessed."

Caleb looked up to see glimpses of ragged black wings against white clouds and blue sky, disappearing against the darker background of aged wood.

"Vampires have entered the castle," he said grimly. "Any idea how?"

Mihail gave a shriek in the background, and began speaking rapidly and incoherently. Alexandru ignored his old servant to ponder the question. As was typical of him, he betrayed little excitement, although Caleb suspected that he must be holding in a great deal of emotion. These two vampires, who had brought together an astounding array of magical weapons and waited patiently for the aid of celestial events, were not simply out for blood. They and Alexandru must be bitter enemies in a way that Caleb, with the disjointed fragments of Arghezi history that he knew, couldn't begin to fathom.

Unhurriedly, the older wizard squatted down and sifted through the dust thickly coating the floor near the library door. He stood and held out his hand to Caleb, showing a collection of beetles, some still wriggling and climbing over one another in his palm.

"I fancy these are responsible," he replied thoughtfully. "They could be induced to gnaw at the roof beams very quickly with the right enchantment. As to how they got here, I believe that the werewolves were made to carry them in last night by some means."

Caleb noted the neutral tones in Alexandru's voice and the careful choice of words. While not an apology, it at least suggested that he did not blame the werewolves for what had happened.

That was somehow worse. If he didn't blame them, why was he incapable of treating the others with the courtesy he showed Caleb?

He had to tell himself over and over that they would fight Cuza first, and deal with Alexandru later.

"Two vampires," Alexandru declared more loudly, turning away from the library door to face the stricken Mihail, clutching at the sides of his cauldron near the hearth. Liszka stood nearby, tensely trying to read the expression on Lupeni's face for guidance.

"We must make what preparations we can," Alexandru continued, throwing down the handful of dusty bugs. With a startling rapidity, he raised his arms and called forth an incantation that uncovered the last of the huge mirrors, each one about twenty feet wide and forty feet high. Now all four walls of the Great Hall sported mirrors.

Caleb, in turn, summoned the sunstone from his room. This small fist-sized lump of rock had served him well against vampires in caves and barns, but he wondered if it would work at all in the large, open hall. Still, they had to use what weapons were on hand.

He stepped quickly over to Liszka and murmured in her ear, "Take the potion to Bela and Grigore, and make sure they're safe."

She looked at him doubtfully—and then she turned her head slightly towards the prison room and gave a long howl. When a cry came back in response, she translated it for Caleb as though he weren't one of them. "They're fine," she said, "they'll lock themselves in. I'm with you, Lupeni. I've come this far."

"But there are vampires here." She had hunted creatures with him many times, but he didn't think she'd ever encountered a vampire, certainly not one who had been a wizard in life. "Powerful ones."

"Vampires?" she shrugged. "They can bite me."

Determined both to protect her and to prove to Alexandru that she should be respected, Caleb handed her the sunstone and told her how to work it. That gave him his hands free to summon objects and to hold a stake.

Meanwhile, Mihail had continued to babble. Something about the look of grim determination on his master's face, combined with Liszka's methods of communication, caused him to lose all vestiges of self-control and fly into a panic. He shuffled from the room as fast as his old joints and fluted ball gown would allow. Although not screaming, he muttered incessantly and disconnectedly to himself. The occasional proper noun that reached Caleb's ears hinted that he was reliving vampire horrors of a half-century ago.

The servant found refuge in the only place he knew—his bedroom, which until last night had been guarded against several forms of Dark magic. Now, his garlic mysteriously vanished, his wolfsbane dried out, there was nothing he could do but lock the door tightly, using the strongest enchantment he knew to block it against forceful entry. He hoped that would be enough.

He could not just crawl under his covers and wait to die. Instead, he sat bolt upright in bed. He did not have long to wait. Soon, as he feared, tendrils of gray mist seeped under the door, creeping across the floor, growing larger and rising into a shape.

A shape that he recognized. He ceased to mutter to himself, only whispered two soft words as the shape took on the features he would never forget: "Ana Maria."

For it was she, the pallor and depthless eyes of the Undead only adding to her ethereal beauty. She parted her lips, a scimitar of a smile spreading across her face, revealing her softly shining, pointed teeth. Mihail forgot he was afraid as she began her song, one that he had heard distantly in this very castle long, long ago.

"Come to me," she sang, and he obeyed.

In the Great Hall, meanwhile, a lone bat came to rest on a windowsill opposite the large mirrors. Alexandru, Caleb, and Liszka stood ready.

"Helios!" cried Liszka, as her sensitive ears picked up the faintest pop.

But the blinding white light was reflected back into their faces, making them squint. A thick fog had appeared suddenly in the hall, its tiny droplets refracting the sunstone's rays into thousands of tiny rainbows. The scene would have been mesmerizing with its beauty were it not for Cuza's cruel laughter echoing around the cavernous stone room.

"How do I turn this thing off?" Liszka muttered, blinking.

Caleb murmured "vesper" and tapped the stone with his finger. Once it was extinguished, the fog no longer entranced them, but they could see no more clearly.

Alexandru had a stake out and was turning around in circles, trying to locate his enemy by shadow or sound. Liszka growled quietly and Caleb knew exactly what she was thinking: it would be so nice to have movable ears. But perhaps that didn't matter—perhaps Cuza's voice didn't tell them his location, as it bounced around from the ceiling to the fireplace to the entrance hall.

"Where am I?" he taunted his ancient foe. "Over here? Or over there? ... Or right beside you?"

Alexandru jumped as the voice appeared to hover over his shoulder, but then it was gone again.

"So many traps," came the voice, and there was a flash of light and a tinkle of broken glass. The vampire-hunters couldn't see what had happened, but they could guess that Cuza was destroying the mirrors under protection of the fog. "So many wards." Another crash.

Caleb and Alexandru came to their senses at once.

The old wizard called Wind, and it came strong and hot, whipping through the Great Hall, stirring up the fog but doing little to disperse it. But at the same time…

Caleb summoned Fire, and the walls began to glow red-hot, the fog condensing onto them and dribbling to the floor like rain.

They could see the vampire now, strutting boldly through the garlic-free, mirrorless Great Hall.

"Boys, boys," purred Cuza, turning to regard them all with a bloodless hatred. "You should know better."

Caleb and Alexandru exchanged a quick glance. What of their magical repertoire remained?

Liszka lit the sunstone once more, but Cuza quickly traced a complicated figure in the air that stopped the rays in their path, focusing them back into a narrow beam that seared her hair and made her yelp. She dropped it like a hot coal, and the brilliant stone hit the floor with a sharp crack, rolling toward the vampire. Cuza casually pointed a foot at the brightly glowing lump and kicked it behind him, his look daring them to retrieve it.

"That's better," Cuza grinned slyly. "Now I feel more at home. Your hospitality was much better on my last visit, Arghezi."

Alexandru drew himself up to his full height, slightly taller than the vampire who stood some twenty feet in front of him. He spat two harsh words: "Get out," raising his hand to cast a spell.

The vampire seemed nonplused. "Has not his hospitality worsened?" drawled Cuza, looking over the heads of all three of his foes toward the door behind them. "What do you say to that, my dear?"

A clear and brutal laugh made all three heads turn.

Not quite as tall as Cuza, equally thin, but rosy-cheeked and swaying slightly with tipsy pleasure, was Lamia. Two trails of blood dribbled from her pointed teeth down her chin and across the white hollows of her collarbone. As she spoke, she drew her tongue around her mouth so as not to miss a drop.

"Lamia!" cried Caleb, not with accusation but with wild grief. The arm holding the stake fell, unable to point it at her. He had just finished defending her, not only because he loved her, but because she stood for everything that he wanted desperately to believe—that darkness didn't have to destroy those it inhabited.

His gesture and the tone of his voice might have gone unnoticed to Alexandru if it weren't for Liszka's response. She wasn't jealous, she wasn't even angry, but she clearly knew what the relationship between Lamia and Caleb had been. It was as if wild wolf had seen her mate trotting down a sidewalk wearing a collar and knitted dog sweater. "You're foaming, mad dog," Liszka grumbled, stomping her foot. "I don't know why I came out here to save your tail."

Alexandru looked quickly at her, paying less attention to her slangy statement than her blazing eyes and flushed face. "YOU!" he roared, losing his temper with Caleb at last, waving his arm in a vain attempt to cover both werewolves and both vampires at once. "With ANA MARIA!"

Caleb gaped at his mysterious lover, who continued to sway, dripping blood. He raised the stake—and paused. He was caught between Liszka and Lamia, two creatures who had only done what came naturally to them until he, mad Fido the monster-hunter, came along to try and stop them. What right could he possibly have thought he had?

In the second that he hesitated, Lamia reached for the sky and hurled a curse at Liszka.

40. Into the Abyss

THICK, BLACK SMOKE BEGAN to fill the Great Hall.

It was not the result of any magical spell but the product of simple fire. The hangings on the wall, colorful tapestries that had once livened up the forbidding stone walls, had caught fire from the blasts of magical energy unleashed by four wizards. Flames licked upwards towards the great wooden roof beams.

Caleb was worried less about fire than about ominous rumblings from the roof above. He watched with horror and fascination as first one, then another of the huge posts supporting the roof came loose and tipped ominously toward the floor. Time slowed, allowing him to trace the path of the beams as they plummeted slowly downward, encumbered by large sections of the roof still attached to them.

Alexandru, intent on hurtling a curse at the back of his nemesis, didn't notice the destruction arriving from above. Caleb shouted to him hoarsely over the tumult of roaring fire and falling roof. In an instant several things occurred that Caleb did not understand clearly at the time. Only months later, after agonizing endlessly over the events of that horrible day, did he piece together the crash and its aftermath.

His shout prompted Liszka to drop the large shard of mirror which she held in front of the menacing vampire. Cuza turned to face Alexandru, a look of ancient, alien hatred or longing on his face—Caleb was never sure if human emotions could be applied to vampires. As Liszka ran toward Caleb, Alexandru let fly a curse that struck Cuza full on, sending him sprawling across the floor.

Caleb had no time to wonder what spell the old wizard had used. He was more concerned with the immediate danger to Alexandru from above, and there was no chance afterward to ask.

If he could somehow deflect the falling mass of wood, the old wizard might escape the ruinous collapse. Alexandru seemed insensible to his shouts, too intent on the duel and on staring at Cuza's fallen body.

Desperately, Caleb thought that together he and Liszka might be able to magically protect the old wizard. They had moved timber before while hunting monsters, although never so much and so quickly.

"Liszka!" he yelled frantically, gesturing upward and trying to create a powerful enough spell.

Her only response was to howl. She didn't need words to tell him that she would never help the human who had callously tried to kill her son.

Then the crash came. Time resumed its normal flow as beam and plank met stone with an earsplitting uproar. Too many noises collided at once to be able to pick out the sound of wood crushing bone. But after several heartbeats, the din retreated and Caleb heard the anguished cries, saw the pained face of his former teacher and friend. Alexandru lay pinned under one of the roof beams, which was finally at rest after a long fall that seemed to take hours.

"Liszka," he pleaded, no longer shouting but still retaining a sense of urgency to his voice. "Help me shift this."

This time she complied, but none too hurriedly, like a fox-hunter removing his prey from a trap. Together they managed to move the huge hunk of wood enough to pull Alexandru free. Caleb knelt beside the old wizard, assessing the extent of his wounds and wondering whether he could heal so much damage.

"Fool," murmured Alexandru, his face drained of color and looking harder than normal, like a rough imitation of a human face crudely chipped out of marble. Liszka uttered a low hiss in the background, but Caleb did not let go. He could not abandon the man who had sheltered and taught him for five years, in spite of the enormous gulf that seemed to separate them.

"Caleb, I was a fool," he whispered, weakly gripping the young wizard's arm, "not to tell you about her. If only you had known."

"Hush, save your strength," Caleb replied. The old man's labored breathing filled him with dread. With a bitterness that took him by surprise, Caleb continued, "I am more the fool for believing her lies. Here, let me help you sit and take care of your—"

"No!" cried Alexandru sharply. "Listen to me now, I don't have much time.

I, too, was taken in by a vampire, but only my pride prevented me from telling you. I could not bear to tell you that I had admitted a vampire to this castle. Under my nose my wife, my brother, and others succumbed while I blindly pursued my own ambitions. You should have been prepared for what can happen when a vampire calls…"

"Nothing could have prepared me," Caleb replied, angry.

"It is your curse," began the old man.

Caleb flinched at the word, sure of what was coming next.

But Alexandru continued tenderly. "Your curse…to be able to see the human in everyone, even in monsters."

Too shocked to speak, Caleb could only stare at his dying friend whose face had become an ashen gray and whose breath rattled hoarsely and shallowly.

"You taught me much," Alexandru murmured, his voice becoming softer and less distinct, as if most of him had departed already. "Apologize to your… family for me. I wronged them as much as I wronged you."

Caleb put his arms around the man's once strong shoulders, unwilling to let him go.

"You must finish—for me. You must destroy the evil that was let—that I let out into the world."

"I promise," Caleb whispered. "I promise."

"Mircea," was all that Alexandru managed to breathe before Caleb felt the life slip away, leaving him holding the shell of someone who had meant more to him than he ever realized.

Gently, Caleb laid the dead man's head on the stone floor, wishing there had been more time for goodbye. At the same time he prayed that the leave-taking hadn't given the vampires the upper hand.

His face was a grim mask when he rose and said to Liszka, "Have you seen them?"

"Think they're buried under that," she replied tersely, pointing to a large pile of wooden debris, at least six feet high and impenetrably dark inside.

The smoke was beginning to get thick, drifting heavily down to floor-level from the burning tapestries above. Caleb hoped that it hadn't spread to the roof and thence to the west wing. He felt certain that Bela and Grigore would be safe from fire in the tower room, but the smoke might still kill them. Then there was Mihail, who was probably unconscious in the west wing somewhere.

Those were his secondary concerns. The primary one was finding the vampires.

He did not have long to wait, as a pair of bats fluttered above the large mass of debris, weaving in and out of the roiling and acrid smoke. Caleb retrieved the sunstone from the floor and levitated it so that its blinding light pierced the smoke. Both bats were stricken. One dropped to the floor several yards from Caleb while the other flew unsteadily away, fluttering out the door leading to the entrance hall.

One at a time, Caleb thought, grateful that he had hit one of them at least. There was no telling how long the effect would last. He wasted no time, ripping several strips of wood from a splintered roof plank to serve as stakes, hardly feeling the searing pain as sharp splinters jammed into his palms.

"Go get Bela and Grigore," he directed Liszka. "We can't stay in the castle much longer."

She looked at him with a rough pride, happy to see the Alpha that she thought had disappeared, and quickly left. Caleb turned to face the vampire lying in a motionless heap on the floor. At first he saw only the folds of the dusty black cloak, not realizing that it was Cuza until he approached and stood over the body. The dizzying sense of relief stunned him. He didn't have to face *her* yet.

Swiftly, he knelt and turned the corpse on its back. With a casualness born of many years' hunting in the mountains of Transylvania, he drove one of the crude stakes through Cuza's heart, feeling the end jam up against the hard stone of the floor underneath. This ought to finish off any vampire, but with all he had heard about Cuza, he had to wonder. He would feel much better after the corpse had been burned.

Before he could finally dispose of Alexandru's worst enemy, however, he had to find his former wife.

Sunstone in one hand and stake in the other, Caleb left the Great Hall in search of the vampire he had loved. Was he mistaken to believe that some of the human still existed within her, and that he had touched it in some way? She was like the smoke filling the Great Hall and keeping pace with him as he strode across the entrance hall, a real presence but impossible to hold for long. He hardly knew what he would say or do when he found her, but he felt a strong compulsion to be with her, whatever the outcome.

He found her in the portrait gallery, limping slightly and trailing one hand along the wall, brushing her fingers over the ornate frames. The dim gallery, a wide corridor with no windows of its own, lay in deep shadow. A smoky haze clung to the ceiling. As he made his way slowly down the passage he remembered a much younger man, drunk on too much wine, stumbling down the same gallery staring at the same portraits.

She stopped near the end of the gallery, her attention fixed on the final pictures in the sequence. Caleb knew them well, knew why she would want to stop there.

Overwhelmed by the darkness, he suddenly called for wisps of Fire to light the candles placed in sconces along the wall. The flames danced and hissed in the smoky atmosphere.

She turned at the sound, raising her hand defensively. From her pale face, half in shadow and half in the flickering yellow light, depthless eyes regarded him impassively. For the first time he looked into their emptiness, without the peculiar lenses she had worn to shield them.

"Cuza's dead," Caleb called softly as he approached, "and so is Alexandru."

His arms hung limply at his sides. Why couldn't he raise his hand against her, knowing now what she truly was?

"You," she moaned angrily, swaying slightly and steadying herself on the wall, "what are you? You are a lie straight through! I thought that you—" She broke off, her hand wavering, but still pointing directly at him. He stopped some six feet away from her. She could kill him any time, but maybe he deserved to die for being such a fool.

"I lied about many things," he replied harshly, "but not about what I felt for you. What am I? A failed human? A failed monster?" At that moment, he could not understand himself any more than he could her. He continued more gently, almost to himself, "And I thought that you had changed. What happened, Lamia?"

Her hand shook more violently as she spat, "Don't call me that! I'm not—I can't be that any more. And you must…not…call me…that…"

Those last words came out slowly, painfully, through clenched teeth. She fought a battle inside herself, evident from the trembling that overpowered her, making her thin frame shake.

She turned away from him, face toward the wall, and gasped suddenly at something there. Caleb approached cautiously and saw that she faced the portrait of the Arghezi brothers: the familiar young, stony-faced Alexandru and his brother, Mircea.

She moaned his name softly, insensible to Caleb now standing beside her.

"He was so beautiful," she murmured after several moments, acknowledging Caleb's presence while staring raptly at the portrait.

He looked at the boy of about eighteen who smiled shyly from the painting. The same deep, dark eyes as Alexandru's looked out at them, but in a softer face, almost beautiful with its sweeping cheekbones and delicately curving smile.

"I tried to find him, you know?" Lamia said dreamily. "Alexandru drove him away. I heard he went to New York or Miami, but I couldn't find him. Alexandru hunted for him over there, so maybe he…"

Lamia turned to him, her eyes seething with emotions, almost human in a way that Caleb ached to touch. Even knowing her history and her crimes, he still loved that part of her that had been—was still—human. "Tell me your name, your real name," she said, her dark eyes once again unreadable to him.

"Caleb O'Connor."

"I loved you, Caleb O'Connor," she stated with a quiet conviction that he would never forget. "If you loved me, there is a gift that I would ask from you."

He understood her words fully as she raised her hands and grasped his other hand, the one containing the crude stake.

"No," he began softly, denial, regret, and horror all creeping into his voice, forcing it to be louder until he shouted, "No! Don't ask me to—"

She appeared not to hear him as she caressed his hand with hers and bent her head down to lick his wounds, tasting him in a way she had denied herself before.

"Now I shall go mad," she murmured with a trace of her old humor. Straightening up, she faced him and said, "I tried, and failed, to live in two different worlds. Sleep is all I want now. That is the gift you can give me."

Slowly he nodded, understanding her need, but reluctant to carry out her request. He felt keenly what it was to balance both the human and the wolf inside himself. Did that even come close to her struggle? He had believed that the Undead should not prey on the living, but should give up their imitation of life for some final rest. Could he give this to her?

He searched her face and found there a trace of her pain, scraps and shreds of human emotion that vampires were supposed to leave behind. He could free her from that pain.

Grigore found him kneeling on the floor, hunched over the still body as the flickering candles threw monstrous shadows on the floor and walls.

"Lupeni," he began hesitantly, "Liszka Alpha asked me to find you. She says we should leave."

Caleb did not answer at first, making Grigore shuffle nervously. Then, without looking up, he said hoarsely, "There are a few things to do first."

He lifted his head and stared up at the Beta with red-rimmed eyes, but his voice was clear as he said, "Find the other vampire in the Great Hall. Take it out into the castle yard and burn it."

Slowly and with great reluctance, Grigore nodded his head, eyes wide with terror.

"Go on," Caleb said, "it won't bite. I will be out shortly."

Despite those words, it was some time before Caleb came stumbling out of the castle, bearing her in his arms, ready to attend to his duty to the living once more.

41. Picking Up the Pieces

CALEB WOKE UP IN a dusty and dilapidated room, covered with werewolf bites. He couldn't see the worst injuries without painfully twisting his neck.

His half-delirious thoughts flowed in odd directions. The graduate students…Mike had been bitten and scratched by many creatures he didn't believe in. He had come to accept that Caleb was part of this mythical world; once he returned to a place free of monsters—New York City, or California—would he come up with a "scientific explanation" for everything that had happened?

A sharp pain…Was it Fang Formula that Mihail had prepared yesterday, or Poultice Potion? The book…well, it had probably been destroyed in the fire. Mihail couldn't help, not suffering as he was from a vampire bite, smoke inhalation, and—Caleb smiled wryly—a good case of the heebie-jeebies. Mihail nearly had a heart attack when Caleb suggested he go to Grigore's cottage with Liszka and Bela, rather than sleep in the granary with the mice. Mice or no mice, Mihail was not about to be thrown to the wolves.

Garlic, ginger, ginseng, spider silk, nightshade, mandragora floated through. That was the Fang Formula, the one Mihail had helped him make years ago for…

…Bela, Caleb put his face into the wadded-up blanket pillow, sick with worry. He saw visions of the dangerously ill little boy, whose throat Vlad had tried to tear out—who later complained that Caleb's potion was too good, because who would believe he was a werewolf if he didn't have a scar?

Now a teenager, this intrepid young wolf had survived the conflagration at Castle Arghezi—but not unscathed. What would become of him now that he had lost a foot? Caleb knew the boy wanted to be a pack leader someday. It was not what Caleb wanted for him, but Bela had the right to make his own way in the world.

The question was too painful. Caleb sighed deeply to clear the dreamlike images from his cloudy mind. He would check on Mihail, and the castle, and then he would worry about Bela.

The chill morning air helped clear Caleb's head as he sat up and tried to plan for the day. His eyes burned from smoke, and a deep breath made him cough. He gingerly stood up and looked around the granary, one of the few rooms untouched by the magical battle or by fire. Mihail slept between two sacks of rye flour, his face pallid from the vampire attack but his breathing steady.

Caleb called out to Mihail, but he didn't awaken, so Caleb gently shook the old man's shoulder. With fatigue so profound even his eyelids were heavy, the servant blinked—then his eyes stuck open in helpless terror as he realized what had happened, where he was, and who was touching him.

"Relax," said Caleb, fighting the urge to say, "I don't bite." How could he think about cracking jokes this morning? "Don't...don't be scared." Even in his role as "Dad," he'd rarely had to say those words. "Um... well, look, you were bitten by a vampire. Only once, you're in no danger, but I thought—if I could brew a potion for you, a blood regenerator, you would get better more quickly."

"Potion...Don't need fancy potion...Drink..." Mihail was winded just saying the few words.

"You want a drink?"

"Don't...regenerate. Drink!"

"You want to drink blood? From a...?"

"Chicken," Mihail murmured, and closed his eyes again.

Getting a glass of chicken blood was easier than brewing a complex potion, but Caleb was not looking forward to the task as he headed for the stable.

Passing by the ruined greenhouse, Caleb saw that the gaping hole was no longer splintered; it had been warped and melted into a twisted orifice by a roaring inferno, ignited by a single spark from the wizards' fight.

The flames had quickly spread into the library, where the piles of books and the abundance of air in the tall room fanned the flames. The lead strips supporting the panels of greenhouse glass had softened, so that the glass fell and shattered on the stone floor, shards melting against hot stones. Droplets of glass and metal spattered the floor, frozen now into tongues and globes; what panels remained in place were cracked in bizarre patterns and hung precariously from their supports. It was beautiful in the way that the tree molds and barren black fields of Vesuvius were beautiful, a testament to the narrow range of conditions demanded by precarious Life. Caleb mourned the loss of the budding, chirping, and snapping plants as he searched through the ruins for signs of Vlad or Grigore.

Caleb was quite certain Vlad was dead, but he had yet to find Grigore, and Cuza weighed on his mind. Certainly the vampire hadn't escaped somehow? He cursed himself for entrusting such an important task to the Beta.

The door from the greenhouse to the kitchens was open, and a black streak of charred wood and leaves formed an arrow across the floor. This was the only damage from fire, as the room was mostly stone, but holes gaped in the ceiling after the struggle to reset the Jupiter wards.

The cupboards containing the potion ingredients were mostly intact, and all but the fresh herbs could still be used—but of course there was no garlic. He filled his pockets with dogwood, ginger, and nightshade, and picked up a small pewter cauldron from the stove. Then he walked out to the ruins of the stable gate and ran his hand along what appeared to be empty space.

It felt solid as a stone wall, and gave off a contented hum as he stroked it, like a cat. Alone, with Alexandru's famous library in ashes, Caleb had successfully reset the Jupiter ward shortly after moonrise.

Both Jupiter and Saturn had been visible as the nearly full moon rose. Caleb's first attempt to disarm the Kronos curse brought the screams of a raven, which raked his hands with invisible claws. He stared at the sky. Jupiter was forty degrees to the right of the moon; Saturn, slightly to its left, dimmed by its red light but by no means occulted.

This configuration favored Caleb's strength. He would create a moonward, and have it deflect Saturn while he called on Jupiter. It would take very little to shift the power balance, as well, for Jupiter was stronger than Kronos.

He began with the simplest ward, the one he'd put on every path into every village for twenty miles in any direction. Then, recalling all of the times he had let entered and exited the castle, he pointed his arm at the stable gate and summoned Jupiter.

Nothing happened; the spell rebounded as before, and he was knocked flat on his back. He exited the gate to strengthen the lunar ward from both sides. This time, the raven's cry was accompanied by a lightning bolt and the whinny of scared horses.

He was a mere spectator in the three-way battle. Lightning struck the roofs behind him, and the screams of unseen birds of prey mingled with the thunder of hooves, the clash of metal, and splintering of wood.

How long it lasted, and how much this magical war contributed to the destruction of Castle Arghezi, Caleb didn't know. His eyes fixed on the stable gate, both hands gripping the wood, he concentrated all his efforts on the side of Zeus. The silence that replaced the chaos was deeper and more peaceful than any he had ever heard.

The magical alarms had ceased wailing. Trying to walk through the gate, Caleb was greeted by the familiar deflection, although he could see through to the forest and the stars.

The triumph brought tears to his eyes, for it reminded him of his teacher, who had spent so many evenings with him under the starry sky. Alexandru would have been proud; he would also, no doubt, have had plenty of suggestions on how Caleb could have done better. Exhausted beyond grief, Caleb made his way to the granary under the light of the Harvest Moon. He held a stake as he slept, fearing a third stage to the invasion, his dreams full of falling timbers, screaming, and the leers of vampires.

There had been no third stage. He and Mihail had slept through the night and most of the morning—by the looks of the sun, it was nearing midday—and a bit of magic would soon put a roof over the bedrooms again.

Only Grigore remained unaccounted for. Grigore—and Cuza.

A trail of blood led to the stable. Caleb's breath caught in his throat, his hand on the stake in his belt.

Had Grigore failed to finish off their common enemy? Had Cuza returned to renew his strength by feeding on the animals? Were all of Caleb's efforts at the Jupiter wards for nothing? Was the vampire now trapped inside the castle?

As he entered the stable, he heard sounds of clattering toenails.

It was carnage. The sheep had all been killed, and most of them carried off. Feathers were all that remained of the hens. The cow lay on one side, gashes along her shoulder, her throat torn out and her belly slit along the bottom to allow access to the tastiest parts.

Caleb relaxed his hand off the stake. Stage three, he thought, the animals. He would have laughed except he did not want to scare whatever lurked in the corners

In all his efforts with the celestial powers, he'd forgotten to set up a few boards or stones to keep away the nonmagical creatures that prowled the hills.

There was nothing left for him and Mihail to eat—it might even be tricky finding him a glass of chicken blood—but Caleb was amused. They had been outwitted not by Cuza and his supply of magic tricks, but by his own cousins: Only one species would open a cow that way.

He sat on the floor and gave a low, friendly whine—one of the easiest wolf sounds to make as a human, and it worked like magic. A small gray wolf trotted out from behind a toppled board, regarding Caleb quizzically with wise yellow eyes.

From the white hairs in her snout, and the stiffness in her hips, he guessed that she was very old—perhaps a leader of others who remained hidden. She would know his kind, he guessed, and he gave her his hand to sniff. He made one more courteous noise and backed out of the room, leaving them to their feast.

"Say hello to the grandkids, old lady," he murmured as he left, hoping that she had some. He felt a small but distinct pleasure at being respected by a simple wolf. Every other relationship in his life seemed excruciatingly complicated by comparison.

He found a scrap of paper in the kitchen and sat on the edge of the stone cistern to compose a letter to Liszka. He asked how she and Bela were doing, whether they'd seen Grigore yet, and to please, if she had time, come by with a chicken. A gust of wind departed with the folded scrap of paper.

Sighing, he rose and started back for the granary, aware that he had nothing for Mihail. He had been unable to summon water from the prison room, but perhaps the courtyard gave him a clearer view of the underground reservoir. Before he could even lower his arms, he was drenched; a slug of water hung over him for an instant and then rained down, soaking his torn and sooty clothes.

He laughed aloud at the absurdity of the entire situation. At the granary, he found Mihail sitting up, his pale face troubled. He was less than reassured by the appearance of wet, grinning Caleb.

Probably thinks I've gone mad, Caleb thought, trying to erase the smile from his face. Mad or not, he had to take care of both of them. At least they had water for drinking and for brewing potions. He sat by the old man's side and murmured the best comforting phrases he knew, awaiting Liszka's chicken.

42 ❖ Forgiveness

HE BREWED THE POULTICE Potion under Mihail's watchful eye. In the Great Hall, less ravaged by fire than the library wing, Caleb had had found two chairs and an iron tripod for the cooking pot. A small magical fire crackled merrily and kept away the autumn chill.

Liszka's chicken—delivered by Vanu, a timid Beta who knew nothing of Grigore—had helped Mihail recover some of his energy and color. He was well enough to speak sharply to Caleb when he failed to stir the mixture properly or to add an ingredient at precisely the right time. In fact, the old servant seemed positively talkative. Something in the experience of the previous day had freed him from his fear and suspicion of the American werewolf.

"Have you added the dogwood?" he asked, trying to peer over the rim of the pot. He was wrapped in blankets like a mummy, and only his worried eyes and sooty cheeks peeked out from the swaddling.

"Several minutes ago," Caleb replied mildly.

"Ah, yes," Mihail grunted. "A few more minutes ought to do it." After regarding the younger man carefully for several moments, he asked, "Being bitten by another...werewolf, does that...I mean, is it different than—?"

"Yes. It hurts more than the bite of a normal wolf or a dog." Wounds from animals vanished almost completely when he transformed back to human.

"For a human...it would be even more painful, I suppose," the old man said cautiously.

Caleb merely nodded. He did not remember his own bite; Bela, who'd been a bit older, only recalled his being out at night one instant, and Caleb's arrival with the potion the next. Perhaps amnesia was one of the side effects, or perhaps the mind was occupied by the change—but he didn't know.

"My mother," began Mihail in a distant tone, "screamed for days, they told me, before she…"

"But you were not present?" Caleb asked, with genuine concern. No child should have to suffer through such an experience.

The old man shook his head, still wandering off in a far country of memory. "I was sent to the castle, to stay with my godfather, the old master…Master Arghezi's father I never saw my mother again."

"I'm sorry," Caleb murmured in response. "It must have been very hard for you."

"They took me in and treated me well," shrugged Mihail, attempting to shake off the burden of painful memories, "and I served the Master faithfully."

The mention of Arghezi's name silenced them both, leaving only the sounds of the fire, popping and crackling under the pot, and of the wooden spoon, scraping hypnotically along the bottom. Alexandru's presence lingered, almost as if his ghost haunted the castle. There was so much about him that Caleb would never understand, so many things that he had wanted to ask. But it was too late.

The old man stood and shuffled over to the cauldron, looking down into the thick, bubbling brew with a practiced eye.

"Ready," he said simply and sat down heavily in the chair.

Caleb stopped stirring and began to ladle the mixture into bottles he had salvaged from the kitchen. As he worked, he thought about the castle when Mihail and Alexandru were young. No one could have known that things would end in this way, that the building would be so thoroughly destroyed after standing strong for four hundred years. But the seeds had been planted a long time ago; he understood that much.

Caleb knew that Mihail would not be keen to see his multitude of scratches and bites. "I'll just go into the kitchens; it shouldn't take long. Will you be all right out here?"

The old man waved a vague hand in his direction, lost in some memory.

The potion did not instantly erase the burning and itching of his wounds, but Caleb felt the pain recede, whispering in the background instead of shouting angrily in the foreground of his senses. His mind cleared, too, freeing him from the urge to giggle insanely. He walked out of the kitchens with a considerably lighter step. Mihail had not moved from his chair.

Caleb put out the cooking fire and called for some water, neatly dropping a blob into the pot. As he scrubbed the dried bits of potion stuck to the sides, the old servant muttered to himself.

"Warned him, yes, but couldn't save him," Mihail murmured.

"Save whom?" Caleb said mildly, although he knew the answer. Caleb looked up from his scrubbing to see the old man holding himself rigidly in the chair, arms wrapped tightly around his chest. "You should not torture yourself," Caleb counseled. "You could not have foreseen this attack."

"No. Not this," responded the aged servant, his voice thick with emotion, "but back then. I was young and they would not believe me, none of them."

"What you are saying," Caleb inquired, wiping his hands carefully on his shirt and taking a seat next to an agitated Mihail, "is that you knew Cuza was a vampire when he came to the castle the first time?"

Mihail shook his head in a series of rapid jerks that degenerated into a violent spasm wracking his entire frame. The memories had seized the old man's body as well as his mind.

Caleb held a cup of water to the shaking lips, coaxing Mihail into taking a drink. After a few minutes, the man calmed slightly.

"I am the only one left," he said dully in a slow, solemn voice, "who knows that happened here, and soon I—"

He broke off abruptly and seemed about to lose control again. Gently, Caleb laid a hand on his arm—pleased that Mihail did not flinch—and said, "Will you tell me what happened? Perhaps together we can make some sense out of it."

Mihail nodded slowly to himself and then motioned for the cup of water. After taking a long drink, he began speaking while nervously turning the cup in both hands and staring at the round belly of the pewter pot.

"The Arghezi family lived here for three hundred and twenty years," Mihail began in a measured, even voice. "Now that line has ended. Master Alexandru was the last of them."

"He had just one brother?" asked Caleb hesitantly, not sure how mention of Mircea Arghezi would be received. But Mihail was eager to unburden himself.

"The old master, my godfather, was a proud man, who wanted the best for his children. He married a beautiful but frail woman, who bore him two sons, Master Alexandru and his brother, Mircea, who was five years the younger. I came to the castle shortly after his birth. Master Alexandru's mother confined herself to bed for the most part after the birth of Mircea. We never knew what illness our mistress had, or even if she had an illness. Much later, when Master Alexandru took her to America to finish the business at the castle, the doctors there could find nothing specifically wrong with her. However, he loved her very much and always tried to indulge her as best he could."

"Oh, for the love of Selene," said Caleb as gently as he could, already tiring of the convoluted and formal speaking style that the normally silent man put on, "you needn't call him Master anymore; Alexandru will do. He was your friend, as well as mine."

Blinking back tears, the old man nodded and continued. "Because of his wife's delicate health, the old master did not want Mas—Alexandru to go far for school, although he believed that his children should receive a good education. Alexandru attended school in Bucharest at the academy there. His younger brother had something of his mother's health and temperament. He stayed at home, taught largely by his father and, later, by Alexandru."

"And you," Caleb prompted, "learned potion brewing and other things as well?"

"The old master taught me, too, until he was killed. When Alexandru was away at school for his final year, the old master died suddenly; we were never certain how or why. Rumors were flying in Stilpescu about some sort of magical curse, but there was never any evidence one way or the other. Some said that the old master dabbled in the Dark Arts and that he went looking for creatures of Darkness. I do not know. I was young then and did not know as much as I do now." He sighed a soft, sad moan that spoke volumes about the trials he must have encountered in the service of Alexandru Arghezi.

"When the M—Alexandru finished school, he wanted to see more of the world. Back then, before all the wars, travel was quite easy. His mother wanted him to be at home, and he wanted to please her, but he could not entirely give up his desires. He spent made many trips to Bucharest and some of the other cities nearby to scour the shops for rare and arcane books to build the library. I accompanied him on many of those trips, rarely understanding the books he bought, but always enjoying the travel."

Mihail took another drink of water, handing the empty cup to Caleb for a refill. He stared into the fresh liquid for some time before continuing, "In Tîrgoviște, he used to frequent the book shop of Mr. Liliescu, so much so that the bookseller would invite us to his home for tea or dinner whenever we came to the city. It was there that Alexandru met the bookdealer's daughter, Ana Maria."

The old man glanced apprehensively at Caleb, gauging his reaction to the name. Mihail had not been present in the Great Hall for that terrifying and revealing meeting with Lamia, but he suspected that Caleb knew her. Caleb merely nodded, revealing nothing.

"She was seventeen, quiet—not shy by any means—and also a powerful wizard knowledgeable in magic as well as in many other subjects, history, astronomy, and the like. He was very taken with her and she seemed to love him, too. They were married a year after they met and she came to live at the castle."

"Ana Maria got on well with Alexandru's mother; she understood her health and moods. Mircea adored Ana Maria, following her around like a puppy. She tutored him, and they often played chess in the library or in the Great Hall. Alexandru continued to travel frequently. I think he was glad that his brother had some company." Mihail paused for a drink and grumbled, "Too trusting, he was."

"Whenever we returned from a trip, she helped sort the new volumes, and they talked long into the night about all the things in those books. Perhaps Alexandru was foolish to think that he could simply bring her here and continue his life of wandering. She never complained, but I saw the signs myself."

"What do you mean?" Caleb asked sharply. He could not imagine Lamia as a teenager. Certainly she had looked young when he met her, probably much as she appeared when she first came to the castle, but she had acted like…anything but a young girl.

"She cried when she thought no one was watching. The maids told me that. And she would stay in her room, sometimes all day, and refuse to eat. Maybe later, after she had become…after she changed, we didn't notice at first because she had always behaved that way."

Caleb was seized by the desire to know what Ana Maria had been like. He tried to imagine Lamia as a human, as the girl who had come to the castle almost sixty years ago, but could not reconcile the images that battled inside him: Her harsh laughter in the Great Hall, fresh blood on her chin, clashed with her wordless cries as she clung to him in her tent. Which was real and which was a lie?

Perhaps he had glimpsed Ana Maria in the portrait gallery: a lonely and scared girl surrounded by the cold, unforgiving stones of Castle Arghezi. He felt a phantom of her last kiss on his lips; already she receded from him. Desperately, he hoped that he could at least hold on to her kiss, and to the hope that she had been human at the end.

The old man coughed, startling Caleb out of his daze. Mihail shook his head regretfully, continuing, "After they had been married for about a year, Cuza appeared, presenting himself as an old friend of Alexandru's father. None of us had heard of him, but he knew a great deal about the old master and had a few items from him that he said were gifts from his valued friend. Whether Cuza had actually been a friend or was the wizard responsible for his death, I cannot say. After we left the castle, Alexandru tormented himself about this very question; he never knew the answer either.

"The family enjoyed Cuza's company; he was very charming. That first time, he stayed for a week; afterwards, Ana Maria became very ill. No one connected the two events at the time. In fact, Alexandru and I left shortly thereafter for a trip to Prague that occupied us for more than a month. But before we left, he assured himself that Ana Maria had recovered from her illness. Oh, if only he had read the signs correctly!"

Mihail's hands were now starting to shake and his voice took on more emotion. Caleb gripped the arms of his own chair tightly, knowing what was coming in the old man's tale.

"While we were on that trip, Cuza came back to the castle on some pretense, worming his way into the family's hearts and staying for the greater part of a month. He had just departed when we returned. Ana Maria seemed well when we saw her, although a little pale. Alexandru was preoccupied with the finds that he had made in Prague and got to work cataloguing all the new books with her help."

"And by that time, Ana Maria was a vampire, wasn't she?" inquired Caleb, compelled to ask what he did not want to know.

"Almost certainly. Was my master blind to the fact that his wife was now a vampire?" Mihail shook his head in puzzlement. "Of course, she lost her appetite and often asked to have meals sent to her room, but she had frequently done that before. Alexandru hoped that she might be with child; certainly his mother hinted that to him. Should I have read the signs better and warned them? I cannot stop wondering."

"It's useless to torture yourself so," Caleb interjected forcefully, as much to himself as to Mihail.

The other sighed, staring into his cup for a time, then continued, "The same strange illness began to strike some of the servants, and Mircea was also ill. I suppose that Cuza must have been sneaking into the castle to be with Ana Maria. The castle was not protected magically as strongly as it is now."

He held his cup out for a refill, his hand shaking so badly that half the water Caleb summoned did not make it into the cup, but splashed noisily on the stones below.

"It was a disease, a cancer, spreading through the castle," Mihail continued after taking another deep drink. "Alexandru and his mother did not notice, but I saw the changes. I was slow to put a name to it and even slower to say something. Oh! I should have warned them sooner!"

"But would Alexandru have believed you?" Caleb wondered. Both men were silent. The rest of the tale lurked, a great sleeping dragon curled up just out of sight, waiting to bring itself to full height and attack.

"Tell me what happened then," murmured Caleb.

"It was the autumn of 1935," began Mihail slowly, his voice beginning to crack, "and Alexandru wanted to take one more trip to Bucharest before the snows buried the castle for the winter. His mother begged him not to go on that trip, even more than she usually did. Did she suspect that something was going on? I refused to go; something was not right in the castle. Soon after Alexandru left, Cuza came to the castle and Ana Maria welcomed him. Now I watched the two of them together closely and began to suspect what he was—and what she had become, too.

"And I became concerned for Mircea. He became ill again and Ana Maria nursed him back to health. I draped garlic around his bed, but someone kept removing all the garlic."

"You protected yourself with garlic, too, no doubt," Caleb said. The thought of the young Mihail, already draped in garlic, with probably a bit of wolfsbane thrown in for good measure, caused him to smile slightly.

"I knew they were in the castle and I protected myself. I heard their songs," replied the old man, the anguish rising in his voice. "Some nights it was all I could do to keep myself in my room when they called to me. It was the same as yesterday, when she—"

"I know. I've heard that song, too." Caleb interrupted hastily. Oh, Lamia, he thought to himself, how could you?

Mihail reached over and gripped Caleb's forearm tightly. Caleb's wounds screamed in pain, but the touch steadied the old man. "An early and unexpected snowstorm delayed Alexandru. He returned late one evening, exhausted from a difficult journey up the mountain in the snow, just as the household was about to retire. Both Ana Maria and Mircea were agitated, although for very different reasons, I know now. Mircea was still very pale and drawn. Something seemed to be preying on his mind. I heard him mumble something to his brother about being quite delirious with fever during his illness and having some residual nightmares."

"Mircea must have known somehow that he had been bitten twice," mused Caleb.

"...Or the sight of Ana Maria made him realize something," concluded Mihail. "We never knew if she or Cuza attacked him first. Alexandru didn't want to believe that she was part of it, but I know she was." The old man gave a snort of disgust, "In spite of all the monstrous things that she did after becoming a vampire, I believe he still loved her."

"Is that so hard to believe?" Caleb asked softly. "I knew her, too," he continued under the harsh gaze of the old servant. "I did not know at first what she was...or who she was. She never mentioned the castle..." Caleb halted as Mihail drew back his hand, making his scars sting afresh.

"I can understand how Alexandru felt," Caleb continued. "She was..." What? How could he express the mixture of longing and frustration? Trying to understand her was like trying to put his arms around smoke.

Mihail eyed him suspiciously, but continued, "The family awoke to screaming, Mircea shouting incoherently. I rushed out of my room to see him fleeing down the stairs. He was by himself, crying for someone to go away. I saw no one—although there were undoubtedly bats trailing after him that I did not see. Alexandru shouted at me to take care of his mother and followed his brother through the entrance hall and up the steps of the tower. We thought that he had relapsed into his former illness, but that was not the case, of course."

"The boy was about to be bitten for the third time, wasn't he? And he woke up just before the act was committed." Caleb shook his head in wonder, thinking of the poor boy Stefan, whom he and Alexandru had rescued from a third vampire bite. Now he knew fully the pain that wracked the old vampire-hunter to hear the boy scream.

"Do you know what happened in the tower?" Caleb asked.

"Later, much later, and only when he was in his cups, Alexandru told me what had happened that night," replied Mihail heavily. "When he reached the top of the tower, he found Cuza, trying to put Mircea under his spell. When the boy saw Alexandru, the spell was temporarily broken, and he begged his brother's forgiveness. Cuza attempted to draw Mircea to him, even as Alexandru raged at him. They fought and the vampire cursed Alexandru, knocking him down briefly. The vampire turned on Mircea and…finished what he had come to do."

"And both Cuza and Mircea got away?"

"Yes, and we knew that our troubles were just beginning. Alexandru told me to get his mother out of the castle that very night, to take her to safety with friends in the village. I left with the rest of the servants, the ones who were still living, that is. Alexandru stayed to confront Ana Maria. I told him all that I had seen, and at last he believed me. He found her in the greenhouse near dawn. I do not know what they said to one another, but Alexandru became very angry. He tried to curse her, but she was as much of a wizard as he. She fought back, and then Cuza came crashing through the glass of the greenhouse. Alexandru could not win against the two of them. He was lucky to escape the castle alive."

"And you went to America then?"

"Alexandru did not succeed in getting back into the castle that winter or spring. Cuza had assembled quite a circle of vampires around him, and they were too strong for one wizard alone. He could not muster enough support from the locals to drive them out. Also, the whole incident had greatly upset his mother. She had cousins in New England who invited us to stay with them. We went, but it was always his intention to return after seeing her settled. But she needed him, she said. Within a few years, the War had broken out in Europe and it was more pleasant for everyone to stay in Boston."

"That's where he met Jonathan Hermann?" Caleb asked, thinking suddenly of the little man who was probably still teaching Freshman Physics to bright-eyed young Einsteins on the East Coast.

"Yes. Mr. Hermann was Alexandru's good friend. When Mircea appeared in New England, they hunted him together for several years. But by that time, Mircea was under the control of vampires even more powerful than Cuza. It wasn't until the end of the war that Alexandru was able to contain these monsters in a locked and warded mansion. At last, the dreadful tale seemed to have ended, and I hoped to live out the rest of my days in peace." Mihail's chin quivered. "Why did we come back?"

Lamia had asked the same question. Why indeed? Either there was no answer to the question, or the answer was so dreadfully complicated that it would take years to unravel. Caleb could not see a path out of that thicket.

Mihail yawned loudly. The height of the moon peeking out from behind the tower told Caleb it was just past nine o'clock. Night had fallen without either man noticing, and it promised to be clear and cold.

"C'mon," drawled Caleb sleepily. "Let's get you to bed."

He helped Mihail stand up and supported him as they shuffled across the brightly lit flagstones to the dark granary. Once inside, Caleb conjured a ball of fire, enough to see the piles of blankets and sacks of flour that served as their makeshift beds. He settled Mihail as comfortably as he could, kneeling next to him to wrap him up warmly in several blankets.

"I will find Mircea," Caleb murmured dreamily. The old man's eyes flew open and he clenched Caleb's hand. "Alexandru asked me, before he—before the end," he said as he took Mihail's hand and tucked it under the blankets, "and I promised him. I will find Mircea."

Epilogue

THE THICK OAK DOOR opened grudgingly, groaning like a ghost with laryngitis. The boy peered into the thick, dusty gloom of the entrance hall. He stepped inside and stopped, allowing his eyes time to adjust.

"Dad?" The word died in the high ceiling above him. He crossed the hall with caution, using his walking stick to probe the floor, remembering the traps. Something chittered to his right, and then scurried across the floor.

"Son of a rabid dog!" he cursed and skipped a step to avoid the…rat, if that's what it was. If it wasn't a rat, he didn't want to know.

The boy avoided looking off to the right, because too many painful memories clung to the iron-bound door that led into what had once been a prison, and proceeded down the corridor that led to the Great Hall. Closer to the double doors of the formal entrance, the floor was littered with detritus: shards of glass, shreds of tapestries, and scraps of furniture. The doors themselves wouldn't open more than a crack, blocked by a charred piece of beam that had fallen from the roof.

He thought he'd have better luck going through the kitchens. Seven months after that night, and none of the rubble had been cleared. Bela wished his own memories could be buried along with the fractured tiles.

Where the entrance hall had been stuffy and dark, what was left of the Great Hall was open to the wind and the sun. Parts of the roof and three of the four walls were largely intact, but the fourth wall, which had separated the Great Hall from the library and greenhouse, was a pile of stones and charred lumber.

"As bad as the cottage, this place is," he murmured, looking up at the holes in the ceiling as if for the first time. "But those beams I could use…" he added with thinly veiled desire, his gaze dropping to the thick roof supports, now lying on the floor.

"You only came for the timber, eh? I hoped for a warmer welcome."

The boy started at the familiar voice of dry amusement behind him.

"Da-…Caleb," Bela said as he turned around. "If you don't need them all…"

"Yes, I'll let you know," Caleb promised. He was wiping his hands on a towel and smiling that infuriating all-knowing smile. "I have been meaning to fix things up this summer."

"We didn't…you know, that night…tear off the ceiling, did we?" Bela asked, suddenly hesitant.

"No," Caleb replied with caution. "It was the next day. After the vampires came. You were spared—you slept through what happened." He put the towel he'd been holding on the back of one of two chairs remaining in the Great Hall.

"Mom helped, didn't she?" Before now, he had never dared to ask for the whole story. He remembered Liszka calling to him, and he recalled locking the door magically with a bit of help from Grigore—but the noises that followed could have been figments of his fevered dreams.

"Of course she did," Caleb smiled. "That surprised the vampires, and gave Alexandru and me a chance to recover our senses. Then…then it was a four-way battle for I don't know how long—an hour, maybe longer. It was high noon by the time Cuza turned into a bat and Alexandru blew the ceiling apart trying to curse him. The bat didn't like the sunlight, of course, and he was forced to transform back. Your mother—Liszka—was waiting for him with a mirror, while Alexandru tried to ambush him from behind."

"Mom never talks about this," Bela said with a mixture of awe and curiosity. "Did you kill the vampire?"

Caleb shook his head. "Not right away. Alexandru's curse hit a stone pillar with not much left to support it, and a section of the roof came crashing down and killed him. All that's ancient history."

Caleb turned to the table next to the fireplace and began putting away the remains of his breakfast. "I didn't invite you here so that you could raid what's left of the castle," he said, pointedly changing the subject. "And how did you get in? I'm sure that all the wards were set this morning."

"The wards? Oh, those were easy to get through," countered Bela with the bravado of teenagers everywhere.

"Hmmm....I've taught you well, maybe too well."

"Picked up some on my own, too."

"Well, that remains to be seen." Caleb frowned for a moment, and then continued, "I asked you to come by today because the baker sent word that something's in his barn. It's upsetting his goats and eating his grain. It might be nothing, but if it turns out to be some creature...I could, well, I could use your help."

"Monsters?" Bela couldn't keep the excitement from creeping into his voice. Monsters had been scarce in the local mountains for the last few years, thanks to Caleb's single-minded efforts. Bela had never seen so much as a hydra.

Caleb shrugged. "It might be nothing, but I want to investigate—"

"—in the name of science?" Bela finished with a grin spreading across his face.

"Yes, something like that." Caleb turned away to get his coat, but not before Bela saw a smile flit across his father's face. "Let's get moving," he called over his shoulder. The conversation ended, as so many of Bela's conversations with his father did.

The gulf of bitterness and obstinacy between the two seemed to have shrunk a little as they made their way down the stone trail from the castle to the village. Caleb pointedly did not comment on how well Bela hiked the rocky trail, considering his injury and the remaining April snow. Bela had let Caleb make an enchanted shoe for him, and the walking stick helped him maintain a decent pace down the mountain. But conversation was difficult for him while concentrating on not losing his balance, so the journey down the mountainside was for the most part in silence.

The sun peeked through the clouds, lighting up parts of the meadows and mountains at random. Soon they came to the upper sheep pastures near the village where they could see flocks scattered across alpine meadows like cumulus clouds on a fine summer day.

Shepherds waved to them cheerfully, and Caleb waved back. Now the trail became a wagon track lined with neat fences; small wooden houses appeared behind the fences, their gardens just beginning to show lilacs and hyacinths. Finally, the conical red roofs of the church with its tall spires came into view.

The burbling of the brook, the croaks of frogs, and the tinkle of bells on sheep were the only sounds that greeted their ears until they drew near enough to the bakery to smell the enticing aromas of Easter cozonac. Caleb patted him on the arm, which Bela knew was supposed to be some form of encouragement.

"He knows we're werewolves," Caleb whispered, "but he really doesn't—"

The words died in his throat. His head snapped up and his eyes narrowed as he stared at a dusty old man emerging from the bakery, stuffing his mouth with rolls as if he hadn't eaten for a week. The man wore simple peasant's clothing, his hiking boots gouged and torn, but somehow he didn't look like a local.

A flash of recognition passed between Caleb and the mysterious traveler, and Bela saw his father's face darken with a mixture of rage, betrayal, and shame.

"Clovis Fintonclyde," Caleb croaked, stepping back as the old man approached him for a closer look. "What brings you here?"

Bela swallowed hard to suppress a growl. Had he been a wolf, his hackles would have sprung up. As it was, he shook and balled his hands into fists. He had heard stories over the years about the old man from Maine who had raised Caleb and then abandoned him.

"I am looking..." began Fintonclyde, answering in passable Romanian as he finished chewing his latest pastry, "...looking for someone skilled in the Dark Arts." He opened his satchel and placed the remains of his bakery purchases inside, then belched and wiped crumbs from his beard. "Do pardon me, it has been quite a journey."

"How?" Caleb asked sharply, momentarily losing the emotional control that so frustrated his son.

"Jonathan Hermann said you might still be here," said the old man, "and he told me a most remarkable tale, one that I would have thought pure fantasy, if it didn't involve my former best student."

"What is it that you need from me?" Caleb asked coldly, having mastered himself, but obviously pained by the reference to the past.

"I have heard that you are the one responsible for ridding these mountains of all manner of Dark creatures." Fintonclyde smiled. He was seemingly unaffected by the suspicious looks from Bela. "I am in need of a...hunter."

With visible effort, Caleb gained control over his expression and voice, which were as calm and detached as if he were chatting about the weather. Caleb wanted nothing to do with Fintonclyde—even his desire for revenge had been dulled by the passing years—but he was intrigued by the request. He probed the old man with questions as Fintonclyde described a monster attack in the States.

"Hundreds of vacationers had to be evacuated and several were bitten," the traveler concluded, switching into English and no doubt thinking Bela wouldn't understand. "We're still watching one of them who may be a vampire…and then, of course, there are the werewolf children."

Disbelief and shock played across Caleb's face. "What did you do?" he managed to get out. "And how many are there?"

"One, at present," Fintonclyde informed him. "There was an older boy, a teenager, but he didn't survive his first transformation."

"It's much harder once you've stopped growing," Bela piped up. "Even now it's hard for me."

The conversation broke, and the two turned to look at Bela, who decided he might as well have his say. "Fintonclyde wants you to go back to America, to Maine, doesn't he?" Bela demanded.

The old man approached Bela, then stopped abruptly and spoke with precision. "We need his experience," he declared, "so that we don't lose our Community over this."

Caleb stepped closer to Fintonclyde as if to take repossession of the dialogue. "Is it the vampires that Toby released from Lilac House?" he whispered.

"Some of them are." Fintonclyde now sounded serious. "But at least one of them is new, and immensely powerful. He may have had ties to those vampires originally, as well as ties to this region. What puzzles me is that he waited so long after the opening of Lilac House to make his appearance. When he showed up, seven months ago, I knew that our Community couldn't face this situation alone."

The words seven months made both Bela and Caleb recoil as if they had been slapped.

"It's Cuza," Bela shouted, reverting to his native tongue.

"Impossible," snapped Caleb. "I staked Cuza and he was burned immediately."

"Who burned him?" Ignoring the old man entirely, Bela lunged forward and gripped his father's shoulder, digging in with his fingers. "Did you do it yourself?"

"Grigore—" Caleb began….

"How many times have I told you that dog is a traitor," Bela hissed. "I told you before, and I say it now." He turned back to the old man, his brain searching for English words. "The new vampire? It's Cuza for sure. You need Caleb, and you need me. We will go to America."

Connie SENIOR

started writing down stories at the age of eight and hasn't stopped since. She lives near Denver, Colorado with her husband and cats. *Only the Moon Howls* is her first novel.